MILENA

MILENA

*

Maggie Ross

COLLINS
8 Grafton Street, London W1
1983

William Collins Sons & Co Ltd
London · Glasgow · Sydney · Auckland
Toronto · Johannesburg

British Library Cataloguing in Publication Data

Ross, Maggie
Milena.
I. Title
823'914   PR6068.o/

First published 1983
Copyright © Maggie Ross 1983
ISBN 0 00 222602 2

Photoset in Imprint
Made and printed in Great Britain by
William Collins Sons & Co Ltd Glasgow

AUTHOR'S NOTE

The story of Milena Jesenka's eventful life has been most movingly told by Margarete Buber-Neumann in her book *Kafkas Freundin Milena*, published in English by Secker & Warburg (1966) under the title *Mistress to Kafka*.

This book, together with Kafka's letter to Milena, formed the foundations of this novel.

ERRATA

The second paragraph of the Author's Note should read:
This book, together with Kafka's letters to Milena, formed the foundation of this novel.

The Czech newspaper *Prítonmost* should be spelt *Prítomnost*.

I

She had been thinking about Milena for a long time now. Whenever she saw the book, the face on the cover, she was moved to open it again. However idly she flicked through the pages, she found herself re-reading certain passages with deep attention. Then she would close the book with the same slight feeling of dissatisfaction and finish by staring again at the mysterious photograph.

It was always the same: she would find herself immersed in the woman as if she had known her intimately, but as if in that intimacy were small areas of shade, private places needing a brighter light. Isolated facts, unrelated images stayed with her daily, keeping her company through long hours of being alone. She found herself trying to pattern them when other work should have been engrossing. In mid-stroke, her pencil would stop over the illustration; the watercolour would dry before the wash was complete and Milena's being would take the place of art. She found herself thinking about her as if about a friend, someone needing help, someone to be watched over because of a vulnerability which was matched, it seemed, by excessive determination.

The woman was excessive, there was no doubt about it. And why not? She had lived in an excessive age. Constantly she exhibited an excess of feeling and expected adequate response. Youth was wild, marriages turbulent, death horror. The history of her era had been well documented. There were millions who'd said what it was like in Europe during the uneasy years leading up to the Second World War. Thousands had told of life under

7

German occupation, and of death in prison camps. There were literary historians by the score who had charted the brief life of the writer whose work, in retrospect, had often been visionary. 'Under Kafka is where to find Milena!' was one of Ernest's coarser jokes. He couldn't understand her interest in a writer whose attitudes, to him, were so alien. Or what was turning into an obsession with the woman who was the first to translate Kafka's works from German into Czech.

'Translators are second-class citizens,' he would say, ignoring the fact that his wife's days were frequently spent giving substance to other people's words. But this was something to which she wouldn't listen. The urge to celebrate Milena's existence had become overwhelming.

'I shall definitely begin with the face,' she'd told Ernest.

The face which she felt she knew as well as she knew her own. Open a book about Kafka and there she was, shining from the pages between Meran and Planá, between the beginning and the end of an intimacy which had burned itself out in three short years. What was left were hundreds of his letters to her, and none of hers. So few words about her. So many from him. So many about him. There was a balance to be righted. She would do it, perform an act of tribute to this distant woman. She would make a portrait of her, building up on basic canvas a collage of her life. For two years now she'd saved every last little piece of information about her time; hoarded cuttings, books, magazines, photos and movie stills of the period – anything remotely reminding her of Milena's existence. She had read avidly the only book ever written about her, by the friend who'd shared her last years. These were to be the foundation on which she'd build a beautiful commemoration to someone who deserved more than the written word.

'I think I'm ready to begin.'

'Why not?' Ernest said. 'Although some might think it dilettante. Get on with it, then, get on with something useful.'

The face was broad, made to seem more so by the square chin and the high curve of the cheekbones. Yet the forehead looked high because of the hair springing upward from a pronounced widow's peak into a plateau of tight curls. Put out a hand and touch that hair and you'd be certain to feel a wiry toughness despite its colour. Her own was the same. And if she stared at the photograph long enough the resemblance grew, until she could feel her reflection in that face and imagine her life as one with the other's. Examine the mouth. Hadn't her own the same generous, heavy upper lip with its well-defined edges? Ernest had marvelled at it. He'd told her that only true beauties had mouths like hers, and had drawn his finger along its curve while staring closely into her eyes. Milena's eyes too were blue, made more intense by the whiteness of her skin. She looked intently at the camera as the photographer took the shot, catching her in the act of holding her breath. She'd been waiting too long for the shutter to click, and had muttered between clenched teeth, 'Hurry up, spider man,' noting how his spindly legs matched those of the tripod he leaned over. Such a business then, having one's photo taken. Such a waste of time, and only undergone because she would mark the twin events of new exile and of marriage. Husband and friends were already waiting in the Café Herrenhoff, her newest home from home.

'These classes are killing me,' Ernest said. He was lying on the sofa, feet higher than his head, flourishing a sheaf of printed notes. 'You've no idea of the effort involved.' Papers were strewn beneath him on the floor. He had flung down folders and notebooks and the coloured pencils he favoured.

'Shouldn't you be there this evening? Isn't it Banking Procedures on Tuesdays? It is Tuesday today.'

He sat up looking aggrieved and half-heartedly threw the notes towards her as she sat on the floor. 'My dear Amy, how am I supposed to work all day and all evening too? Try to grasp the fact that we're not all like you, lying around

9

most of the time. Some of us have regular jobs to go to. The Daily Grind, we call it. So there are occasions when we don't feel like going out again in the evenings to tax our brains.' His voice was beginning to rise. 'And Heaven knows, I've had my share of taxing! Furthermore, how am I supposed to have time for my real work?'

The question was rhetorical. Keeping low on the floor was the best counter to Ernest's wrath. Bend over the sheaf of cuttings and pretend not to feel the hurricane of his frustrations. He had taken off his glasses and was bouncing them in time with his words. 'Writing about other people's money all day isn't exactly wonderful. Wouldn't be so bad if some of it occasionally came my way.' He looked down at the front of his immaculate shirt. 'Look at me. Just look at me! Thirty-four years old.' His fist against his chest. 'Heart attacks happen to people like me.' His fist on his forehead. 'Penury. Ignominy.' The choice of words pleased him. Replacing his glasses he took up notebook and pencil and wrote them down. Then, with a sigh, he lay back on the sofa murmuring, 'If I weren't so exhausted I'd give you my Desperate Poet speech!' At his laugh she looked up at him and smiled.

'Honestly, Amy. You really must try to see things from my direction sometimes. All this is all very well . . .' his gesture dismissed what was on the floor '. . . but will it earn us Hard Cash?'

'As much as your excursions into philosophy.' Below the belt but necessary: Ernest in attack could demoralize to the point of paralysis. She saw the glint of his glasses. He leaned heavily from the sofa and gave her his Ernest stare.

'I'm quite sure that from your superior position –' she was on her knees '– you can divine everything! And that discerning brain of yours can assess which of us is more likely to produce something of value.' A pause. 'Which cannot always be equated with money.'

A longer pause while he thought. 'Which, I might add, some of us spend rather too freely when we've got it.'

'I want to see her as a whole,' she said. Sometimes the change in conversation worked. At others it merely served to increase his irritation, giving rise to subsidiary paragraphs about lack of breeding and a butterfly mind. 'She must grow, don't you see?' The child into the woman in that strange middle-European setting of the first part of the twentieth century.

To see her at all within the context of an age so little understood, against a background more felt in the bones than comprehended – despite all the assiduous reading, despite all the staring at pictures of Vienna, of the collapse of its empire, despite the sight of Hitler's minions raping Prague – to see her at all was like staring down at the rain-washed road, seeing first the road, then the window spotted with rain. Then the drops of rain themselves reflecting road. Then the images of herself inverted minutely in each separate drop. And, last, her own flat reflection in the darkly spotted glass, surveying everything.

Somewhere in the confusion, in the welter of events there was Milena spanning the gap between that comfortable, eternal pre-war existence and those terrible years of confinement, carnage and death. Kafka never saw the deaths. His was mercifully early, but he knew of the possibility. He'd felt it inside and tried to communicate the pain, describing in his special way how a man might spend his life trying to persuade himself that his road did not lead down one of those dark corridors, only to discover that he'd been in one all the time. Milena shared his vision for a while, asking to be, and becoming his faithful translator. So devoted was she that her feelings had to embrace the man as well as his work. This was self-evident. And naturally he in his turn must reciprocate.

Ernest was deflected. 'Why not turn out a nice, naturalistic portrait of her? Throw in Mr K. looking over her shoulder, and it's finished. Sell it to one of your magazine friends. Do it nicely and I might write an article round it, to give it a bit of depth.'

She looked at him in alarm and saw he was waiting for the reaction. 'Fine,' she said carefully. 'I'll do the picture my way. Meanwhile you can do some research. Most of the books you'll need are here . . .' She picked up two of the heavier ones. 'The passages where she's mentioned are marked. But you'll have to search for corresponding history of the period.' She thumbed a page. 'Martial Law is in Chapter . . . Three, I think. When she was twelve. Walking home through lines of soldiers with fixed bayonets.'

A frightened girl going home to the sad flat in Prague, where her mother lay alone for hours propped up in bed with pillows.

A heavy sigh from Ernest.

'Her father neglected her, when he wasn't behaving like an overlord. She had to kiss his hand each morning. Can you imagine! Always so pleased with himself. He liked women under his thumb.' She laughed. 'A little like you, I think!'

'And what does that mean?'

'He fancied his chances – as they say!' Ernest was displeased. 'Never mind. He stood up for his beliefs. Once he acted quite heroically.' She paused, watching Ernest's face.

'Well, go on. What did the fellow do?'

'He stood up against police cordons, that's all.' She began to peer at scraps of paper now dim in the fading light.

'Don't mystify, Amy. The first principle of conversation is clarity.'

Hoping to bore him, she began recounting the story of Dr Jan Jesenky's stand on the Příkopy facing a line of rifles; how he stayed alone tending a wounded man. 'If you like,' she said, 'I'll mark the pages about Czechoslovakia's fight for independence against Austria. This – ' the book under her hand ' – is about her pre-Kafka years. The Minervists, and so on. She had a very enlightened education, which I suppose you could thank her father for. He probably regretted it when she married Pollak. Too independent.' She found a chapter. 'The letters to Kafka are mentioned here, but I have a complete set of them edited by Willi Haas.'

Ernest groaned. 'It was only a suggestion. And it wasn't going to be some great, definitive biography.' He put up a weary hand. 'Although why I should bother at all I don't know.' He flung an arm across his ruffled hair. 'Look at me! Money in the morning. Philosophy in the evening. And –'

'Sex at night!'

She had definitely gone too far. He pulled himself upright. Despite the low light she saw him clearly. His glasses made him look older than his years, she thought. Once she'd told him they made him look noble. His eyes were malevolent and small.

'Is that all you can do – make pathetic remarks? An offer of help, a suggestion which might turn your efforts into a work with intellectual merit – ' his eyes rolled ' – and you hide behind what I'm forced to call bourgeois deviation.' He drew a deep breath. 'Perhaps, once in a while, you might find the . . . compassion to listen.' He had his feet on the floor. 'One can't expect consecutive thought processes from you. As for compassion . . . you have none.'

'So now you want sympathy for your night rides?'

'See!' he shouted at the walls. 'She hasn't heard a word. I've been desperately trying to move the discussion away from the petty, and she's still wallowing in her own little pit! Two years I've been trying. Two whole years of the inalienable right to grow.'

'Spare me the sermon, Ernest.'

Too late altogether to withdraw. It was the big decision, whether to fight or retire after the first few sallies. But how to fight this time from a stand based only on something deeply felt inside? The Freedom lecture was high-minded and logical. Nothing new. It had been his battle-cry, part of the attraction. In it she'd seen the means of escape. Part of her still saw the rightness of it. Nobody had the right to fetter another. If one person chose to live with another –

13

marry him even – the argument was still valid. Ernest had said that only on those terms could each be sure of the strength of the attachment.

He was so devoted then. Hadn't he proved it by marrying her? She'd thought him so brave against the opposition. No father and no religion could stand in his way. They were part of the conventional world which together they would leave behind. Hadn't adversity increased the resolve and brought them closer? It should have done. Unless her father was right after all. He'd said that Ernest was nothing more than a social climber, a pseudo-intellectual with a taste for young girls. All it had done was increase her resolve to marry the rootless Jew as fast as she could, in the face of threats of disinheritance and locking her up. Such excitement in their meetings. And joy in the final escape. The relief of distance from which she could tell her father how his money and his sensibilities were nothing compared to what she'd got in exchange.

But what she had got was hard to pin down. A bank worker. A poet? A Jew who had relinquished his Jewishness for a philosophical ideal. A lover of profound sensitivity. An unreliable friend? A hypochondriac? A dandy. Someone to pit your wits against, who would take up all your energies and all your time if you didn't fight him every day.

'We all know the excuses you make in the name of freedom,' she said.

'Amy, you haven't got it in you to understand, that's quite clear. And tonight I can see that whatever I might talk about will automatically be reduced to your lowest common denominator.'

'Oh! I thought sex figured high in your book.'

'Not at the level you wish to discuss it.'

'But I don't want to discuss it.'

'You do nothing else.'

'If I do, then it's your fault, Ernest. If you weren't so obsessed with it we could live in peace.'

14

He stared at her blankly until a thought came. 'I practise and you preach!'

Better not to answer. Nothing to be gained from wails about betrayal. Neither could she reasonably pursue the argument she wanted to: that all his promises had remained unfulfilled. He'd sworn she'd never feel the loss of him through sharing. Freedom meant more love for everyone, not less, he'd said. His statement, "We must open our beds with our hearts" had, at the time, only caused her mild amusement. She wanted to feel the same again.

Her decisions lately had taken on new clarity. An end to masochistic self-indulgence. For if she thought honestly about their arguments it was true to say their very nastiness was often enjoyable. Certainly Ernest loved a lacerating fight – the better if he won – and had taught by example how digression, deviation and displays of emotion could win the day. In private all was permissible as long as she remembered they were taking part in sport. For someone blessed with memory, compassion or a real desire for a real conclusion, these fights sometimes sickened. Philosophers argued harshly, she supposed, but did they aim to injure?

There must be no more fighting for fighting's sake. It was wearing her out and making her thin. The adrenalin was rising so frequently that often the mere sight of Ernest entering the bedroom in the small hours would start her quivering. He was eroding dignity. That was it. She was beginning to think of herself as without hope. A lost cause trying with futility to regain whatever she'd had before . . . No. Not quite right. She didn't want the pain. But there'd been more than enough pleasure to balance it. In memory it glowed like the summer sunset they'd watched together. Nothing mean to mar the view. The man bringing her such joy that all else was insignificant.

Everyone had to know. Alert the whole hotel. Wake friends from sleep and give them flowers in celebration. Run barefoot down the corridors laughing like a wild thing. Tell Stacey and Jasmine their lives too have changed.

From now on the trio will be four. And the foursome must be two pairs, for they can only share him if she will allow. And she wants him for herself.

But don't tell father. Sex isn't included in this daughter's education. Nor Judaism in the curriculum.

Could Ernest's influence have been so bad on someone in need of a guiding hand? A new father willing to condone her flights of fancy, a listener to her outpourings, the one who might channel her energies into usefulness. And his was a loving hand, not the authoritarian knuckle which had tried for twenty years to rap submission into her.

'Come on Amy, be a good girl and get me some tea. And a bite to eat.'

He had an essentially child-like air about him; a way of appealing as if he relied upon her totally. His look implied that thinkers needed doers to get them through the daily maze. She thought of another thinking man, and the heat rose in her face.

'There's nothing. Didn't you eat earlier, at the café?'

A pause. 'That was hours ago. Surely there's something?'

'Conrad's been here.'

'What! That bloody Lipschitz. I hope you kept your eye on him.' He stood up and went to the door. Suddenly the room was flooded in light. 'Trust you to feed him.'

'He had to eat. He was here so long. I told him about my portrait. And he actually understood. He suggested making it in two panels. Peace and War. He clarified a lot for me. Said I shouldn't be afraid of abstraction.'

'He's never been renowned for clarity so far!'

'I know. But he's nice. And funny.'

Ernest looked sharply at her then quickly round the room, taking in the top of the bookcase where the ash-tray stood.

'We did smoke a little,' she said.

'So I suppose you haven't done any real work today.'

'I finished two drawings this morning. Laurie doesn't want them until Thursday.'

'So when's pay-day?'

'We've had it already. Don't you remember? We bought the Neurath book.' She wasn't criticising Ernest: she would read it too. 'But since Laurie doesn't want anything until next month at the earliest, I thought . . .'

'Next month!'

'I thought I'd give the time to Milena. Conrad suggested bordering a panel with white tiles. Clinical, like her father's surgery.'

Ernest was groaning softly, his eyes raised ceilingward. She caught a glimpse of the soft fur of his belly through the gap in his too-tight shirt. 'I suppose,' he said, 'we could sell something.'

By that she knew he probably meant the flute. 'No, not that.'

'You never play it.'

'That's neither here nor there. I played it yesterday evening, if you must know. To these four white walls.'

He was at the bookcase, poking about among the books. 'Ah well, there's always dear Father. We could try the twice-yearly letter a few months early.'

That she wrote more frequently to her father was unknown to her husband. But sometimes the need to reach him was so strong she put down her feelings without constraint. Wasn't there the slightest hope he might respond in a miraculous way?

'Tell him categorically we're flat broke. Be explicit. He may come round if he thinks we're grovelling.'

'No. You'll just have to cut down on your cheroots, your women and your billiards – not necessarily in that order.'

To her surprise he laughed loudly and went into the kitchen.

Milena stared up at her from the floor, the visible upper part of her body leaning forward slightly and rigidly. The sepia photograph was made paler by the plastic skin stretched over the cover of the book. The dark dress, the shadowy background. The shadows round her eyes made

17

her too serious, too grown-up. Where was the beautiful *Backfisch*? A way must be found to give her colour and make her shine.

On the first panel she would put down a ground of translucent blue the colour of Bohemian glass, cracked all over like grandmother's porcelain with its wire staples. She would find a blue like the colour of the marbles she played with as a child; like the dark poison bottles ranged along the surgery shelves; the blue that changed through grey to lilac to purple in the dresses she favoured later. Put her against a cold blue sky in which the clouds are high and racing. She is already shadowed. She is just sixteen.

As she stands waiting for the train she is not aware how much she loves her father. The water tracking from her eyes comes she imagines from the wind and not from thoughts of hurting him. She doesn't cry for her dead mother even though she truly loved her. Her going was a release from the seemingly everlasting task of being nurse. And being it alone, while father paid infrequent, per-functory calls, then sought company elsewhere. Great professors cannot be detained by family ties. Before he leaves the flat he tells her to be less noisy, refrain from wearing deliberately flamboyant clothes, concentrate more upon her studies and see that the dogs are groomed and fed by one of the more reliable servants. Adjusting his monocle he nods approval when she asks to be allowed to visit her aunt, not thinking, as she should have, to question the request. The front door slams and she hears his foot-steps echo on the stone stairs. She is left alone.

The tears are for his neglect. Then she smiles at his stupidity. Her hair strands across her face. She likes her situation. She has chosen the view of bright domes and spires and a scudding sky above the diminishing track. The wind blows fresh enough to push the tears across her fur collar, and keep her hands inside her sleeves. Is it so very Dostoyevskian to stand in the silence of an awaited train?

Or is she thinking of Anna Karenina? She stamps her feet, then strolls towards two waiting passengers. She is eyed curiously. What if she is recognized? She smiles at the sheer joy of being at the start of another adventure. She is in love with a young man with a sensitive face. They discovered each other a week ago. Since then they've been frantic for meetings away from the others. They have met on street corners, by the steps of the school. They have walked in the labyrinths of the Kinsky Gardens and talked of Life and Music and Medicine. He has promised to sing for her. She will read him passages from her favourite poets whose lines she'll speak beautifully while he lies in her lap and she strokes his thin hair. The sound of the fountain will accompany her words. No! Like the waters in winter the poor boy will freeze. December in Prague is no place for lovers. In any case her father will hear about the affair and pack her off skiing on the Spičak.

Ernest was crashing about in the kitchen impersonating a starving man. She heard him shake the can of dried beans. Shortly he would appear at the door and beg for bread.

'I'm not even asking for margarine.'

'None of that either.'

'Cruelty, that's what it is!'

'Conrad had to eat something.'

Ernest held out a firm and healthy forearm. 'Take it, if that's what pleases you. Give him my arm! Everything else has gone. Give everything away! See if I care.' He waved dramatically. 'Look! You've missed something . . .' A vase had caught his eye. 'And what about that picture?' He went to it and stared hard at the landscape with figures in its dull gold frame.

'That picture is mine, Ernest. We are not selling it.'

His eyes widened. 'She gives my life's blood to all and sundry and denies me even a crumb. She'd move mountains for anyone else. But me? Nothing.'

'Shall I ring up Irwin and ask if he's got any bread?'

'No!' He was startled.

'Why ever not?'

'He's not the sort you can ask.'

'But you took him out for a meal last Friday. You said he almost begged . . .'

'Please Amy, don't go on about last week. Now it's this week, with this week's problems.' His chin was out: she knew it was a sign of rapid thinking. 'Besides . . . one act of that sort shouldn't necessarily have prominence over another. . . Looked at logically, if a fellow is so poor he can't afford to buy himself bread, it's highly unlikely he'll keep surplus quantities at home!'

'Since when could Irwin remotely be described as poor?'

Realizing that Ernest might try a variety of hypotheses in an effort to remove them further and further from the subject, she got to her feet. 'I'll try anyway.'

'No, Amy! No.'

By the set of his face she knew then she'd trodden unwittingly on forbidden territory.

'I'm seeing him later, anyway,' he said.

'How much later?'

'Are we cross-examining again? Does it matter how much later?'

'I suppose not. Except that yesterday you told me you were going to see Morris tonight after your class.'

A pause. 'So what's wrong with that? I'm seeing them both. At Morris's flat . . . possibly.'

She felt a sudden pang of sorrow.

'We'll be going over one or two points which he feels Irwin is qualified to deal with.' He began to collect his papers from the floor.

Should she now tell him that Morris had 'phoned earlier saying he hadn't seen or heard from Ernest for several weeks? And she'd bewildered him by mentioning this evening? Perhaps she had misunderstood it all.

'Morris 'phoned today.'

Ernest stopped what he was doing and looked at her

20

coldly. 'I presume you've only just remembered he'd
rung?'

'Of course.' She watched his expression.

'Next you'll be telling me that Irwin rang.'

She felt a slight tremble starting in her knees. She
clenched her hands and said 'No. Only Morris. He says
the work is going too slowly. But since there are so many
facets, and so many . . .'

'Next time someone calls, be so good as to tell me straight
away, will you?' Jacket already on, he moved quickly across
the room to the door.

He had his hand on the door-handle when she said
hastily, 'And what do I say when Morris 'phones to ask why
you haven't turned up?'

He looked at her blankly. 'Please observe the rules, Amy.'

'What rules? What rules?!' She followed him into the
hall and down the corridor. He took no notice of her shouts.

'Is honesty anything to do with rules? What am I supposed to say to your so-called friends? Shall I explain
exactly why you don't see them? Or would you rather do
that yourself?'

'Please, Amy. Please!' He had located his keys and was
at the front door. It was dark in the hall, and quiet as if
all activity in the entire house of usually busy flats had come
to a standstill. He opened the front door and a shaft of dim
light revealed his face. 'Don't wait up for me,' he said. 'Go
to bed and get some rest.'

'Is that what you tell them all when you leave?' She
felt the weight of his kiss on her cheek.

'Come now! For whose sake do we perform this charade?'

When he'd gone she stood with her back against the
wooden panelling trying to drag air into her cramped lungs.
She felt ill. The pain was definitely physical. It ran sharply
through her chest and constricted her throat. Strange
pulses beat in her neck. Upstairs the sudden wail of a baby,
stopping as suddenly in mid-cry. Footsteps in the hall

below; on the stairs; the landing; coming past the door not stopping, going up. She opened the door and looked out onto the empty landing. Another door banged upstairs. From somewhere high up came the clatter of rain on glass. And laughter from the Italians on the top floor. The hall air was cold and smelled of dust. It was good to breathe from an area through which so many people had passed. With each breath she would draw in the collective strength which made them able to carry on their daily lives. She had to be part of a working world from which panic, of necessity, had been excluded. She had to keep her body subdued and her mind clear. It was time to continue.

On the floor of the living room in a circle of light were the piled parts of her own private puzzle. But the room was too empty now, too high, too white. It was no longer filled with all the evidence of their systematic support of the modern arts. She had often persuaded Ernest to sacrifice comfort in favour of the *avant-garde*: new designers had to be encouraged. But in two years the flat had been denuded, as piece after interesting piece had either been sold or given to what Amy considered deserving causes. Glass and stainless steel straight off the drawing board, with cutting edges and a cold feel stood isolated in all their intractability.

The anteroom was empty, save for the sofa bed and a simple desk which had escaped notice. It would be a kinder place for her to work than the echoing cube in which she stood. What little remained there seemed, in the cold electric glare, a positive block to progress. She stared round her looking for a way to break the spell. A kick at the glass table top produced an E and an echo. She would fetch the flute and play a table tune ... summon a sound, any sound to fill the chill atmosphere; to still the noise of water dripping outside on the balcony. Rain dripping irritatingly onto leaves. The plants were drowning.

With an effort she unbolted the outer window, stepped out and was met by a storm. Water hit her sharply in the face. Bouncing drops jumped off the marble as she bent, hitting her ankles, legs and arms. Dragging the heavy pots inside in a backward crouch, she felt wet leaves on her wet face. Her dress was clinging to her knees. She was fighting the rain forest, able to see nothing beyond the green and wet, gripped by vines whose leaves flapped and tossed and stuck to her skin. There was mud on her hands, and grains like sand-fleas leaping and rattling the window panes. Plants inside, she fought with the windows to close them, and wiped her wet face on the curtains. She laughed loudly to the empty room, telling it how cold she was as she tried to rub warmth into her damp and freezing limbs.

Then gradually the return of silence. Her standing with her back to the windows, hearing the rhythm of the rain outside. Dim sounds of traffic on the ring road far away; the small noise of dripping leaves inside, sending trickles of water in tracks across the boards towards her precious hoard of cuttings lying waiting on the floor.

Milena's face looked up. She stared down at it, and it stared back at something just above her left shoulder: a beetle crawling down her neck like a rivulet. 'All I want,' she whispered, 'is a little latitude.' She would try to do no violence to her.

She kicked at the book seconds before the rain river reached it, ploughing papers with her toe and scattering them.

Wet carpet underneath, and the edges of mutilated hands. Her pink fingertips grasping a row of hands drawn in outline: they would demonstrate the ferocity of an un-guarded cutting blade. Palms facing her in macabre benison. In the top left corner of the panel would go this curious, bloody fence surrounding the smallest and faintest picture of Kafka she could find. She would overprint his smiling face with the office stamp of Industrial Accident Insurance. Confine him within the circle of his job – the conscientious official worrying about the problems of workers' welfare, trying to arrange adequate compensation for them. Hands with missing fingers held out for pittances. His desk the symbol of slavery, yet symbolizing for him the admirable calm of an ordered existence. Nothing so irritating as symbols. Kafka holding the only things he needed: pen and paper. Write, correct, modify in case there should be the slightest uncertainty about what he was expressing. To be exact. The very exactness examined, further explained for fear he might have been partially understood or presumed to think life simple. His admiration was for the confident, self-assured, comfortable, well-covered persons from whom he might try – and fail – to hide his unworthiness. Yet he smiled. In nearly every photograph he looked out with sharp eyes, his lips often verging on a smile.

The humour of the terrible struggle. The scale of it. Fighting at the dining table and not at Marathon. Fighting maternal suffocation and paternal tyranny. The smile of someone guilty of being loved; being loved far beyond his deserts. What a muddle he'd been in with girls, in spite of all the headaches, insomnia, grey hairs and despair. Was it not comical to be concerned over the trivial choice between marriage and solitude? Especially since he'd really chosen long before the last attempt at engagement. And how could so sick a man become a husband? A father? She saw him so certain in his uncertainty. A protected corner of the collage would be a safe place for him, curled up like an old mole in a subterranean hideaway.

She would find black for him: bright, ink-blot black of unusual intensity, spreading out from the centre of his head like a Rorschach test, and trailing off into spidery lines. At the outer limits words would begin to take shape, forming into that curious handwriting of his with its left-handed lean, its long loops and heavy horizontals. Reams and reams of paper covered with his words to other people: *Dear Herr Wolff*; *Dear Max*; *Dearest Felice*; *Dear Frau Milena*. The risk of contact. The risk of being half comprehended. The risk of being understood. Mundane events, feverish dreams, intense feelings, positive advice all went into his letters. He had to try the recipient's strength; draw from it some for himself. And being perceptive, he must have known that correspondence was a substitute for contact in the real sense. Yet the dialogue was necessary as fuel for his imaginative work, allowing him to contest and expound without the dangers of physical proximity.

Rain was still beating on the windows. There would have to be a window. Somewhere in the pile of Geographicals was the picture of an eastern European window opening onto a bright blue sky with clouds. She thought it might adequately represent the Czech nation's history of defenestration. Or maybe for Milena it might have more to do with anything but itself. The sound of Ernest's ironic laughter was in her ears. She could almost hear the irritation. 'Why can't a window merely be a window? Why must it always look out? Or in?' From her window she could see nothing but tracks: tracks forming a great Star of David around Milena. Lines of railways, lines of roads, leading from her, leading to her: Prague to Vienna to Meran to Prague to Buchholz. And the one-way route to Benešov to Dresden to Ravensbrück.

Now what was the matter? She was crying. The smoking was beginning to affect her tear ducts. She ought to stop if she couldn't cope. It was only thanks to Conrad she could afford to smoke at all. They certainly couldn't afford the luxury of her being ill. She sank onto the scattered clippings and felt something biting like a bullet into her leg. It was the pencil with which she'd been writing before Ernest had come into the room that afternoon. She removed the half-written letter from beneath the pile of cuttings and quickly re-read it. Now she must recollect what she'd been trying to say . . .

It is so difficult to do justice to your work. Like climbing a beautiful hill, from the top one sees something wonderful. But how to get there? There are so many stops along the way. So much to see. Yet if one dares make a mistake in the recording of a single detail, I have the feeling that when I get to the top I will

25

have spoiled the view. So I keep trying.

Be patient, dear Frank, and think how much you are helping me. Here, where I'm unable to breathe, I can be sure to forget myself when I take up your work. And I shall continue with it, be certain of that. There are few things on this earth I consider more worthwhile. It is gloomy here. Never mind! All I have to do is go on board ship again, and all is well. My worries at the moment consist of translating this magnificent stoker of yours into the stubborn personification of frail family you see so clearly. But should I draw him with the face of someone rejected? I think he shall stay in shadow.

And I'm not surprised that you can't remember me well. Why should you? I suspect that at the time I was in Ernest's shadow. Perhaps you saw someone resembling one of the more animated statues of ancient Egypt! I think of you often in your hotel, and hope the climate is improving your health. Definitely it wouldn't here. Nothing but rain, rain, rain. No real spring at all. Yet the flowers still know it's time to grow. How do they do it, I wonder? Their internal clock must be more precise than mine. My dear grandmother always set her clock by the sun. Perhaps she was right, and we would all be healthier if we did the same . . .

There was so much to tell this strange man. But how could he bear to hear it? It was astonishing that he hadn't been alarmed and repelled by her first outpouring. It was on one of her bad days when she'd first taken it into her head to write. Better not to think of the state she'd been in: half-demented with lack of sleep, worry over money and Ernest's behaviour. She'd had to write. Frank's story had been so new, so strange, so powerful that when she'd read it, it had come down on her like a great silence. The only moment of taking a quiet breath.

He had to know how she felt. And to do that she had to explain who she was: not just anybody sending praise, but someone already known to him. She was the wife of an old friend. Surely he remembered? If he didn't, then it was necessary to describe herself: the tallness, the frizzy hair, the blue eyes, the big hands. Perhaps he'd seen some of her illustrations? She had a modest reputation. And their meeting? In the coffee house, with Ernest doing all the talking to a crowd of admiring listeners. Who was there? William. Irwin. Paul. A fair-haired girl called Uschi in a flame-coloured dress which bled her skin of all tint. She remembered being deep in conversation with Charles when Frank came through the door with two or three others whose faces she couldn't now recall. Thin, emaciated, he looked around with lively eyes. She remembered noting his ears: strange winged things whose upper edges seemed expressly shaped to take the twin swathes of dark hair which fitted over them. She saw his slight smile and mistook it for one of self-assurance. But he said very little, addressing his remarks to . . . who was it? Leon, sitting beside him. It was the first time she'd felt really well after the 'flu. And the first time she'd gone to the café since being ill. Afterwards some of the party had gone to a concert, leaving Frank and Leon talking. She hadn't enjoyed the evening, being irritated by Ernest's insistence that the girl in the flame dress should go too. And his extravagance in buying her ticket. They'd sat on either side of him, and he'd complained in a loud voice above the Schönberg that the audience were philistines. When was the last time they'd gone to a concert? When parties, and visits to galleries and theatres were customary? Had the change been gradual? A certain order had somehow been eroded without her knowing how. Perhaps correspondence with this now-distant stranger could stabilize a life that was collapsing into bits.

. . . . . My days are topsy turvy now. Sometimes we go to bed as the light is creeping round the blind. Then poor Ernest has to go to work with a buzzing head, and I gather what strength I can from coffee. But what pleasure to know that when I start work, it is yours I can turn to . . . . .

Say nothing more to alarm him. Find a few reassuring words to prove that she was truly only interested in doing her best for him.

. . . . . Perhaps this letter will doubly reassure you that I took no

27

offence at your criticism of my first efforts. I found your notes constructive and enlightening and, whatever you may fear, encouraging! So I shall persist. I am in the mood to work despite peculiar pains in the chest which erupt in bouts of coughing. But the present calm I feel is a good omen. Write to me meanwhile and tell me how you pass your time. Is it pleasant there? What do you see from your window? Artists always want to picture things. Write nothing long or tiring, merely a line or two from a place not quite as grey as it is here . . . . .

She would post the letter as early as her head would allow after half a night's smoking, saying nothing to Ernest about it. Not that there was a vital need to be secretive, rather it was a slight apprehension he might ask her why she should feel it necessary to correspond with someone so unimpressive. When she'd read Frank's story for the first time, she'd made the mistake of reading passages aloud to Ernest. 'Too low-key for me', he'd said. 'A bit like the fellow himself.' And he'd returned to his paper on Modern Science as a Source of Clarity in Language.

It was the difficulty of having to explain the need to do more than just illustrate the work. But when she'd read his story, she'd taken on the man. Here was a friend, one especially hers. Someone holding the same view of an irrational world. She felt she so clearly understood what he was saying that she must tell him so. It was an almost physical need to grip his fingers, look into his sharp eyes and put the strength of her convictions into his very blood.

2

Rain all week. Every day she got wet going to the post office. It became a matter of principle not to go home until she'd returned at least once to see if a letter had arrived by a later mail. Once she caught sight of Mrs Kertesch standing in line for her pension. She waved, but didn't go over as she should to ask about her arthritis. There was a danger Mrs Kertesch might mention rent, having surely noticed the large bunch of flowers in her hand. But who could live without flowers? She'd bought an orchid on Thursday to put on Ernest's desk, and guiltily made drawings of it to justify the purchase. No-one came to visit them that week. It was as if the rain had finally driven everyone underground and pinned them there. When it turned to day-long drizzle, darkening the hours into gloom, she turned up her collar and went out looking for someone to talk to.

She found Laurie, usually bright and busy in his little office, cast into voluble misery by the state of the magazine. He said it was a sign of the times – the rain, a manifestation of the national disease. And the readership was failing. Printers weren't bothering to deliver on time. Unions were wanting higher wages which, in theory, he agreed with. No mention of more work. She showed him a drawing of the orchid, and he handed it back with a shake of the head. He was cutting down pages and, for the time being, leaving out illustrations. So borrowing a pen she wrote 'Hello!' on the back of the orchid, addressed it to Stacey and gave it to Laurie to put through the firm's franking machine.

'Since you've still got more money than me,' she said, 'I'll take an early advance on my next work.' He hesitated, eyebrows raised in mock horror. 'Come on, Laurie. Don't be mean.'

'How can she ask such a thing?' He addressed the fuzzy outline of a typist behind the frosted glass partition.

'Didn't I have to wait a whole month for my November fee? And didn't I have to go to your house to collect it? Imagine if I told people that!'

He rolled his shirtsleeves tighter and looked offended. 'I was sick at the time, Amy. And I do not take kindly to blackmail.'

'There you are! Didn't I nurse you back to health?'

'With a little help from chicken soup. And my wife!'

'Grapes and flowers. Magazines from America. They cost me a fortune.'

He placed his hand over his stomach and smiled. 'Shall I ever forget?' Then with his special mocking voice: 'My dearest princess . . .' he took her hand gently, 'there are times in a person's life when all he wants is a little peace. Like then. Like now!'

'You gave me the 'flu. I nearly died,' she said accusingly.

He turned her hand over in his and stroked it. 'You should look after yourself.' With his thumb he marked the dark places under her eyes. 'Shadows like ink. I've been hearing things.'

The telephone rang. She waited while he gave the caller as good as he got; rang off; made another call of similar volubility and length, while at the same time giving her the benefit of loud asides.

He banged the 'phone down. 'That's how to deal with them. Agents! What do they care about Literature? If Moses had an agent we'd be one Commandment short.'

'I'm sorry Laurie, I don't follow.'

He tapped his head in aggravation. 'The brain, girl! The agent would have kept ten per cent for himself!' He thought again: 'Or made him write another Commandment!' His mood was brightening. 'Now that's what I call a good, well-rounded joke.'

'Laurie, I really must have money,' she said.

'From me? Why have I been so honoured?'

'Because you're the simplest person to get it from.'

'Simplest, no. Simple-mindedest, yes!' He put his hand in his trouser pocket and brought out a few notes.

'Good!' she said. 'Now we shall have coffee and cigarettes. Then I shall do something useful for you . . . like filing.'

'Spare me more troubles,' he said. All he wanted her to do was go home as quickly as possible, get into a warm bed and stay there until her cough had disappeared.

She sat drinking coffee with him in his office until it was time for the second post. She left him standing at the top of the office stairs, plucking his braces as he watched her descend.

'Do you know which Commandment the agent took?' he called when she'd reached the bottom.

'Which?'

' "Thou Shalt Not Steal"!'

By Friday the cough had settled on her chest in painful tightness. The rain had turned into thick, grey mist. It clung to her clothes and soaked her hair. She blinked it and breathed it. She found it in shops; in the post office; the library. It hung over the ceilings and round the shelves where she poked about, hoping for insight into Milena's youth. At home the canvas was blank save for a solitary window hovering centre top, its panes filled with the bright blue of an impossible sky with toy clouds. She sat dripping over photos of Prague, trying between coughs to make sense of an architectural jumble of spires and domes and crenellations. A foggy city, close-packed and shadowy: a grand Baroque showcase for a dead emperor. Might as well look for a needle in a haystack. She wouldn't find Milena there. She'd left and gone to Vienna, glad indeed to escape confinement.

Kafka stayed longer, but longed for release from his special demons. Behind which anonymous shuttered windows did he sit at night, waiting for sufficient quiet to write? Home from the office noise to sleep a while. Or try to sleep, with a hammering head and the din from the kitchen of the maid and mother shouting. Dinner *en famille*, father giving everyone the benefit of his wisdom. Don't do as I do, do as I say. He should eat good meat. He should help more in the business. He shouldn't mix with no-good actors. 'He who lies down with dogs, gets up with fleas.' He should join in more. The terrible, noisy games of cards at which he sat like a stranger. The longing for quiet. Variations on the theme of the search for peace. Was he fit to live alone? Fit to live with? To be engaged? Hedge the marriage possibility about with infinite provisos. No homely evenings sitting opposite the wife with gold-capped teeth. No cosy, conjugal bed. At night he had to write alone. No chance, no hope of children. Too late. Already tuberculosis had been diagnosed. And welcomed? It was a pardonable wish: to be so ill one was forced to relinquish a conventional existence. Left in peace to fight the blank page, and keep the body at bay long enough to set down the vision before it was too late. The longing for normality returning to plague him from time to time. His letters to women only promises of shared love. His affairs with them sufficiently disastrous to be the catalyst of future work.

Library cold and hunger drove her into the streets which, to her surprise, had vanished in a khaki haze. A real fog come down over an unready city. Traffic sounds came through the gloom, muffled and slow. She bumped into strangers shuffling their way along the sides of buildings, before disappearing into the dark. She hadn't experienced a fog like this since she was a small child, when a simple outing had turned into a nightmare of being lost; her only anchor the hand of her nurse which she'd hung onto with simple ferocity. At last the front door, her frantic grand-mother snatching her up and gagging her with her head-scarf, then rushing her upstairs to the warmth of the stove. Was it the day of her baby brother's funeral? Memories merged. But a day with grandmother all to herself . . . She

32

pushed her face into her coat to avoid the sting of fumes. To stop the tears. Lonely. She would go and find Ernest.

At the bank they said he'd already gone home on account of the weather. They recommended she did likewise. But she knew where to find him. Slowly she made her way to the café gleaming dimly in the dark; the glow from neon lettering touching the tops of the Ionic columns, and the miniature trees in their boxes outside.

The place was emptier than usual. One or two solitary customers were trying to read their papers. Someone was playing billiards in the back room. The waiters were wandering between the tables flicking imaginary crumbs with their cloths. Albert said hello as he passed into the kitchen carrying a tray of empty coffee glasses. Ernest was sitting with a group in a corner by the far window. It was risky coming on him unawares; he didn't like it. Not that he ever said much to her in front of his friends. The best she could expect was a quick, hard look noting her present condition, and a pat or kiss before he went back to talking. She'd learned long ago to regulate any amusement she might have felt when listening to his public pronouncements. If she often thought his listeners were more respectful of his pocket than his views, she tried to keep her misgivings to herself. He acknowledged her in his usual perfunctory way. Irwin and Morris waved at her and continued arguing. The discarded pieces of a chess game lay between them among papers, books and ash-trays. Charles seemed noisily at odds with Rose. Three strange girls stared at her coldly and went back to Ernest.

Jasmine made space for her and immediately told her she looked ghastly. She agreed, and was glad Jasmine's mind had already moved on to the ballet she'd seen the previous evening. She said she'd demonstrate the experience, and stood up. Nobody but Amy took any notice as she propped herself against the nearest wall. She began to wave her arms. There was little grace in such dangerous swaying. As she collapsed there was laughter. She was stoned. Conrad winked at Amy.

More coffee was served, the whipped cream falling over the edges of the tall glasses. No wonder Ernest was getting fat. There was cream round his mouth which the girl beside him wiped off with delicate fingers. Why did he always need so many girls: girls wearing ponchos who painted neo-realist nudes; girls with large arms who pummelled clay; well-dressed girls like the one beside him whose manicured fingers smoothed his cheek? On the table in front of him lay the silver box which held the cocaine. He played with it as he talked. They would wait for Albert to finish fussing, then settle down to the ritual passing of the powder, the ritual rolling of the tube, and the heavenly snort.

After that it was easy. She could enjoy everything: listen to William's jokes; lose to Charles at chess; comfort poor Rose who, when she could take her mind from him, liked to indulge in private explanations of why she couldn't yield her virginity. She said that only Amy bothered to defend her against the others. She'd never forget how Conrad had tried to lace her tea with acid: she'd been grateful to Amy ever since for stopping him. She'd do anything for her, she said. One day she'd even take her home.

No-one noticed the approach of evening, except to comment that fog was clouding the chandeliers. So good to feel heedless of time, to feel witty and light-hearted. Her hunger was gone. The cough merely punctuated the repartee and went unnoticed. It was the most enjoyable, the funniest, the sharpest evening she'd ever experienced. Until the next evening when the silver box was passed round. The same pattern and variations as friends came and went round the central figure of Ernest, who could always be heard insisting he couldn't waste his valuable time just sitting and talking. But he was one of the regulars who always stayed until closing time when Albert would serve nothing more. Then he'd cry 'My God, another day gone!' as he and the stragglers were herded onto the pavement.

It was a recognized custom that the last of the party

should see each other home. Conversations were wound up, further meetings arranged and arguments concluded as they walked the night streets arm in arm. This night they were happy to make for the flat, taking everyone with them and hoping the fog would be gone by morning. They clung to one another with Ernest leading the way; Charles and Conrad linking arms through Amy's, holding her up. She could feel the lift as they pulled her along, her feet dragging. She was swimming in a green sea. Conrad gave her his scarf. The cough shuddered through her with new force, bending her double. But Ernest said onward. Yard by yard they blindly followed him, desperately plunging into each intersection. Twice he led them the wrong way, swearing he knew the route like the back of his hand. And not a sound in the streets; nobody except a man sleeping in a doorway under a cardboard box, who woke with a curse as they stumbled into him. He took without comment the money Charles gave him, and went back to sleep without a word of thanks.

By the time they arrived at the flat they were soaked to the skin and smelling faintly of sulphur. She fell into bed with no thought for the others, not caring who it was who removed her wet clothes and tucked her in like a baby. She slept instantly. Then woke. She was cold. She was hot. When she tried to call out the pain in her chest cut like the point of a *poignard*. She wanted something to kill the pain. She wanted Ernest.

Later she woke and thought she saw Conrad standing beside the bed in the dark, wrapped in the hand-woven rug. Then Jasmine and Charles came and went, flickering and fading in a misty dream. She thought she heard them whispering together by the wardrobe where the fog was thickest.

She woke again when the light went on. It was too bright and she was still in pain. Pillows were being pushed behind her. Someone was pulling at the straps of her nightdress and she was fighting them off. It was Conrad and he was hurting. His voice was telling her to be quiet. She saw his serious face above her. 'Sit up,' he said. She sat up. Something sticky was being rubbed across her shoulders, and moving up to her neck. His voice was quietly pleading with her to let his wrist go. She smelled camphor and eucalyptus. He was pushing her head forward and holding her down. He was a beetle crawling along her spine. She tried her best to beat it off, but it crawled across her shoulder blade and over her collar bone. He was telling her to stop yelling; telling her to lie back and be still.

She felt his hand press into her chest and felt it move between her breasts. 'Where's Ernest?' she said. His palm moved rhythmically, rubbing in the breathing balm. It moved in a circular motion, wider and wider across her breasts. 'Where's Ernest?' She could feel the heat of his hand as the rise and fall of her shallow breathing met its pressure. He was kneeling close beside her; bending over her; gripping her hard by the shoulder and rubbing and rubbing her chest. She could see the gleam of his skin, and feel his breath on her forehead.

His hand began to move from one breast to the other.

'Where's Ernest?'

'Asleep,' he said. 'Go to sleep.' His hand continued making circular movements around her breasts. His fingers hurt. 'Lie back,' he told her as he began to knead. He was kneading and squeezing her breasts; slower and slower, his head so close she could see black pupils and gold flecks in his eyes.

'Conrad . . . ' she murmured, 'I want something to . . .'

'I know,' he said, and kept kneading.

'I must have something . . .'

'You'll get it. You'll get it.' His hair brushed her face as he bent his head.

'In the desk drawer, Conrad.'

His fingers stopped momentarily. 'In the what?' Then he began to pummel her breasts more urgently.

'Please . . . under my peasant scarf.'

36

'What? What?' His muffled voice stopped as his lips closed over her left nipple. She could feel his tongue.

She grabbed at his hair with a weak hand. 'Please!' Feebly she tried to pull him away.

He looked up at her wildly. 'Can't it be later? Plenty of time.' His lips went back to her nipple, his hands moving over the contours of her thighs.

'Please!' With a supreme effort she sat up straight, knocking him into her lap. Her breathing rasped with the sound of a saw. 'Get me an aspirin, Conrad. Get me three!'

He collapsed, rolling over her and down her legs until he was lying across her feet. 'Goddamit, Amy!' he exclaimed.

She looked at him warily. 'I feel awful.'

He pulled a face. 'How do you think I feel?' He drew in deep, dramatic breaths and began to rub his mouth. 'That stuff tastes terrible. Killed my tongue.'

'Doesn't feel so good either!' She pulled the bedclothes up to her neck and looked at him seriously.

He rolled over onto his back and lay with his legs in the air, tucking his shirt into his trousers. 'Do you good though,' he said. He waved his legs experimentally then got up.

'Maybe. Where's Ernest?'

He looked at her with his head on one side. 'Where do you think?'

'Go away,' she said. She didn't want to think.

He was smiling broadly at her as he went to the door. Hand on the light switch he said, 'Shall I kill him now? Or later?' Then he turned off the light and went.

She lay in the dark for a while, staring at his after-image before dropping into precarious sleep.

In the morning she coughed up some blood but said nothing to Ernest about it. Conrad came to say the fog was clearing.

When he too had gone she sat up in bed and read and re-read Frank's words, trying to see him on his balcony in the sun, watching the lizards scuttling over the warm walls. She told him about the blood, knowing that he would feel immediate sympathy. She wanted someone to care about her tiny existence and listen to what she had to say. To him she'd be able to speak without restraint, convinced – without proof – that this man she hardly knew would be incapable of passing judgement on her. He could be told anything; it wouldn't matter. He wasn't frightened of what she was. He'd replied to her first letters, and that was sufficient for her to feel sure a link had been forged between them. He was a writer of honest prose, with the instinct to know another's honesty.

Her thoughts went onto paper in a long, rambling stream of words which she didn't bother to correct or re-write. She felt too weak to care if she was making total sense.

In her ramblings Ernest was the figure her thoughts centred round: his worried face, the constant enquiries about how she felt. She wasn't so sick she couldn't carry on, she said. He had to be looked after. There was breakfast and clean shirts and clean boots and reassurances. She liked him sitting on the bed beside her, eating apples and drinking her tea. He'd sift his small change on the quilt and wonder whether he had to walk to work, or whether he was fit enough to go at all. He came out in sweats. He wasn't able to breathe. There was a terrible tightness in his chest. It was touching the way he behaved. She could see why the sight of her helplessness should move him so. For his sake she'd call the doctor.

When Ernest was out she added more to Frank's letter: how she'd spent one whole, wet afternoon trying to finish the illustration and had ruined the Captain's face during a bout of coughing, by putting her fist in a patch of wet cerulean. But what she wanted, she said, was Frank to send her all his work. She must have it, not necessarily to risk illustrating it but to confirm what she already knew, that his were very special qualities. Nothing facile. People were as he saw them, full of contradictions and absurdities. Like

38

her life. One day she'd speak about it. Her life now was hard compared to the comforts of home. Home? Here was home. Her choice. Eyes closed. A vision: tea and apples with Mother. Ernest gone out, daily from two until eight. Watch the clock, try to sleep. Get up. Read the manuscript. Shuffle the parts of the Milena mystery. Read the manuscript. Had she said thank you for it? Thank you again.

The doctor said she must have rest and warmth and good food. She must worry less. Not worry about the blood which he didn't believe was serious. He left a prescription for iron pills. No doubt Ernest would take them and they'd both feel better before the week was out.

By the weekend she was on her feet again and feeling human. Another visit to the doctor confirmed that she was mending. The weather was clearing. She looked at the sky: blue after weeks of not being there at all. On days of pure blue everything seemed simple and clear.

A walk in the park with Jasmine clinging. Like old times. There was the same familiarity between them, but confidences from now on would come less easily, now Amy had something to hide. The old law was broken. They were fully grown.

Leaning her head on Amy's shoulder Jasmine said she wished that Stacey wasn't so far away. The perfume she was wearing obliterated the smell of the cut grass. They walked towards the edge of the park where it was still wet under the trees. Beyond them undulating open land broken by clumps of trees showing the first touches of spring: tree reflections in the still waters of a necklace of small lakes lying in a dip in the landscape. In the distance the trees had a reddish tinge where they grew closer together and taller until, across the sky-line they became the solid mass of a real wood. Amy called it her forest because of a block of fir trees – perhaps part of an older plantation left after the park had become public property – which lent a storybook look to the view. Beneath the firs it was quiet, protected and dry, even on stormy days. There were alleys and cross-paths set

39

like a maze in which one could wander for hours, or slip between the tall trunks and lose oneself.

Ernest had been amused by the woman turned child again because of a few pines. Soon after discovering it, she'd led him there, with trepidation, knowing his distaste for exercise. Beneath the trees she'd waited in vain for his look of amazement and pleasure. She'd told him it was her special place, and he'd put his arm round her, told her how much he loved her love of nature, and suggested they go back for a beer.

'He's asked me to marry him,' Jasmine said.

'Who?'

'David, of course.'

'And what did you say?'

'Well . . .' Jasmine kicked at a twig with an immaculate shoe. 'There are lots of difficulties.' She didn't look up. 'There's his family, for a start.'

'And what do they say?'

'They don't know yet. He's waiting until I make up my mind. To tell you the truth, I think he's terrified of telling them.'

'Naturally he is. But wait until they meet you. They're bound to like you.' She squeezed Jasmine's arm.

'They have,' she said miserably. 'Last Friday week.' She looked at Amy with desperation. 'It was awful. Well, bits of it were. I liked his mother. At least you know where you stand with somebody who looks you over absolutely blatantly. Remember what you used to say? "Just smile a lot"? I did. And I took her a massive box of chocolate liqueurs. I think she was impressed.'

'Were you wearing something grand?'

'Purple silk. Frightfully restrained. His brothers thought I was rather splendid. They were all there. Like peas, but frightfully good looking. We all sat on the edges of our chairs. His father shouted a lot.'

'At them?'

'Who? No. It's his style. They don't seem to take any

notice. It must be the machinery he works with all day. Factories. He wanted to know what sort of business I had. He kept giving me advice on how to run it. They stopped him in the end.'

'Well, it sounds as though they were on your side.'

'I suppose so. His brother's girl friend was there, wearing a diamond as big as . . .' she pointed to a knot in the tree they were passing '. . . that. But she didn't sit with him, much less talk to him.'

'Surely you could tolerate segregation for one evening?'

'Well, I had to sit and listen to her going into raptures about drawing room curtains. There's a limit to what one can say about curtains.'

They'd reached the wet grass, skirted it because of Jasmine's fragile shoes, and made for a bench beneath a tree.

'Honestly, Amy, it was excruciating. You should have seen David's face. I couldn't decide whether he was pleading with me to keep a straight face, or whether he was hoping I'd start one of my fabrications.'

'Oh, you didn't hurt her feelings, did you?'

'Of course not. Luckily we went into dinner.' Jasmine was staring miserably at her feet. 'Oh my goodness, the memory!' She laughed without humour.

'We got through all the prayers and things quite safely. Naturally I'd gone prepared and knew what it was all about. Then we had one of those huge meals that stick in your throat. It was all dry – except the soup, of course – dry chicken, and roast potatoes like nuts. No gravy or anything. And the sweetest pudding you've ever tasted.' She sighed. 'They gobbled it up, with David's father shouting at me to eat up and grow fat.'

'Sometimes one has to sacrifice oneself!'

'I know. I was doing my absolute best. But I still blench at what happened next.' She put her hands briefly in front of her face. 'After the meal, you see, I naturally took out my cigarettes and offered them round.'

'And they don't approve of smoking?'

She bit her lip. 'I was at the far end of the table, right next to the candles. So of course I lit my cigarette from one of them.' She pulled a face. 'I leaned over and just lit my cigarette.'

'Oh, my dear!'

Jasmine nodded. 'It went deadly quiet. They all simply stared at me. Then David leaped to his feet and rushed me from the room. I couldn't believe it. I was taken away!' Her eyes were round at the awful memory. 'There was the most terrible hubbub coming from the dining room. I swear his mother was screaming. And I was so upset being dragged away like a leper.' Her face was pink. 'What a nightmare!' She put her hand on Amy's. 'David just hadn't explained that one never touches the Sabbath candles . . .'

'But surely they understood you'd made a genuine mistake?'

'Worse than that, Amy.' She rolled her bright, brown eyes. 'He hadn't told them I wasn't Jewish! I was furious. It took half an hour to get me back into that dining room. His mother had calmed down enough by then to have me there! She kept saying "My own son! My own son!" And I kept saying "How could you?"! Then I left.' She shook her head sadly. 'I wouldn't see him for days.'

'But wasn't it brave of him to take you there in the first place? He must have thought they'd be bound to love you. Not like Ernest. He never even tried.'

'Well, David's family aren't all that strict. Not like Ernest's.' She rubbed Amy's hand. 'Are you cold?'

'No. Someone walked over my grave!' She patted Jasmine's arm. 'At least he's asked you to marry him. That's noble.'

Jasmine had lowered her head. 'Now we come to the other bad part . . .' She was staring at the patch of concrete beneath their seat. 'I know it sounds ridiculous, Amy, but you're not to laugh.'

'Oh, come on Jasmine! You know me better than that.'

Her face took on that confessional look which Amy knew so well. 'It's circumstances really,' she said. 'And we haven't known each other all that . . . Well, we haven't – David and I – not to put too fine a point on it . . . well . . . slept together.' She sounded defiant. 'Oh, I love him a lot. I really do. Otherwise I wouldn't be talking about him at all, would I? He's absolutely amazing, in lots of ways. So intelligent. You see, first of all, there haven't been too many opportunities. And secondly, he's been a bit reluctant.'

'With you? How could he resist?'

'I rather admired it. Such a nice change. And you know we both like serious men. Men with something a little bit . . . unattainable? Unfortunately he's dropped this bombshell about wanting to marry me.'

'Against his family's wishes?'

'Oh no. They've all to agree. He says they will if I'm willing to change my faith.'

'Does it matter that much to him?'

'I'd willingly do it for his sake if I knew for sure.'

Jasmine put her head close to Amy's. 'That's why I need your flat!'

A pause. Amy laughed.

'One afternoon, that's all. Three until five would do nicely. My free afternoon – next Tuesday week.'

'Of course you can have the flat.'

'Oh, Amy, aren't you wonderful?' She kissed her cheek. 'Are you sure you're not chilly out here?'

'No, Jasmine. Next Tuesday week is fine. No-one will be there. Ernest stays out until late. And I've got an appointment until six.' Already she was wondering what she'd do until six.

Jasmine's face was shining. 'Just think how good you'll feel knowing you've helped your dearest friend to make the biggest decision in her life.' She got up. 'Shall we go back?' she said.

'You've never regretted marrying Ernest, have you?'

43

'Never.'

Arm in arm they walked back towards the café, while Jasmine agonized over her Arab-sounding name.

With the coming of the warmer weather the cough subsided, leaving her weak and unable to concentrate except for short periods upon the completion of Frank's work. Originally she had envisaged making wood cuts, but gave up the idea as being too laborious. She could see harsh black and white, overlaid with washes of sea and sky: jagged outlines depicting people in uncomfortable situations. The immigrant in an unknown harbour unable to land, still trapped on board in confrontation with strangers. She gave him Frank's piercing eyes.

The letter she sent him with the drawings was insistent that her work was more for therapy than publication. Should he, on the other hand, want to use it, she would be overjoyed. These days she was so uncertain.

With the sealing and sending of the letter came the physical dread of emptiness as it fell from her fingers into the post box, and was followed, as she went home, by regret for what she hadn't managed to say.

The next letter would be different. In it she would express the power she felt inside to accomplish anything. It was there somewhere, hiding for the moment, but still able to return. It was the move away from home; the sudden change of status from rich to poor; from girl to married woman; the being a late developer. She still wasn't ready to face the bleakness of it all. One had to have continued strength in order to survive.

Below the flat in the street a man was repairing his car. Bonnet and boot both open, pieces of engine strewn on the path and road, the car looked hopeless. No hint of helplessness though about the man, neatly dressed in clean jeans and shirt, polishing something with a rag. Why did he look so certain he'd be able to get it back on the road? She wanted to hang over the balcony and ask him. Did he have a degree in Advanced Car Mechanics? Was there behind the open

44

front door through which he went from time to time, a qualified engineer who was giving him expert advice? He wasn't going to have the thing ready in a matter of minutes – for all she knew he might be days yet – but his shirt showed no traces of sweat, his hair was brushed and smooth, each gesture neat and considered. Should she go down and throw herself on his mercy, begging him to give away his secret? She knew for sure that if night fell before the car was back in one piece again, he would go indoors quite happily to eat an orderly meal and sleep soundly, not concerning himself about the wreck outside. He would have the kind of mind that put things in compartments. Hers, she felt, was like Pandora's Box: open it and out would fly ideas, dreams, half-thoughts, worries and hopes in never-ending clouds. They'd buzz around her ears for days, not letting her sleep, not allowing her to work. What was missing was a central, stabilizing core of something or someone. As in the old days.

Then it had been school which had held the pieces together. Curious to think of it now with such nostalgia. At the time she knew how privileged she was supposed to feel, being sent to such an expensive and progressive place. Reasons enough to hate it. But, like many girls before her, she'd succumbed to its blandishments. She'd been cared for and cared about, more at home there than with her family. The wild illegal excursions to cemeteries and the like with Jasmine and Stacey, the illicit sorties across the river, the breaking of countless house rules were censured as if the three of them were naughty children who, given time, would grow up to be solid citizens. Nobody openly mentioned the drugs, with the exception of Stacey's father who truly believed his daughter was under an evil influence. Her own father never questioned the disappearance of surgery supplies, or the bills he paid for the clothes which Jamine wore, charged to his account. Her father was far too busy to notice his well-dressed daughter.

Had the strength she felt then been an illusion? Poor

Ernest. He thought he'd run off with someone strong and brave. No wonder he'd lost interest in this weak, pathetic scrabbler after security. One look in the mirror was sufficient. Her thin, pale face stared back at her. She knew by the lowered eyelids that this had all the makings of a rotten day. Let go, and soon the rest of her face would droop downwards as if she was being sucked to earth by gravitational pull. The chest and stomach would cave in and curve; the weight in her legs increase until, like a deep-sea diver, she'd hardly be able to drag herself towards the bedroom. It had happened many times before under the influence of this and that. Now, under the influence of nothing more than desire, she could make it happen. If she wanted to. The luxury of it: to shrivel and shrink into nothing the apparition she saw before her. A smile fluttered at the corners of the spectre's mouth, hovered a second and disappeared. She was wearing joke clothes. So much for inner harmony! If Frank could see her now he'd pass her by as a stranger. It wouldn't do. He was her hope. She would change her clothes, eat some food and write to him.

Their letters crossed. His pleased her by its pleasure at her work. And by its length. Of course he'd send her more of his work. He'd arrange for it to be sent via Fox, his publisher. The fact that she liked what he wrote gave it some value for him. Such a nice way of expressing himself in a polite, slightly distant way which seemed to promise greater intimacy. As to the question of his engagement, he'd been engaged three times, if one took into account the fact that he'd been engaged to the same girl twice. She spent considerable time pondering why he should still be engaged yet feel, as he put it, that there was no prospect of marriage. His remarks that women always suffered innocently but that men suffered perhaps more, caused her to wonder what kind of woman attracted him. She could ask him: it was clear he had no inhibitions about answering personal questions. She sensed he might reveal more of himself on paper than face to face. From what she could remember of the café encounter, there'd been a warning in his demeanour not to come too close. With the written word his sensitivity could be protected from physical contact. But he was ill. She'd forgotten that she was thinking of someone sick who perhaps longed for a normal life while being afraid it would be denied him. She must tell him how life was never normal. Eddies and whirlpools. That married life was an ocean full of hidden hazards.

She would tell him her history from the time she could remember at home, until the misery of here and now. Misfortune/Fortune, always both sides of her card. There was a law about her life that whatever she received in joy was to be paid for in pain. So many instances. After the death of her baby brother she'd been her mother's only, best-beloved child. At thirteen she'd been deprived of her mother . . .

There is no argument, Frank, that law for me exists. It has been a consistent force in my life and it's still in operation.

The more love she'd tried to show for her father, the more he'd demanded her obedience as if the two were synonymous. She had gladly forsaken him to live with Ernest, who now treated the action as if she'd come out for a stroll . . .

The life we lead here is unhealthy in the extreme, both in terms of physical and mental well-being. Those first few months of unbelievable happiness are now counterbalanced by what can only be described as moments of real horror. But please don't pity me. I'm only trying to tell you the truth of matters here in this emotional hothouse. Things at times have been so desperately fraught between us that once I ran away. Neither of us seems to know how to handle the other. Nor do we even understand the simple art of living within our means.

Now you can see what sort of person you're writing to!

She enclosed a reproduction of a painting by Böcklin, cut from a magazine. It had been intended for Milena but she thought the struggling bodies caught in the swirling

47

waters of a rocky river might underline how she felt.

It was strange how writing to Frank had the immediate effect of making her feel better. Once she'd overcome the urge to send yet another letter speeding after the first, she could put her mind to some simple task. Cleaning the flat was long overdue. Dust hung in glistening clouds in the shafts of pale, spring sunlight. It deadened the shining surfaces of glass and steel. The mystery was where it all came from. Mrs Kertesch told her she lacked routine and a proper respect for such evidently expensive furniture. Ernest concurred, forgetting that he too had come from a home where dust had been miraculously removed by unseen hands. He complained too about her cooking, dwelling on the past delights of *latkes* and *helzel* and something he called *goldene yoich*, which summoned up pictures of a yodelling cook. He wasn't to be blamed for taking himself off to the nearest restaurant to dine, since the only thing he might find in their refrigerator was one egg. If she'd tried to make such dishes she knew their reception whatever the result: he would express surprise that she'd bothered, spoon in the soup as fast as he could, complain it was too hot and go out immediately. Possibly he might not even sit down to eat, but stand nervously staring over the steaming plate at the bricks and blind windows of the house next door.

She thought of Frank lying quietly in his deck chair in the sun, a glass of milk in his hand, her letter in front of him, wondering why anyone should think him so valuable a person, and so worthwhile a writer. He owed it to her to get well. She wouldn't let him sit there, his breathing becoming shallower and quieter until it couldn't be heard. What she should give him was the will to live, and the promise that his living could be joyful. She'd send him her favourite, most energizing postcard, the one which would make him feel better instantly. She hoped he too would enjoy the decorative and formalized tree against which the couple were standing; the golden whorls and the magic eyes and the curious flowers underfoot.

Not until the card had been pushed through the post office letter box did she realize he might read more into the picture of the man and woman in close embrace above the word 'Fulfilment' than she'd intended.

She went in search of Charles for his cheerful company, and the possibility that he'd sold something and might still have money. His mother kissed her fondly and sent her down into the back garden where he was working on a maquette of a seated Thing – or so she said. Oblivious of her shouts not to spoil the plants, he continued throwing lumps of clay the armature from a bowl overflowing with dirty white water. The table on which he was working was already awash with slip, most of it disfiguring his preliminary sketches. He was standing in a pool of whitish mud which had left a tide-mark on his ancient tennis shoes. The laces trailed over the wet grass which in parts was almost submerged by water trickling slowly into the nearest flower bed. His mother screamed from the balcony that he was killing her bulbs. When there was no reply she pleaded with Amy to make him listen.

'Ignore her,' he said. 'It's a mania with her, tidiness. She combed the grass this morning. And dusted that cherry tree!' He was staring at Amy. 'You look a mite better than when I last saw you. What's up? Are you ill?' A bird in the tree suddenly began to sing. He threw a lump of clay in its direction and went on with his work.

'I'm on my way to Fox,' she said. 'He may want me to illustrate some of Frank's work.'

'Good for you. Good for him.'

'What's the girl that Frank's engaged to like?' she asked as casually as she could. She felt his sharp glance.

'Two arms, two legs, the usual appurtenances. A bit rough by all accounts, so that's in her favour.' He rubbed his wet hands down the front of his already wet shirt. 'And his family don't approve, so that's in her favour.'

'Why won't he marry her?'

He was struggling to reach a packet of cigarettes in his

shirt pocket. She rescued it and lit his cigarette. He puffed on it and handed it to her. 'I suppose he's a professional fiancé! Likes the business of getting engaged. Sometimes even I feel the urge.' He looked hard at her. 'Here! Don't go getting like the rest of them. Nothing to do but gossip. You're made of better stuff.' He took the cigarette from her lips and it went out in his wet fingers. 'Damn!' He threw it onto the garden.

'May I come and pick some of your daffodils?' she said.

'Help yourself. Use the studio door, and you won't run into Mother. She doesn't like her arrangements spoiled.'

From the balcony above came the sudden cry of his mother, leaning over the balustrade and shouting excitedly at him to go and pick up the cigarette end which lay like a dead star on the fresh peat of the borders. Then other voices coming from above: unseen visitors arriving and calling out.

'Oh dear,' Charles said, 'it's Aunt Sylvia. That's all I need. And Aunt Grace. And little Malcolm!' His mother turned to welcome them. They came out from the kitchen and stood beside her looking down from the balcony. He waved to them briefly and began to back towards the studio wall pulling Amy with him. When they were out of sight they could hear his mother saying how Charles was busy with his latest sculpture, and didn't like to be disturbed. They heard the ring of heels on metal as she led her visitors onto the top steps of the staircase to get a better view of the *oeuvre*. He pulled a terrible face and made a gesture for Amy to listen to the conversation going on over their heads:

'Wonderful! Oh, I really like that, don't you?' somebody exclaimed.

'Now that's what I call magnificent!' a man's voice said.

Charles raised his eyebrows in surprise. 'Never been known before,' he whispered. 'Usually they can't make head or tail of my sculpture.' He peered upwards, trying to see. Cries of delight were still coming from the balcony.

'Perhaps we'd better go and have a word with them,' he said in a kinder voice.

Holding Amy by the hand he stepped into view.

At the foot of the staircase they stopped. Above them were his four relatives, backs turned, leaning over the balcony rail and looking down into the garden next door.

'We've always wanted a fishpond with a fountain,' his aunt Sylvia was saying. 'And lions . . . *couchant* aren't they? But no gnomes.'

'What does it say on that plaque, Malcolm?'

'"One is nearer to God in a garden than anywhere else on earth".'

'How nice!'

Charles gripped Amy's wrist and held up her arm like a boxer's. 'Amy's here!' he shouted. 'An original!'

The four people above turned and looked down at them.

'She's my inspiration,' he called. There was silence except for the singing bird. Then his mother hastily began to shepherd her visitors back through the kitchen door. Aunt Grace stopped and smiled coyly down at him.

'Is she your model, Charlie?' She adjusted her hat as though she needed to busy herself, having said something risqué. She pointed to the dripping maquette with its skeleton of exposed wires. 'Can't see much likeness!' She laughed.

Charles pulled a face at her departing back. 'We'll go inside, Amy,' he said, 'and let the rabble cry to the wind.'

He took her into the studio downstairs where they sat smoking in gloomy silence, broken only by the chirping of birds and occasional bursts of hysterical laughter from upstairs.

'Did you get paid for the Butter Man, Charles?' Amy said at last.

'Please! I can only take so much Philistinism in one day.' He sighed. 'As a matter of fact, I did.'

'Then give me half.'

'Half?' He was amused. 'I should give you half my hard-earned money?'

'Why not? I'd give you mine if I had it.'

He looked at her serious face. 'That's perfectly true. But why should you think I don't need it myself?'

'Because you're fat and well fed. And there's Mother to look after you. And you always pay for your drinks.'

'Unassailable testimony, my dearest!'

'Then give me half.'

He pulled a face, stared at her for a moment's considera-tion, then went over to an ancient coil pot in the corner. Putting his hand into it he brought out a wad of notes. He counted out half and gave them to her. The rest he put back in the pot and covered it with a dirty rag. She thanked him with a smile, but said nothing. His expression was still morose.

'Am I really fat?' he said.

She considered. 'Quite fat.'

'Then my sculptures will have to get even thinner! Sort of Dorian Gray syndrome. Use less bronze too. Perhaps I'll get to be as famous as the renowned Irish sculptor Jack O'Mettti!'

'Why do you want to be famous?'

'So that I can keep you in the manner to which you wish to become accustomed!'

He put out a thumb and dabbed her chin. 'You've got such a sad face. Like six volumes of Dostoyevsky!'

What was wrong with that? He was one of her favourite writers. Frank's too.

'Since when this sudden interest in Frank?' Charles was frowning.

'I've illustrated one of his stories, that's all.' She wanted to be honest. 'We've written since.'

Charles began to kick the dusty floor. 'Don't believe too much of what he says.'

'I believe every word he says.'

'Why? What has he said to you?' He was suddenly agitated. 'Did he mention my work?'

'No, Charles. Why should he?'

With unusual seriousness he explained how he'd sent

Frank several photographs of his latest standing figure, 'only to keep the blighter in touch'. In reply he'd received what he described as a dissertation on the truth of a work being in danger of disguise beneath inessentials, unless the artist was vigilant.

'He knows nothing about it,' he said. 'Bloody cheek!'

'He meant well.' She knew for sure he meant well. In a letter to her he'd spoken in the same manner, and she'd taken him to task for the implied patronage. 'He says nothing lightly,' she said.

He looked concerned. 'It's terrible when someone always says what he means.'

'Isn't that the only way?'

'There we are!' He clapped a hand to his forehead and left the mark of clay between his brows. 'Here's another of them! People like you and him could disrupt the entire universe with your honesty.'

She looked at him fondly. 'So you do take him seriously?'

'He gets under my skin.'

From upstairs came the sounds of preparation for afternoon tea. Voices were raised in animated conversation.

Charles studied her face. 'He's like you, you know. And yet he's not. For instance, he knows nothing about how to lie. And we all know that you're a terrible liar!'

She laughed. 'Don't save my feelings, will you!'

'That's it,' Charles said. 'You lie to save people's feelings.' He raised a hand to stop her remonstrances. 'I know what you really think of my stuff. And usually there's some truth in it. But you bother to tell me in such a way that I love you for it.' He was looking squarely at her. 'Now Frank . . . He hasn't got the knack. If you ask, he tells you straight out. If you don't, it's worse. He just looks. Have you ever seen him "Just Looking"?'

She wished she had. Charles lit another cigarette.

Loud laughter came from the kitchen above. Charles pointed at the ceiling. 'I bet you like all of them. I bet you even love them!'

'Your mother has great qualities.'

'She puts up with me for a start?' He leaned sideways and put his face close to Amy's with a grimace.

'Do you realize that if I started trying to understand my mother I'd have nothing left of myself at all?' He grinned. 'Don't sit there laughing. Why don't you try giving *me* more of your understanding? Stop piling it all on undeserving persons like her. And that old man of yours.' He was looking at her out of the corner of his eye. 'He was here the other evening, charming the pants off Mother.'

'He never said . . .'

'And boring the pants off me with his "Science coming to the rescue of Artists". There's something about me that makes people want to lecture me.'

'What did he want?'

Charles had his arms behind his head. 'Killing time, I suppose. Said he'd gone somewhere . . . or something . . . and somebody wasn't in. Or something!'

'Please, Charles.'

'Truly, Amy.' He let her see how honest his expression was.

'Don't lie to me. If you want me to know that Ernest was here, you want me to know why.'

He pulled his chair closer to her so he could reach her hand. 'I'm not lying. But if you want the painful details they are: one, he came here because the female he's currently interested in is giving him the runaround. Two, he came because he couldn't face going home. And . . .'

'But why?'

'Says you make him nervous. Says he doesn't know what you're going to do next. Says he's coming out in shingles. Says you're giving him the bad end of your tongue.'

'Wouldn't you?' She let Charles stroke her hand. 'What am I supposed to do?'

'Get to know *me* better!' Little flakes of drying clay fell from his fingers onto her lap. 'I'm very good company. I do funny tricks.'

'What else did he want, Charles?'

'Should there be something else? Are you implying that I'm not good enough to visit if you can't think of anywhere else to go?'

'He wouldn't have come unless he'd wanted something.'

'Don't make him out worse than he is, poor chap. No wonder he won't go home.'

'I know Ernest. And I know what you want me to think of him.'

'Then I can't win, can I?' He released her hand and stood up. He stretched, then stood in front of her, looking appealing. 'Shall I do the Extremely Difficult Headstand for you? Women have fallen over my feet after it!'

She watched as he took his stool and placed it in front of her. He lay across it on his stomach, his legs raised. 'Maybe I'll swim a little. Tone up the stomach muscles.' With loud grunts he began to flap his arms and kick his legs in an imaginary breast stroke.

She stood up. 'I'm going, Charles.'

He stopped swimming and hung over the stool, motionless like a rag doll. 'Don't go, Amy,' he muttered.

'Then tell me why he came.'

'He came to borrow money,' he said in a muffled voice. 'And when I wouldn't give him any, he turned the charm on Mother.'

She felt her face redden. 'And you let him?'

'He's a grown man, fully responsible for his acts.' Raising himself from the horizontal, he stood up looking miserably at her. 'Did you want me to give him some?'

Pity made her hug him. 'If you'd done that, there'd be none for me, would there?' she said. She released him before his attempted kiss reached her lips.

'We'll go upstairs, shall we? I can hear the kettle.'

She stayed so long talking upstairs that the visit to Fox didn't happen. The best thing might be to telephone him first to ask for Frank's work.

3

On the easel set up in the anteroom she'd begun to piece together the first panel. The only way to cope with such a dauntingly large area was to divide it with pencil lines into sections on which she could work independently.

Now she was trying to concentrate on one small part at a time. The painted sky shone like the sky outside the dim room. She wanted tiny birds in flocks flying above the faint green of trees bordering the great and winding river Moldau. On an island in the river she set down the child and gave her a bunch of violets to hold. So that she wouldn't seem alone, she stood beside her a watchful aunt, correctly dressed in the Prague fashion of 1910, with what was to be a look of slight disapproval on her face. The Austro-Hungarian empire was still intact but cracking up visibly: Czechs no longer communicated with Germans – or so she would have her niece believe.

She began with the child's face. Twice she tried it; twice she blotted it out, finding the simple business of putting down the exact expression of knowing innocence impossible. First she was too young, then she looked too old and careworn, as if she'd suffered prematurely. At last she fetched a mirror and drew her own face, trying to see herself as a child without the lines and shadows which even the low light couldn't hide. Looking so long at her face had the effect of estranging her from it. And as she drew it fatter, younger, healthier it ceased to be hers. Painted, it ceased to belong to anyone, not even to Milena, and became simply a shape she'd scribbled on. The third dimension was gone.

She told Frank about it, as she told him everything now,

good or bad. She told him she'd seen nothing more meaningful in the reflection of that unknown person than written on notepaper. She saw little meaning in the letter she wrote. She was utterly useless. She told him she couldn't work when Ernest's words still sounded in her ears: 'You don't understand me.' And happening at the very moment when she'd been trying to make things right between them. No shouts, no hysteria, no accusations. She had decided to ask no more why he left her all day, and often all night, and why he looked at her like a stranger. She was ready to tell him she'd accept him as he was, because the sight of him still moved her. It was to have been a new beginning, until he'd cut through her hopeful conversation and told her she was wasting her time. She didn't understand him.

So she wished herself onto a sunlit balcony beside the friend who would understand. He wrote two letters in reply, making her feel instantly better. And filled with remorse for burdening him, she changed the subject and told him of her visit to Charles. She sent more sketches, but as an afterthought asked for them back with the excuse that she needed them urgently. He mustn't look at them too long and discover their superficiality. She knew she was capable of better work, and that work would be for him.

Each day as the sun grew stronger she found herself filled with hope. She urged him to think himself better so that his own work would come more easily. He must not look at himself with such disgust. Each day at the post office she found replies which caught her mood, questioned its causes, asked how she was thinking, what she was thinking. He wrote of his confidence in her, and proved it by telling her his deepest anxieties and dreads. And nothing that he said was left unanswered. He marvelled at her openness and understanding. He said how crazy was his passion to hear from her.

Of Ernest he said he'd built his own picture, of the most reliable, understanding, almost exaggeratedly paternal, though inscrutable of those in the coffee house circle. What

57

he'd particularly liked, he said, was the way Ernest was called to the telephone several times during the course of the evening – presumably by someone who dozed by the 'phone, and who started up from time to time to telephone him. If only she could have shown Ernest the letter.

Now the first daffodils were out. In the shops the first jasmine from the south. She bought huge bunches to lighten the anteroom where she wrote her letters on the desk among piled up paints, books and Milena clippings. If she spent more time writing to Frank than continuing to paint, she spent as long staring at the white canvas with its tracery of pencil lines, thinking herself into the other woman's life. When Jasmine excitedly 'phoned to remind her of Tuesday's plan, she told her how she'd bought her name flower to stand beside the bed.

It wasn't easy to work in the anteroom. Like the rest of the flat it had been too carefully designed. It had been a mistake to suppose that because it was smaller and less clinically white than the living room she'd find it more congenial. It was too silent. Lack of traffic noise caused her constantly to stop, listening to small, unfamiliar sounds coming from other parts of the house. She was for ever bringing in lamps and experimenting with their direction; pointing them at her writing, the canvas, the flowers. It was too restrained a room for lovers. It needed more colour. And more flowers. She saw Jasmine and David lying together surrounded by them like the couple in Klimt's paintings.

On Tuesday morning after Ernest had left, she went to Charles's house and let herself in by the studio door. The garden was in first flower. She picked daffodils and narcissi, the first small spikes of tulip, and handfuls of pink and yellow primroses. She broke off branches of spiraea to make a bride's bouquet, and took all the forsythia she could see. To perfume the room she took buds of viburnum blowing by the fence in the shade where she found a few lilies of the valley. She picked the leaves of those plants not yet in bloom until her arms were so full of flowers and foliage she could barely manage to carry them back home.

The anteroom was transformed. She made up the sofa into a proper bed, and put on it her grandmother's quilt with its cover of alpine flowers. From the attic upstairs she brought down someone's embroidered cushions, and a fragile chair of faded brocade celebrating strange, courtly love. Then she tidied the desk, took paper and pen and all Frank's letters tied in a bundle, put the key for Jasmine under the front door mat, and left for the library.

During the long afternoon she sat reading and writing, or watching birds dart past the big windows and through the spring leaves which tapped the glass. She took books from the shelves and flicked through them, their strong smell mingling with thoughts of couples in love with no place to go; couples with no love, and people separated by long distances whose letters never mentioned love but were full of it just the same.

In one letter she'd asked Frank about the Girl. Why not? Why shouldn't he know how cruel it was to keep someone waiting for a marriage that was never to take place? Since his letters barely mentioned her, surely it was to be assumed that she held little importance for him? It wasn't pleasant to imagine them sitting together talking about weddings. She could hear the rattle of pots and pans in their talk, and could see the neat little domestic nest the Girl was mapping out for them. She told him this wasn't the kind of life he'd tolerate for longer than it took to put the new kettle on the stove. He answered quite clearly that now the Girl would be free of him. But he still wrote to her. When he left the hotel and went home after convalescence, he might still see her and be persuaded to change his mind. He was too kind.

It was kindness, she thought, which had moved him to suggest she leave Ernest for a while 'because of your illness, his nervousness'. After all, he'd written, she'd left him before. When had she mentioned this fact to Frank? Had Charles been writing to him and telling him prejudicial things? Were there other stories being spread about her? Or had she, in one of those late-night, barely readable scribbles confessed to escaping once? People must, she told him, when driven too far run away and find a calm corner before all strength deserts them. She told him that neither would she leave Ernest, who needed her, nor would she accept offers of money. She told him she thought the offer was insincere, half-hearted, and hedged about with qualifications. He was trying to come between Ernest and herself while still wishing to stay uncommitted.

As she wrote she knew where the cause of her anger lay: he'd said he thought it best if he neither personally interfered nor showed himself. What cowardice! She was supposed to be grateful, she supposed, for the peace he was giving her. Did he know what kind of peace that would be? One solitary hell-hole in exchange for another. Didn't her Furies pursue her wherever she went? Yet he had the temerity to stand aside, leaving her to struggle on her own, thinking he'd done his best. He was supposed to be her friend. But if he saw her as someone to be patronised at long distance, then she'd reject him.

On the way home she slammed the letter in the post box. But by the clock above it was too early to go home. She went instead to a quiet coffee house where she knew she wouldn't meet Ernest or his friends. Over coffee it dawned on her that the letter had been too harsh and she must instantly make amends.

She got to a stationer just before closing time, hastily grabbed a card, rushed back to the café and wrote:

You do see the difficulty? Isn't one always longing for it, but afraid of it just the same? But surely there are more important things. We should be thinking of you and your well-being.

Feeling quite light-hearted she posted the card, made

two circuits round the block and decided it was safe to go and find out what had happened at home.

There was a powerful scent in the hall. Three vases of flowers stood outside the door to the anteroom. The smell had pervaded the living room where she found Ernest sitting at his desk writing under the light of a single lamp. He ignored her entrance and greeting.

She went into the anteroom and was met by a perfume so strong it made her feel weak. The bed had been remade into a sofa, the quilt neatly folded on top. The embroidered cushions had been stacked on the fragile chair. On the floor stood all the vases of flowers, arranged in neat rows. The curtains were tightly drawn, the window closed. Someone had turned the easel to the wall and piled the Milena cuttings in heaps on the desk.

'Nice, isn't it?' Ernest was standing beside her. 'Reminds one of a funeral parlour, doesn't it?'

'I thought you didn't have flowers at your kind of funerals.'

He ignored this. 'Pity you didn't get here sooner while all the fun was still going on. You might have helped clean up.'

She noticed the wet patch on the rug.

'Water,' he said. 'A vase or two fell over. The blue one broke. I suppose it wasn't saleable?' He sounded ominously restrained. 'She didn't offer to replace it, and I didn't ask. After all, there are limits to what one can say under the circumstances.'

'There were no "circumstances", Ernest. They had nowhere to go, so I . . .'

'Save it!' he said. 'I've had to listen to that hysterical friend of yours for nearly half an hour. I don't want any more.' He rubbed his eyes behind his glasses. 'Not to mention that dreadful man.'

'That was David. You know David.'

'No. And I don't want to know him. There's nothing I hate more than racial *camaraderie*. It's enough that I entertained them for half an hour. Or more. It's enough that I didn't throw them out for being here unasked. It's enough that I was put in a very embarrassing position.'

'You didn't come home early?'

'I did not. Neither did I come in here. Thank goodness.' He waved a hand in front of his nose. 'Let's get out. The smell would bring down bees.' He went back into the living room. She went after him.

'What position were you put in, Ernest?'

'It wasn't funny, Amy. I came home to do some work. I was sitting right here . . . when I heard the lavatory chain being pulled. I thought it was you. So I called you. When you didn't answer I went into the hall and bumped into your dear Jasmine coming out. Literally bumped into her. She hadn't a stitch on.'

'That must have pleased you!'

'It didn't please her. She screamed. I mean *screamed*. Then someone came leaping at me from nowhere. The next second I'm on the hall carpet and grappling with a naked fiend.'

'Your reputation preceded you!'

'It wasn't at all funny. He came hurtling out of that room like a tiger on an elephant. Have you ever tried grappling with a naked body? You can't get any purchase.'

'That's why ju-jitsu fighters wear those baggy pyjamas!'

'It was not funny, Amy. He could have killed me.'

'He knew who you were. You've met before.'

'But not quite so intimately! Luckily I overpowered him quickly.'

'You didn't hurt him? You weren't horrible to them?'

He pulled a face. 'Yes, if spending a long time calming them down, giving them coffee and listening to them complain about you constitutes being horrible.'

'Were they happy when they left?'

He sighed in exasperation. 'You really are the limit! Were they supposed to be happy after what they'd been through? That ridiculous room! Did they really ask for it

to be filled with flowers? Do you know you nearly asphyxi-
ated them?'

'I'm sure they loved it,' she murmured.

'Heaven knows what they were doing in there. But it
looked like a hurricane had hit it when I went in. Jasmine
said they'd opened a window to get rid of the smell. Your
stuff got blown all over the room apparently. She said she'd
rescued most of it. What possessed you to let them in there
in the first place? And who paid for the flowers?'

'They had nowhere to go, so I said they could . . . They're
going to be married.'

'So that makes it all right. Whatever you say makes it all
right, doesn't it?' His voice was icy. 'You can embarrass
me, embarrass your friends, and think you're some kind of
ministering angel. Some angel!' Abruptly he turned and
went back into the sitting room, ignoring completely her
explanations.

While she was washing up, the telephone rang. She heard
Ernest answer it, talk excitedly to the caller, then call her
name in an ominous voice.

'It's Charles,' he said, handing her the 'phone.

And while Charles berated her for desecrating his
mother's garden, Ernest wandered back and forth listening,
with an I-told-you-so expression on his face.

She went to bed early followed closely by Ernest, who
continued telling her how stupid, thoughtless and in-
considerate she was. He reiterated the many ways she'd
failed him. He repeated Jasmine's complaints and Charles's
tirade, threading the accusations through with so evident
an anxiety about Charles's mother that she pitied him. Once
into his stride he might talk for a whole hour, pausing occasionally to make sure she was listening. She replied with
yes's and no's, knowing that he might shake her awake if he
felt neglected. The last words she heard before sleep were
that they couldn't afford to make enemies.

Under the circumstances she felt it best not to mention
the affair to Frank, who wouldn't at that distance be able to

understand. If the phrase 'fat old Charles' crept into her letter, it was only because she wanted to forewarn him that his friend was capable of being unnecessarily malicious about her. When he said that her letters were sometimes terrible, then he must realize the life she lived was sometimes hard to bear. To her the word 'terrible' had another meaning, one fraught with the essence of fear which might be mistaken for ecstasy. If one looked at the paintings of Delacroix, or read the works of Kafka, then one knew something of that meaning.

Did he ever dream? She had looked down on forests and deserts, and seen movements of people rushing from unnamed catastrophes. Did he know the paintings of Genovés? They came closer to her dreams than most, yet they remained metaphors. He who never used metaphor as embellishment might still be able to understand the terror of her dreams which she could so easily re-enter when awake.

She painted in the flight of birds. Around the child with the strange face went a wall of white surgery tiles giving off an odour of novocaine. She was enclosed in a box like the one her father had locked her in for being disobedient. Undoubtedly Jasmine had turned the canvas to the wall because she'd been disturbed by the tiny face that refused to stay fixed. The head had a body, yet it looked bodyless and legless: one fixed point in a floating ectoplasm from which, the longer one looked at it, gauzes began to swirl, drifting into thin tendrils like smoke solidifying; like the smoke of the cigarettes she constantly rolled; twisting and dropping into a series of changing patterns. Under the child's chin there floated a bunch of violets once taken but never proffered to a man lying in hospital. Seeing the bandages over his eyes she'd kept the flowers and given him a kiss instead.

Lines coming from her, lines going to her. She covered the canvas in pencil marks, drawing in the severed hands and taking them out again; putting in three schoolgirls and

64

taking them out again. She stood for hours, pencil in one hand, cigarette in the other, drawing and erasing, drawing and erasing. Finally she chose to portray them as the Three Graces, one of whom (according to Frank) was the final judge. She drew them graceful enough in their self-conscious way, standing as if watched by an unseen audience of admiring young men. They were the first Czech girls who dared to cross the provincial boundaries into the excitement of the German literary world. And as she smoked and drew, erased lines and drew them over, the Graces began to lose their composure. Their bodies began to tense, their fingers stiffened at their sides, their heads twisted this way and that, and their eyes started from their heads. She was drawing in an increasing fury three women outside convention and morality, who changed under the pencil into mythical beings with powers to pursue and pass judgement; beyond pity, inexorably sweeping aside the irresolute.

'What the devil's that?' Ernest was standing in the doorway.

'I don't know. Leave me alone.' The pencil with a life of its own was furiously putting in a crown of writhing snakes round the head of one of the girls.

'Is that supposed to be Whatshername?'

'No!' Her hand began to tremble. 'Maybe. I don't know.' She couldn't see what she was doing. She felt faint. With a sharp crack the pencil point went through the canvas.

He came over and took the cigarette from her shaking hand. He sniffed it then ground it to nothing in the ashtray. 'Try breathing some air instead,' he said. 'Your eyes are bloodshot.' He looked at her closer. 'And your nose is running!' He backed away in disgust.

She wiped her nose and smiled at him. It was good to see him, although his presence made her realize suddenly what a curious shape he was. His little round stomach was protruding like a comic-book pudding. 'You do look funny, Ernest!' she said.

He sat down heavily on the sofa. 'I wasn't aware this was your room.' He sat back and closed his eyes. Two silver coins were resting on his eyelids. 'What a day I've had of it.' He stretched his legs. It made him look even funnier. 'That ghastly report. Took me all morning.' She could feel the laughter rising. It always happened – first the smoking, then the laughter.

Ernest was sitting up primly. 'I don't think you can see the seriousness of what I'm saying. The Foreign Division's worth working for. Pays a few debts.' He stared down at his boots, then lifted one for her to see the hole in the sole. She began to laugh again.

'What debts?' she said.

'Oh, nothing to stop you laughing.' He was quite good humoured. 'Only the milk bill and the grocery bill and the back rent and what I've borrowed from Morris and what Irwin lent me. And the telephone bill!'

It was hard to compose herself when the sight of his cracked and carefully cleaned boots kept bringing fresh bursts of laughter.

He watched her for a while, then brought a postcard from his pocket. 'From Stacey and her husband,' he said. 'Are you in any condition yet to read it?'

She stared at the picture of the yellow house in a bleached field. She tried to walk through the foreground of tall thistles. Grasshoppers leaped from around her legs. 'This is last year's card,' she said.

'They've only just got there.'

'Fields should be full of flowers there now.'

He smiled broadly. 'I think it would be better if we avoided the subject of flowers for a while!'

She collapsed on the sofa beside him, and he finally joined in her laughter.

When calm had returned he took the papers and the tin from the desk, took the block of hash from its foil, and rolled a cigarette. They sat sharing it, while he told her more about his office problems. She lay back and let him talk.

66

Another cigarette was followed by another, and his voice became an orchestra from which she could pick out the assured, the weak, the frightened voice as if he were several people talking in unison. Hash clouds spread in the small room, curling round the canvas, filling the air with a powerful and bitter fragrance. She could hear him telling her how he needed her support and how she could give him strength to carry on; the slow, deliberate way he spoke giving enormous weight to his words. And because her own words wouldn't come, with weighty nods and shakes of the head she managed to assure him that she wouldn't fail him.

They slept together cramped up on the sofa and woke to a dark room with the window a square of purest violet. The effects of the drug wore off slowly, making them calm and considerate of one another. They drank quantities of sweet tea, smiling at one another over their cups. He wanted her to play the flute but she said her lungs still hurt her. He said he supposed she smoked to deaden the fire.

In the living room he lit a candle and stood it on a low table. No other light was in the room, apart from the mild orange glow of street lamps filtered through the curtains. They sat and watched the almond flame, listening to the sound of the traffic on the ring road becoming fainter and more intermittent as the night wore on. The flame flickered and reflected a thousand times in the surfaces around them. She saw it in Ernest's glasses and in his eyes. She watched it diminish and fade. Her body felt heavy and totally at peace. She was a life-sized rag doll with non-articulating limbs and a stitched smile; no will, no desire, no needs because this was all there was to existence.

That evening was an oasis in the desert of following wasted days. Days spent in trying to work; going again and again to the post office in futile search of letters from Frank. She feared she'd lost him. She went back to his stories to look for clues to his character. She then covered sheets of paper in charcoal scribbles, trying to metamorphose men into beetles, men into dogs. She wrote to him in misery of her fears that he might have misunderstood her, and of a new loneliness. She called him 'My Dearest' in an effort to catch him before he receded too far. It was alarming how quickly she had attached herself to this stranger, and how much she now needed to hear from him.

There was a letter awaiting her the next morning. She ran home to read it in the secrecy of the anteroom, fearing the worst. But an immediate lightening of the spirits came with his first words. Here he was telling her how he was walking between the lines of her letter, under the light of her eyes, in the breath of her mouth as in a beautiful happy day. What a day! She could feel it flickering through her as if spring had just started its upward course through her blood. It was so joyful a feeling that with it came alarm that he could bring out such strong emotions in her: like someone in love. At his next sentence she was already fearful: he was telling her he was shortly to go home. The convalescence had nearly ended.

What a risk. No more the calm invalid, he'd be the worried working man, surrounded by family, colleagues and fiancée, with a piled-high desk of work awaiting him at the office. She knew she was right. Or why else did he end his letter with the request that she should go on caring for him? Already he was distancing himself in preparation for his return.

Then came the seemingly light-hearted postscript – that hid and yet didn't hide what he was trying to say. He was asking if there was a chance they might meet before he became embroiled in matters back home. Why shouldn't he take advantage of that which had fallen into his lap?

Anything is possible, she wrote, as long as we remain true to our feelings.

In celebration she went to the café with the hope that she could sit beside Ernest and transmit to him some of her cheerfulness. She stopped at the door when she saw him deep in conversation with Irwin at a table in the corner. There was something about their flushed faces and the way

68

Ernest was gripping Irwin's arm that told her they weren't talking about philosophy. No other friends were present. One cup each, and Albert hovering near the kitchen door watching with a worried expression.

A hand on her shoulder, and Rose was standing beside her, looking in.

'Hello, Amy. Are we coming or going?'

'We can't go in,' Amy said. Firmly she steered Rose out through the doors and along the street, trying to explain how ignominious it would have been for Ernest to have been caught in the act of arguing about money. 'It's not right,' she said, 'after all he's done for Irwin.'

They went to a café with outside tables, where they drank coffee and talked. Ernest wasn't poor, Amy said. In fact he was as rich as Rose's own family. Or at least his family was. Ernest's trouble was his pride which forebade him asking for allowances overdue, or making do with handouts meanly given by friends who, in times past, had taken more than they should from him. Why shouldn't he now expect them to give instead of lend?

Rose looked embarrassed. 'Money doesn't necessarily mean happiness,' she muttered, seemingly afraid to look Amy in the eye. Amy stared at her for the cliché and saw how ill at ease she was. She kept fingering the petals of her collar as if trying to hide its opulence. Amy remarked on how grandly she was dressed, and asked if she was going somewhere special. The reply was vague, hinting that her parents had insisted she go away with them for a holiday. When pressed she admitted that the plan meant living in a villa by the sea because, as she put it, her mother needed more colour in her cheeks. Since Rose's mother was noted for the amount of colour she applied to those cheeks, Amy wondered what a dose of sun and sea would do to them. Rose admitted she wasn't keen to go, sensing matrimonial machinations in the air. She'd heard talk of young men being invited. It wasn't fair. Only offers of new clothes, and some of her mother's jewellery had persuaded her.

69

'Look,' she said miserably, revealing a brooch hidden under a fold in her collar. Amy stared, remembering the time at the opera when she'd seen Rose's mother wearing it. Pearls and enamel gleaming beneath fur. She'd thought the cherub might suffocate under the long-haired fox. It had amused her that his arrow pointed precisely at the wearer's left nipple. Now she saw that from its tip hung a diamond like a water drop. Rose fiddled with the safety clasp, unpinned the brooch and put it on the table between them.

'I don't even like it,' she said, poking it with her fingertip. It sparkled different colours. 'And Charles hates things like this . . .' She had blushed.

Putting her hand on Rose's shoulder, Amy said gently, 'He wasn't there today. But there's still time to go back and see if he's arrived. Perhaps Ernest and Irwin have finished by now.'

She knew that Rose had no appointment with Charles. He rarely made them with anyone unless a commission for work was involved. For Rose he wouldn't have bothered. 'Standard Rose' he called her. 'Well-trained and pruned'. But his indifference didn't deter her. She tracked him down, and having cornered him was often content to enjoy his presence in silent admiration. Poor Rose.

'No, it's no use. He won't be there.' She looked at her little diamond watch. 'Besides . . . I always make the same mistake.' She sighed heavily. 'I tell her I'm going out. And she asks me where I'm going. And I say I'm going to meet someone. So she guesses it's a man because I won't tell her who it is . . .'

'Why don't you lie?'

'Somehow I can't. You know what she's like. I swear she's got some sixth sense. And I can't bear scenes. So I try to keep quiet in case she gets hysterical. Then she says I can't go out in rags. She says I look like a trollop.'

'What a lovely old-fashioned word!'

'So then I go back upstairs and get all dressed up. She's

pleased. I hate it. And I come out looking like this.' She looked into Amy's eyes. 'Honestly, Amy, I hate myself.'

'If you stood up to her once or twice she'd gradually change.'

'It's not worth it. Father's always telling us we've got to keep her happy. He's afraid she'll have another breakdown.'

'Vicious circle!'

'Oh no! Today she was so pleased I looked nice . . .'

'And pleased you agreed to go on holiday?'

'Yes. To tell you the truth I could do with a holiday. There's a swimming pool. And tennis. It doesn't take much . . .'

'Well, there we are! Go and enjoy yourself! After all, there are worse things than being swamped with clothes and diamonds!'

They stared down at the brooch gleaming in the sun.

'It's so vulgar,' Rose said. 'But what could I do? She rushed upstairs and fetched it, and pinned it on me before I could say a word.'

'You don't have to wear it.'

'No . . . She forgets half the time what she's given me. I've got drawers full of the stuff.'

The sun suddenly went behind a cloud. Amy sat up. 'I know what we'll do,' she said. 'We'll go and look for Charles.'

'Oh no! I couldn't do that.'

'We'll pretend I've got to ask him something.' She smiled. 'Actually there is something I ought to talk to him about. He's just what you need, I think.'

'Amy, honestly, you're the kindest person I know. I don't know anyone else who's so understanding.'

'Let's go then!' She picked up the bill and handed it to Rose. 'You'll have to pay for this, I'm afraid. I have a slight cash flow problem at the moment!' Her attention was caught by the sight of someone across the street. 'Isn't that your father?'

They looked, blinded by the sudden emergence of the

71

sun. A tall, grey-haired man in a dark suit was standing on the street corner opposite in earnest conversation with a woman.

'I don't think it is. He's at a board meeting.' Rose looked again at her watch. 'He said it would take all day . . .'

Amy noticed with some alarm that the man who was certainly Rose's father had reached out his hand and briefly caressed the woman's face. She hoped that Rose, busy paying the waitress, hadn't noticed. 'No,' she said. 'It's not him. Funny how people look alike from a distance.'

Rose stared across the street, shading her eyes. 'It *is* him,' she said. 'How lovely! He can take us both to lunch.' She got up hastily and fastened her handbag. 'Come on Amy. Let's catch him.'

She was on the pavement and moving before Amy called, 'No, Rose! What about Charles?'

Rose stopped and looked at her, making a small gesture of resignation. 'He wouldn't like it,' she said. 'And I couldn't go like this.' She had turned and was waving across the street, trying to attract her father's attention.

Amy saw the woman's head go up in surprise, and saw her speaking rapidly to the man. He looked around fearfully, recognized his daughter, and waved to her while taking a step back from his companion. Then with great formality they shook hands. After a few hurried words the woman walked rapidly from sight round a corner.

'Come on Amy, he's waiting.'

'No. You go, Rose. I've got things to do.'

At the kerb Rose faced her friend for the last time, a look of pleasure on her face. 'All right. I haven't seen him alone for ages.' She waited for traffic to pass. 'You won't be going to Charles, will you?'

'Of course not. Not without you.'

Rose crossed the street. 'I'll see you when I get back.' She hurried towards her waiting father.

'What about this?' Amy picked up the brooch and held it high for Rose to see.

'Oh . . . You have it!' she shouted excitedly from the other side of the street as she began to run towards the man already stretching out his arms.

Amy watched father and daughter meet in a fond embrace. She saw Rose point her out. She smiled at his wave of recognition, then watched as they walked away arm in arm, already deep in conversation until they were out of sight.

She wrapped the brooch in a paper serviette and put it in her pocket. As she sat for a while, feeling the sun on her face, all the morning's pleasure disappeared into sadness. She felt tired and lonely. She went back home.

The flat was cold after the warmth of the street. The outdoor brightness made the anteroom seem darker and very stuffy. Already the sun had moved away from its single window, leaving behind the usual gloom. Once again she took out Frank's last letter and read it. No joy now, only irritation. This time she noted how he'd questioned her running home on his account. He'd asked if this meant he no longer needed to worry about her health. How dare he! She must put the matter right . . .

Was this all that bothered him – whether she'd recovered and was keeping it a secret? Did he believe she was capable of hanging onto illness to keep his sympathy?

Believe me Frank, I say not a single word that isn't well considered. I see that you're going home at last, and I really do want to know if this means recovery. Perhaps you might even consider you'd gain more strength should you make a slight detour on my behalf. It's not impossible, you know. Think about it!

The stuffy smell in the room was growing stronger. Dead flowers. She lay full length on the carpet and looked under the sofa. A scatter of stray petals in the process of shrivelling. One or two blackened leaves. A dead spider like a brown crown. She blew it into the line of dust against the skirting board. For a while she lay with her chin resting on the rough pile of the carpet. Dusty smell, musty smell. Too

73

tired to move. No light. The smell of confinement. No more fresh flowers. No more friends. No Jasmine. No Milena.

Off to the river one day to join her friends, she'd never arrived. She'd been ambushed by men in grey coats who'd gripped her arms and held her, while someone (surely not her father) had jabbed a needle into her arm to calm her down for the journey. No doubt they told her it was all for the best and she'd thank them when she got older. God knows what they gave her, or who signed the papers committing her to Veleslavin. Her first incarceration a kind of rehearsal for what was to come twenty-two years on. A first warning that people with power could use it arbitrarily.

Eight months in the dubious peace of a mental institution, while war was being waged in France. Long days and longer nights of not knowing what was going on at home or abroad. Eight months of fighting the injustice of a place she saw with the clarity of sanity. What else could she do but be troublesome, with a lover waiting for her outside? Her father, when questioned, most surely replied that his daughter was resting in the country after suffering a mental breakdown due to her studies at school. He'd been sorely tried, he said, by the way she could never make up her mind – changing from medicine to music – symptomatic surely of the lessening of her grip on reality. Why hadn't she wanted to be like him? Why did the son die and the daughter survive to plague him? Sons could love whom they pleased without causing alarm, while girls had to be watched over until they'd been placed with appropriate husbands. He locked her up. She retaliated by escaping to marry the lover in 1918. Had he not imprisoned her, she may not have felt such an urge to wed. She might have stayed a few more years bearing the loneliness and his overweening ways for love of him.

The carpet pricked her face. She rolled onto her back, kicking the easel as she turned. It clattered, wobbled and righted itself against her steadying foot. She could feel the brooch in her pocket. She examined it. No damage. She put it on the floor and the diamond drop hung sideways from the arrow of the little gold putto with the worn-out sex. He was set round with pearls, small and misshapen between what looked like rubies and diamonds. She liked the pale, settled look of these stones, so unprepossessing and so old. She rubbed a fingertip over a stone and the diamond quivered like lightning. Always fingering things, Rose's mother, as if she were continually feeding imaginary mice hidden behind the fox fur. She fetched a silk scarf and polished the stones and the gold and the cyan-blue enamel with the rose-coloured edges, then wrapped it up and put it back in her pocket. She wouldn't look at it again, afraid of becoming too fond of an article destined to be sold to the jeweller who'd give her the very best price.

She looked up and saw the child staring down at her. The eyes followed her as she rose and went to the door, taking Frank's letter with her from the desk. They looked so knowingly at her from the white blob of face above the curious, disconnected body, she wondered whether to paint them out. Who could bear so penetrating a gaze? But that was how she was, and had always been. Best to leave her. But the little girl needed company. She might put another child beside her – Milena's own daughter. When she felt less tired. Or when she'd heard again from Frank.

In the hall downstairs she met Mrs Kertesch struggling against the outer door with a huge bag of food. She helped carry it into the tiny flat, conscious that Mrs Kertesch was not looking at her in her usual cheerful fashion. They stood facing each other in the kitchen.

'You shall have the rent very soon,' she said.

Mrs Kertesch looked relieved enough to smile. 'It's not for me, you understand . . .' she snatched a carrot from a bunch poking out of her bag. 'Have one. Vitamins. Good for you, plenty vitamins.' She said Amy ought to eat nourishing things and not sit all day in the dark. 'I hear you walking about and sitting down and walking about,' she said, wagging a crooked finger.

'Talking of sitting,' she continued, 'have you seen my little chair lately? The one what was given me by my late husband's mother, God-Rest-Her-Soul? Such beautiful seat work, in tapestry with people on it coming and going, in love.' Amy felt her face turn warm. 'Only, should you see it my dear, then you should put it back from where it came. Not for me, you understand, but on account it belonged to Mrs Kertesch, God-Rest-Her-Soul.'

She lifted up a neat pile of ironing and offered Amy a seat. 'But not a chair to take weight, you understand. Not a fine, big woman like Mrs Kertesch . . .'

After putting away the shopping, she spread a tablecloth, set cups and saucers and plates, then put on the kettle as deftly as her crippled hands would allow.

'What I ask myself,' she said, 'is why a fine, strong young woman like you were when you first come here, should go so thin. And then I say to myself, "Mind your own business, Pearl."' She shook her head. 'But it won't go away, the curiosity.'

The room was so small that kettle steam instantly clouded the windows. She made the tea. 'Some might think you was dawdling away to nothing, *mamala*.' Amy hid her smile. 'But no. You won't. You'll live.' She placed a tea cosy over the pot. 'You and me always want to know what tomorrow will bring.' Her hands were cross-hatched with fine lines. 'But we can't afford to wither, can we?'

Lemon was sliced, sugar put in Amy's cup without her consent, and chunks of rye bread cut from a loaf Mrs Kertesch conjured from an invisible cupboard.

'No biscuits today,' she said. 'But a nice bit *wurst*. You'll like it. You see.' From another cupboard she produced a frying pan, cooking oil, three eggs and a slice. She spent some moment locating her handbag which they eventually found on the floor under the table. From it she took a large, red salami wrapped in brown paper. As she cut it she continued talking, not waiting for answers: 'If you buy the best you should look after it, I say. *Nu!*' Into the pan went the

76

oil which she heated over a tiny flame. 'You got a good body, so you should look after it, yes? You got a wonderful talent, so you get letters from famous magazines . . .' She looked up, smiled and shrugged as if pleading that examining her tenants' letters was an excusable pastime. The *wurst* crackled as it dropped into the hot oil. 'So you look after the body what holds the talent, eh?

'But what you should do first is pour the tea for us so it don't curdle the tongue. Right? Then you should open that little drawer there . . . and find us two big silver knives that Mrs Kertesch, God-Rest-Her-Soul, gave to Mr Kertesch and me from the set.' She cracked the eggs into the pan and stirred them vigorously. 'We should have got the set, but something moved her to be mean at the last minute.' The eggs steamed. 'Find the forks, Amy dear. And a spoon for the sugar.' Smoke began to rise and cloud the coloured lampshade above the table. 'I never held it against her.'

She stood up and stretched her back and regarded Amy seriously. 'Remember that, *mamala*, never hold things against people. That way you don't get lines!' She laughed and her face puckered.

She brought the smoking pan to the table, set it down on a mat, sprinkled salt and pepper liberally on the contents, cut them in half and put one half onto each warm plate.

'I think I know one thing for sure,' she said, munching the *wurst* and egg appreciatively. 'They don't change. They never change. *She* never changed . . .' (indicating the knife she was holding). 'Give with this hand. Hold back a bit with that hand. You should see the parts of sets I got. Sheets, towels, pillowcases. One set white, one set blue with embroideries it should be. So it should be. But no! She gives us one blue sheet and keeps the other, one white pillowcase, keeps the other . . . My husband, God-Rest-His-Soul, ask her one day why she did it. And she tells him, "Why not?" One day she thinks maybe she needs the other one!'

She pointed at Amy's untouched plate. 'So eat! Delicious, yes?' Amy took a mouthful.

77

'See that?' Mrs Kertesch pointed with her knife through the open door of her sitting room, where a large and ornate vase stood on the floor beside the tiny fireplace. 'One of a pair,' she said. 'Naturally! But could she part with the other one?' She shook her head sadly, broke off a piece of bread and stuffed it in her mouth. Amy wondered whether the miniature sitting room would have held another such vase.

'Where is it now?' she asked.

Mrs Kertesch seemed to think the question irrelevant. 'I should know?'

'But didn't your husband inherit it when his mother died?'

Mrs Kertesch stopped eating and laughed, her mouth wide open, displaying chewed remnants of *wurst* and bread. 'When grandmothers go to concentration camps, who knows where their vases go!' She shook her head. 'That's why I say, "Look after the living while they're here."'

'And what if they don't want looking after?'

Amy was treated to a sharp glance. 'Then look after yourself!' Mrs Kertesch cleaned her plate with a piece of bread. 'Eat,' she said. '"So from hunger you won't starve" – as they say!' She leaned across the table and gripped Amy's arm with a birdlike hand. 'But don't think to change him. They never change.' Her hand went up to pat Amy's cheek. It felt like being scratched. 'Nothing to do with selfish or not selfish. If they're like that, they're like that. One day I tell Mr Kertesch, "If you don't look out, I find a lover who look so like you, I don't tell the difference!" So he said to me, "If you don't know the difference, then you deserve each other!"'

'Mrs Kertesch . . . I can't tell whether you think one ought to go off and find a lover, or stay at home and make do with what I've got!'

'What difference my advice?' Eyeing the *wurst* left on Amy's plate, she made a stab at it with her fork. 'So you think you might want a lover? Who doesn't?'

She ate the *wurst* then threw her fork on the table with a

78

satisfied cry. 'Ah! At times like these, nothing's so desirable as a smoked salmon sandwich!' She laughed so heartily her eyes became slits in her creased, brown face. Then slowly her laughter subsided and she became calm. She looked at Amy keenly. 'But for you, *mamala*, I wish only the best from inside you. If a man will do that for you, then take him.'

Impulsively Amy removed Frank's latest letter from her pocket.

'No! No! No!' The old lady's waving hand stopped her. 'Secrets out now is sorry later,' she said, hastily rising from the table and brushing past the outstretched hand. She busied herself refilling the teapot.

'We're still strangers,' Amy said. 'Two people talking to each other from different rooms. Trying to get close, but afraid. We met once, that's all. In a café . . .

'He's a writer. I think he uses these letters to me to say those things which have nowhere else to be told.' She took the cup from Mrs Kertesch's uncertain hands. 'Odd, how much better one feels, being able to say things – anything one wants – to a person.'

Mrs Kertesch began to struggle with the slicing of a lemon. 'I tell you, Amy . . . The best thing in the world is to talk. And if, by great, good fortune at the same time you happen upon lying next to the man – and it's been good with him – then you can never wish for better!' She handed Amy the knife. 'Why is it,' she said, 'that men don't want friendship with a woman? Such joy to lie and talk quiet with a friend . . .'

Amy felt the tears rise, and was surprised to see Mrs Kertesch dabbing at her eyes with the edge of her sleeve.

'That's what I miss,' Amy said, slicing the lemon.

'That's what I miss,' was the reply.

They drank their tea in companionable silence. Afterwards Amy helped clear away and wash up. She swept crumbs from the table into a brass tray ornamented with flowers. She folded the cloth and put it into a drawer.

'You go post a letter now?'

'Yes.'

At her door she kissed Amy on both cheeks and said, 'If, by chance, you should come across cushions with birds on . . .'

'I'll put them back.'

'Ugh! It's not so important. I got a better idea. You find a pretty dress and put it on. Look better. Feel better. Plenty hot days to come. Swallows fly high soon.'

4

How strange that he was a Jew. How strange that the thought had never occurred before. But why should it? It had been a long time since such differences mattered. Now she no longer considered Jews so outside her experience that she thought of them, as did her father, as aliens. So beyond the pale were they in the world of her childhood that the existence of their entire race was acknowledged only by rare words of contempt. Only once did she remember her father mentioning a certain clever dentist working in Vienna as being – surprisingly – a Jew. She now wondered why she'd never queried his singling out of the Jews for such treatment: she a child who questioned so much. Her childhood was almost devoid of Jews and, for that matter, any other race, apart from the odd child at school with the slanting eyes or coffee-coloured skin. They'd come to class for a few short months of intense examination by the other pupils, then leave for some other paternal, diplomatic post, never to be seen again.

There was Muriel Harris, of course, who professed to own the biggest refrigerator in the universe. None of the class had the chance to see it since her home, Muriel said, was out of bounds to non-Jews. She did her best to describe to Amy the differences between their home lives. There had been something exciting about the prospect of entering forbidden territory where curious rituals occurred. But the nearest Amy managed to get to them was Muriel's garden wall, from which could be seen the complications of curtain drapery at the windows of a house which looked no different from its neighbour. About Jewish boys Muriel was more coy. She said they were different from Christians and she preferred them. When asked why, she replied they made better husbands.

Laughable. But through childhood and through college later, Muriel's words had threaded their faint way through encounters with the opposite sex. And Jeffrey Rose's kiss had caused more reverberations than he was ever aware of.

She still thought of him with fondness: at thirteen the first boy to kiss her, after meeting her from school one dark afternoon. At her door he'd suddenly confronted her and asked in a rush of acute embarrassment if he could kiss her. She'd said yes without a second thought, immediately curious to know how this quiet, intelligent boy would achieve such a novelty as a kiss. What courage! She'd admired the courage he'd shown in walking home with her each day from school, in the face of some jeering from his friends. She liked him for his gentleness, and the way he enjoyed her constant talk. At her door that day, Jeffrey had grasped her shoulders, bent his head and planted a perfect kiss on her lips. Later she knew how perfect it had been. And while he kissed her, he was shaking. She'd been amazed to feel him trembling against her, locking her into his trembling as if they were windblown branches of a tree in a storm. It had lasted only briefly and, for some reason she didn't remember, had never been repeated. Although she'd wanted that kiss again, something had made her fearful. All she knew was that she'd been the catalyst for a powerful passion which had repelled as much as it had attracted her. Perhaps he'd felt the same. Or the one kiss had been sufficient. After that he avoided seeing her home, although sometimes she managed to catch up with him on his solitary walks in her direction and they'd shyly talked a little. Her father, having seen her once or twice with him, told her not to mix with Jews, thus confirming that Jeffrey might be the representative of an entire nation of passionate tremblers.

But she knew that because of those three factors:

Muriel's assessment of Jews as husbands, Jeffrey's promise of passion, and her father's embargo on commingling, she was attracted to Jews more than any other race. And it had been no accident that of the men who shared with her a taste for intellectual pursuits, Ernest was the one she'd finally chosen.

His passion for her, although omitting trembling, was sufficiently powerful to persuade her that his need was overwhelming. Neither at the time talked much about their differences. They were in love. At last, he said, he'd found a worthy companion, but said it with an amused irony which made her laugh.

He would not, he claimed, have anything to do with bourgeois wives who ran their homes like clockwork, and made their children's lives a misery of over-indulgence. He wanted, he said, discussions on family matters, food and feelings kept within the confines of the kitchen where, if she thought she was happiest, the Jewish woman could fatten her loved ones into an early grave without the aid of his presence. He would have nothing to do with ceremony, believing that all ritual was meaningless: it had lost whatever significance it once had through centuries of mindless practice. Language too had lost its way, to the extent where many of his race neither spoke nor understood the words of those ceremonies they most cherished. He said the hierarchy was at fault for wanting the people kept in subservience and ignorance.

The fights with his parents which ensued were as harsh as hers with her father. Never had he suggested that she meet any of his relatives, nor did he seem to have visited them since marriage. He'd cut off all communications with ease, save the legal ones which supplied him with a little extra money. He dismissed her talk of family feeling as sentimental superfluity, and suggested that the quicker she forgot to love her father the better she would be. They lived in a racial no-man's-land in which the fact that he'd been born a Jew and she a Christian were of no account. The

83

word 'faith' had become in Ernest's eyes merely the subject for debate with Morris and Irwin, who shared his view that Metaphysical was Nonsensical. He wished, he said, to live in a world in which all knowledge derived from experience, the structure of which was reflected precisely in language.

Now here was Frank telling her that because he was a Jew this necessarily made him different. His road, he told her, had been even longer than his thirty-eight years because of it. She must bear in mind how he had come to her, and how, on an apparently accidental turn of the road, he'd seen her when he'd never expected to. He was warning her of his innate weakness and inability to respond to her calls.

Into her replies she put a lecturing note, sensing he needed a strong response. She told him he abased himself unnecessarily, suspecting that when he said how far below her he felt, he was speaking from a greater height.

But such a cruel reply, written in some moment of heat couldn't be allowed to rest. Straight away she had to rush back to the post office and scribble a telegram to him, saying how anxiety had made her speak hastily. All she'd really wanted to say was that they should meet on his way home.

Why couldn't he come? It was time they met to put an end to uncertainties about each other. They were writing daily now, and becoming more confused. Surely he could see that face to face they could resolve all his anxieties? Not for much longer would she tolerate the vision he had of himself as the unworthy, wandering Jew. She would shake the pessimism from him. There would be a new beginning.

And now he was saying he couldn't come because the disease of the lung was nothing but an overflowing of his mental disease. It frightened her the way he was making the obstacles greater. Now he was claiming that she was almost a generation younger than he. He was white-haired; had headaches, insomnia. He'd made two girls unhappy, the first having suffered (and successfully survived) a battering of five years. He was saying he wasn't capable of marriage, despite desiring it desperately.

84

Mentioning the problem of her own marriage had obviously triggered off in him the most deep-seated fears and hopes. He reminded her of a fly fluttering against the glass, unaware that the top of the window was open and all he had to do was go upward to freedom. If she'd written that two hours of life were certainly worth more than two pages of writing, it was only to convince him that he could go beyond the words into a wider world of which she was one member.

Daily she bombarded him with letters, furiously trying to make him act decisively about the Girl waiting so hopefully back home. She drew for him a night scene of a bachelor sitting over his lonely meal, one hand poised above it as if to cover the shame of eating on his own; behind him an open door revealing a lighted room. The light penetrated the bachelor's darkness enough to touch the rungs of his chair and his bent back. She sent him another picture of a man in the act of juggling. His arms were raised as if he were praying, his fingers bent either in throwing or catching objects invisible to the observer. Underneath it she wrote the title: The Clumsy Juggler. She told him she was happiest (or unhappiest, whichever way you looked at it) while trying to control the welter of images that came when she read his work. He was to her the clearest of writers; yet in the absolute clarity of character, incident and description of place there remained the mysterious quality which she was trying to transpose into illustration.

One morning she asked Ernest what he thought of Frank's work. But his interest was more in the size of the telephone bill. She told him she'd telephoned Fox, who'd mentioned the possibility of illustrating Frank's stories. She didn't say she'd already started.

'You must keep after him,' Ernest said. 'Get yourself done up a bit and go and see him.' He was gingerly opening the next letter.

'What's it like, being a Jew?' she asked.

He looked startled. 'What do you mean?' he said, then

went back to examining the letter. With a sigh of relief he saw that it wasn't another bill.

She persisted. 'Are you still a Jew?'

'Of course, You can't stop being one.'

'Not even if you're married to someone like me? And you don't follow the Laws, or keep the festivals?'

'Why are you dragging all this up now?'

'Why do Jews always answer a question with a question?'

A pause. Ernest smiled at the old joke and responded: 'Do they?'

He continued sorting out his letters. 'I'm a Jew because I was born one. And I will die one.'

He looked up at her with interest, unsure of her mood. 'One is still homeless, if that's what you mean.'

'Even living with me?'

Ignoring this, he continued. 'But it doesn't bother me. Perhaps it's true to say it bothers me less and less. Too much else to think about.' He threw the letters onto the table. 'I can't possibly cope with this lot.'

'You once used to say that all Jews were outsiders.'

'Did I? Without defining the word "outsider"? I apologize! Nonetheless . . .' He got up and went into the kitchen. She wandered after him and watched as he began the usual search for shoe polish and brush '. . . it's still true for me. I'm not one to believe in a Promised Land.'

'They had to settle somewhere, surely?'

'And look what's happened. The inevitable. Nothing's worse than rampant nationalism, to my mind.' He began attacking his boots with the brush. 'Look what it's leading to – the same kind of repression the Jews themselves have suffered from for centuries.'

She wondered why the sight of his bare neck beneath the whiteness of his collar so moved her. Taking the brush from his hand she began polishing his toecap.

'Anyway,' he said, 'I'd rather be an exile nowhere than a settler in someone else's land.'

'The land was barren when they got there . . .'

He tapped her on the head. 'There is a danger that if it's easy to grab land, then one grabs more.' He took his foot from her brush. 'Where are my keys?'

She rose from her knees and pointed questioningly at his pocket. He found them. 'What happened to bring on this great interest in Judaism?'

'I'm curious, that's all. I forget you're a Jew at all. And when I ask myself what makes you one, I don't know the answer.'

He collected his briefcase from the table in the hall. 'I can't help being one. It's as simple as that. The only way I could stop being one would be to take another faith – become a Christian, for example. And since I'm an atheist, that is an impossibility.' He looked at his watch, checked his reflection in the mirror. 'I shall be late again,' he said.

'Frank's a Jew!' The words came out too hastily.

'Ah!' He stopped. 'Insight is required into the Jewish mind.'

'Would you say his work's essentially Jewish?'

'Never read any. I don't care how the fellow writes, as long as we can earn some cash from it. Morris goes on about his stuff being "Universal".'

For the first time she wondered whether Ernest was capable of simple jealousy. Again he noted his reflection in the hall mirror, removed a loose hair from his suit, then opened the front door.

He went towards the stairs.

She leaned over the bannister and called to him: 'What's so special about being a Jew, then?'

He looked up at her, clutching his briefcase to his chest. 'We have infinite patience, tolerance and wisdom!'

'Does being one make you feel distant from me?' she asked.

'Only when you stop me getting to work on time!' He hurried down the stairs and out of sight. She heard the front door bang behind him.

She stood in front of the canvas and thought the child

still looked lonely. Around her she put in the border of white tiles, painted meticulously with a realistic shine and the grouting lines between. The effect was remarkably three-dimensional. She was good at her work. She was beginning to enjoy the act of painting. Picking up a pot of red paint she dipped the brush into it. With a flick of the hand she spattered the white tiles, watching the droplets run and coagulate like blood. Then she stood for a long time looking at the child and the red-spattered border and the three wild, pencilled-in women and the sky with the flight of birds. All it needed now was music to bring it to life. Milena loved music.

She searched in the desk drawer and found A Little Piece for Flute by Schubert. Now she dipped another brush in black to transpose the piece to canvas. The music would come and go between the three Furies – for this was how she was beginning to see them – half hidden by their limbs, emerging to sing out with clarity as if, after all the sadness, there had come a time of happiness.

She sorted through the cuttings, looking for photographs of surrogate men for Milena. No photograph of Father; no lovers lovingly autographed. No wedding groups, no holiday snaps. Did she lead an unrecorded life? It seemed improbable. It would have been easiest to make her the centre of a flower whose petals were composed of those artists, writers, musicians and the like who crowded her life at that time. Easy and trite and not right. Neither would it do to substitute a row of eligible-looking young men, similar and handsome in the manner of the times. Hadn't she once said that all the men in her life had been weaklings? After the slow breakup of marriage there was the young aristocratic Austrian officer, Count Schaffgotsch, who began as lodger and ended as lover. He couldn't keep up with her talent and energy. She loved and supported him, but put him in the shade. So in the shade he must go, standing small to one side of the picture; out of uniform now, with the new red star on the suit which seemed too big for him.

His face is indistinct. His arms are weighted down by some passenger's heavy luggage. He is caught up in the smoke and smell of goulash stew of the Franz-Joseph station in Vienna. He and she carry bags to earn a living because Austria in 1925 is suffering such inflation that neither will survive without the most determined efforts. But he is weakening. He takes her to Buchholz to live for many months on an island both literal and metaphysical. He writes plays and fairy stories, and she increases her fame as a journalist. But hard times have left their mark on her, and she turns her thoughts more to politics. And Prague. When the move back home is made, her journalism earns enough for them both, and he slips slowly into the shadows.

She sang the notes as she painted them, her voice lowering to the faintest hum as they went behind the three women, where nothing but the leger-lines kept the tune from dissolution. Standing back from the work she saw how she was still painting barriers. Nevertheless she'd devised a small block of cheerful sound which ended on a happy note and left her singing it to the empty room. She sent the last note to the ceiling and echoed it to the corners where the flowers had been. To it she added another note, then a third, searching for a fourth to make a tune to hum. It was a joyful jazz tune that Milena might have danced to, loving jazz as she did, and revelling in dancing. With her new-found status she was self-assured and happy and the centre of a crowd of friends; sufficiently secure to ignore her detractors, for there were those who found her too intense, her tongue too sharp and her past too colourful.

Somewhere in the desk was a postcard of some café dancers: clutching couples in sophisticated clothes enjoying themselves (as far as she could remember) in a bar in Baden-Baden. She might use the couples as a kind of frieze, putting them along the lower edge of the picture, in counterpoint to the grim trio above. The card came to light hidden beneath others she'd lately been saving with thoughts of sending them to Frank. At the time of buying it she'd thought he might like the cheerful scene. But when she looked at it again she knew she'd been mistaken. The dancers were having a terrible time. The women, stiff-armed and severe, were holding onto the hems of their frocks with disdainful expressions; the men were staring over their bare shoulders at others more desirable on the far side of the floor. Neither tiaras nor pearls could revive the ladies' sad rigidity. The men were only there because it was the place to be seen. Despite the bright colours of the card, the atmosphere was heavy with *ennui* and fatigue.

The war has been over for seven years. In Germany the Nazi party has been re-formed by Hitler and its power is growing. Prague is now the capital of an autonomous, sovereign Czechoslovak state with vulnerable frontiers. Prosperity has briefly returned. Yet the gaiety is soon to be exhausted. The couples dance as if they're in a marathon, and their strength is slowly being sapped by the music's relentless rhythm.

She gathers up her evening cloak and the new bag with the thin gold chain. She glimpses her powdered shoulders and her crimped hair in the mirror as she passes. She wears her clothes with the *panache* that becomes one of the city's most admired fashion correspondents. After seven years she is back in Prague and intends to enjoy it. It is late, and her friends wait to escort her out into the night streets to yet another party. They walk together in a group, she holding up her skirt from the mud, stepping over puddles in her satin shoes. As they head towards the old town they pass a large house whose windows are open, letting out the sound of music and laughter. When they reach the corner there's a noise behind them of a heavy door slamming. She looks back and sees someone roll into the gutter. She insists on going back to see what's wrong. The others reluctantly agree, more to humour her than from concern.

Nezval the poet is lying groaning in the kerb, his hair already matted with mud, his shirt blackened and the smell of drink rising strongly in the night air. She bends to see if he is injured. The others say she should leave him and come on, knowing how much she dislikes the man for his weakness and indiscretions. A small crowd forms, saying how disgusting it is to see such a sight in a public thorough-fare.

Someone drags at her arm but she pushes them away. 'You go if you want to,' she says. From all sides they are nagging her to leave him lying, but she refuses. Someone calls him a 'filthy, wallowing pig!' and her mind is made up. The first person that kicks him receives a blow from the sharp point of her shoe. She sends her friends away and has time to notice how eager they are to quit the scene. Until the ambulance comes she stands beside the drunken man's head, defending him against all comers; trading abuse for abuse; hitting out with her fists, the bag already wrenched from her arm.

Later when someone asked why she protected a man she so detested she said, 'Because he needed help.'

She tried to close the drawer as best she could; it refused to shut. In the corner lay the crumpled paper napkin from the restaurant, still wrapped around the brooch. She took it out, looked at it quickly then put it in her pocket.

She left the room, let herself out of the flat and walked hurriedly towards the centre of town before resolution deserted her.

The sale of the brooch proved more difficult than she'd supposed, due, she later realized, to the state of her clothes. Two jewellers refused to take it, saying that such an item was too rare to sell readily. The third, after questioning how she'd come by it, and receiving the haughty reply that the brooch was an heirloom, presumed she'd come upon hard times. She concurred, but declared she was unwilling to sell it unless the price was right. After some haggling the deal was settled, and she left the shop clutching a large wad of notes.

She went straight to the building where she knew Irwin

worked, climbed the innumerable stairs to his floor, knocked on his office door and went in. He took what was owed him, but seemed uncomfortable to have her there. To her questions about his work he replied in monosyllables while looking at his watch. She decided not to prolong his discomfort and said she must go. He escorted her thankfully to the outer door, shielding her from the gaze of office girls who stopped typing as she passed. After apologizing for not being able to take her out to lunch, he shut the door on her hastily and left her to make her own way down to the street.

Charles's mother wouldn't let her past the front door, but softened at the sight of money. She accepted Amy's profuse apologies for the ruination of her garden, but backed away from her kiss. At her call, Charles came through from the studio, wiping his hands on his shirt. She stood close beside them listening while Amy asked how much Ernest owed, and watching while the money changed hands. After telling her son he should never lend money, especially such a large sum, she nodded goodbye with a slight smile and went upstairs, leaving them standing on the doorstep.

'Amy, you are the limit!' Charles was exasperated. 'What on earth possessed you to do that?' Not waiting for an answer he continued irritably, 'Now I'll never hear the last of it. "Neither a borrower nor a lender be!" You should know what she's like . . .'

He stared at her. 'And why can't Ernest come and pay his own debts?' He saw the stubborn set of her face. 'Doesn't he know about this?'

She shook her head.

'So where did you get it?' The money in his hand was covered with clay. He sighed. 'No. I really don't want to know.'

'As if it was any of your business!'

'True. But it's my business when you start coming here and fouling up my life.' He thought for a moment. 'Oh no!

Now she'll make me spend this on mending the roof!' He raised his eyes upward. 'I think I'll emigrate!'

'And I want you to promise you'll not lend Ernest any more.'

He laughed. 'Your old man could wheedle blood out of a stone! Look at the way he gives you the runaround.'

'Please, Charles!' She handed him the bundle of notes. 'And do you know who else he owes money to?'

'I have a fair idea. We money-lenders compare notes!'

'I want you to pay them back for me. Tell me who is owed what, and take it now.' She took a step inside the door, but Charles stood his ground.

'Sorry, Amy, but I've promised the old lady I won't let you in . . .' his voice trailed off in embarrassment.

'The trouble with you, Charles, is that you're weak. All you do is complain about her, but you never stand up to her.'

'And what do you do, may I ask? Stagger around making trouble.'

'I've already apologized to your mother about the flowers. And she was gracious enough to accept my apologies. But if you're going to bring it up time and again from now on . . .'

'I'm not the one to bring it up. All I get are other people's complaints. Mother accusing me of having vandals for friends . . . And Jasmine ringing me up accusing me of setting the whole thing up as a joke . . . Going on about having confidences broken, and all sorts of nonsense. She said you nearly ruined her engagement.'

She began to cough.

'Are you all right, Amy?'

The paroxysm subsided and she caught her breath. 'It's only nerves,' she said. She grabbed the notes and began to peel them off. 'Just tell me how much you think Ernest owes, and I'll give it to you and go!' She felt tears in her eyes. 'Irwin's already been paid, by the way. And I don't suppose you want to give Rose her money? That is, if he's borrowed any from her . . .'

93

'He has. And I don't! Anyway, she's on holiday. I got a card from her yesterday.' He stared mournfully into the distance.

'Is she enjoying herself?'

'How do I know? All it said is that she'd been playing tennis with hundreds of men.' He pulled a face. 'Long may it continue!'

'Let's get this settled,' she insisted. Into his hands she counted notes, with the instructions that he was to pay Ernest's debts as quickly as possible, and ask the recipients not to lend him any more.

'I'm sorry I disturbed you, Charles.' He looked shame-faced. She began to walk down the path to the front gate.

'Don't forget to go to the wine merchant. I bet old Ernest owes a goodly sum there!'

She closed the gate.

'And the bookshop. They've been asking me where he's got to lately!'

On her way to the department store she called at the bookshop and paid Ernest's bill. At the wine merchant's they told here there was little outstanding, another lady having settled the bill the last time they'd been there. She bought a miniature bottle of gin and surprised the man behind the counter by drinking down the contents in one gulp and leaving him with the empty bottle.

At the store she went straight to the dress department and spent her energy trying on every beautiful dress which caught her fancy.

The dress felt good. It clung as soft silk should. She decided to keep it on. She saw the colours flickering in glass cabinets and counter mirrors as she passed on her way from the hairdressing salon. She'd been there a long time. Now her newly hennaed hair shone above the blues and greens like a chrysanthemum. Matching shoes and bag, and the old clothes left behind in the ladies' room. Before departing, she'd made up her face as carefully as she knew how, surprised at the loveliness of her reflection.

In the coffee house Ernest was sitting in his usual place among the usual group. She could see his thinning hair as he bent forward over a newspaper. Those close to him had their heads thrown back and their arms clasped as if they were listening to him. There was laughter and the sound of billiards coming from the back room. A few people were sitting at other tables. She stood by the door and watched Ernest joking with Albert as he changed the coffee cups. They were like old friends. Next to him was Conrad. Irwin was there, and William with yet another girl; several girls unknown to her lighting each other's cigarettes; a man in a leather coat leaning heavily over Hannah. No Paul in sight. Ernest continued reading aloud above the shouts of his companions. It was the same easy, noisy scene on whose fringes she'd sat so frequently during their better days.

Before he finished the paragraph she must walk quickly through the café, go up to him and say a calm hello. Before anyone else saw her and had a chance to nudge him she must put him to the test. One look at his face on seeing her in these incredible clothes would tell her if he still felt the same way about her. This time it wouldn't be creeping in to take a distant seat, grateful for any proximity to him, and he hardly acknowledging her presence. This time she'd be at the centre, astonishing the lot of them.

The waiters stared at her as she entered. People at tables looked up. As she approached the corner table, the laughter died. Only Ernest's voice continued above the click of the billiard balls and the conversation in the back room. Someone whistled approvingly. Ernest stopped reading and looked up.

She halted in front of him and stood, defiantly smiling and holding her head high.

He looked the new dress up and down and raised his eyebrows in surprise at the hennaed hair. 'Well,' he said, 'how smart we are today!'

Before he'd had time to go back to his reading, she'd struck him smartly across the face – swearing later that the action had been entirely reflex. 'When you find out where it all comes from, you'll be even more surprised!' she said.

She left the coffee house as fast as she could, afraid less of the waiters who began to descend on her like a flock of angry rooks than of the girl with the cropped hair who screamed abuse at her as she ran.

Afterwards she regretted the gesture. Cinematic and trivial. Ernest had stayed away for the night, and she'd sniffed cocaine to give herself a good reason for not being able to sleep.

Nervousness the next day was increased by a letter from Frank.

He mentioned the proposed wedding, saying how the plans for it had been exclusively his – and this in parenthesis, while telling her how he might have sent a letter to the Girl on the back of one of Amy's letters! Who was he trying to frighten? Himself? What a tightrope he was choosing to walk.

The letter crackled under her twitching fingers. She'd tell him categorically not to marry the Girl. It wouldn't be because of jealousy on her part, but from the conviction that a writer of his stature and sensitivity shouldn't waste himself upon a person of whom he was so unsure, and who seemed (even from the little she knew) so unsuitable a partner.

She gave him little rest, raining down on him during his last weeks at the hotel long letters full of pleading and threats, interspersed with others full of hope and future possibilities. If only he would come. She told him how Ernest's nervousness was increasing with the burden of work he'd lately taken on. This made itself felt in his treatment of her: disregarding her feelings, and the state of her health which, unfortunately, had taken a turn for the worse. It was true she'd been coughing again lately, especially at night when she lay in the big bed watching coiling shadows, waiting for Ernest to come creeping in during the small hours. If he came at all.

Whenever she wrote about her health Frank responded, saying how closely he with his illness was bound to her. Her peaceful letters, he said, made him immeasurably happy and came as rain onto his burning head. To those which began with exclamations and ended with he knew not what terror, he reacted with fear, actually trembling as under an alarm bell. He searched for furniture under which to hide, praying she might fly out of the window in the same way she rushed in. He said he couldn't, after all, keep a storm in his room. Sometimes she wished she knew for sure when he was making jokes and when he was deeply serious. She had to get to know him better.

One evening while she was writing one of her calmer letters, Ernest came home early. So intent had she been on what she was doing that she barely heard him turn the door handle and enter. When he asked her what she was doing, she replied honestly that she was writing a letter to Frank. He raised his eyebrows, and she saw by the droop of his shoulders that he wasn't feeling particularly joyful.

'We've been writing for quite a while now,' she said.

'Are you working for Fox?'

'Not properly. I'm going to see him soon.'

'What's this? Preliminary research?' He was staring at the sheets of written paper, a gleam of interest in his eyes. She placed them under the one she'd just started.

'His work's incredibly good,' she said. 'The more one reads, the more there is to find in it.' Ernest made a slight noise of disbelief.

'A bit esoteric for my tastes. To my mind he's going the wrong way.'

'And which way is that?'

'Towards the metaphysical, I should suppose.' He pushed his glasses up his nose.

'And what, exactly, have you read of his?'

A pause. Ernest stood in the middle of the room. 'I probably know as much about him as you do.' He waited while she laughed. 'Once was it, you met him?'

97

Normally he would have put more venom into the attack. She looked at the clock. It was unusually early for him to be home.

'What happened?' she said. 'Did you get tired of playing with your friends?'

'I have work to do,' he said, not moving.

'So have I.'

He still stood looking at her. 'I wouldn't have thought you and Frank had much in common.'

'How strange you should say that. You of all people. You and he are very similar, surely? Same age . . . roughly. Same education. Same family background.'

'Ah!' He was suddenly interested again. 'Well, I can tell you for certain he's not like me at all. He's the rabbinical type. Head in a shawl. Hypochondriac too, I seem to remember.' A smile touched his lips. 'Up in the mountains, searching for Tablets!'

'At the moment he's a little cut off from people because he happens to be ill. That's one of the reasons I write to him.'

'Aren't we all?' He sank onto a chair and put his head back with a sigh. 'Amy, come and unknot me . . .' He was making circles with his head. 'Banker's Shoulder, that's what I've got!' He was making a pleading face at her.

She went over to him and put her hands on his back, feeling for the pain. His shoulder felt hot. 'You've only met him once, haven't you?' he asked very casually.

She began to massage the back of his neck, pinching it, pummelling his dorsal muscles. 'Maybe . . .' she said.

When her hand moved over his shoulder, he made a grab for it and held her by the wrist. Moving it towards his mouth he opened her fingers and kissed her palm.

'Can't you take it, Ernest?'

He mumbled something into her hand, pulling her by the wrist, trying to grab the other one and turn her round to face him. After a small struggle she ceased to resist and let him pull her down onto his lap. After kissing her on the mouth with more passion than she remembered for a long time, he murmured in her ear: 'It was only once, wasn't it?' but she knew he was smiling.

'I have a beautiful idea . . .' he said. As she relaxed, he released her hands and began to stroke her arms gently, with tiny strokes, as if she were an animal. 'Beautiful Amy . . .'

His arm round her shoulder he led her slowly into the bedroom, head close to hers, whispering those endearments first formed on a hillside where wild flowers were growing. The sound of his voice, harsh from the climb, came clear to her through the familiar phrases, and she replied as she used to do. Now, as then, he knew how best to please her. If she was cold he warmed her; if she was slow he slowed too, sensing each way as if he were still among the flowers, afraid to break a single stem. With waning detachment she recognized again the subtlety of his seduction, and warmed to it as past hurts and resentments left her. Any reluctance she might have felt at daily indifference slowly mattered less and less as she allowed herself to be carried into his passion.

While making love his concentration on her was absolute. It was as if she was the first woman he'd ever loved, and certainly he'd never love another. Nothing gave her the slightest cause for doubting it. With his body over her she could look into his eyes and see nothing but the reflection of herself, naked and desirable, and hear nothing but his admiration, devotion and need. His hands told her how much he wanted her, while he spoke so gently and looked so lovingly, with so profound an emotion, that she could only meet him with her deepest feelings. To her whispered, 'Why can't we always be like this?' his reply was that they could, they could. He loved her. He needed her. She was the most marvellous woman in the universe. All she had to do was arch her beautiful body and respond. And she did so with equal vehemence, all the love she still felt for him in her reply. And as he pinned her and penetrated her, she

99

loved him so completely that only afterwards did she realize again the mistake she'd made by telling him so.

It had always frightened her that Ernest's sensitivity should manifest itself most forcibly in the act of making love. He brought to bear on it such a concentration of intelligence that she felt the slight chill of realization only afterwards. When she lay with him in the quiet of the bedroom she was certain, instantly certain, of her love for him, and then as instantly sure of his lack of love for her. Thoughts came and went, confusing her by their contradictions: what she called his sensitivity was only selfishness: he needed her and she must reject that need: it was simply that they loved one another and he showed it best in bed, away from the worries of daily life: she often confused neglect with single-mindedness: if he made love to other women it was because of the beliefs he held so dear. If she stayed quiet when panic threatened, then he would come back to her of his own free will. He couldn't, after all, do without her.

Like a mother with a baby she noticed everything about him, every curve, every mark, each daily change in his colour and the growth of his hair and beard. What surprised her more than was reasonable was that he noted so little about her. When making love he gazed at the whorls of her ears and adored them, stroked her high forehead and kissed her brow, ran his hands along her arms and outlined each nail of her fingers. But he never seemed to imprint them on his memory. Perhaps she was for him, as she'd frequently suspected, archetypal Woman, to be caressed and fondled and fucked as efficiently as possible in order to extract the maximum response. It wasn't a thought she enjoyed, but she was quite aware that to gain the most satisfaction from someone there had to be an initial effort. They had been living together for a year before he said one day, 'You've got a scar on your chin!' in a critical tone, as if he'd only just discovered she was less than perfect. It had bothered her. She cherished his physical imperfections: his poor sight, the way his front teeth were slightly crossed, his rounded belly, his thin coating of black fur, and the mole shaped like Cyprus underneath his arm. She'd told him that if circumstances separated them for hundreds of years, she could identify him instantly by listing all those beloved signs of his individuality.

Before going to sleep he made love to her again, taking her more than willingly into a precise and violent act which left them slippery with sweat, marooned on the stripped bed like two exhausted wrestlers. Cruelly she'd once told him that practice made perfect, nonetheless his skill bound her to him in a way of which he seemed aware, yet took for granted. It was only appropriate that she too should bring the same seriousness to what for him was of the utmost importance. And she knew he took it very seriously indeed. When discussing it with friends, he'd often talked of making love as a continuing experiment, to be analysed and researched in order to get the best performance. The conversations had sometimes disgusted her with their unfeeling tone. To hear his discussions with Paul and Irwin was to hear herself, and all women, reduced to machines which, with the correct amount of lubrication, could run sweetly. Her remarks to this effect were greeted with disdain. If that was how she saw herself, Paul had said, no wonder women were still struggling to free themselves. Being outnumbered at the time, she'd agreed to change her way of thinking. Once she'd threatened to find a lover of her own, knowing before the sentence was complete what the reply would be. Ernest would welcome the idea, he said. The sooner the better for him. As he began proposing names she'd run from the café with her hands over her ears.

She woke early with him gone from her side. The pale dawn light made her shiver. She could see herself in the mirror near the bed – a woman with an expression whose blankness turned to alarm as she heard Ernest's voice from the living room, and knew he was speaking to someone on the 'phone. Through the open doors she could hear his insistent murmur as if he were trying to persuade. She stared at the crumpled heap of clothes which lay on the floor from door to bed marking their passionate progress last night. At the sound of the receiver being replaced, she threw herself down in a sleeping position and closed her eyes. She heard him come into the bedroom and take off his dressing gown. He got into bed and huddled close to her, running his hand along her side, evidently surprised at how cold she was. He sat up again and searched for the duvet, covered them both, then lay down with his knees tucked behind hers, his arm enclosing her. In a short space of time he was softly snoring, leaving her staring at the far wall where the light slowly continued to brighten. At seven-thirty she woke him with a cup of coffee.

'I'm not going to work today,' he said. 'I don't feel well enough.' He lay back, exposing the soft hair under his arms.

'If you like you can go and buy me a newspaper – with your new-found wealth!' He smiled at her and she went to get dressed, glad she'd have him to herself for a whole day.

When she got back he was sitting up in bed, a book propped on his knees and her bedjacket stretched uncomfortably across his shoulders. She'd bought bacon and eggs to make his breakfast, and a loaf of bread for toasting.

She sat beside him watching how greedily he ate. Between mouthfuls he read the news to her, pointing with his fork at particular items.

'Inflation's getting worse. Up two per cent since last month. Believe me this isn't the end. If jobs in industry are going, then white collar jobs are bound to follow.'

'So you choose today not to go to work!'

'Have sense, Amy. When I allow a job to dictate to me, then I'm really one of the manipulated masses.' He licked the egg from his knife and wiped it on a piece of bread. 'What we've got to watch for is how the Government controls money demand. It may set the level of interest rates ...'

'Or more likely let market conditions set them. The working man doesn't stand a chance today.'

'You can't have money flowing outside the banking system, Amy. It's too risky.'

She said he was getting as bad as his employers.

'Have you ever heard of bankers taking real risks? All this talk . . .' she tapped the article derisively '. . . is so much self-protection for the most protected breed on earth! I shall be glad when you get out of all that into something more worthy of you!'

He looked at her mildly. 'I'd really like some jam.' He laid the cold knife flat on her wrist and ran it across the back of her hand.

No jam in the kitchen cupboard. She ran downstairs to Mrs Kertesch who gladly donated a tiny jar. When she got back upstairs she noticed that the door of the living room was now closed. Ernest was still sitting up in bed as before, but the jacket was now upside down on his shoulders.

'Have you been in the living room?' she asked.

He smiled without replying. 'Get undressed and into bed, and I'll make some more toast.' He got up quickly, stopping to kiss her lightly on the cheek. 'Let's have a day here together.'

She did as he asked, settling beneath the covers with a pile of books picked at random from the shelves; listening to him being noisy and cheerful in the kitchen. She opened her favourite Flaubert. He came back humming a tuneless tune, a pleased expression on his face. 'It's going to be a lovely day indoors today!' he said. They shared the toast and jam, then put the tray on the floor among their cast off clothing.

The sun slowly lit the room, sending flickering shadows of spring leaves to pattern the walls. They sat side by side weighed down by books, papers and journals. From time to time she found herself glancing at him. He looked slightly ridiculous naked, with his glasses perched on the end of his nose, and the beginnings of a beard. If she bent her head sideways she could see the bristles gleaming quite white in the sunlight. She put out her hand once to touch the roughness, and watch his reaction. He neither noticed her touch nor deviated from his reading.

Only when the telephone rang once, then stopped, leaving its echo behind like a ghostly tune, did he stiffen slightly and look up, then go back quickly to his studies.

'Are you expecting any calls?'

'I'm always expecting calls,' he said without looking up.

'Some more than others?'

It was no use wishing she hadn't spoken. She knew by the deeper silence between them that she'd overstepped the bounds again. Closing Flaubert she grabbed another book, sorry that Frederic Moreau's problems seemed less real than her own. She began to read Chapter One of *Lovers' Yearning*, as if her life depended on it. Nervousness slowly subsided as she became absorbed in the silly plot. For a mindless day in bed it couldn't be bettered. Once or twice she laughed aloud, causing Ernest to raise his head.

'"I want to love you so much," he said, that I tire of you quickly. My passion will overwhelm me. I shall see you every hour of the day, make love to you all night. And so this very flame which burns within me will naturally falter and quickly die. It will leave me free of you. Only in this way can I rid myself of the terrible inner turmoil I am suffering.'

'What do you think of that?' she asked him.

'Such rubbish you read.' Ernest had turned his head and was staring at her coldly.

'What an awful thing to say.'

'Well, it is rubbish, by any standards.'

'No, no. I mean what an awful way of telling a woman you're in love with her. First you say you can't live without her. Then you say it's only a stage you'll have to endure in order to come out of it in one piece!'

'I don't see the problem.' Still only half listening, he put down his book. 'Who says they're in love with you?'

Exasperated, she began again: 'This man professes the most consuming passion for this lady . . . Flora. He woos her, gets her into bed because he's so passionate she can't resist him, then he tells her that!'

Ernest took off his glasses with a sigh. 'What?'

'That he wants to get the affair over and done with so that he can get on with his life!'

'Sensible chap!' He was trying to offend her. 'Other females to fuck. Lots of fish in the sea.'

'Being crude doesn't suit you, Ernest.'

He slid down his pillows and pulled the sheet up to his chin.

'Wake me when he's decided to become a monk!'

No longer interested in Flora's fate, she joined him under the sheet.

The sound of the telephone ringing once as the receiver was replaced, woke her from a deep and unremembered dream. She opened her eyes in fear and saw Ernest standing at the bedroom door in his dressing gown, bright sunlight taking all the colour from him. At once she felt her skin tingle with apprehension. The muscles tensed. Despite the warm room she felt cold.

'What were you doing?'

'Looking for this . . .' He came towards her holding out a tray on which was the small, silver box and the tiny spoon he kept hidden at the bottom of his desk drawer. He slid into bed beside her, opened the box lid and carefully unfolded the square of tin foil inside. 'See the way it shines?' he said. 'Good stuff this – not much residue. Let's have a little, private party!'

5

It was still that irritating touch of distant superiority in the tone of some of Frank's letters which annoyed her. He seemed at times to be passing judgement on her from some high vantage point which made him untouchable. In one letter he'd even called her 'little child'. But in the next he was talking about himself as being a Jew unworthy of consideration beside that other, stronger Jew with whom she lived. He should know how she lived.

For him to say that when she'd married Ernest she'd taken a large step down from her level, was to set her wondering deeply why his race had sunk so low in his eyes. And when he said that is she came to him she'd leap into the abyss, she wondered about his sanity. Could he not see how terribly he belittled himself and all Jews to talk as if he were the lowest of a mean race? She wouldn't allow it, as little as she'd acknowledge that the whole idea of their meeting at all was doomed to failure. Why not, she asked him in panic, come down from the judgement seat long enough to see whether it was possible? Then he'd see in reality whether she had time for him or not.

It was so sad. And irritating. She knew how her nerves were stretched. Fox had noticed it when she'd gone to collect Frank's manuscript. She saw him eyeing the way she twiddled the pens on his desk. He'd grabbed a chair far too hastily and asked her to be seated. The difficulty was that he hadn't been what she'd expected. She told Frank. Such an accent. And seemingly so superior in his manner. How foolish to have fallen into the trap of believing him stupid when, after only the briefest of conversations, she'd discovered him to be intelligent and acute. The fact that he was willing to publish Frank's work at all, which had been viewed with suspicion by other publishers, was in his favour. When he'd spoken to her about the work, stressing that her illustrations should be evocations of mood rather than realistic, she'd lost some of her tenseness. And he was so tall. She stood under him as if under an elm, wondering while she cowered there whether he could see dandruff in her hair. In his office she'd sat beneath him while he talked about style and its dangers to an author. Then he stopped in mid-sentence and sat down facing her, to say very quietly that he thought she was beautiful. A strange man. Did Frank know him well? He was at once so formal and polite, yet was capable of saying that. When they met, Frank shouldn't expect her to have become what she never was. But Fox had seemed so sincere that her nervousness had evaporated, and she'd replied that she was never beautiful, really not, perhaps sometimes pretty. After that the discussion turned quite naturally back to the subject of Frank's stories. He said he couldn't let any harm be done to them by insensitive illustrators, as if she wasn't included in that group.

It would be easy for Frank to recognize that with a few rare people there was the possibility of passing in seconds through the formalities of first meeting to real understanding. She didn't, she said, include their friendship in this category since their intimacy had grown like a fast-blooming flower through constant communication. But Fox was a surprise: a few minutes after her arrival, he was her friend. She had sensed the increasing intimacy. Neither his tone had changed, nor what he said in any great way, but he looked at her with a straight look, perhaps a little fearful in case he'd made a major misjudgement, but willing to risk it. You see, she wrote, some people take risks which for them may be large ones. Why should your coming to see me not be a risk as large as his?

She would have liked to continue her dissection of Fox

for Frank's benefit, but she suspected that using the attractions of one man to persuade another to love her, might offend his sensibilities. Fox bothered her. He'd been able to calm her. She didn't write to tell how the new, calmer mood began to change again to one of frustration when she recognized the limits already bounding this new friendship. With someone like Fox, so obviously raised and schooled impeccably in the old-fashioned style, it would be difficult for him to change from the superior-sounding aristocrat with the reticent manner into the spontaneous, approachable friend she required. His very height was against him. It had lent enchantment to her first view of him, for she'd thought him excessively handsome. On closer inspection his face had revealed spots and large scars which, for some reason, detracted not at all from his good looks. She was, she knew, looking at a face much in type like her own, with its high forehead, regular features and small mouth. He might have been her brother. Such a change from Ernest's Hasidic features or, for that matter, Frank's.

The problem she thought was one of loneliness. She could do with a reliable friend. As simple as that. Frank was a friend with whom came so many complications that, for an instant in his office, she'd looked at Fox with real hope. As they'd talked, now and then their eyes met with a look other than straight: a man and a woman sizing each other up for sex. It was then that she'd taken flight, deciding to go before she'd gone too far.

Poor Frank. She'd definitely gone too far in castigating him. Feeling as usual immediately sorry, having posted the letter she sent flying after it a bunch of tulips so large it would cause him terrible problems when he was ready to leave. On the accompanying card she wrote: Ignore all the words except the one that spells Love.

One had to love somebody or one was too alone. Her father didn't love her, she thought. None of her pleas to that distant figure could shift him from his intransigent position. When she held in her hand the crisp envelope

containing the coldly written card stating that having made
her bed she should justly lie on it, she could feel its chill
creeping up her arm. She could see him sitting at his
mahogany desk with the green leather, arranging the card
to sit squarely while he wrote, then putting it into the envelope and sealing it with the watered pad. She knew that
only shame on his part for his daughter's behaviour pre-
vented him from dictating the thing to his secretary. Her
eyes misted over. She was getting to be like a Pavlovian dog,
trained to cry at the sight of certain hand-writing. These
days she cried too easily. She dabbed carefully at her nose;
it had a tendency to bleed. She'd bought a nasal spray and
kept it hidden from Ernest, in case he should suspect how
much cocaine she was actually snorting on her own during
the long days. Frank's letters too were still hidden, the
problems becoming more difficult daily as their bulk increased. Not that Ernest was the type to pry, rather his
vision might suddenly clear as it sometimes did in moments
of idleness. So she'd taken all the letters, thrown away
the envelopes, tied them up with string, and put them
under the sofa in the anteroom, out of sight in the deepening
dust.

There was a film of dust on the painting. She moistened
a piece of rag with spike oil and gently rubbed it over the
child, watching the way the small, strange face began its
intent stare. But how to start again? A mad woman's
scribblings covered a quarter of the canvas, snake locks
emerging here and there from the beginnings of a terrible
face. Somehow she must find a way through the erasures
and the web of crazy pencil lines back into Milena's life.
She stood back as an artist should, trying in her mind's
eye to see something approaching a visually pleasing
composition, just as she'd been taught. As if it mattered.
To celebrate someone who took chances when they came,
and was never fearful of the outcome, one had to emulate
her, not caring too much if fact and fantasy intertwined
should bring about chaos. Nevertheless, she picked up a

ruler as if to belie the idea and began to draw careful lines, neat parallel rows of them at right angles to Schubert.

She'd build something an architect in 1927 would have been proud of. Of concrete and glass and steel, incorporating the revolutionary idea of a cross wall system suitable to brand new materials. It might resemble the Olympic building in Prague, or the Czech Pavilion at the Paris Exhibition. It would be highly functional, decoration an intrinsic part of structure, with a beauty·of proportion clearly discernible to those who knew about Loos and Gropius and Le Corbusier. A strong and delicate building with which to celebrate another new beginning. A building taking flight like Milena's career as author, contemporary commentator, and editor of an *avant-garde* magazine: or the great plans of her new husband to make truly twentieth-century cities. If Milena and Jaromir lived in far cosier quarters than those he proposed for the new urban dwellers, at least it showed that here was no parochial thinker. Somewhere in her file were collections of poems, odd translations of stories with unfathomable plots, dialogues and dissertations on what constituted the New at that time. But some were already lying dog-eared on the floor where feet had trampled them. Later she'd use them to give Milena's two years of real happiness a truly substantial form. First she must set the foundations solidly, making the building grow from a first meeting among the rural scenery bordering the river Vlatava. At the bottom of the canvas she painstakingly drew in the outline of a Bohemian landscape where lovers discovered one another. She worked upward with the pencil loose in her hand, trying to move her wrist freely in harmonious curves away from the ruler's restriction. How difficult now to imagine someone else's happiness and wonder how it passed so fast. But easy to see that hard work would come easily in such an atmosphere of optimism. They were a group of people intent on regenerating society, to whom everything was a challenge. Russia was building a new society in the East, on the wreckage of an unjust regime.

In Europe the time hadn't yet arrived when frontiers were fearful barriers. It was a time to talk about new beginnings and put them to the test. It was a time for making new lives.

A dream. She stopped. The ruler's weight brought her hand down to her side. A dream as powerful as any of Frank's, which had stayed with her for two years and wouldn't be suppressed. She had been walking in her dream down an old alleyway between the high brick walls of two public buildings. Beside her walked a small girl of perhaps two or three, holding her hand. In the dream she knew that the child was her own daughter.

Milena's daughter was born after eight months of fighting against pain. The diagnosis of sepsis came too late to prevent the agony or the cure: being a doctor what else should her concerned father give her but repeated doses of morphia?

She placed the ruler back on the canvas. The pencil scratched along the metal edge. Instead of curves it began to block in units of separate dwelling space, spreading out sideways like Radiant City. She drew in lift towers and balcony zones, working out the correct scale for standardized, rationalized living volume per capita. An architect could lose himself in such a white, glassy world: a child could get lost in such a maze. With her face not inches from the surface of the work, she drew up and up, planning mad multiple storeys in a City for Three Million. On top of the highest penthouse she would place a tiny Jaromir; modular man, his arms wide in helpless appeal while his wife far away in hospital lay crippled and drugged into addiction. Not until the light in the room began to diminish did she stop and look at what she'd achieved.

It wasn't what she'd intended. The skeletal construction rose and spread across one half of the whole, taking over and distorting the music; crossing the blood-stained tiles; piercing the birds in blue flight, and sectioning off the child with the violets, whose aunt was now isolated inside a perfect cube. The tiny Count Schaffgotsch, wearing his red star, had almost vanished behind the structure. Its horizontals bit into the first of the Furies, leaving her with lacerations. They attacked the body of the second and cut her head into parts, and finally became entangled in the dark incisions making up Medusa's sinuous locks. Amy sat down heavily on the sofa. Feeling suddenly cold and exhausted she raised her legs slowly until she was lying flat, still gripping the pencil and staring at the ceiling.

Somewhere down below gypsy music is playing wildly, its high-pitched insistence attacking her nerves like hot needles. Against the lighted square of the window she can see the silhouette of her husband looking down into the hotel courtyard. His shoulders are hunched, and she knows his fists are tightly clenched. She had told him to say no to all her pleas and he says it repeatedly, until it sounds like an accompaniment to the violins.

As she throws herself from side to side on the bed, hitting the wall with the flat of her hand, throwing her hands up to her ears to block the noise, rolling back and glimpsing his obdurate stance, the gasps of pain which come from her mouth turn to screams of despair. He must listen. He always has. He must go and buy it for her. Now. Can't he see she didn't mean it? How can he bear to see her suffer? How can she bear this totally unexpected glimpse into hell?

The music plays on as she writhes and sweats and her knuckles grow raw from beating them on the wall. If she had the strength she'd crawl from the bed and claw at him until he does what she wants. He is torturing a sick woman who came to be cured of an injured knee, not pushed into madness for lack of a simple drug. She asks him again for morphia. His head goes no from side to side in rhythm with the violins. Hers beats the wet pillow until she weakens and sinks into exhausted sleep composed of demented, asphyxiating dreams punctuated by hysterical awakenings.

If only the terror would engulf her totally, taking her for always out of the unendurable. She has forgotten her child. She screams out her pleas to the empty room where she looks in vain for him in the shadows. She knows he is hiding round the walls. He's hiding in the wardrobe and clattering the hangers with the noise of a *csárdás*. He has drawn huge light circles on the ceiling, meant to frighten her into calm. He is hiding under the ruckled rug so that she would fall and break her bad leg if she left the bed. He has closed her in an airless room leaving her lit by a single lamp. He has left a shining revolver there, close to her trembling hand. He has gone down to eat cold turkey in the restaurant below. He will dance to the music of the gypsy band with a trio of young and healthy girls who will accompany him on his travels.

Ernest turning the light on woke her. 'Not again,' he said in a low voice.

'Not again,' she said, unable to see him in the dazzling light. 'What time is it?'

'Time you were in bed, by the look of you.'

'I am in bed.' She struggled upright, trying to shake off the deadness of apprehension. She saw he was looking at the painting.

'You might have left a light on. Nearly broke my leg in the hall.'

She saw he was wearing an overcoat. 'Is it cold out?'

'Cold enough.' He peered at the canvas, his nose nearly touching it. He dabbed it with his thumb. 'Why isn't the 'phone working?' he said.

'It's not wet. They're pencil lines.' She sat up and put both feet on the floor and tried to smooth her dishevelled hair.

'The 'phone isn't working, Amy,' Ernest said heavily.

'Maybe Conrad left it off the hook.'

'When did he ring?'

'I spoke to him this morning . . . No. Then Stacey 'phoned. They're back. She said the holiday was wonderful, but the office is in a mess . . .'

'So it was working . . . when?'

'This afternoon, I suppose.' She looked at the mass of pencil lines behind Ernest's head: St Sebastian.

'It's the bill!' He looked at her accusingly. 'Have you paid it? You have paid it, haven't you?'

She thought for a moment, and knew the bill was lying next to the card from her father on the desk. 'No. I haven't paid it. I paid most of your debts, Ernest, but not that one.' How she hated the telephone. 'And I don't think I can.'

'For God's sake!' He raised his head in despair. 'I can't go on!' He sneezed violently, and frantically searched in his pocket for a handkerchief. He sneezed again and coughed loudly. 'That's all I need,' he said. He wiped his eyes which she could now see were watering copiously. 'Can't you do something? Can't you see I'm ill?'

She watched him undress and get into bed, wondering without asking how he'd come by two long scratches across his back.

Ernest stayed in bed the next day, surrounded by books, magazines, folders of work and notepads. She went out once at his request to notify the office of his condition. Her day was spent mainly in the bedroom. If she tried to return to the picture in the anteroom, Ernest's voice would call her back, asking what she was doing. He requested constant cups of coffee, flasks of lemonade, a little nourishment so his strength wouldn't desert him. Knowing of old how much he enjoyed his illnesses she quietly gave him what he wanted, glad to sit and listen to him. He read her his current banking reports, sections of yesterday's papers, and his comments on the manipulation of the news. He was in top form. He showed her a literary magazine where Leon's name was mentioned. When he slept she crept away to write to Frank in a hurried hand.

A strange sensation, she said, to look after someone ill. How it brought out the best in her. How it increased her feeling of helplessness. How it brought to mind the country doctor in Frank's story who so fatally misunderstood his patient. Watching her father treat the injured with such meticulous care had made her sure for a while that she too would join the medical profession. But she'd discovered it wasn't enough to nurse them carefully, perhaps cure their bodies completely, yet see them wrecked emotionally by experiences often outside her comprehension. Her father was (luckily for him) either unaware or oblivious of his role as psychological healer – look at the way he behaved at home – and had often been blind to the damage of the work he did himself. Having successfully mended the jaw of a man wounded in some battle – her father told this story himself with great irritation – but unable to make the man's saliva glands function as before, he'd sent him home with a bag round his neck to collect the dripping saliva. The patient had committed suicide. Good work gone to waste!

These were things about her father, and her feelings, which she'd never told anyone before. Not everybody, and especially not Ernest, could understand how such events – sometimes not even events, maybe merely a word brutally spoken – could mark one as surely as if someone had inscribed them with a machine of torture. She would have liked to write to Frank of happier things, but who else was there to tell of what was deepest inside? Who else could understand the guilt, from which she'd never be able to free herself?

The next evening Irwin came to visit Ernest. He threw a pile of scientific journals on Ernest's knees and talked his way through preliminary complaints about night sweats, dry coughing and incredible weakness of the limbs. But lured from his woes by the prospect of interesting hours of analysis and discussion, Ernest visibly began to improve. She stayed until she sensed the conversation was slowing due to her presence, then left them talking, noticing as she reached the door that Irwin had taken a letter from his jacket. She closed the door on the image of Ernest smiling broadly as he tucked the letter inside his pyjama pocket.

When she left the flat to go and post her letters to Frank, she could hear them deep in discussion about the problems of language in science.

The evening was warm enough for her to feel pleasure

at being outside, able to look up at the sky, still pink, promising another warm day tomorrow. The light, touching projecting pillars of offices and shop fronts, gave their lines a Gothic look, their severity broken only by patches of colour where window boxes bloomed. She walked slowly through the streets, keeping to the outskirts of the commercial centre, happy to be aimless; to wander down unknown side roads where hedges were newly sprouting and laburnum trailed cadmium over walls. She passed blocks of flats in neat green squares, their windows setting off fireworks of bright light. Soon she was passing houses in terraces with identical doors and symmetrical windows, in which it seemed everyone had welcomed spring by placing there a plant or two. She'd so nearly missed the spring, the season of them all she most loved. Everything seemed new and fresh, from the bright green of young lawns to the woolly buds of chestnut trees already visible in their circles of leaves. And as the houses became larger and their gardens more grand, the light increased, flooding rooftops and walls with a pale and theatrical pink. The evening was dying as fast as the first of the early flowers, sending shadows of tree trunks in broad bands of indigo across the roads.

She turned into an avenue of chestnuts, where great houses lay in their own well-kept grounds. There was the scent of lawns and dug earth. She reached the corner where two avenues met, and stood irresolutely in front of the last house. Ahead were a few more isolated dwellings then open playing fields beyond. Where the road wound upward out of sight was the first sweep of parkland. It offered an uninviting prospect. In the lengthening shadows she stayed for a while, leaning against an iron gate and looking at the trees' shimmering leaves. With a sudden creak the gate opened, sending her in a slow circle onto the gravel of an unweeded drive. For no real reason she began to walk towards the house, liking the resolute sound of her footsteps.

At the huge front door she stood for a moment wondering whether to knock, and why she should do so. It was something to do with one of Frank's letters that she badly wanted it open. He'd imagined the two of them on either side of a room tugging away at separate doors, each closing theirs when the other was opened. But only after she'd twice lifted the heavy knocker did she realize that the sound reverberated in too hollow a fashion. The house was silent. Above her head a perfectly painted portico held the weight of a wistaria whose flowers hung in clusters from a twisted vine which wound across the walls and round the shuttered windows. Upstairs there were no shutters, only curtains hanging straight, cutting into the reflection of the darkening sky and deadening it. Small balconies with ornamental iron-work jutted out from each window. She walked through fallen petals along the neat stone paving to the side of the house, where she could see lawns with white urns from which yucca sprouted, a tennis court beyond, and the bor-ders of what looked like another garden.

It was darker at the back of the house, the sun already casting a massive shadow which blotted out the colour of all the border flowers, except the white ones which shone like stars. She made her way to where the light was still illumi-nating rows of bright glass cloches, and someone had sowed seeds in fine green lines. She stood inhaling the smell of soil. A flight of sparrows flew low over her head and settled in a tree, their quarrelling making her suddenly nervous. She walked between the rows, embedding footprints as she bent to examine the crops. Weeds were already beginning to appear among the vegetables. Beneath the frames were lettuces already succulent and half-grown, and the fronds of new carrots packed close like ferns. Putting her hand inside the frame she pulled a few carrots from the bed, but as she extracted her hand, the sharp edge of a piece of glass sliced across the top of her wrist, leaving a thin bleeding wound. She departed hurriedly, grasping a bunch of carrots.

It was almost dark by the time she got back to the flat. Irwin had left, and Ernest shouted at her from the bedroom that while she was in the kitchen she should make him a bite to eat. She stood for a long time in the dark, running cold water over the wound, and thinking about the well-ordered lives of a family with a home, who would return from holiday to know the pleasure of walking again in their garden.

Ernest found her in the kitchen crying and eating carrots. He bound up her wrist which she said she'd cut on a broken bottle, said he couldn't trust her for five seconds not to get into trouble, and raised his eyes in mockery when she said that spring was a fugitive season. He went back to bed carrying a tray with coffee, boiled eggs and toast. She stayed to water the dying plants, then write another letter to Frank.

Only come, and you shall see how easy things will be after all your fears. Come and see how this woman you have the temerity to call 'little child' can explain things to you. Nothing is impossible you know. Being well is possible. Beind loved.

At night Ernest shifted his bulk in great rolling movements across the bed. Intermittently he snored. Her wrist throbbed painfully. When she closed her eyes she saw in rapid succession visions of Frank arriving by train and coming in search of her flat; him going in search of Ernest; Frank with the Girl coming to talk things over; Frank so ill he had to be brought to the safety of the flat where she would tend him until recovery . . . she felt as beset by anxieties as if she were high on coke. Good thoughts rushed crazily after bad until she was forced to leave Ernest deeply sleeping and go back to the anteroom to write down her fears.

The one thing he mustn't do was surprise her, she said. She must know when he'd arrive, the very train, the place where he'd stay. There were certain plans she herself would have to make in order to give him her time. Because she hadn't spoken lately about her own work, he mustn't suppose she was being idle. Apart from the illustrations which Fox was waiting for, there was Milena's portrait which, he must realize, was very important to her. As for earning other sums of money, she'd seen an advertisement for someone able to teach portrait painting to an afternoon class of retired people, near the West station. What better place to keep an eye on arriving trains! She added the post-script that because her 'phone wasn't working, he'd have to be doubly sure to let her know his plans in good time.

She found Ernest in the bathroom next morning, tweaking the grey hairs from his chest. Despite the cold he seemed in a very pleasant mood. He said he was going to practise mind over matter, and proved it by sitting down to a breakfast suitable for two. It was still early when he left, sniffing and coughing but declaring he was perfectly well. She wondered what had persuaded him to wear his best pin-stripe suit, brand new white shirt, finest tie, and to polish his toecaps like glass. It wasn't until she left the flat herself to go to the post office that she realized it was Saturday and that he couldn't be going to the bank as he'd said.

One letter waiting for her at the post office. She tore at it hastily, scanned it for signs that he'd decided to come. All he talked about was a dream he'd had. She went to the nearest café to study the letter more carefully: there had been occasions when a second, or even a third reading had revealed a well-hidden irony, or a subtle joke at his own expense. The tone of this letter was all too evidently serious. They had met again in his dream and he'd failed, he said, to hear her voice speaking expressly to him. But he said the message of the dream was not that he'd failed to hear her, but that he couldn't anyway have answered. She blinked back tears of frustration and read on, finding no comfort in being compared to a fiery column holding him encircled. Such a short letter to cause such extended panic.

She sat watching the crowds pass. If she closed her eyes all she could see with clarity was Ernest hurrying merrily off somewhere. She wanted someone to confide in who could be relied upon to give sympathy, however superficial. Jasmine's day had no doubt already been ordained. By now she'd be sitting in the segregated ranks of the synagogue toying with an upside-down prayer book. Stacey was far away and married to her own special Jew with whom, so she wrote, life was wonderful.

There was always Charles to go and visit, although lately he had seemed a little distant. When she'd congratulated him on winning the commission for the new fountain, he'd accepted her pleasure coldly. No. He'd been happy to speak about the project, until she'd made the mistake of moving the conversation too hastily round to Frank. On that occasion he'd actually asked her if she was trying to upset him. Poor Charles. She'd try to be nicer to him soon. But not today, for if she visited him again she'd find the subject of Frank springing to her lips unaided.

Her lonely state was getting worse. If she could find someone to talk to. Laurie came to mind. At least he shared her interest in Frank's work.

As she climbed the stairs to his office, she could hear a typewriter, and his voice calling instructions. When she entered she saw he had his jacket on and a manuscript under his arm.

'What's up, princess?' He came and put his arm round her and led her back to the door. 'I'm just off. It will have to wait until Monday.'

'Can't we go in and talk a bit?' She tried to keep the urgency out of her voice. 'I liked the piece you did on Robert Musil.' But he seemed in a greater hurry than usual.

'I promised faithfully to get home in time, Amy. For once I'm going to make it!'

'I'm doing a series of illustrations for Fox,' she said to his back as he made for the stairs.

'Thank God,' he said. 'I thought you were after me again for money.' They were at the landing when he caught sight of her face. Quickly he tapped her cheek. 'Sorry, Amy. No offence! Maybe I'll have something for you soon . . .' He started walking down the stairs. 'Maybe Tuesday week.' She followed him closely. 'I'm supposed to be taking the family to the Zoo . . .'

'Oh Laurie, how could you!' They had reached the bottom, and were crushed together in the small vestibule. 'Fancy a man of your sensitivity wanting to gloat over trapped animals.'

He peered hard at her, putting his nose close. A powerful aroma of garlic hung around him. 'You joking, Amy?'

'Joking! One shouldn't even imprison a fish – trap it and force it to go round and round. And what about birds? Can you imagine being hardly able to stretch your wings? A prisoner for life in a tiny cage? And animals . . . Have you seen the distance a creature like a leopard runs? And the jaguar . . .? It catches its dinner on the move . . .' Laurie was edging towards the door. 'And look at the giraffe . . .'

'No, Amy! You look at the giraffe!'

For some reason her eyes filled with tears.

He looked at her with another 'What's up?' put down the manuscript and pulled her towards him. He held her close, his jacket grazing her face and the garlic smell almost overpowering her.

'I have a ridiculous need to talk to somebody,' she said in a muffled voice. She blinked away the tears. 'About anything.'

'You tell that old man of yours from me that I'll come and put ground glass in his coffee!' He held her at arm's length. 'Why he should do it, I don't know. You've got more than all of them put together. Including brains.'

'Can't we just go somewhere and chat, Laurie?' she said.

'Sorry, Amy. I've got to go. Lunch waiting.' He put the manuscript under his arm. 'I tell you what, though. It won't last, this one. Believe you me, he's bitten off more than he can chew this time!' He held the street door for her. As she squeezed past him in the narrow opening he said in her ear, 'Somebody's husband wields power in high places!'

They walked together to the car park, Laurie still talking as though she were totally informed. She gathered that Ernest was deeply involved, and the woman perhaps less so.

At his car he shook her hand warmly and told her to come and see him on Tuesday week. He told her firmly to keep off cocaine, and winked at her surprise that he knew.

'Small world!' he said. 'Try asking that husband of yours how much he values that nice little job he's got!' As she opened the car door for him he noticed the ragged bandage around her wrist. He cried out in horror and grabbed her arm. 'What is it? What is it?' He was clearly deeply upset.

'I cut it on a piece of glass.'

'Don't tell me the gory details. I'm likely to faint.' He shook her. 'And don't lie to me.'

'I honestly cut it on a piece of glass while I was . . .'

'Why, Amy? Tell me why? Nobody's worth it. Nobody!'

She calmed him only by showing the wound. He looked mistrustfully at it, not totally convinced that only the most inept of suicides would have cut the upper part of the wrist by mistake. Then gingerly he helped her cover the cut, which was already showing signs of healing.

'You'd better come home to Mona,' he said. 'No knowing what you'd get up to out there.' He motioned vaguely across the car park. 'Better to come home with me than wander around, wondering whether to turn that thing into a bracelet!' He got into the driver's seat and started the engine with determination.

Mona wasn't especially surprised to see Amy, being used to Laurie's ways, she said. She kissed her, held her hands, immediately noticed the bandage, gazed into her eyes with a questioning look and began talking about lunch. The children were called in from the garden: they came running, voluble and enthusiastic at the chance of telling somebody new about how they'd started proper school. They fetched paper and coloured pencils for Amy to draw them interesting things just like the last time. The news that they wouldn't be going to the Zoo after all brought no great reaction. They were already satisfied with Amy's promise to draw a complete menagerie of animals for them to colour, as long as they could start straight away.

Lunch was a noisy affair and composed, Amy thought, of leftovers from strange and tasty dinners perhaps previously served to more rarified guests. Afterwards Laurie took the children in the garden to play, with the promise from Amy that she'd follow them shortly. She and Mona sat with their elbows among the dirty plates and smoked a quiet cigarette.

There was something pre-Raphaelite about Mona's rounded face, deep-set eyes and cloud of hair that quite belied her less than languid behaviour. Her animation extended to the need to make physical contact as she talked.

'Laurie works too hard,' she said. 'Such energy. Look at him now . . .' Outside, Laurie could be seen lifting his younger son high above his head so he could climb on the shed roof. 'Even at home he can't stop!'

'But you don't seem to see much of him these days.'

'Enough.' Mona patted Amy's arm. 'It's not true! But he wants me to go and work in the office, now the children are at school. In that pandemonium! I tell him it's only the free labour he wants. No, I'm thinking of getting a proper job again.' She pulled at her ancient cardigan and laughed. 'Did you know that I used to be a fashion designer? Would you believe!'

'I can imagine Ernest's face if I told him I'd got a job in his office.'

Mona looked rueful. 'Yes, but your old man's a bit much, isn't he?' She clapped a hand to her mouth. 'Oh dear! There's Laurie gone out tactfully with the kids so I can be a comfort to you, and look where my big mouth's leading me.'

'Ernest does work very hard.'

'True. At everything, it seems.' She patted Amy's hand. 'What a good thing you know how to handle it all.'

On the point of saying she didn't know how to handle anything, least of all Ernest's infidelities, Amy changed the subject back to children. Screams of excitement were coming from the garden. She said that Ernest had always wanted a child; was instantly annoyed at Mona's explosive

'Whose?' and instantly forgave her. Mona agreed that sometimes even the least likely of men had been known to settle down to family life once a baby appeared on the scene.

'But I'm a natural pessimist,' Mona said with a smile. 'So I don't hold much store by miraculous changes of character. My old mother used to say, "Blessed is she who expecteth nothing" or words to that effect. Especially babies of straying males! That's why I married Laurie. I didn't want any nasty surprises.' She paused and thought. 'That's one reason, anyway. And now he's so busy working he hasn't time for anything – what do you say? – extra-marital.'

'And what would you do if he did?'

'I don't honestly know.' Her cigarette burned a long ash while she thought. 'It's happened to so many friends of ours, in so many permutations that I should be well prepared.' She laughed. 'Classic solutions – take a lover. Or kill him. Or both!' She nudged Amy's arm. 'No. Afraid not. Haven't got it in me. I suppose I don't really care enough.' In this Amy detected a small note of bravado.

Mona put out her cigarette and lit another. 'Now you,' she said, pointing it at Amy, 'you care. And anyone can see how hurt you get. But you always act so . . .' she searched for the word, '. . . so noble.' She leaned back in her chair and glanced outside. On the shed roof three figures were cavorting wildly.

Mona obviously hadn't heard about the incident in the café when she'd slapped Ernest. Amy decided not to tell her.

'Your best solution, in my opinion,' Mona continued, 'is to get out more. A party or two, or a nice, dark little bar. Find somebody you really fancy and pop into bed with him. Very therapeutic!' Her translucent, holy face looked strangely at odds with her words. 'There are an awful lot of men around who'd be only too willing.' She drew hard on her cigarette, noticed that Amy's was out, and offered her another. Amy refused, surprised to see her smoking so heavily. 'You could have Laurie, but he's a bit preoccupied. And it might be hard work getting him to catch your drift!'

Amy wasn't sure how much Mona was joking. 'It's wonderful for the morale,' Mona said. 'And when it's over there's no breast-beating and gnashing of teeth. It's best with strangers . . . no names, no pack drill!'

'You sound as if you're speaking from experience!'

'Naturally!' Mona looked surprised. She saw the slightly disapproving expression on Amy's face. 'Good Heavens, Amy. Laurie was out six nights a week, when he wasn't abroad somewhere. Or at yet another wretched book fair. And when he's here he's usually got his mind on work. Not that I'd want it otherwise, mind you. He's devoted to his work. And to me and the kids. What more can one want?' The thought amused her. 'But it's rather curious . . . now they're at school and I've all the time in the world, I don't particularly want to go gallivanting. It bothers me.'

'Why should it, Mona? You said you married Laurie because he's the faithful type. Isn't there something to be said for being the same?'

Mona's eyes widened. 'Come on, Amy. Don't make it worse.' She got up from the table and stared into the garden where three figures were squatting close together on the shed roof. 'To tell you the truth . . .' and from the downward droop of her lovely mouth Amy could see it was going to be the truth, '. . . I'm beginning – just beginning, mind – to fall in love quite desperately.' She flicked ash deliberately onto the carpet.

Amy felt the same sinking of spirits she'd have felt if Mona had told her she was seriously ill. 'Who with?' she asked, not really wanting to know.

'Him, of course.' Laurie's head could be seen above the boys, talking excitedly. He looked up, saw his wife and waved. 'I even caught myself the other day looking at his photo and wondering whether he was thinking of me.' She looked at Amy with sadness. 'He's so good,' she said, 'it makes me feel terrible.'

'But you said you didn't care . . .'

'If I started caring,' Mona said with spirit, 'I'd wind up like you, wouldn't I? And anyone can see how awfully unhappy you are. I'm not noble either, so I'd rather not start getting all steamed up. If he let me down after that, I'd really go to pieces.'

'I can't see the problem, Mona.'

Mona sighed heavily. 'What makes it difficult – and a bit easier at the same time – is that he's fair-to-middling in bed. Which probably accounts for the fact that he's never strayed.'

'I suppose there might be an equation between being undersexed and being faithful.' Amy stared at the man in the garden. 'But perhaps Laurie's a man of principle.'

Mona's hearty laugh caused a cry of 'Come out!' from the party on the shed roof. Laurie was standing precariously close to the edge, gesticulating to her. 'Age doesn't improve him,' she said. 'He's getting to be a Leg-Over man!' She went to the corner of the room and picked up several badminton raquets and a shuttlecock. 'I wonder what he thinks I've been telling you,' she said, stepping out into the sun-drenched garden.

At six they had supper outside because the evening was unusually hot. It had been an exceptionally warm spring and the forecast was promising. At eight when the children had been put to bed by Amy, after prolonged conversations about space travel, animals, motor cars and preferences in sweets, other visitors arrived.

She welcomed the fact they were strangers; they were cheerful and came with wine. The men were brothers, Mona said, and they entered talking as loudly as if they were at home. Their wives, carrying on a separate and no less noisy conversation, had an air of affluent unconcern which Amy remembered sharing in the not-so-distant past. Mona and Laurie seemed delighted with their guests and treated them all evening with flattering attention.

Amy sat as silently as politeness would permit, only

joining in when directly addressed, her mind frequently wandering to thoughts of Frank. She noticed a tendency towards hysteria in the company, and put it down to the amount of alcohol being consumed. There was something about the evening she wasn't enjoying, perhaps due to her own nervousness and insecurity.

Towards midnight, when Mozart had taken the place of talk, she wondered why the sense of unease still persisted. She thought she might be getting out of the habit of enjoying company, and began to dislike her own introspection.

When his visitors had gone, Laurie said that if Mozart couldn't manage to break through to them, nothing could. Then he laughed, said he couldn't help liking simple-minded people – especially when they were advertising agents – and went to bed.

Mona asked Amy to stay the night, giving her the living room sofa to sleep on. She gave her blankets to wrap round her, and pushed unnecessary pillows under her head.

'You know, there's something about you that scares hell out of a certain type of man,' Mona said.

Amy wondered if this was going to be one of those night-long sessions of heart-to-heart searching, so deliciously fulfilling in the old days, but now only an impediment to sleep. Mona gripped her foot and gently shook it. 'People aren't used to it,' she said.

'Used to what? No. I don't want to know. Mona, do let us get some sleep . . .'

'The sight of you made them nervous.'

'I'm sorry I forgot to hide the bolts in my neck!'

Mona's eyes rounded. 'You don't think they always behave the way they did this evening?'

'Why not? People should be themselves whoever they're with.'

Mona put her hand over her mouth to check the laughter. 'Poor things! You're frightfully unrelenting. They had to keep justifying themselves in front of you, don't you see? They were frightened of you.'

'Frightened of what? I hardly got a word in edgeways.'

Mona thought carefully. 'It's your manner, I think. You're one of those rarities who actually listens to what people say. And you have the unforgiveable habit of taking it as the literal truth.'

'What's wrong with that?'

Upstairs the thump of Laurie's feet on the bedroom floor, and the creaking of boards as he got into bed. 'With you there's no leeway,' Mona said.

'Lately I'm always hearing things about myself I don't want to hear!'

'People get swept away by you, Amy. And they either fight it and get nervous, or they go under and become your slaves.'

Amy leaned forward and grasped Mona's shoulder. 'You know how much I love you and Laurie. I wouldn't do anything in the world to upset either of you.'

Mona's smile was slightly uneasy. 'You make me feel so dreadful having said all that, Amy. Especially since Laurie thinks you're not well, and I'm supposed to see that you stay calm.' She nodded at Amy's wrist.

Amy removed the bandage and showed Mona the thin line of puckered, healing skin. 'I've never been happier.'

'Now you're lying in your teeth.' Mona threw herself back on the sofa and raised a weary hand to her forehead. She looked like Ophelia. 'God, I'm tired. Why don't you leave him?' You're wasting yourself. Laurie says you've got enormous talent. Ernest's eating up all your energy. He'll not stop. And there'll be nothing left.'

'It's not like that at all, Mona.'

Perhaps it was the lateness of the hour, or a sudden flow of affection for someone who seemed to care, but she came to the decision that Mona should be the first to know.

'I am also in love,' she said carefully.

Mona sat up with a new light of interest in her eyes.

The next hour passed in rapid questions and answers, Mona crouching low over Amy's feet, the blanket enveloping them both. She'd never heard anything so fascinating before: a long-distance love affair taking place from the beginning on paper. Yet an affair so passionate that both parties were prepared to commit themselves, having hardly met.

'You're both mad,' Mona said. 'Can I tell Laurie?' She said that since he knew Frank slightly, he might be able to throw some light on his motives and intentions. Amy begged her not to say too much, and omitted to tell her that Frank still hadn't completely made up his mind to visit her on his way home from convalescence.

After Laurie had thumped several times on the ceiling, the conversation slowly came to a close. Mona went reluctantly upstairs to bed, leaving Amy to sleep more peacefully for having been able to share the secret.

6

Ernest had created the problem by insisting of late on sleeping in the anteroom. Nothing was said. She discovered him one morning when she thought he'd been out all night, tucked up under the floral coverlet, blue shadows on his chin and under his closed eyes. It wasn't good sleeping alone. She'd told him so and he'd laughed dryly, saying that one was always alone when asleep. She hated the way he'd hung his tie carefully over the painting, its point ending over Radiant City. She'd thrown the tie at him too, then picked up his boots which had been pushed under the bed – far too close to the bundle of letters lying in the dust – and tossed them into the hall. It had made no difference. The next night and the next, he'd slept in the anteroom, taking no notice of all her pleas.

'You'll have to get out of here completely,' he said.

She refused. She said the anteroom was hers by right. She said she needed privacy to work. He said he needed it to sleep. She pointed out that lately she'd been doing work for Laurie and for Fox. In reply he showed her the worn toecap of his boot. She felt, as usual, instantly sorry. Had he not in the next breath mentioned the telephone, she would have gone there and then to the landscape in the sitting room where she'd hidden the remainder of the money, and given him some.

'Get it reconnected,' he said, bringing back the old anxieties. She wondered if it was in his mind to do a deal – reconnection of the phone in exchange for use of the anteroom. She wouldn't have put it past him. How ignominious to have to bribe him to sleep with her.

'Why do you want to sleep in here anyway?'

He said he came in too late at night to disturb her. She said she usually wasn't asleep anyway. How could she sleep if she was worried about how and where he was? He told her that he couldn't stay at Irwin's flat because it was too small, implying that it was with Irwin he spent his evenings. He said he didn't like the way she tossed and turned all night. Besides, it was better not to sleep with a sick person, he said.

'But I'm not sick, Ernest.'

'I am,' he replied. He rolled up his trouser to reveal a purplish bruise on his skin. 'You did that last Wednesday week, and its not gone yet. It's a sure sign I'm weakening . . . getting weaker every day.'

She laughed, but could see how serious he was. Then she realized that he was, in actual fact, speaking the literal truth. He was going downhill. Not only were his nerves being pushed to the limits of endurance by her troublesome behaviour, but she and some unknown woman were making demands on him at the same time. Poor Ernest was on the sexual treadmill.

'Have a little backbone, Ernest,' she said. 'If you will lead such a rackety life, you'll have to be fitter than this!'

He was frowning, having detected a new note in her voice. Should she tell him immediately, she wondered, that there was someone to take his place? She knew with the deepest certainty, and quite beyond reason, that he needed her. Of Frank she wasn't so sure. Did he need anything but his work, she wondered, even though he'd asked if she still wanted him to come. But the peculiar passion of the second Saturday letter was evidence that he was in the throes of something almost out of his control. As if something unspoken had been settled between them, he asked how they should continue to live if she said yes to his letters. He told her it would be impossible for her to continue living there. From it she might have gathered he was saying she should think of living with him. By now she knew enough of the way his mind worked to see the inner turmoil. For him nothing was simple, least of all committing himself yet again to a woman. Yet the idea was fatally attractive. He'd moved close to her, backed away and then moved slower. Each time a little closer, yet still with one hand held straight in front to fend off possible attack. She'd told him this.

Ernest was walking about the room, pushing back the curtains, peering out at the gutters and down-pipes of neighbouring flats, all lit by a strong evening sun. His face was an orange silhouette. Small fires flared in his glasses. 'You'll have to move that easel,' he said. 'It will be in my way.'

'What are you going to do in here? Dance the tango?'

He put his hand on a pile of cuttings, resting his fingers on Otto Wagner's fascia for Vienna's Westbahnhof. 'This,' he said, 'represents nothing more than your inability to come to terms with reality. It is an excuse . . . a long drawn out excuse for not standing on your own feet.' The papers on the desk fanned out under his hand. She caught a glimpse of Valli and Elli in their ermine tippets.

She pointed to their gentle faces. 'They weren't as tame as they look. People never are, are they? I might put them in, if there's room. Especially Ottla. She was his favourite sister. She had the spirit he thought he lacked. I think she and Milena were alike in some ways. I wonder what they thought of each other . . . if they ever met.'

'Have you no interest, Amy, in what I'm saying?'

'Yes, Doctor Freud!'

He went on, 'You're talented and reasonably intelligent. There is no reason why you can't put these . . . er . . .'

'Attributes?'

'. . . attributes, to better use.' His voice became reasonable. 'Make a concerted effort to work in a sustained way. Be business-like. Forget all this dabbling. All this harking back.'

Her voice was sharp. 'Aren't I earning enough for you, Ernest?'

'For instance . . .' he was still being reasonable, '. . . now that Stacey's back you could find out the state of the market there. She's bound to have connections. Isn't Jay somebody's brother-in-law? Surely he could put you in touch with more work?'

She laughed and stroked his cheek. He backed away from her hand as if she'd tried to scratch him. 'I'm the rescuer am I? The one who has to come up with the money to pay your more spectacular debts?'

'I don't wish to discuss it, Amy. What's gone is gone.'

'Why? Are you afraid you'll hear something you'd rather not?' His expression changed to one of slight anxiety. He backed away further from her, his face flushing with anger.

'That will do!'

'Shall I tell you where I got the money to pay your last lot of bills? You've never asked, have you?' He didn't answer. 'I got it,' she said, 'from . . .'

He put his hands over his ears as he walked towards the door.

'I got it from Rose!' she cried loudly. And 'Rose!' again louder as he went into the hall. She let him go.

When he'd left, a peculiar numbness came over her, as if she couldn't decide any more what she really felt. Was she fond of him? Did she love him deeply? If she did, she thought, she also possessed an alarming facility to step back and regard him with dispassion, aware of his every weakness and disliking each one. Once she'd loved him with such fervour that she'd been incapable of standing one tiny centimetre away. To him she'd poured out all her deep feelings and all her most secret thoughts; all her past miseries and hopes for the future. For a time he'd seemed to reciprocate in the same, uninhibited way. How naïve he must have thought her. That same painful intake of breath came as always when she remembered the first time he'd betrayed her.

He'd come in later than usual, looking more pleased than usual, and somehow healthier. Without his saying a word, she knew instantly what had happened. When she attacked him with questions he told her only that he'd met someone else. To her cries of 'How could you?' he'd simply expressed surprise that she should find it so upsetting. He'd thought she was above such base notions as jealousy. If not, she ought to be. Instead of keeping calm she'd launched into attack. She would never forget that first time and the way her fury raged day and night, increasing in strength as she realized her own impotence. Ernest retired into the safety of silence at home, and spent more time away from her lashing tongue. Only once had he made the mistake of speaking about that other woman, to say, 'The moment I saw her I was done for.' She remembered his words still, with an almost physical hurt.

Stacey had written to her to be careful, or she might lose him altogether. After that she had reservations about her friend. But she'd write to her again now and perhaps, by some devious route, arrive at mention of Frank. 'Wouldn't it be nice,' she could say, 'to look up an old friend (a mutual friend) who happens to be going through a period of ill health?'

She turned the easel round to catch the full glare of the evening sun, thinking to work on it a little before the light died. She liked the way the colours yielded their strength to the orange glow, muting the violence of purple and blood red, bringing out the blackness of the musical notes and making them dance. She mixed carmine and burnt sienna, then drew with great rapidity a small star in the top right hand corner of the canvas. It would be hard and bright – matching that of Milena's Austrian count – burning briefly with the fervour of a convert to Communism working hard for her adopted party. Having seen the way the world was moving, she had a choice to make between blindness and commitment. The star was six years of trying to remain convinced that everything could be put to rights by working within the only party which could see the threat of fascism. And work was possible, even in the face of increasing unhappiness at home and her battle against morphine addiction. In front of the star's points she would place Milena's troubled face, her hair flecked here and there with tiny spots of red, its gold taking up and diffusing the power of the stronger colour. She picked up the photograph with its now curled edges. The face was as flat as the paper on which it had been printed. If she'd taken a magnifying glass to it she knew she'd be able to see only irregular masses and blotches of black and white and grey. Nothing recognizable of Milena would be left intact except the shape of her eyes. The black pupils with their white highlights stared at a point directly above her shoulder.

There is a wild look in her eyes. She stands in the office doorway and waits to be recognized. Vanek looks at the unkempt hair and the shabby coat, obviously borrowed from a male inmate of the sanatorium, walks towards her questioningly then realizes who she is. She knows that someone with her political affiliations shouldn't be seen in the offices of a Social Democratic newspaper. But she's long past the point of caring. She needs work, she needs money for Jaromir and Honza. She is hungry to the point of starvation. It has been too great a strain travelling there, and she must try to stay calm long enough to explain that her talent to write is still intact, and she is cured.

She starts to say how much she wants a chance to write for his paper, but breaks off suddenly as faintness overcomes her. If only he will buy her a small cup of coffee then she will start again the well-rehearsed phrases, about how she will write articles for him as good as they used to be. They go to a nearby restaurant where the light is dim and a corner table will hide her. She watches the waiter pouring their coffee at the counter, beside plates of eggs and sausages and piled portions of ham on poppy-seed bread.

'I'll have a couple of hot sausages instead of coffee,' she says as casually as she can. Vanek watches her wolf them down, appalled by the sight of someone so hungry. She thinks she's never tasted anything so wonderful before.

But when he orders more, she turns on him and says he's trying to insult her. While they drink their coffee she allows him to persuade her that he has ordered the sausages for himself.

Wary now, he tells her that he will let her write for him not out of friendship but because she is one of the best journalists he knows. To avoid trouble she agrees to write under several pseudonyms. She will send Honza to his office with the articles, so that others won't recognize her. Jaromir, immersed in trying to get to Moscow to become an architect of the new Socialist Society, has little time to be displeased that she has put practicalities before Party. Soon, in 1934, he will leave her and the child behind in Prague and find himself a new love in Russia.

With great care she cut round the photograph of the face, then stuck it in the top right hand corner of the picture, overlapping the right hand edge of the window frame, and blotting out some of the criss-crossed pencil lines below. She drew the lines in again over the chin, through the neck and into the outline of the cheek. The lower point of the star cut into Milena's hair. Between the strands she touched in red with her brush as if it twinkled there to disappear behind the solidity of the head. Both star and head stood out too starkly on the light coloured canvas. She began to mix up the blue of Bohemian glass, spending so long in trying to find the exact colour that she barely noticed the fading of the light. While it lasted she continued to work, stopping after one or two brush-strokes fearful of making a mistake. With Milena safely in place, she felt that each mark she made must be so full of truth that anyone seeing what she'd done would stand before it and accept the statement as inevitable. Faintly, so faintly they'd hardly be visible, she would put in the rooftops and cupolas of Prague – not flying in all directions as in Kokoschka's picture, but standing still, despite internal conflict, miraculously intact.

And over them she planned to put the terrible roads and railway tracks which, for the time being and until real

136

strength returned, would have to wait. Why was everything so difficult? Was it so difficult to mark in territorial boundaries which could be crossed only with the correct stamps in one's pass, or the right blood in one's veins? Three neatly printed maps were spread out on the desk, parcelling out the land in pink and brown, purple and green to the scale of one in one thousand. Europe Historical. The last map, dated 1918, showed a brand new Czechoslovakia cutting into Germany; a fragment of what was once the glorious Austro-Hungarian Empire. No more Emperor, only leaders of little lands pretending to unity, their fragile frontiers lasting a mere twenty years before they were breached. Twenty years of increasing economic instability and frustration, making them the more vulnerable to the advance of a dictator.

Ernest's presence lingered in the room. She fancied she could detect the faint aroma of a cigar. It was stuffy, and smaller than usual, due to the narrowing of space by the opening out of the sofa bed.

Pushing the upholstery into position tired her. She sat down heavily on it, leaning her head back. Sweat was running delicately down her temples. She closed her eyes, trying to breathe some warmth into herself, trying to calm the slight sensation of panic that always came with awareness of surrounding silence. No sounds from the Italians upstairs who were usually at their noisiest in the evenings. No footsteps clacking up the marble stairs. No radio or television echoing round the wide funnel of the hall. She went into the sitting room to reassure herself that traffic still ran on the ring road and that people were walking in the street below. The orange light of the setting sun had given way to the diffused orange glow of city lights, spreading so strong a colour into the night sky that it might have seemed to the uninformed that some distant disaster had taken place. She switched on all the lights in the room and let down the blinds over the balcony windows. This room too seemed stuffy. She had a weak desire to rid herself of ancient odours

137

and gathered dust. Spring was a time for clean sweeps; it enabled her to face up to problems more resolutely.

Two problems faced her now, neither capable of resolution. And spring almost completed its cycle of bud into blossom while she prevaricated. It wasn't her fault Ernest strayed. Was it? It wasn't her fault Frank couldn't make up his mind. Sometimes she was less certain of the latter, given that it was she who'd begun the relationship in the first place. What did she want from him? She didn't know. Friendship? Frank was already a friend. Love? From his letters it seemed he already loved her in one sense. Someone to live with, perhaps? Perhaps. She thought she understood him more completely than she did Ernest, yet he'd told her she didn't. He'd further confused her by saying that the 'Jewish question' was only a silly joke. He had no right to say he joked when in actual fact he didn't. Trying to comprehend Ernest's attitude to the question was difficult enough; now here was Frank presenting her with yet another facet of the Jew's complicated crisis of identity. It irritated her only slightly that neither Frank nor Ernest gave much attention to her own non-Jewishness except in relation to themselves. In the early days of marriage she'd gratefully joined in Ernest's condemnation of her father's bigoted attitude to religion. She could only agree it was un-Christian in the extreme to denigrate someone born into a different faith. As a child she'd frequently said prayers for 'those less fortunate than ourselves', quite aware of the unspoken assumption that the less fortunate were of a different race. Strange that she was beginning to feel like one of the less fortunate to the two men closest to her.

Word had it that Frank and his greatest friend Leon were avowed believers in the State of Israel. It was Charles who'd told her. He'd said to beware of people with strong feelings. There was nothing in Frank's letters to suggest fanaticism. Rather he saw himself alone in the world – a poor, unworthy Jew too advanced in years and too ill for radical behaviour of any kind. Was an alliance with an ex-

Christian so radical? She wanted to ask him face to face. How many letters could she write per day, asking all the questions that occurred minute by minute? Wasn't she overdoing the correspondence already? It seemed not, since he still wrote back, wanting to hear more. The worst that happened was that he put off reading her more vituperous remarks until morning so he might sleep easier at night.

She went to the balcony window, put up the blind and opened it, letting in a rush of stale, warm air from the street that brought with it the faint mixture of automobile exhaust, evening meals cooking, and a hint of perfume from some invisible blossom-laden tree. She leaned on the rail and looked down into the street, sensing again the excitement of the time of year. As she'd been capable of marrying Ernest against the heaviest of odds, so she'd be capable of forming another equally important relationship with someone even more complex. What that relationship would eventually become depended more on the result of their meeting than on any conjectures about religion.

The next morning, she went to the park to read Frank's letter, feeling certain the sunlight could do only good to the words she knew would hold some darkness. He told her she'd awakened all the old demons who sleep with one eye and with the other wait for their opportunity. It was a long letter which, at the first reading she skipped over, merely glancing at details of his trip with the engineer and the continuing problem of sleep. What she looked for and quickly found, and as quickly re-read, was his insistence that he hadn't written thoughtlessly when he'd told her to get out. On the paper in front of her was his offer: what he earned, he said, would be enough for both of them provided no illness interfered. She smiled slightly that, as usual, he'd had to include a proviso in the offer. He wasn't afraid of the material burden, he said. He had another kind of fear; an inner conspiracy against himself which she might understand better when she read his letter to his father.

She stared blindly at the burgeoning trees across the lawns, endeavouring to see the predicament. He wasn't talking of practical problems, or if he was they were so hedged about with metaphysical fears that the two were interchangeable. If only she knew of what exactly his fear consisted. That it existed she didn't doubt. Yet he could still make proposals which for the moment totally pleased him. In the next sentence he said so, stating that the idea he'd suggested was the only unquestionable thing, free of morbidity, making him completely happy.

On the back of the letter she found what he'd written the following day, obviously in a different mood. He said he should certainly not be coming to her. If he came (and he knew he wouldn't see anyone but her) it wouldn't be before Tuesday. He'd wait for her at the South station at five o'clock.

She stared at the words, transfixed by their purity. It was as clear a statement of intent as if he were already standing there.

It took a third reading of the letter to discover the usual ifs and buts. 'If' he came it would certainly not be before Tuesday. He 'could' wait for her at the station at five o'clock. Even the footnote about the food arranging itself contained the word 'would'.

She began to reply . . .

There's such joy in the knowledge that you'll come, it almost overwhelms me. Hasn't it been a long time until this meeting? There's so much to tell you, to ask, to show, that I shall take no notice of your little hints that you may not come after all! I shall meet you at the station because that's the very best place. You must promise to stand and wait for me should I be late for any reason. Not that I will be late. But don't on any account think of coming to the apartment, for there you'll be bound to find difficulties.

If you see coming towards you a tall, thin person wearing a dress of blue and green, it will be me. Don't be surprised if since that time we met I have altered. But should there have been some change in you too, it won't stop me from recognizing you. I have the image of you sitting in that café engraved on my mind. Your letters have set you deep inside me, so I know you. When I work on your writing it brings me so close that sometimes I wonder you don't feel the tiny touch of a hand on your arm there. And when we meet I shall tell you about my work plans.

And I shall tell you again about Milena. She stays with me not quite as constantly as you do. What a beautifully pure Czech name she had. Somebody once told me it was a German name, but I'd rather believe it was Jewish. If you asked me why I should want it so, I could only answer that for me at this moment all things Jewish are of the utmost fascination. I have so much love for your race that even Ernest can be included! I'm sitting in the warmth of the most wonderful spring sun you've ever felt, trying to send a little of it to you. The blossom is so thick now that birds are lost in the branches. A few brave ones are hopping round my feet, not looking for crumbs, but drawn to me by the visible heat of my pleasure . . . . .

She ran to catch the mid-day post. Then slowly back through streets lit by an extra-bright light, where passers-by all smiled at her as she passed.

She found Conrad, who had let himself into their flat and was sitting in the kitchen drinking coffee and staring out of the window. She told him he was blotchy and getting fat, to which he replied that he wanted it that way.

'You're looking very pleased with yourself,' he said.

She laughed. Between them on the table lay her bag with Frank's letter in it. He noticed her glance at it. With a sudden movement his hands grabbed it before she could stop him. Unable to speak she watched with fascination as he rummaged through it. Finally he shook the contents onto the table, pushing aside bus tickets, make-up, Kleenex and coins. Frank's letter lay on top, Giving the bag a final shake, Conrad threw it roughly to one side and looked at her.

'None at all?'

'None what?'

'What do you think? Coke? A fraction of hash? Uppers? Downers? A chew of tobacco . . .? Anything.'

She shook her head. 'Nothing, my dear.'

'All gone?' He was surprised. 'How have you been managing?'

She tried to keep her eyes off the letter, Frank's handwriting uppermost and visible. 'It's not totally my way of life, you know. There are other things to think about! But there's some tobacco in the desk. In the anteroom. Do you want it?'

He said yes. When she returned he was holding the letter and turning it over in his hands. She gave him the tobacco and papers and gently took the letter from him and put it out of his reach.

'I didn't know you knew Frank,' he said.

She felt her face blushing. 'A bit. I'm working on illustrations of his work now, for Fox.'

'He used to be a good friend of mine,' he said. 'I actually started him writing.'

She tried to keep the astonishment from her face.

'A long time ago now,' he continued, 'I wrote an essay on the advantages of a healthy life, and he admired it.' He looked at her keenly, trying to decide whether she was taking him seriously. 'We used to do a lot of swimming together.'

'When you were at school?' He shrugged. 'And all of fifteen!' she said, laying a hand on his arm to show there was no ill will on her part. Why was he such a child; boastful and foolish, yet capable of so much generosity and kindness?

'He was so skinny then, he didn't cast a shadow!' Conrad said. 'But you should have seen his father. Huge man. We were scared of him. Frank included. We'd all be talking nineteen to the dozen, then suddenly Frank would go quiet. You'd look round and his father would be standing there. I swear he'd been listening, hoping to catch Frank saying something he shouldn't. Funny bugger.' She held her breath, hoping for him to continue.

'Social climber, his father.' He paused. 'Don't know about the mother though. Only seen her a few times.'

'Does he . . . does Frank resemble her?' As she asked she wondered if she was giving herself away.

'They look very much alike, come to think of it,' Conrad was enjoying himself. 'He's got sisters too. One of them's a real cracker.' He began to roll a cigarette. 'Got a touch of the Chinese. Hard to describe . . . Nice mouth and a round chin. Hair up in a sort of backward roll . . . No! God! I'm supposed to be a poet and I can't fit a description to a face!' He licked the cigarette paper in disgust. 'I once wrote her a poem. Not about her face!' He put the cigarette to his lips and left it in his mouth unlighted. 'Something about a living fire, I think. Most poetical. Good though.' He leaned forward confidentially. 'You remind me of her.'

It was preferable to change the subject. 'Did you look at my postcards? There's a panoramic view of Prague there, in 1937. Just streets and hundreds of buildings. Sometimes I search all over it trying to decide where Milena lived. It must have looked very modern then. Up in the air on the sixth floor – she and Honza and masses of flowers. I imagine her standing on the balcony in the "hanging gardens of Milena", staring out over the city and wondering how to sort out her life. I suppose she believed, as we all do, that she had the final control over her future.'

'Come on, Amy. She surely wasn't as simple as that! I thought you told me she was intelligent . . . and politically astute. How old was she by that time? Forty odd?'

'Yes, you're right. She was. And to write for *Pritonmost* you had to be good. She must have known what was coming. Germany began rearming in 1934. In '38 they took back the Rhineland. And already she'd seen them try to take over Austria. One look at the map would have told her they'd try again. And after that . . .'

'Poor bitch.' He was staring at her again.

To avoid his gaze she stood up and began to make more coffee.

'I must go soon,' he said. 'Got to get organized for the Great Leap Forward. Packing and all that.'

She waited, wondering where he of all people might be off to.

'Might visit Frank while I'm there,' he said casually.

She started visibly. 'You're going *there*?'

'Sure. Didn't I tell you?'

She wondered whether her own face was showing as many emotional changes as his. Now his expression was one of bravado. 'My fiancée comes from there.'

'Who? Oh, I didn't know.' She poured coffee from the pot and brought the cups to the table.

'Will you live there when you're married?'

He gazed over her head. 'Don't know yet. I'm sounding out the situation. Seeing her parents and all that sort of thing. Looking them over! She wants . . . they want a proper wedding. I've agreed.' He was trying to look nonchalant. 'Can't do much harm. And you can't blame them for wanting to see the prospective son-in-law. Make sure the whole thing's legal! I'm not everybody's cup of coffee!'

She was torn between telling him to call the wedding off before it was too late, and wanting to ask the exact day when he thought he might be paying a visit to Frank's family.

'Frank's convalescing at the moment,' she said. Conrad looked at her in surprise. 'I mean,' she said blushing, 'you'll not find him at home . . . if you go to visit him, that is.' She could feel how warm her face was, but he was following his own troubled thoughts.

She went with him to the door. 'You'll be fine, Conrad. Don't worry about it all. Just try to remember you're not marrying her family! Think about her.'

'Don't say any more, Amy, or I'll call the whole thing off.'

'I'll go instead,' she said, 'and leave you and Ernest here together!'

'You! Leave him!' He snorted. 'If I could see half a chance of that happening, I might – just might – stick to poverty.'

144

She hustled him out of the front door and down the stairs before he could begin to question the seriousness of what she'd said. As he reached the bottom of the stairs he called back to her that he'd be putting a packet on her doorstep soon. He told her not to leave it hanging about. He was gone too fast for her to refuse a gift she felt she'd outgrown. No more drugs. She wanted clarity of mind for the days to come.

She couldn't believe it. In a few lines he'd dispelled all
further doubts. He would definitely be coming on Tuesday.
She stood in the post office clutching his letter as if it might
disappear from her hand. People were staring at her. A
whole line of them had turned their heads and were wondering why the woman with the incredulous smile had been
allowed to intrude on their sanity.

She went home quickly, calling Ernest's name in the hall.
There were signs of his having been in, although the sofa
was still intact. A dirty shirt lay tossed over it, and one
black silk sock which she didn't recognize.

The painting in the living room glinted in the strong
light, the gleam of small brush strokes visible under the
coating of heavy varnish. Her fingers searched the back of
the frame and found the envelope with the money in it,
where she'd tucked it so carefully behind one of the wedges.
Still enough left to buy Frank something substantial: a
watch perhaps, if he wore one, or a pen for real ink. She'd
think of something for him to carry as a reminder of her
love. A point in the painting caught her eye. She looked
closer wondering why she'd never noticed it before. Hidden
in the clump of trees which formed part of the background
she could see what looked like an eye peering from the
undergrowth. She looked closer to make certain, and saw
another. Definitely eyes. The unknown artist had touched
in with minute dabs of white paint the glint in the eyes of a
creature (or person) looking out from among the leaves. All
these years and she'd never noticed it before. Twelve to be
exact. Her mother had never mentioned them when she'd

given her the gift, or she'd surely have said, 'Watch out, child, those people are running into trouble.'

She remembered the ceremony beside her mother's bed, the unwrapping of the tissue, the gleam of the gold frame, her mother's thin, white fingers smoothing the fragile paper backing as she read the copperplate 'Flight Into the Grove.' And there they were – three people in classical draperies which flowed behind them, such was the speed of their running, escaping from Heaven knows what. And they were already in another danger zone. The dog beside them running on its hind legs (for reasons of composition, she supposed) seemed as unaware as they did of what they were about to meet. Poor things. She laughed and put the picture back on the wall, glad to see that the eyes became less visible as she backed away. On the other wall she saw her reflection in the mirror, and smiled at the sight. Would he like the look of her? Surely the same worries were going through his mind exactly at that same moment. And he was the traveller, braving a strange place in order to see her. She was asking a lot of him.

She decided to spend all the money on him in one last expensive fling. A ring perhaps. But he'd had his fill of rings having pushed them, on three separate occasions, on two female fingers. By now he either hated the symbolic gesture, or regarded it as commonplace. Somehow she couldn't imagine him wearing anything on his own fingers. Frank's hands would be bare and thin and beautiful. At last the idea of buying him cuff links came to her. Charles had once said that Frank always dressed formally so as not to give offence. So why not let him wear the weight of her friendship on his wrists?

She spent the rest of Saturday wandering around the more expensive shops in the centre of the city, fussing over trays of baubles, rejecting these and those, and aggravating numbers of patient shop assistants. At last she found two circles of gold engraved with rays like the shining sun, attached to two smaller circles with fine oblong chains.

She went back home by the longest route, passing the synagogue, and saw Jasmine standing with a crowd of people under a chestnut tree. As she approached, Jasmine came towards her with less than her usual enthusiasm. They talked for a moment about the weather, and the astonishing colour of Amy's hair. Jasmine seemed reluctant to answer questions about her forthcoming marriage, but said it might be soon. She was clearly eager to rejoin the others, turning her head to them constantly. Still speaking she backed away, the note of apology in her voice tinged with what sounded like irritation.

'Is anything the matter?' Amy called after her. She received the reply that if she didn't know, then nobody did.

'Do tell me,' she said.

Jasmine stopped. In a furious outburst she described her anger and shame at those dreadful flowers. 'And not one word of apology from you!' she cried. 'Really, Amy, you're beyond redemption!' She turned smartly on precarious heels and went back to the group. Amy stood where she was protesting her innocence in a loud voice. How could Jasmine so misunderstand? And why was she still complaining? Standing in the kerb she watched them all hastily dispersing into cars with loud banging of doors and revving of engines. She saw Jasmine sitting at the wheel with stiff back, looking straight ahead. Severe faces stared at her from car windows as they drove away in a rattle of exhaust fumes.

During Saturday evening she worked to try and finish the last illustration, the smallest of all – a mere scrap of a sketch she'd been puzzling over for days since. The drawing board, already covered with calligraphical representations of the harrow, looked like one of Yuan Tzu-Tsai's rejects. It was impossible now to face up to the horror-filled pages of something so evidently written in sadder times. Fox had said the story was deeply pessimistic, but would he understand that between the writing and the publishing of it was a gap so large she truly believed that

Frank might now disown it? She would have to find out. She looked for writing paper, but Frank was unreachable. She would have to wait until Tuesday.

She went to bed early and slept sweetly, waking but once to the sound of voices coming from the kitchen.

On Sunday morning she met Ernest in the hall, wearing his dressing gown and looking fragile. He claimed he wasn't feeling well again, and said he might have to have a few days off work. He said his temperature had gone up a point and a half. Holding back the desire to mention that he might be suffering from a hangover, she told him to get back into bed and went to prepare his breakfast. Revival, although not instantaneous, came gradually throughout the day, so that by afternoon he was on his feet, dressed and complaining again about the condition of the anteroom. It was evident that he'd slept, however briefly, on the sofa bed, his clothes scattered dangerously near wet brushes and palette. She said nothing, but tidied the room, checking nervously that the bundle of letters was still in place. In the evening after he'd gone out wrapped in an unnecessary scarf, she washed her hair and his clothes, had a bath, ironed the dress of changing greens, then tried to concentrate on finishing the illustration. When it was late and getting dark she took a short walk in the neighbourhood. She paid a call on Mrs Kertesch who welcomed her warmly, saying that people were always preferable to television. Talk of the weather was to neither of their tastes, and it was obvious that Amy had something on her mind. She mentioned Fox and led up to Frank's work, revealing finally that he was her letter-writing friend. Then she launched unhesitatingly into the whole affair, ending with his impending arrival. Mrs Kertesch nodded, listened seriously and made little comment until the end. Then she said, 'Such a great adventure! You got troubles, my dear.'

Brushing aside such thoughts, Amy warned that if a tall, thin man with a searching gaze should be seen in the street outside, or in the lobby, he should on no account be allowed upstairs. 'A man of thirty-five has his own ideas!' Mrs Kertesch said mildly. She said she'd fight back the urge to take him in and give him a nice cup of bortsch, for he'd surely need a lot of energy before facing such an enthusiastic friend. She said she'd send him back to his hotel.

'You'll like him, I know you will,' Amy said as she kissed her on both cheeks before going back upstairs to sleep.

On Monday the clock hardly moved at all. Minutes and hours stayed suspended in a procession of meaningless acts. The only good thing was Ernest's decision to go to work as usual, as usual these days wearing his best suit and newest shirt. After visiting the post office where no late letters awaited her, she went on to Fox's office to deliver the illustrations. It was her hope to find him in the mood for talking, but his secretary said he was busy and she'd give him the work herself. The office was as hot as the street where she wandered for a while, unable to make up her mind how best to kill time. She drank endless cups of coffee in cafés, tried to eat a sandwich at a bar but found it stuck in her throat. She fed it to the pigeons in the park, admiring their boldness and thinking of Frank on his balcony. A heatwave had come down on the city making even the open parkland unbearable. Shady trees afforded little protection from the sun's sharp rays. Only the lake where boating children screamed and splashed gave off a little steamy coolness. She sat with her feet in the water, staring over the hazy heights of far-off hills, at steeples and domes and high-rise blocks all caught like her in timelessness.

Later she wandered back to the city centre, thinking to visit Ernest at the café. It was packed, every window and door open. She could see the fans circling in the ceilings, and make out among the crowds some she recognized: Charles, looking fatter than ever; two or three of Jasmine's new friends; by a window Irwin in shirt sleeves; William lolling near the front door. People were overflowing into the street, sitting against the columns, crushing the orna-mental trees. She nodded at a perspiring Albert collecting discarded glasses from the steps. The waiters, rushed off their feet, held their trays over their heads as they pushed through the customers. No sign of Ernest. She gave an answering wave to somebody she didn't recognize, then wandered away down the street past other cafés and pubs where thirsty customers were making more than their share of noise. And finally home, keeping to the shady side of the street.

The evening died slowly, moved along a fraction by the act of preparing a postcard to send to Stacey. On the front she drew a white bird in flight against a blue sky, and wrote on the back: Don't be surprised by new developments in my life. As always you'll be the first to find out. You know him well! Miss you as always. We must try to bridge these distances. Love to Jay. Keep your fingers crossed for me. Ever, your loving friend . . .

She took Flaubert to bed with her and lay gripping it firmly under a bright light, trying to enter into the troubled life of the vacillating young man as eagerly as she'd managed it on previous nights' vigils. It was still in her hand when she woke in the early hours to the sound of Ernest unlocking the front door. How little it mattered now where he'd been. She turned out the light and lay listening to the sounds of him getting into bed in the anteroom.

On Tuesday morning it was hot soon after sunrise. Another sweltering day ahead. Ernest had gone before she dared risk getting into the newly ironed frock and best sandals. Although it was early and Frank might not be at the station until five o'clock, at least it was Tuesday. By nine she had forced down a large breakfast, cleaned her teeth, run out to the corner shop for more bread, come back and cleaned her teeth again. Half an hour was spent carefully making up her face, only to wipe it all off again when she'd decided it didn't look natural. She tidied the apartment so there would be no complaints from Ernest, freed her handbag of months of accumulated rubbish, put the box with the cuff links back into it, and left the house as the clock on city hall was striking a quarter to twelve.

At the post office the clerk handed her a card. She signed for it with shaking fingers. Its postmark was the city stamp. Frank had arrived. The time on the stamp was ten a.m. He was sitting, he said, in a coffee house near the South station drinking coffee and eating a pastry. He hadn't slept for two nights and wondered whether he'd sleep the third in the hotel near the station beside a garage. She felt faint. The words blurred. The ink shifted under her damp hand. He said he expected her at ten on Wednesday morning in front of the hotel. He begged her not to surprise him by coming at him from the side or rear. She laughed aloud and the clerk gave her a strange look.

Noon now and no time to waste. She certainly couldn't wait until Wednesday. Anything could happen. He might take fright and run; his note sounded apprehensive enough. It ended by saying he'd probably go and look at the sights, naming her street as one of them. But surely he'd wait near the station? He was ill. He couldn't walk far before getting tired, especially after two sleepless nights. What to do? Would he walk a little, then go back to the café to sit? He'd go back to the café. Or the hotel. Or the station.

The station. For a minute she stood indecisively, saw a taxi and waved at it. It went on. She saw the word 'Station' on an on-coming bus and ran for it, waving frantically at the driver. She scrambled aboard, sank into a seat and mopped her face, still clutching Frank's crumpled card.

At the station entrance she paused for breath, holding onto a rail for support. Hundreds of steps to climb. Hundreds of people to study. She stood frantically looking. No Frank. Not one person remotely resembling how she remembered him. She had toured all the platforms before it came to her: she was in the wrong place. She was in the West station instead of the South.

A quarter to one. No bus this time. No taxi. The quickest way was to run, through the small, less crowded side streets in as direct a line as possible, praying her breath and her sandals would hold out.

Nearly two o'clock when she reached the side of the South station, stopping to lean panting against its dirty walls. Her clothes now were clinging, her breathing difficult. She felt as if she were drowning. She gulped stale air, then walked the wall's length slowly, keeping her hand against the brickwork like a blind woman. At the main road the sun's glare hit her.

He wasn't waiting on the front steps of the station. But why should he be, since he wasn't expecting her until the following day? She looked for him in the main hall; in all the waiting rooms, and in the dingy buffet. She tried all the platforms, and lastly the bookshop. No sign of him. Back to the station entrance again, wondering what to do. Out past the taxi rank on the forecourt and along the road, past rows of mean shops. She could taste the grit of the place. The noise was terrible. She had walked a block when she saw among the projecting signs cluttering upper storeys the words Hotel Riviera hanging vertically in the broken vestiges of ancient neon. Over the din of the traffic could plainly be heard sounds of welding and panel beating. She stopped, wondering whether she dare go up the steps and ask for his room number. She hesitated and looked around, trying to ignore the palpitations in her chest. On her right was a small café, its window covered with an almost opaque layer of dust, every speck of which the sun picked out.

She thought she heard a tapping sound. As it grew louder and more persistent she turned her head. Inside the café a fist was knocking on the glass. First she saw the fist, then a faint face, looking out through the peeled and faded lettering. It was unmistakably Frank. He was standing and smiling at her, his hand raised. Opening his palm he placed it flat on the dirty glass in a greeting. She put her palm over his and covered it, with the glass still between them. Then he beckoned her inside.

She sat down opposite him, smiling. He smiled back. For a few seconds they sat smiling at one another as if a miracle had been performed in which neither had had a part.

He'd been for a short walk, he said, but found the heat trying. Rather than go to his stuffy hotel he'd decided to return to drink yet more coffee and read a book. It lay beside him on the table. She was glad for him that the place seemed wholesome. He spoke in a low, hesitant voice, looking at her directly from under thick, black eyebrows. He had clear, grey eyes, in them a hint of expectancy. She knew he was hoping she wouldn't find him unacceptable. His face looked thin, making his narrow forehead seem higher than it was. He ran a hand over his heavy thatch of dark hair, recently cut and standing out in thick swathes which ended abruptly over his ears. She spoke about the excitement which had made her go to the wrong station. She held out her arms to display the ruined dress, telling him how her thoughts had been befuddled by heat, antici- pation and apprehension. Yet as she spoke she could feel a calm coming over her, because of his calm and the way he looked at her; not asking inconsequential questions, only content that she'd come. He himself looked cool enough despite the dark suit, the hard-collared shirt and formal tie. He sat with hands folded, seeming completely at ease. She continued speaking about why she'd come a day early and how it had been during the preceding days, letting the words flow as they would, taking up the thread of her letters as if there was no difference between talking and writing. He nodded agreement, pursed his lips or wrinkled his brow and smiled from time to time, renewing that wonderful knowledge she'd always had that she could say anything to him, and whatever she said would be understood.

They sat talking while the coffee got cold and the sun sent pale shadows through the window. He talked of the difficult journey, his fellow passengers on the trains, the hotel where he'd been convalescing. He spoke simply and clearly, and in his talk she could hear now and then the cadences of his writing. Their conversation flowed through gentle and familiar channels, stopping at moments while they negotiated unknown curves, then moving on to encompass all those shadowy areas of their daily lives which in their letters they'd passed over too rapidly. He asked few questions, having little need since she supplied him with details unasked, picking up the sense of the question by the look in his eyes. Her enquiries he answered freely and seriously, pausing to consider what she'd asked, sometimes leaning back and answering with a gesture, as clear as if he'd spoken. She could see there was nothing of the performer in him. Everything came from him naturally. She asked what he would do when he got back home. Slowly at first, then with a precise, unhesitating manner he began to describe the life which awaited him. He spoke of the work which he did so badly, and for which he was paid too much; of the generosity of the directors who tolerated such an invalid. This he said with a smile, not of irony but of someone truly amazed by the kindness of his fellows. He thought himself an imposter there who might one day be found out and asked to leave. She said she thought it might be better for the world if he did leave and spend all his time writing.

At this first mention of his writing he began to blink rapidly in some agitation, until she said she'd lived so close to it that it was hers as well as his. And since they were sharing it, she had a perfect right to decide when and how it was accomplished. She spoke of Fox's efforts on his behalf, and how everyone who understood the work longed for more. Some were afraid of its power, she said. Others talked about it without having read a word. Her only excuses for putting drawings to words which plainly needed nothing more, were her wish for a wider audience for him, and the baser desire to earn herself a living. At this he laughed and she thought how young he looked. By now any small strangeness between them had gone.

She tapped his arm while she was talking, feeling the boniness inside the sleeve. Once she brushed his hand, and saw how tanned it was, and wondered about the rest of his body. Her feelings for him, never sisterly, were becoming a strange mixture she'd never experienced before. The sight of him moved her not with the pity she sometimes felt when she looked at Ernest, but with what she presumed was another of love's variations: desire and tenderness taking turns with amazement at his uniqueness. He seemed so simple, in the best sense of the word. Only once before had she come across the same kind of man who had instantly inspired in her similar feelings. But he had been very old; a truly religious, very old man with whom she'd once had an important conversation in the flower-filled confines of the cloister of the church where her brother was buried. The old man had spoken to her not as if she were thirteen years old, but as if speaking to an equal, perfectly capable of comprehending everything. And she was. She'd known and appreciated the sense of what he was saying. She knew he knew about her wildness and that it didn't matter. She knew he knew she was grieving, although all she did was run like a demon around the gravestones, scandalizing the mourners. She knew he loved her when he held her hand and put his fingers to the side of her face. He hadn't mentioned her dead mother and why they were there that day. He'd said none of the usual things about having to grow up and face the world early and take on the responsibility of looking after her father. He'd said that animals and children had no need of death. That was all she could remember, except the thinness of his ribs when she'd hugged him impulsively, and the gasp he'd given because of her strength. Stirring in her then had been the same urge to make contact; body to body being the simplest way not to lose him.

When the sun had left the front of the café and traffic had changed direction outside, they stopped talking long enough to order some food from a grateful proprietor who'd long given up hope that his only two customers might help pay the rent. They ordered omelettes because they might safely be assumed to contain no meat. When they came, Frank examined his, looked concerned and said he thought he could see pieces of ham. He considered the problem for a moment before calling the proprietor over with an apology.

She sat back in wonderment as he carefully explained the reason why he couldn't eat it. He had an aversion to the killing of animals for food, he said. He realized he should have made it clear what his needs were, although there was no mention of pieces of ham on the menu. The bewildered proprietor was further confounded by being offered the price of the meal in recompense for the misunderstanding. Both he and she looked hard at Frank in case the joke was a deep one, but he was perfectly serious. The proprietor took the plate away to the kitchen, returning a few minutes later with another omelette on a sparkling plate wrapped around with a serviette. He served it to Frank with a flourish, looked into his face to see if he was satisfied, brought fresh coffee unasked, then went behind his counter where he stayed beaming at him over the top of his newspaper.

After the meal, during which he spoke little, concentrating almost entirely on the food, Frank asked her about her father as if the thought had been on his mind. She said there'd been no change in the relationship, and that sometimes she felt it might be better to finish trying to keep it alive. And yet while the pain continued she knew her feelings hadn't calcified, and therefore she must persist. When his cards came, laying down guidelines for the kind of life he thought she ought to be leading, paying no attention to her feelings or the reality of the situation, she said she despaired. How could any father forget so thoroughly he was speaking to another human being whose rights had to be treated with respect?

'I've asked myself that question too,' Frank said. He smiled and put his hand gently over hers. 'Fathers are a special race. I'll tell you more about mine when I've found the strength!'

Heads closer together they spoke familiarly about their families, talking of problems with sisters and friends, but leaving out for the time being their deeper worries concerning Ernest and the Girl. They had four days, he said, in which to find a little mutually inspired peace. He wanted to see the city in which she lived, and check that it was doing her no harm. His memories of it weren't particularly good, and had something to do with the holding of a Zionist congress. She said she'd take him to her favourite places which nobody else knew about. He could give himself safely into her hands, because she knew exactly what he needed. He smiled at her wryly.

They left the café after another altercation with the proprietor, this time over the cost of the meal. Frank, against all refusals, insisted on paying for three omelettes, but he haggled over the price of the coffee, counting the cups on his fingers to establish the number they'd drunk. It wasn't the cost which bothered him, only the fact that here was a problem with only one solution which could be right. She stood waiting while he sorted it out, watching him treat the transaction as if it were one of life's great mysteries. She shifted from foot to foot, not knowing whether to laugh at him for his parsimony, eventually realizing with amazement that he was unaware that matters might be handled differently by those less fastidious.

Although the evening was still remarkably hot he put on a new dark grey trilby. When he stood up he was almost as tall as Fox, but he walked as if his height was a bothersome thing to be overcome by stooping and looking at her from under his brows. As they went towards the hotel she found herself unable to stop comparing him with Ernest. There were the same good manners and gentleness of speech, the same tendency to use gesticulation in place of words. Both were able to make the most formidable phrases sound simple and natural. Even their humour bore comparison – though Ernest's was blacker – having a fine edge to it that she felt was essentially Jewish. Not that she could have imagined this 'long, thin creature with the friendly smile' (as he'd described himself in a letter) enjoying Ernest's latest and favourite joke about the man who, when asked by a lady why he was so good in bed, replied that he practised a lot on his own. And their differences? Not all the worries of daily life could defeat Ernest's essential optimism. He really was the man Frank imagined him to be, as substantial in spirit as he was in body. She walked beside Frank and wondered whether his resilience was as frangible as his form, or whether the very act of being beside her denied this.

They stopped in the foyer of the Hotel Riviera. She raised her eyebrows at the shabbiness. The walls were hung with blotched wallpaper and overlayed by tattered photographs of French seaside resorts. In the corners hung bunches of plastic grapes with faded leaves. A sign stated *Definitely No Visitors in Rooms*, to which Frank pointed apologetically. They sat for a while on frail wicker chairs, unable to recreate their former intimacy in a place which smelled so sour. She asked why he'd chosen it, and he said rather it had chosen him. But it would do. When she said there was time to find another, he explained that he'd already put his name in the book, as if this was an end of it. She said no more, but noticed that his face in the yellow light looked drawn underneath the tan.

When she suggested he might want to rest after such an exhausting journey and so exciting a day, she knew by the relieved look in his eyes that she must leave him. They'd meet tomorrow at the hotel. She'd come for him. They agreed on ten o'clock. Before going upstairs he escorted her to the door, made sure she didn't want him to call a taxi, and shook her hand with a formality that took her by surprise.

She went home slowly, wondering at her own state of exhaustion. Not until she was indoors and chewing greedily on a large slice of bread did she realize the cuff links were still in her handbag. Before going to bed she washed the green dress carefully, had a shower and removed the city grit from her hair. She searched the wardrobe for something suitable to wear next day, and found a blouse and skirt which she thought might just pass muster.

She neither heard Ernest come in, nor did she see him the following morning before he went to work. On the kitchen table, propped up among the ruins of a hasty breakfast, she found the note he'd left. It said that Rose had been looking for her.

She took a bus to the South station, arrived comfortably at ten o'clock, and waited in the hotel lobby without attracting anyone's attention. At ten fifteen a young girl came sidling down the stairs with a guilty look in her direction before scuttling out. Nobody came to enquire what she was doing there, and there was no-one to ask which was Frank's room. He arrived looking apologetic a few minutes later, as clean as the day before, having shaved and put on the same smart suit. In his hand he carried a thin book which he presented to her with a slight, deprecating shrug. He thought she might like it to look at some time. It was about the desert. He'd read it on the train. She needn't bother to return it. She asked if the traffic noises had bothered him in the night, but he said his problem was always the same, noise or none. The inability to sleep, to which he couldn't resign himself lay he supposed in the constant shuttling back and forth in his mind of every memory he possessed, and some he couldn't even remember having! He warned her that lateness was one of his weaknesses, brought about by uncertainty in this case, since he couldn't plead extenuating circumstances. She said she'd arrive late herself next time, thus making him early.

Without agreeing where they should go, they left the hotel and went over to the shady side of the road. She suggested they might stroll in one of the parks where the air would be cooler.

They walked side by side through the iron gates and down the alleys towards some unspoken goal. Ahead on a slight rise was the pattern of pierced stonework of an unfinished palace, white against the blue sky. Below it lay the formal lawns beloved by royal builders, the green grass decorated with strapworks of begonias. They spoke about the city, its people and the difficulties of being alien. He told her there was such a thing as feeling foreign anywhere. She noticed he walked easily with no hint of the invalid. Neither did his breathing seem laboured. Only the nasal quality of his voice made her think he might have a slight cold. They sat down on a stone bench under a cypress tree. From her bag she took the jeweller's box and put it into his hands. He opened the box slowly, stared at the contents a long time before taking out the cuff links and holding them on his broad palm. He spent so long looking at them that she had to bend down and peer into his face to see the reaction. There were tears in his eyes. 'How could I have deserved these?' he said. She told him the gift wasn't especially important or valuable, just something she'd bought because she'd like the golden rays.

'Perhaps symbols are silly,' she said, 'but you're here, and the sun's shining, isn't it?'

He put the box in his pocket, saying it was a long time since he'd been given such a present so sweetly offered. He asked her if it had cost her much money, and she shrugged her shoulders. But he persisted, saying that for someone as poor as she was, the cuff links represented a great deal. And he wasn't worthy of them. She said she spent money as it should be spent: how and when she thought fit. Then for no reason at all she lied, telling him that she'd taken the teaching job by the station, so he wasn't to worry unnecessarily. He replied that her finances would remain a mystery to him. She felt slightly dissatisfied.

They spent a long time walking in the park, keeping to the gravelled pathways, wandering in the long alleys of clipped trees, resting now and then on a bench to talk and stretch and ignore the view while they contemplated one another.

He asked about mutual friends, mentioning Charles in an admiring tone. She said he was essentially weak, having never freed himself from his mother's hold. 'I suppose many of us fall into that category,' was the reply.

She told him about her childhood, forgetting what she'd already said in letters, and pleased when his knowledge of her life showed how carefully he'd read them. They went on to talk about the town where they'd both been born; its cramping, stultifying atmosphere from which an escape was so necessary. She'd made hers, he said. His was yet to come.

'I would like to have children,' she said.

He said nothing, but took her hand in his and held it. She felt extraordinarily happy.

When the heat began to strengthen they walked to a cooler side of the gardens, among flowering shrubs where the odour of moist earth mingled with the heavy perfume of magnolia and rhododendron. He said he wasn't particularly keen on flowers. She couldn't live without them, she said. Sometimes she bought them instead of food. At heart she was a peasant. If he wanted she could take him to another place, much wilder and quieter, and they'd pretend they were the first people ever to have set eyes on it. As they walked he kept her hand in his quite naturally, but with a certain shyness as if he might be wondering whether he was taking liberties.

By the statue of the boy with the fiddle they stopped, deep in discussion again of friends separated and those with whom there had always been contact. She was amused by his summing up of some of them. He had a discerning eye, but spoke about their faults fondly. Yes, he remembered Conrad and the swimming parties; his wild claims that he could swim any river. In his exaggerations was a theatrical element which, he remembered, he'd tried to copy. He would be glad to see Conrad again, he said. They went onto the grass and sat shoulder to shoulder, his hand covering hers. She spoke at length about Conrad's activities, keeping nothing hidden. She spoke about drugs and he listened carefully, making no comment. But when she paused or perhaps her expression changed, he patted her hand several times and nodded for her to continue. She told him she still missed Stacey who had been so much a part of her growing up. Maybe he'd meet her again himself, and find her just as lively and intelligent as she used to be in the days they were like twins. He talked about Leon, the most constant of his friends, who seemed, he said, to possess more energy and enthusiasm than anyone he knew. She felt mildly jealous of Leon. His capacity for work was endless. Into each day he packed study, work, discussions with friends, meetings and his latest literary endeavour. He'd even found time to get married, he said.

'Getting married is comparatively easy,' she replied. 'It's the continuation that's difficult!'

It was time to talk about Ernest. She led him to a more secluded lawn under an ash tree. Squirrels scampered behind its trunk as they approached and sat down. From somewhere hidden came the quiet murmur of voices, and the quick gasp of a woman's laugh. He already knew a great deal about Ernest, he said. She wanted, she said, to fill in the gaps in her letters, so the picture of her life would be simply and totally clear. There were constant changes, she said, not only in her own attitude, but in Ernest's. In fact the only unchanging factor was Ernest's habit of being unfaithful to her a hundred times a year. The trouble was that it was all too easy to understand how women found him fascinating. He kept them, and herself, under a kind of spell from which it was difficult to escape. She thought she might have offended Frank deeply. But his eyes brightened into a reverential look like somebody admiring an impossible feat superbly achieved. 'How does he do it?' was all he said. He was like a child being told an absorbing fairy story. Then he lay back, putting his hands under his head, looking up at her face while she spoke about being left alone; the worry of working under such circumstances; the additional problem over the anteroom and Ernest's trying to take it over. Furthermore, she told him, neither of them could find ways of making ends meet, and this caused perpetual wrangling. She put it down to her lack of proper education in the matter – too much time spent on Latin and Art – and to Ernest's natural extravagance. Only when Frank closed his eyes for a second as if the sunlight had hit them, did she stop talking about Ernest. She apologized for being slightly addicted to the subject.

'I think we should eat,' he said.

Trees gave them shade as they went through the shrubbery, scattering pigeons in the undergrowth. Rounding a clump of rhododendrons they heard whispering and rustling ahead of them. Someone grunted. They were in time to see a pair of feet in pretty patent-leather shoes being withdrawn from under a bush. More whispering, then the unmistakeable sounds of people scrambling to their feet. In the clearing in front of them a man and woman were standing flicking dead grass from their clothes. Frank averted his face from the scene and walked on. What held Amy temporarily transfixed was the tall man with the grey hair and the military bearing who was staring at her with dismay. It was Rose's father, brushing himself down in a flash of gold rings. She saw him turn swiftly to the woman beside him who was completing the pulling down of her blouse. Looking straight at Amy he raised his chin and pulled up the corners of his mouth in the semblance of a smile. As he nodded good-day to her his hand went down to check his flies.

They made for the café at the end of the gardens, where tables with umbrellas were set out on the gravel. They both agreed that it was bad luck for Rose's father, well aware that the same situation might be applied to themselves. Except, Amy said, she had every intention of telling Ernest about their relationship when the time was right. Frank said he found it impossible to lie. 'People who do it must be so clever.' Again the same admiration in his voice for those who managed what to him were prodigious feats. She felt herself blushing at the thought of the non-existent teaching job.

They ordered and ate a salad each. She noticed he ate

everything put in front of him, including bread and several slices of cheese.

They walked towards town when the heat in the park became too oppressive, keeping in the shade, with frequent stops for discussion. She wanted him to see the art gallery, and he seemed pleased to comply. He bought her an ice from a man with a barrow, but refused one himself. She accused him of trying to show up the difference in their ages by subtle means. His reply was that hers were even subtler, for until the moment when she'd cleverly reminded him, he hadn't given it a single thought. She told him that if he hadn't made such a fanfare of it in his letters, it wouldn't have occurred to her to think about it. She didn't like worrying about people's ages – a tedious pastime that interfered with getting to know them. Take Mrs Kertesch for example, a lady who looked exceedingly old. But it was irrelevant. They were friends because they liked one another.

'And what is "exceedingly old" to a person of twenty-four?'

'Do I seem so young to you?'

'With the sunlight on your face you look like a child. Sunlight does that to people,' he said. 'It either makes them look young, or worn out.'

'It suits you very well,' she said. 'But it's not a crime to be either!' She took his arm delicately. He looked pleased. 'We might go to the cinema,' she suggested. 'Air conditioning. And there we needn't look at anything but the screen!'

He refused. He had no taste for cinemas now, although once he said he used to go frequently. Now only the posters pleased him. Another sign of old age! Films made him feel he was no longer in charge of his sight. She thought it strange that one whose writing was so cinematic should say such a thing.

At the gallery she helped him up the steps with mock concern, and he gracefully obliged by clinging to her arm. They wandered through the airy rooms content to be aimless. Now and then they stopped to look at pictures which caught their eye, enjoying the act of moving in unison with one another as much as the sight of familiar works. At Rembrandt's small self-portrait they stopped and stared and couldn't believe the perfection: age breaking up the lines of the chin and wrinkling the space between the brows: so perfect an application of paint that there was no intermediary between sitter and viewer. 'Such insistence on life,' Frank said. She took him on to look at another old man: Saint Jerome in Penitence, with owl and parrot depicting the melancholic and sanguine temperaments. He stood looking at it for a long time, then remarked that they were dependant upon the experts, but with luck might avoid their conclusions. Saying nothing she led him next to 'A Hermit's Meal in his Cave', and watched the way he carefully perused it. He looked at her and smiled.

They moved on through the calm, bright rooms, their footsteps echoing on the boards, their quiet conversation amplified by the comparative emptiness. Light filtered down through thin muslin stretched across the ceilings, giving a softness to nearly all they saw. Rubens's Head of Medusa caught her glance, looking malevolent in a corner. She turned her head and hurried past it, afraid to be drawn back into Milena's turmoil.

They stopped again in front of Tintoretto's 'Portrait of an Old White-Bearded Man', she inspecting it closely to hide her grin. She felt her arm tightly gripped. Frank's breath was in her ear as he whispered softly, 'All right! I've got the message!' His face was so close she felt the excitement of him rising inside. She turned to him at the precise moment he was aiming a kiss at the top of her ear. It missed and his lips brushed her temple. He released her and stood back, his brown skin diffused with blushes.

They spent from afternoon to early evening exploring the entire extent of the building. He said he thought the artefacts might remind one sometimes that they might safely consider the past dead but not buried. He was smiling.

Outside where the evening air was cooler and traffic had thinned, he asked whether she shouldn't be getting home to Ernest. When she said that Ernest was probably sitting in his favourite café beside his current girl, his look changed again to one of admiration.

'Shall we go to a concert?' she said.

'Leon understands music. He's with musicians constantly.' He sounded wistful. 'It would be wonderful to hear you talking about music together. But concerts aren't for me.'

They began walking past a row of expensive shops, their windows covered by small, curved canopies. Through open doors they could see late customers busy over purchases: someone holding up a glittering necklace to the light: a woman pointing along a row of porcelain jars: money being counted into held-out hands. Rose's father came into Amy's mind.

'Music overpowers me,' Frank said. 'Like the sea. Endless waves. I'm afraid I'm a poor swimmer.'

She could think of nothing better than to drown in sound, she said. Playing the flute was for her a way into the best kind of oblivion. He said he'd never learned to play an instrument. In fact he'd never ever learned anything remotely useful. All machines from typewriters to cameras to cars were mysteries to him.

A car came past them and slowed, its horn hooting. She saw an uplifted hand and Laurie's face above the wheel mouthing a greeting. She waved back as the car went on.

'Laurie,' she said. 'Another admirer of yours. Don't be surprised if he asks for another of your stories.' She looked along the road to see if the car had stopped, but it hadn't. Frank was already several steps ahead. He had stopped in front of a restaurant and was stooping to read the menu outside, but she could have sworn he'd run for cover.

Inside it was fairly crowded, but they were given two seats in a corner, away from the central brightness and noise. 'You must eat well,' Frank told her.

As during their last meal together he concentrated on his food, chewing each mouthful carefully and with enjoyment. A couple sitting opposite seemed unable to take their eyes off him, even watching the way he replaced his knife and fork on his plate. At some point during dinner he spoke a few words to them. Afterwards she couldn't remember exactly what he'd said, but the result was startling. The man's face became animated and relieved as if he'd been waiting for a chance to speak. He launched into a description of what life was like in his office round the corner, saying it was so terrible that he'd rather it didn't exist at all. The woman joined in and hardly waiting for replies which, when they came, amounted only to nods of the head or the briefest of remarks, they presented Frank with a blow by blow account of their respective daily existences. The duet lasted until coffee was brought, subsiding into the final calm of those who have passed through a memorable disaster. When the pair left they shook hands warmly, saying how pleased they were to have met them.

'Will Absolution last until next Sunday?' Amy said.

'You can't suppress a fever,' he replied.

The encounter had obviously exhausted him. His face looked darker and drawn. She said she was going to make sure he didn't get lost by going back with him to his hotel. He made no remonstrances and allowed her to see to the bill, which she paid for with his money.

On the hotel steps she wondered whether he'd ask her in. Instead he kissed her on both cheeks, then on the fingers, said goodnight, hesitated, then asked if she'd meet him tomorrow.

'I'll come for you,' she told him.

8

'Have you seen Rose yet?' Ernest asked. 'She seemed fairly agitated the other evening. She and Jasmine had their heads together for hours.'

'Rose can wait. Whatever it is, I haven't time today.'

He raised his eyebrows and pushed up his glasses. 'You know best,' he said. 'There's a parcel for you in the sitting room. Looks like Conrad's handwriting.'

She said that too could wait. Grabbing her handbag she made for the door.

'See you this evening!' he shouted at her as she left.

She found Frank waiting for her in the café near the hotel. He looked relieved to see her, but said nothing about how late she was. She asked how he'd slept and he said the night noises had been fairly unbearable. Was there somewhere quiet they could go?

They walked slowly across the busy city talking about books. She liked his way of speaking, amused by the deep voice coming from so thin a throat, and the way he considered the subject with the same care he'd given last night's menu. She asked if the Girl shared his literary tastes, and he bowed his head slightly before saying no. She took his arm, encouraged by a slight movement he made with his elbow. It was difficult to know how to speak about his fiancée without offending him. He seemed so sensitive to anything she said that her first fear was of appearing too censorious. How much easier it had been to write about the Girl in letters. But he continued talking about her, giving her credit for her good qualities, measuring them against those he found less to his taste, speaking almost to himself, yet turning now and then to emphasize particular points about her. He spoke sadly, saying how affectionate she was, amiable and unselfish, always going out of her way to please him. He was sorry he didn't like going to the cinema with her, or to the comedies she so much enjoyed. To Amy's 'What does she look like?' he said she had a certain kind of beauty coming as much from her liveliness as from her looks. But he thought she looked and acted younger than thirty. She had a special line in racy slang which he found very funny. His father thought she was vulgar. He was totally against the marriage. It was dangerous, she said, to listen to fathers, and difficult not to go in the opposite direction in sheer defiance. He shook his head. He said she might understand his feelings more when she'd read his letter to his father. It had always been a source of wonder to him how a father could hold a son in such contempt. How could he believe him capable of falling for a woman because she'd put on a fancy blouse and made a pass at him? Of course he could understand his father being sceptical about any attempt to marry, after the last two fiascos. It couldn't have been easy for either of his parents to witness two broken engagements to the same girl, two renewals, then the breakup of the whole affair. The noise of traffic drowned the sound of his voice from time to time. She strained her ears, not wanting him to have to repeat words which were so obviously paining him. She heard '. . . the impossibility of it all, because he rules there.'

They crossed into a side street, leading them towards the northern suburbs. She pointed out the building where Ernest worked and said he'd taken the day off because of the weather. 'He must be very good at his job,' Frank observed, then suddenly added, 'How can anyone take his place?'

She said that since he was in some ways already sharing it, he was half way there. Now it was up to both of them whether they continued. He told her there was no way of escaping someone who spread such a huge shadow. She thought he was overestimating the power some people possessed. Strength always came to one's rescue if one tried hard enough.

'There's not a corner that is mine completely,' he said. 'And never can be.'

She squeezed his arm. 'You're forgetting that I'm good at driving away demons, Frank!'

He gave her a quick, sideways look and continued. 'From my earliest childhood he's done nothing but bewilder me. All of us. Always raging against someone – in the warehouse, the shop, at home . . . Never wrong himself.' He laughed dryly. 'An utter paragon!' He patted her hand. 'It's still the same. But now each of us has learned a different method of self-protection. At least superficially. But he's still here . . .' He thumped his chest with his fist. 'Who would want to take that place?' She said nothing. She suddenly realized they had been talking at cross-purposes.

Soon they were walking in quieter streets, some lined with trees whose fallen blossoms they trod underfoot. Sunlight had taken the colour from everything – trees, rooftops, cars and pedestrians. A shimmering heat haze marked the road ahead where she was leading him. Above it could be made out the first faint outline of rising hills. And to the right, trees marking the edges of the wide, wilder parkland. He walked cheerfully beside her. As they began to go up the steeply sloping road taking them to the outer gates, he looked at the trees on the sky-line and said, 'This is more like it!' increasing his pace and taking her with him.

Oblivious of the scorching sun he hastened her through the gates, off the melting tarmac and onto grass. She pointed out the string of lakes glimmering in a dip in the green, the distant trees now emerald with summer foliage. Then the black block of fir trees, looking slightly bleached in the strong light. He wanted to walk and walk, he said. These last few days his legs had been prisoners. He wanted to walk the way he and Leon used to.

Out in the middle of the park and where city rooftops

were hidden by its undulations, the grass grew longer and wilder, signs of discolouration beginning to mark its growth. They negotiated areas of scrub growing so close they had to walk in single file, disturbing flocks of quarrelling birds which rose complaining to the sky. They sat for a while on the softer turf of a gentle hill looking out towards the west. Their shoulders were touching when she put her head slowly and carefully close to his. She had the sensation of handling a sensitive animal which might bolt if she made a clumsy move. He kissed her temple and his lips were warm, but he kept his eyes on the view. He said how much he loved the emptiness of the landscape. In her memory there flickered the image of a man's face over hers, his body locked to hers; behind his head hazel trees against a summer sky.

She said, 'I had an art teacher once who used to say, "Don't let the parks fool you into thinking they're real country. They're not. A park is only a copy of the country in a nice, iron frame".' Frank said he could find no criticism of that day's picture.

By late afternoon she had led him in an arc from the lakes, round in a huge half-circle, then up again towards the banks of taller trees they'd first seen on their way in. She was taking him, she said, to somewhere special.

He didn't speak as they entered the forest, but looked around at the dense trees which blocked off interior light and cast deep shadows. He looked up at the branches where little flashes of light like stars came and went with the slight movement of a far-off breeze. She watched him. They walked the length of a wide alley, then turned into one of the smaller tracks so that finally the forest was totally enclosing them. He put out his hand to her again and they walked close together, looking up at the dark green umbrella covering them. Brambles and small bushes grew at the feet of the trees among pine needles which lay thickly covering the forest floor. There was a deep silence broken by the occasional snapping of twigs under their feet, the soft scampering sounds of hidden creatures high above them. Once they heard the rush of flight of a frightened bird, then the faintest ringing of a far-off bell. She took him along familiar paths, knowing they were nearing the part she loved best. As their eyes became accustomed to the gloom they saw each other more clearly. He was smiling. She stopped in a small clearing surrounded by the tallest trees, their great trunks going straight up over their heads to a glittering sky. Beneath them the floor was dry and felt warm to their feet. A powerful and heady perfume pervaded the still air.

'What a wonderful place,' he said.

She told him how she'd found it and kept it secret and special, not mentioning the time there with Ernest. He spread his jacket on the ground and sat down, pulling her by the hand to sit beside him. They sat in this way for a long time, staring round them at the enclosing trees. He said it was the first time he'd met a woman with whom he could share so much. There were no misunderstandings or areas of incomprehension. She thought of the letters in which he'd said she didn't understand him. With the others, he told her, he separated in his mind that which they and he could share, and that which had to stay private. Understanding his writing was a case in point. What had always troubled him was how to reconcile the solitary business of being the kind of writer he was, with the enforced companionship necessary to marriage. What he had to offer any woman was an almost monastic life of unshared loneliness. Unless she had the strength and resources to continue her own life, acknowledging his selfishness and prepared to tolerate it, she would be totally unhappy. He asked if he had the right to inflict this on anyone. Not waiting for a reply he said, 'Perhaps it is possible . . .'

He began to stroke her arm, his touch tingling her from fingers to shoulder. His hand went to her waist, smoothing the fabric of her skirt, moving up to her breast, over its curve to her exposed neck. She sat very still, afraid to do what she most wanted – to grasp his head with both hands, push him down to the ground and kiss him passionately. She felt his fingers pull her blouse down over her shoulder until it was bared. Then he laid his face against her flesh and she could feel the heat coming from him. Putting her arm around him she took him slowly back with her until her head was resting on a bed of pine needles, and his lay on her barely covered breast. She stroked his springy hair, feeling its thickness, running her fingers over the convolutions of his ears, listening to his voice through a pleasurable haze. She felt his hands moving over her chest and stomach, feeling the contours, retracing their path, making circular movements over her hips, going down between her thighs and trembling, but not lingering there, going over her thighs and back up her sides to her breasts. She thought she heard him mutter '*Maman*' into her flesh. She held him close, feeling the sharpness of his backbone through his shirt, and the protruding wings of his shoulder blades. She lay very still until his hands stopped moving and stayed holding her close while she stroked his hair. She remembered he was supposed to be an invalid.

Presently he sat up and bent over her. He had a slight cast in one eye which made his face more beautiful to her. 'You're the first Gentile I've ever loved.' It sounded slightly ironic. He said it frightened him, but freed him a little at the same time. And she was so young. He couldn't believe such wisdom and intelligence. 'There's absolutely nothing vulgar about you, Amy.' She wondered about other women. She wondered whether he'd ever gone to prostitutes.

'Give her up,' she said.

'But how can I? She's done nothing wrong. *I* have wronged her by leading her to believe in a future together.'

'Then put it right by telling her explicitly you can't marry her. It's kinder.' She looked at him hard. 'Tell her about us.'

He brought his knees up to his chest and held them together, his head low over them. 'She doesn't deserve it.'

They argued about the Girl for several minutes, he taking her side and pleading like her defence counsel.

At last he said, 'You're right. Better to get it over with as soon as possible.' He hadn't imagined prolonging the agony. She replied that she too hadn't imagined it differently.

He was silent for a second. The discussion seemed to have exhausted him. She said he'd feel better having done the deed, but there were bound to be scenes with the Girl at first. He didn't respond when she said she could see a pending storm which, if he acted promptly, would be over fast. He said he thought it was getting cold.

They left the forest quickly, emerging into evening brightness and warmth. As they walked towards the gates they'd come in by, Frank mentioned Ernest. He compared himself unfavourably with him, saying how purposeful and determined he sounded. She didn't agree. She knew, for instance, that the battle over the anteroom couldn't last long. Like his love affairs his minor fixations were short-lived.

'What a lovely evening,' she said. She didn't want talk of Ernest to spoil it. She could smell the faintly lilac perfume of chestnut trees wafted towards them on a rising breeze. The closeness she felt to Frank, the feeling that their future lay together came over her like the scent itself. She wanted to hurry him back to the hotel, go upstairs at long last, and spend the night making love.

He seemed incapable of walking at more than a slow amble, leaning slightly on her arm. She would have been happy to continue in this way had Frank not said suddenly, 'I'll take you home', at the same time raising his arm to a taxi coming towards them through the dark arch of a baroque building. Completely taken by surprise, she allowed herself to be helped into the taxi, but stopped him getting in beside her. 'I'll go by myself,' she said, trying to keep the anger from her voice. He merely nodded, smiled warmly at her and closed the taxi door.

'The park tomorrow?' he said through the window.

175

'The park.' The taxi moved off with a lurch, throwing her against the back of the seat. It had all been so sudden that she was at her own front door before she could really realize they'd parted.

She found Ernest waiting for her when she got in. He was sitting at the kitchen table, his hands folded in front of him. He came to the point sharply and without hesitation.

Rose's mother had accused Amy of stealing a valuable brooch. Rose had been to him with the story that the brooch wasn't hers, she had only borrowed it for the afternoon. Yet knowing this, Amy had taken it from the café table, thus leaving Rose in a terrible predicament. Her mother had missed the brooch and asked her daughter where it was. For days now Rose had been trying to contact Amy to ask for its return before her mother got too agitated and called the police. Everyone knew, Ernest said, that the mother was notoriously unstable, and quite capable of doing anything once she got the wind in her tail. Bloodhounds weren't beyond her capabilities, he added with a smile. He asked Amy what she'd done with it.

Her first reaction was one of extreme irritation. Why hadn't he tried to defend his wife rather than believing she was capable of thievery? Her voice growing steadily higher with frustration brought about not entirely by this affair, she railed at him for his partiality, succeeded in side-tracking him into a fierce discussion about whether truth was necessarily only formal or factual, then flounced off into the bedroom where she threw off her clothes and went to bed in a temper.

Friday morning was slightly cooler. She had woken early and gone to the shops. Ernest was still sleeping in the anteroom when she returned. The parcel from Conrad was still on the sitting room table. Wrestling with it for several minutes yielded a broken nail, and a mixed collection of hash, grass and cocaine. The poem accompanying it, evidently written while Conrad was either drunk or high, explained that this was his parting gift to her who had

176

deserted him for another man. She put the parcel on a high shelf and went out as quietly as possible without disturbing Ernest.

She waited for Frank at the park gates which they'd entered the previous day. But growing tired of waiting there, and wondering whether he might have come early, she began to look for him. She made for the lakes from which a faint mist was still rising, then back to the forest, not convinced that Frank would be waiting for her there: it was too dark and uninviting, damper than before. A slight nervousness made her look over her shoulder and start at the slightest crack of a twig; even the creaking of her leather belt irritated her. She left the place quickly and stood on its edge staring out over the hazy landscape, hoping to see his thin figure appear over a rise. To make certain he wasn't anywhere in the park, she tramped over those parts they'd visited before, fighting her way through unnecessary thickets and getting scratched by brambles. Then back to the beginning to sit and rest in the sun's increasing warmth, keeping her eyes on the gates at the top of the slope.

She knew that she was childishly waiting for him to come looking for her. She watched the pigeons and noted the cloud beginning to mar the deep blue sky. She took a great interest in three dogs shadow-boxing each other into frenzies. She walked past the place where she could see the gate, taking the longest path to the kiosk. There she bought a sandwich she didn't want. Still he didn't come. Maybe he was sitting in another park, looking at the beds of begonias and the building of Maria Theresia yellow, not bothered a bit that she wasn't with him. For people with only four days at their disposal they were somewhat vague about place and time. They were both to blame.

She thought she ought to go to the other park and look for him, but Frank was nowhere to be found in the formal park. She walked briskly through the many lanes of the shrubbery, plunged across damp lawns looking for the particular ash tree under which they'd sat. All she saw were a couple standing close up against its trunk, the man pinning the woman to it with both arms. She ran before they had time to notice her, although she wasn't certain.

The café next, but closed and boarded, a giant padlock across the door, and a sack of uncollected garbage in front of it.

Then in increasing panic back to Frank's hotel.

The hotel said he'd left at eleven-thirty. A disinterested grey-faced man grudgingly told her the time was half past two. How had she spent so many of their precious moments unable to find him? He hadn't left any message for her, so she presumed he'd definitely gone to one of the parks. She decided to walk back.

Although not as hot as the previous days, it was warm enough. She could feel the sweat start under her armpits. Her forehead was damp. She was exhausting herself. It wouldn't do. The sensible thing would be to stop and take stock of the situation before real panic set in.

She went into an uncrowded café recently vacated by office workers, where she ordered iced tea and a sandwich. Forcing herself to eat slowly while she thought, she came to the conclusion that when Frank had said 'the park' he must have meant the one they'd just left that evening. The problem was whether he really thought of it as a park, or did he only equate formal paths, clipped hedges and statuary with the word? He was no fool. But she wanted to protect him. How many women had already worried over him? Living with him would be full of anxieties. And love.

She looked up into the face of a young man who'd sat down opposite her, unobserved. He had his cup to his face, so his mouth was hidden. He must have been there some time. All she could see were his eyes looking directly at her over the rim. They were sharp, brown eyes which were staring at her with a directness for which she was unprepared. She felt herself start to blush, fumbled in her handbag to regain her composure, wiped imaginary crumbs from her lips, then looked straight at him with a slight smile. Putting the cup down he smiled back, revealing white and even teeth which reminded her of pomegranate seeds. He was very attractive. On one side of his face was a small, badly healed scar. While she was examining him, his eyes were exploring her face, evidently liking what they saw. He looked quickly at her lips, her dimpled chin, her cleavage. She could feel the nipples harden against her blouse. She pressed her knees together, and tried to finish the sandwich as quickly as possible. She asked for the bill, and while she was groping in her bag for change, the man leaned forward and put his hand on her wrist. Shocked by her response, she hastily withdrew her arm. 'I'll pay,' he said in a tone of voice already possessive. Instantly she liked him less. With a perfunctory word of thanks she got to her feet snapping her bag shut, and went from the café as fast as she could into the crowds outside.

She finally found Frank sitting in the park of the previous evening, within sight of the lakes and the forest on the slopes above. On his lap lay an unopened book. She thought he must have been sleeping, for when he heard her approaching steps on the gravel he gave a start and looked around as if wondering where he was, before he recognized her with a relieved smile. He said he'd never doubted she'd come, and kept telling himself this in the face of opposing thoughts which asked why she should bother. He also wondered, he said, whether she oughtn't to be at her portrait class. She hugged him and said it was a day for trying to overcome their problems, not least that of arranging satisfactory meetings. His hands felt cold to her touch. She said they must walk.

Once more they set off over the grassy slopes, until they were out of sight of fences and gates, walking briskly and avoiding the trees' shadows. Yesterday's thin wisps had given way to thicker clouds, building up on high in rippling patterns, and threatening more to come. She took him through open fields, past pools and miniature mountains, holding him firmly by the hand, urging him on, sensing in him the slightest touch of sadness. He had little to say, merely passing odd comments on the lie of the land, or expressing surprise at the variety of the terrain. Some of the time his thoughts seemed far away. As they trudged on she settled her mind to the fact that it was as good a place as any to be, considering the mood he was in.

By late afternoon they had arrived at one of the farthest fences where the gates led north. The air was definitely cooler. She shivered and clung to him, wrapping one half of his jacket round her. His heart was beating vigorously. He held her close with his lips to the lines on her forehead. 'Shall we go for a ride?' he said.

'Not if it means I go home afterwards!' In reply he hugged her tighter.

A taxi wasn't hard to find. They told the driver to take them round the entire city at a slow pace.

The drive took as long as they intended. They sat huddled together, arms round one another, mouths sometimes meeting; sometimes staring, each out of their respective windows at the city, diminishing in size as daylight faded, and being dramatically re-illuminated by flaring street lamps.

'Your Sabbath is starting,' she said quietly.

'It doesn't mean much, I'm afraid.'

'Surely you celebrate it?'

'Any celebration in our house is a travesty. It's always been. I've written to him about it. You'll see.'

The sky had darkened. She grew tired of the constant change of colour from black to orange as they drove back into the centre.

'I'm hungry,' she said. 'We haven't eaten for hours.'

She chose a restaurant she knew, ordered the meal for both of them without intervention or mishap, while Frank looked at her with admiration. He ate contentedly, giving her occasional glances as if she had achieved something wondrous. He told her she was his guardian angel – and not only of him, but of all Jews everywhere. She told him he was mixing her up with Milena whose record for rescuing them was a matter of history. He gave her the money to pay the bill, watching with delight the way she handled the change and tipped the waiter.

'Now I'm taking *you* home,' she told him. It was then or never.

He acquiesced without a murmur.

Once inside the hotel foyer she resolutely followed him up the stairs. As they climbed higher it became dingier and the smell more powerfully musty. On the first landing the light went out with a sudden click, leaving them in the dark. He had to ascend to his room alone, turn on the light and leave his door open for her to find her way upstairs.

The room contained a medium-sized bed, a table and bentwood chair, a matchwood wardrobe and bedside table on which were a pile of books. The table held two open notebooks, several pens and a bottle of ink. There were no curtains at the window, but since the view consisted of a rooftop patched with metal squares and bitumen, she guessed there was no need of them. The light in the room was a murky orange, giving their faces a sinister hue. The room horrified her. Again he said it suited him, and that he was only staying another day and a night.

'And you've managed to work.'

He said he kept a diary: sometimes it was only a line or two, thoughts which later might become parts of stories, or might find their way into the novel he'd been planning for so long. She wondered why talking about his work always made him so nervous. At least, he said, the room had the necessary solitude. 'What more can a bachelor want!'

She sat down on the bed and held out her hand to him. He came and sat down beside her.

'Writing's a dangerous comfort,' he said.

She kissed him, pulling him down with her to the pillow,

trying to restrain herself from too great a display of passion. He kissed her lips, her chin, her eyes, looking into them with his clear gaze as he held his head away from hers. His breathing was short and shallow, and he was beginning to tremble violently.

Slowly she unbuttoned his shirt, running her hand across his surprisingly smooth chest, then directing his fingers to the buttons of her blouse. She led him as gently as she could into the act of undressing her, stopping from time to time as his trembling became so violent that the bed rattled. She held him tight until the paroxysm passed, telling him it would be all right, as if he were a frightened child. When they were both naked she pulled the covers over them, still trying to control his convulsions which were evidently composed of anguish, not ardour.

The fragility of his frame surprised her too. She'd grown used to Ernest's bulk – the physical mass of the man beside her in the bed. This man's thin and bony body with its fine skin caused a shock as great as the way he reacted to her touch. He was experiencing a pleasure so obviously mingled with distaste that only by frequent pauses between caresses could she lead him towards the excitement she already felt. He made love to her in total silence, breathing none of the endearments, the jokes, the dirty words that Ernest used in the game of sex. This was no game, but a deadly serious affair and a risky one, for a man who was suffering. Again and again she calmed his convulsive trembling with reassuring words; waiting for his passion to return, while hers came and subsided, came and subsided until she had to stop herself from crying out to him for help. He went through what seemed like hours of laborious climb, and when he finally entered her, his trembling came again and grew into quivering, frantic climax with a speed which left her amazed and unnerved. When he lay beside her, finally calm, she shook with frustration and self-pity.

They lay on their backs side by side in the dark for a while, not touching. Then she realized he was crying. At once she took him in her arms. She wanted to tell him he needn't worry, because the next time would be better for both of them. They would learn one another's needs.

Her words were never spoken, for he began a long and bitter castigation of himself, spoken into the darkness. He likened himself to an animal wallowing in filth. He said he couldn't bear the terribleness of life; the sight of flesh; the whole business of living. He'd been this way for many years, and as he grew older the fear increased. He feared for everything, and lost his way because of it. She lay quietly staring at the moon becoming more visible in the window's purple oblong. Earthshine showed a faint half-ring and she thought how remote everything was.

'There are ways of conquering fear,' she said. 'One way is to lie quietly now, imagining nothing. Here we are, the two of us, looking at a moon which takes twenty-seven and one-third days to revolve around the earth!'

He said he'd always believed in the magical effect of women on the moon. She stroked his forehead and closed his eyes with her fingertips, telling him to sleep. He said that sleep would be the best birthday present in the world. It was his birthday and he hadn't told her.

She lay, her arms around him, watching the moon's progress until it disappeared from view.

Lamplight in her eyes woke her, and Frank was bending over and kissing her temple, telling her it was now July the fourth. There was a nasty taste in her mouth. She was chilly. As she put up her arm to push the hair from her face, he saw the scar on her wrist. She told him the fuss it had caused. He said he couldn't imagine a less likely suicide. She got up and washed her face in the cracked basin, knowing it was still true that she loved being alive.

Frank insisted on taking her home in a taxi. Before parting they made precise arrangements to meet at the café beside the Riviera Hotel the following afternoon. Frank said he had to go and see Fox at last, having put off the disagreeable task as long as possible. But he would do it in the morning, giving her time to catch up on needed sleep. He said he thought he too might sleep for once, thanks to her. Before she left the taxi he kissed her passionately and boldly with no trace of trepidation.

Ernest was lying full length on the carpet in the sitting room wearing his floral dressing gown, silk pyjamas and leather slippers. By his side was an empty glass. He looked as though he'd either been drinking heavily or had just woken from deep sleep, and asked her in mock heavy tones where the hell she'd been until three in the morning.

His 'I suppose you've been having it out with Rose's mother' decided her. She said no, and went on to say that she'd been with someone known to him. She told him how she and Frank had spent the last three days together, saying that what had begun as friendship had grown, and was growing daily, into love. Reasons for this were many, and included Ernest's own lack of interest in married life. There was no blame to be apportioned, for faults were obvious on both sides. From now on, she told him, her life would be more tolerable, and his freer from accusation.

He got up, grabbed the brandy and poured two large drinks. She took the one he offered her.

He came to sit beside her at the table, his eyes revealing that he was doing much rapid thinking despite the foolish smile on his face. Hadn't he always told her, he said, that love should be shared? But he was regarding her with a new look which, if she liked to interpret it one way, could mean he wanted to ask her questions he daren't: 'Is he good in bed? Is he better than me? Have you discussed me together?'

'He's an incredible person,' she said.

'When I knew him he couldn't even button his coat straight!' He was jealous.

'I can't talk about it any more, Ernest. I'm exhausted and I've got to get to bed.'

He got to his feet. 'Quite. Quite.' He drained his glass, set it down on the table with an attempt at a flourish and left the room. She raised her eyebrows at this unusual behaviour, and continued sipping her drink, trying to think. Turning over and over in her head what they'd done, what they'd said, where they'd been, what they'd written, what they'd said, what they'd done, always she came up against the last four awful hours in the awful hotel. To-morrow would be better. She would make it so.

She went into the bedroom to find Ernest peering at her over the bedclothes, a winsome expression fixed rather drunkenly on his face.

'Lost my way!' he said.

She got in beside him and turned out the light. She lay waiting. In the dark she felt the familiar hands come for her and she let them, slipping towards him in relief and release. She knew why he would make love to her so blatantly. Had she resisted him then there would have been another time. He knew her weaknesses too well, and knew too surely he was one of them. 'Why not?' was all she said to herself. If Ernest could be unfaithful, so could she. She would leave guilt until the morning when the furious, physical need for him had been assuaged.

They woke late. She tried to persuade Ernest into a little more quiet love-making but he refused. He hid his head under the covers and claimed he felt too fragile. She brought him breakfast in bed which he left untouched. He didn't rise until noon, in time to see her fully dressed and combing her hair in front of the sitting room mirror. She told him she was going out and that he shouldn't wait up for her.

'Give him my regards!' he shouted childishly as she went out of the door.

Frank was waiting for her in the café next to the hotel. He looked extremely cheerful, greeted her with a slightly more proprietorial air than previously and ordered coffee for her. He said he'd seen the flags in the streets and thought it only right that the day was one of celebration. His mood was catching, and she began to respond to the enthusiasm with which he talked about what they should do on his last day. In view of the change in the weather he thought they ought to avoid all parks, and perhaps concentrate on a few more museums or galleries. And he would like to buy her a present. He said he wanted to buy her a proper pen. She couldn't refuse, since if she did he'd think she didn't want to write to him any more.

Buying it took patience on the part of two mystified assistants, good humoured intervention on Amy's part, and all of an hour. At last, Amy having selected the perfect pen, they came to the question of paying. Frank demurred at the price so they began the laborious business of choosing another pen. Finally he paid for it and put it into his pocket.

They spent some time wandering round the store, but she could see he had something on his mind. She saw him take the pen from the box and examine it. He'd decided, he said, that he'd made a mistake. Since the other pen, her first choice, had been the one she'd really wanted, he thought she should have it.

Another lengthy parley took place between him and the manager who, with a final hopeful gesture, wrapped up the box with sellotape and string before presenting it to Amy with a strained smile. They had only gone a short distance from the stationer's when Frank stopped, looking worried. He said he'd made a mistake. He said he ought to have bought her a spare nib. With difficulty she persuaded him not to go back to the shop but take her somewhere to eat instead.

Lunch passed without mishap and she was left wondering what kind of malady he had which enabled him to eat so heartily. They spent the rest of the afternoon wandering the galleries of a museum devoted to ethnic studies, deep in talk about his work.

They sat in the American gallery and she said how the first story of his that she'd read captured perfectly the immigrant's isolation. He dismissed it as juvenilia, and said it was only a sheer imitation of Dickens. She said it was dangerous to underestimate his own work; he might close off the already narrow way ahead. Selfishly she wanted him to go on writing forever. He confessed to feeling unusually optimistic – in itself a bad sign – and able to listen to her words with hardly a qualm. She looked from his long fingers to the grey hair at his temples, from the aquiline nose to the beautiful jawline, loving him deeply.

Later she mentioned money to him and he offered her all he had, saying that when he got back home he would send as much as she required. His own needs were minimal. All she had to do was wire the exact amount she wanted. She was greatly moved by the offer, but said she'd rather get out of the mess herself and not weigh him down with additional problems. If the worst came to the worst she could always play the flute in a tunnel with a hat beside her on the ground.

Slowly she was realizing the tone to adopt with him: that his inner melancholy could be pierced by an optimistic and positive manner. There was no denying that his view of the world was black. He thought himself old when he wasn't. He'd said he was very ill, but she couldn't detect any tubercular signs, unless one counted his excessive thinness. His attitude towards his own race was ambivalent to say the least, ranging from opprobrium to excessive esteem. He needed constant reminders that all could be well with the world, with his health, with his work, with his sexual life. And who else apart from her was there to handle them all?

At five-thirty in the Indian gallery, in front of a case containing several lingams, she came to the conclusion that it was she who must take the initiative from now on. Hopefully the sight of all those athletic creatures performing complicated asanas with one another might inspire him to take her back to the hotel and try again. But she found him studying a ritual flaying knife, totally ignoring the Coco-de-Mer vulva beside it. There didn't seem any further point in staying.

She led him quietly from the building into an evening

overcast but not yet raining. He showed no surprise when they reached the steps of his hotel. She took his keys from the board behind the desk and went ahead of him up the stairs. The smell was, if anything, more powerfully pungent than the day before, and overlaid with hints of curry and onions. He said it could put one off food for life.

They opened a window in his room, after a struggle. A slight breeze touched their faces, and they stood side by side looking over the asphalt and broken slates of the roof to the slate-grey sky.

'I'm tired,' she said, undressed quickly and got into bed and under the covers before he'd stopped looking at her in surprise.

'I'm so tired,' she said again. She put her arms over her head, covering her face. A few seconds, then she heard the chair creak as he sat down. Shoes were removed. She heard clothes being taken off and methodically placed over the chair. The rattle of coins falling to the floor from inverted pockets. She ventured a quick look to see what he was doing, and saw only the peaks of his narrow, white behind upraised as he knelt searching.

'Damn!' she said.

'What is it?' He was standing now, naked but apparently unashamed. She noticed one of his toes looked deformed.

'I've been bitten.' She pulled back the sheet to reveal several red marks on her thigh.

'Bed bugs, I think,' he said. 'I'm the same. I mentioned them to the landlord but he seemed to think them quite natural. Called them "Mahogany Flats", as if they were pets he'd bred himself!' He laughed and got into bed beside her.

She turned her face to him, looking into his eyes; waiting a while before touching him, then putting her hands softly round his thin wrists. Instantly the shaking began, but not so violently as the last time. She stopped until he was calmer, then took his wrists again and moved his hands over her body. Trying to forget her own need, she concentrated on quelling the fear which could so easily turn to repulsion. She ventured reassuring words, spoken so quietly they were nothing more than an accompaniment to the whisper of the breeze outside. He responded slowly to her gentleness, stroking her body, kissing her with small, dry kisses while keeping his eyes averted from hers. She held him close each time he began to tremble again, waiting for the change in his trembling by which she could know he was moving nearer to genuine fulfilment. When his climax finally came it did so, as before, in a brief, gasping rush of emotion which ended in his throwing himself away from her and putting his hands across his face. She brought the sheet up over them both, stroked his arms and shoulders until he could bear to look at her again. She tried to keep on her face an expression of peace she wasn't feeling, while she spoke in a low voice about her love for him. He asked her not to think too badly of him, and not to leave him. She said she wouldn't. She held him and waited while he slowly fell asleep in her arms, the look of an exhausted child on his face.

She stayed awake for a long time, listening to the noise of the street and the garage next door; to footsteps and raucous voices on the stairs. Now and then shrieks of female laughter came through the thin walls, and later she thought she could hear the rhythmic bounce of bedsprings. When her arm began to grow dead with his weight, she withdrew it carefully and lay huddled against the curve of his back which was brown and mottled with tiny sun burns.

It was dark by the time he stirred. He sighed heavily, then sat bolt upright as if afraid. She told him where he was and that she must leave shortly. He made no further attempts to make love to her, although she tentatively tried to encourage him.

She took her time dressing, trying to disguise her need to depart. He said he had to leave early the following morning, and she promised to be at the hotel by half past six. She was trembling slightly when she kissed him goodbye. She shut the door on him quietly and groped her way down the dark stairs wondering why she felt slightly unwell. A man sitting in the vestibule glanced at her suspiciously as she slunk past him as fast as she could. Out in the street there was the refreshing feel of light rain.

Ernest asked no questions when she arrived back home, but looked at her quizzically, saying little. While she took a bath he came and stood in the bathroom doorway looking at her soaping her breasts. She let him take the sponge from her hands and continue washing her. She stepped into the towel he held and allowed herself to be dried. Soon after she had gone to bed he followed her into the bedroom and lay down beside her. He made love to her in an intense and calculated way of which she loved every minute.

Frank was standing outside the hotel complete with luggage at his feet and trilby hat, when she arrived the next morning. He said she was late. She had put on the dress of changing greens in the hope he would remember her more clearly when he found himself back again in the grip of family. She knew she looked good. Her hair and cheeks shone. All the food she'd consumed in the last few days had made her feel fatter. All the sex she'd had had made her more aware of her body. For the first time in many months she felt truly alive and back to her old form.

Rain had given way to bleak sun which lit the streets with silver light. She liked the shining grey pavements, and the coolness of the air on her skin. It was going to be a beautiful day. They walked past the café where they'd first met. Then through the station forecourt with lines of taxis already waiting. The day seemed unnaturally silent after the week's familiar hubbub: nothing but the muted station roar sounding like the ocean above the twittering of hundreds of waking starlings roosting along the ornamental pediments of the façade.

Inside she was astonished by the number of people up and ready to travel at that hour on a Sunday. She felt a longing to join them. The stairs were crowded and the buffets beginning to fill. Frank's train was already standing at the platform, its doors wide open. People were jostling at the barrier where a flustered inspector was trying to keep order.

After attempting, and failing, to find a platform ticket, Amy stood gazing at the confusion of travellers, then gripped his arm hard.

'This is awful,' she said. 'I can't stay. You will write, won't you?'

He nodded. He looked at her with his bright, grey eyes, then bent and kissed her gently on the mouth at the exact moment she was backing away. 'Goodbye, angel.'

She walked rapidly from the barrier, not turning until she'd reached the top of the stairs. There was no sign of Frank. Thin beams of sharp sunlight in which dust danced were illuminating the scene. She thought of Piranesi.

9

'Why I should be dragged into this I don't know,' Charles said.

The fact that he was there at all, sitting opposite her at the kitchen table looking fatter than ever, with a morose expression unusual to him, meant the affair was serious. He said that Rose had pestered him every day until he'd promised to do what he could to put matters right. He said he was cross with Ernest for washing his hands of the matter, and felt that Rose was justified in asking for explanations.

'And why are you suddenly taking sides?'

'If you did but know it, Amy, I'm trying to defend your position. She's been crying to me all week about your avoiding her. That ghastly mother of hers is having fits and threatening all sorts of ridiculous things. It's serious.'

She began to remonstrate but he cut her short. 'After all, we're not talking about junk. That brooch belonged to her mother's great grandmother . . . or some such venerable person. So give it back.' His fists on the table were pink and dimpled. She thought he looked unusually well-dressed.

'I've sold it,' she said. 'So there we are! I've sold it. Now what are you going to do about it?'

She told him how Rose had given her the brooch at the outdoor table of the café.

'But it wasn't hers to give. It was her mother's.'

'Her mother gave it to her. Then it was mine. Then the man's in the Pop Shop!'

'You've gone too far this time, Amy.' As he shook his head his cheeks wobbled. His eyes looked like green buttons in an upholstery of pink fat.

'How's the sculpture business these days, Charles?'

He told her not to change the subject. He repeated Rose's warning that the family was contemplating police action. Only her father's common sense had so far averted it. 'And he's a very powerful man,' Charles added.

It dawned on her why he was there pleading Rose's cause. 'Isn't her father a councillor?'

'What's that got to do with it?' he asked crossly. 'I've never met anyone as infuriating as you, Amy!'

She persisted. 'Isn't Rose's father on the committee planning the new piazza?'

His face red with anger, he stood up. 'What a low-minded and indecent thing to say!' If she was inferring that he'd had ulterior motives in coming to see her, she could think again. He had no need of patronage, since his work was in constant demand. At that very moment he could be working on a commission. She asked what had happened to the jolly friend who always took life so casually. Life wasn't such a great game. If she'd been thinking ahead for a change on the day she'd taken the brooch, she might have realized the consequences. Taking it was folly enough. Selling it was sheer stupidity.

She asked him how she was supposed to pay Ernest's debts without selling it, and he said he'd have let him stew in his own juice. 'Besides,' he said, looking at her malevolently, 'what's wrong with him taking a bit more from that high falutin' lady of his? Her husband can afford it!'

She felt her face flushing. She said what Ernest did was no-one's affair but his own.

'You can say that now you've got somebody else to think about!' He read the question in her face: 'Ernest told me about you and Frank. Good old loyal Ernest!'

'And what were you talking about that brought on this telling of tales?'

'If you must know, I was defending you as usual. Told him you weren't a thief, and so on. That's when he told me about Frank. Know what he said? He said, "So you can

193

stop all this concern about my wife. She's capable of lots more than you can imagine." By that he meant stealing brooches as well.'

She put her head back and laughed. 'Charles, you're a dreadful hypocrite. You've been trying to take Ernest's place for ages!'

'If that's how you see my friendship, Amy, then it's no wonder you're in trouble.' His expression was dignified and hurt. 'I shall tell Rose what you've said and wash my hands of the rest.' His face became sad. 'The funny thing is that when Jasmine told me how unscrupulous you were, I wouldn't believe her.'

'You *have* been busy, Charles. I wonder you find time to work!'

Saying no more he left instantly, cracking the front door behind him. Her regret was instantaneous, but quickly forgotten as she went back to more absorbing matters.

Charles had interrupted her reply to Frank. The journey, he wrote, had been difficult and exhausting. He'd seen the Girl and explained the position concerning marriage. He'd also told Leon. She stared at the words, not knowing whether to be pleased or dismayed. Their love affair was becoming common property. Leon now knew. And, of course, the Girl. She could see the scene, and felt all the pity Frank had felt when the Girl told him she couldn't leave him unless he sent her away. He'd agreed that she could send Amy a letter, for which he was preparing the way.

Furiously she replied that it would have been better if he hadn't involved her. Then she tore up the letter and wrote a reassuring one to allay all doubt that she could handle whatever the Girl might say to her. She pondered a long time over a strange note at the foot of the page in which he remarked that he couldn't find his way between two facts: her illness, and when she'd told him the battle over the anteroom couldn't last very long. So he'd remembered something she'd said in passing, idly chattering

194

away not even sure he'd been listening. He'd probably heard and taken seriously every word she'd uttered. And she and Ernest were still sharing her bed.

She took what she thought was the wisest course of ignoring the footnote, keeping his mind occupied with talk of the book he'd promised to send, the letter to his father which hadn't arrived yet, and Conrad's imminent visit to him. Her head had begun to ache. Too many people making demands on her. Ernest claiming he was going down with yet another unspecified illness which he said was interfering with his work on reform of the monetary system. And Mrs Kertesch wanting rent. And Fox sending work she didn't want to do because she couldn't get excited about alpine flowers.

Milena stared at her from the canvas and mouthed a few words about getting down to the business of painting the yellow gentian. She looked at the text resentfully. Who was Oswald Heer who originated the term *Schneethälchen* for small hollows and northern slopes where the snow lasted a long time and where the ground was saturated with ice-cold water? Milena shut her lips tightly, taking on the determined expression of someone who knows she can negotiate a dangerous descent.

The sunlight is bright and she can see only by narrowing her eyes against the glare. She wishes she was wearing goggles like her father. But she'll manage: her boots are good, and she's been on skis since she was able to walk. The only time that *Tata* is bearable is when he's beside her on the run shouting instructions to her as she begins her twentieth downhill rush. The snow is the only thing they love to share. They can happily spend all day out in it together, for it lubricates the friction. Back at the hotel he spoils it all by lecturing her on lack of control. He tells her she may stay up until nine, and further tells her not to mix with undesirables, especially those who look foreign.

She lifted the panel and held it away from her. There were gaps like snow valleys everywhere. In them might go the remnants of Milena's pre-war happiness: a view here of the Prater, complete with swing-boat man; the faces of cheerful friends; there a line or two from an article about the unbridgeable gap between Czech and German. But later would be soon enough. She laid the canvas face uppermost against the far wall and stood staring between the diagonals of the easel at the cluttered desk beyond. Now she had to look outward from her own small problems to those of her country. So much work to do in the space of a day. Lover and daughter had to be left to fend for each other while she went to see for herself what was happening between Czech and German, and to write about it as honestly as she could. Constant travelling while Henlein gained power in the North and Masaryk looked helplessly on pleading democracy. Optimism foundering on the knowledge that after Chamberlain's second meeting with Hitler on 22 September 1938, the Sudetenland was lost.

Too many photographs in piles on the desk, too many pictures of upraised arms with swastika bands and faces turned adoringly to the high podium of power: Speer's monumental monstrosity. The scudding clouds sped swiftly past her eyes, leaving only the huge circular swastika. Rows of troops marching: marching first into Austria, then into Bohemia, Silesia and Moravia. Photos of ardent citizens welcoming the invader with salutes, flags on sticks and flowers. Cut round the outline of a Nazi soldier, leg outstretched in classic goosestep, gun held rigidly across the shoulder. Trace him on stencil card, cut him out and clone him. All round the borders of the virgin canvas a frame of strutting military men coming in their thousands behind the tanks. The tanks arriving when the ink on the non-aggression pacts was hardly dry. And the refugees. She riffled slowly through a second pile, looking for them in the dust and finding them too easily. Where the lines of soldiers stopped there began the lines of pathetic families on the move, their wake littered with discarded furniture, utensils, clothes and toys they no longer had the will to carry. And they were fleeing to only temporary asylum which in a few months would be no more.

In her flat in Prague a huddle of Czech officers and air-men hid and waited to be smuggled out, while she wrote about Jewish refugees left waiting on the Polish borders in No-Man's-Land. Whatever else there was to do she had to make sure the people were informed. To inform she had to know. To know she had to find out for herself, and to do that she had to forget about fear.

A cigarette to slow down the marching feet and halt the fear. Long and steady inhalations to calm the nerves, while she writes a reply worthy of a country about to be invaded. It is February 1939. She is answering a German Nazi who claims the right to be a National Socialist, and sees the rebirth of the Czech soul as an urgent necessity. Rebirth, she writes, can only take place organically. She tells him her nation is a bridge between no-one but themselves, never so ambitious as to think of things like *Lebensraum*; content to breathe its own air and cultivate its own land. But she knows – being a realist – that her country can only submit. The conqueror mistakes subservience for defeat and forgets who gave birth to a certain Good Soldier. And no-one comes to arrest her yet.

In four weeks' time she will go into the early morning streets of Prague to witness the arrival of Hitler's army. Afterwards she will write that although the people were profoundly silent, no-one gathered in the streets to talk, or raised their heads from their desks. On the pavements nobody turned to look. Only the German population welcomed the army of the Third Reich. On the grave of the Unknown Soldier that day was found a mound of lilies of the valley.

And time kept standing still. Twice she wondered why the scissors weren't moving in her hand, and twice she'd gone to the sitting room to check the clock. An hour later she'd gone back again to find the clock hands had only moved a few minutes. Taking a random handful of cuttings with her she sank onto the sofa, putting her head back with a sigh of relief. Then she opened her closed fingers and risked a glimpse at what she'd grabbed.

On one side the man in the dark overcoat and the wing collar waving a piece of paper at a hopeful crowd. On the other, the mutilated report of a man who had hacked his wife to pieces for reasons off the page. She turned each cutting over to see what was on the back. People winning races; buying and selling; getting born and getting married, and some of them hacking at their wives and cousins. Advertisements for corsets and tooth powder and motor cars: mysterious, captionless scenes taking place in printers' fog. And all the scraps of newspaper crumpled and folded with age and maltreatment. Like that they ought to go into the second panel, stuck at random with their edges overlapping or torn, demonstrating how, until the very direst of events intrudes, people go on living their unplanned, random lives. Only a few possessed the foresight to know what might be coming, and they had to stay in order to help when needed.

She knew Ernest needed her. He'd said so time and again. Now part of her said go to Frank, and part said, stay with Ernest and have his child.

Her next letter came from the guilt she felt at the sight of Ernest powerless. He wasn't used to being the victim, he'd had no training . . .

I feel that you and I have betrayed him. Up in the forest I tried to explain how much he relies on me. I know it even though things might appear to the contrary. And others (those who might mention him to you) are wrong, or misguided in their opinions. You know things are never as they seem. And you're an old friend of his. Frightful things go through my mind of what we might be doing to him. The appearance of strength is no more than a veneer. If he is shattered by us, and I think he will be if he knows how deep our feelings are, then we will be responsible. And you are his friend. He is burdened with worries. Anyone can see that these problems take up all the time not given to women and recreation!

198

Forgive the unnecessary irony Frank, for aren't we . . . am *I* not behaving in exactly the same way he is? All my time is taken up with thoughts of you, your work, your health. The two of us then, the pain of three of us now – *torture à trois, à deux* – the weight of what we are doing. It has happened to others before, I know. Histories to make one shudder. The man who hacked his wife to pieces, then his cousin, and had the corpses disappear in some way. I'm afraid of what is to become of us. You and me. Me and Ernest. You and the Girl. I wait for her letter with trepidation. Yet I feel that whatever we plan, we must for the moment decide to keep silent. Please, Frank. He isn't strong enough yet. Neither am I.

She wasn't strong at all. She gravitated between sleeping too lightly, and bouts of drugged unconsciousness from which she dragged herself as if from the ocean. The old pattern. And now here they were, falling into another old pattern by following letter with letter, one countering the other; postcards proclaiming deepest love, followed by regret and uncertainty. There were telegrams sent to quiet his fears that she'd deserted him, or taken offence that he'd allowed the Girl to write.

He said he was in his sister's flat for a while, since an uncle from Paris was staying at his parents'. It meant he was alone – time and again he returned to this need to live alone – yet at once came the qualification that he meant it to be only temporary.

He contrasted his quiet apartment with those communal ones where in every corner illicit affairs, improper, accidental things occurred, illegitimate children were begotten: there was noise, lechery, the incest of the dissolute, uncontrolled bodies, thoughts and desires . . . he positively wallowed in the words as if he'd forgotten he was speaking to someone other than himself. She could still feel his trembling beside her.

Letter after letter, each giving her something to ponder over or be frightened by. The Girl's letter a pathetic thing of pleading and hidden threats, to which she didn't know how to reply. What could one say to someone who supposes she is the centre of a simple problem about whom to marry?

Complications were coming so thick and fast, she didn't know which one to dodge next. Stacey and her husband were both coming to see her – or so they'd told Frank – and wanted to have the whole thing out with Ernest. Conrad had been pumped surreptitiously by Frank for facts concerning her, but had spoken mostly about his imminent wedding. Then there was Leon who no doubt was putting in an adverse word or two. There was the puzzling state of Frank's health, with the doctor saying the disease hadn't cleared, and threatening him with injections.

At home her energies were being forced into thinking more about Ernest whose complaints about illness were growing louder.

He said the office was wearing him out. He had pains in his back and his legs felt weak. Discussions were wavering about a transfer, but he was coming more and more to the conclusion that he ought to get away from all the aggravation.

'No wonder I feel ill,' he said.

One night he was sick and complained of feeling feverish. The spots appeared later and put him in a panic. He knew he had chicken-pox. The doctor confirmed his diagnosis and told him he'd live if he went to bed, quelled his hysteria and changed his eating habits. It was decided he should sleep in the anteroom again to prevent Amy catching the disease. He made a great fuss about his installation, insisting that Milena be removed to the sitting room along with paints, brushes and all the paraphernalia of her short life. From the sofa bed, propped up by pillows and surrounded by books he began immediately issuing instructions and making plaintive pleas while Amy ran here and there, complying.

The worst of it was the lack of time in which to think. Frank was writing again about fear, and his obvious anguish couldn't be ignored. Only when she got to bed at night after running around all day for Ernest, could she find a small moment to concentrate on her own pressing problems.

First, there was the letter from the Girl to be answered. Amy felt she had to lie. She wrote that Frank had neither written nor spoken of her, and therefore her fears about this were unjustified. The answer looked a miserable thing without hope or comfort, but she sent it, glad to have found the courage to face up to at least part of the trouble that was Frank.

For the first time she seriously considered the fact that he might be really ill. What had frightened her was what he'd written about diseases of the lung being usually the most amiable of all, reminding her of those times when he'd talked about extracting from the disease the most sweetness possible.

She wrote a hasty panic-stricken note to Leon asking for information about the real state of Frank's health. To Frank she could only say that the best thing for the time being was to wait. She told him he was outside all blame in the matter, being essentially a person who had no idea about such things as duplicity and adultery. What caused self-torture and sleeplessness was the thought that she herself might really be the cause of all the suffering. The only small ray of hope was that she might be Frank's saviour in the matter of his fear . . .

For what is this fear of yours? Is it something so beautiful to you that you must hug it close? One can see that. And see the necessity. Without it one is naked and cannot look into the future at all. With it the future (of a kind) becomes possible again. I know this. Yet dear Frank – and I must hold you while I say this, for you mustn't misunderstand me – this fear is not of ultimate value since its loss (or casting off) would still leave you whole. Now don't laugh. We're all falling to pieces aren't we? You are not the only privileged person!

Ernest received several visitors during his weeks in bed, none of whom seemed afraid of catching the disease, except Irwin who, on his first visit, stood firmly in the hall with his head round the anteroom door carrying on a conversation about Wittgenstein's *Tractatus Logico-Philosophicus*. He consistently refused to receive anything from Ernest's hands before it had been baked for ten minutes in the oven. Once he closeted himself in the kitchen with Amy, giving her the benefit of his opinion on wives who deserted their husbands for the sake of writers of expressionist rubbish.

Paul, too, chose to call; he said he'd heard it from Charles who'd heard it from Rose that her mother was definitely going to prefer charges for theft. Privately he told Amy she might be in need of legal advice. He asked her why she'd written such an undiplomatic letter to Rose's mother, thus making it almost certain there'd be a court case. She said she knew nothing about it, and he must have got his facts wrong; somebody must be lying.

But how could she think about trivialities when there was so little time to think about herself and Frank? One crisis had been averted by replying promptly to Stacey, thanking her and Jay for their thoughtfulness. But Ernest was ill with chicken-pox. So she must reluctantly give up the idea of seeing her friends for some time. She enclosed an old photograph of herself, begging Stacey to show it to Frank as proof of her continued existence.

Still he wrote about fear, telling her how she was right in thinking it had been the root cause of their problems during the four days. He didn't know its inner laws, but he knew that if she'd been completely convinced by him she would no longer be with Ernest. Not that he needed proof for her, he said, for she was beyond everything clear and safe for him. But it would have been proof for himself, and that he lacked. On this, he wrote, fear occasionally fed.

He was accusing her obliquely of not loving him. But hadn't she explained that she loved Ernest too, especially Ernest helpless in bed with whole galaxies of suppurating spots? The only practical thing to do at the moment was to see that he got well. Emotions were another matter, like wind-socks changing course a dozen times a day.

Why had it never occurred to her before that for the twenty-four years of her life she had always been in thrall to a man? Now, having said she couldn't, for the time being, go to Frank, and having asked him in vain to come to her, she had begun to see herself in a different light: not in harness with any man, but individual and free.

Yet there was still her father trying to control her from a distance with threats and I-told-you-so's. She knew his power. Hadn't he once confined her to a mental institution? The fight with him was still on, and because of it she knew she hadn't freed herself yet. What she most needed was time to herself away from all of them.

She wrote to Frank of a plan in which she'd leave Ernest when he'd recovered, and spend perhaps six months on her own, trying to put her life into focus.

Meanwhile Ernest, in bed under a coverlet of papers, files and books, issued his instructions unaware of this subtle change in her. Visitors were constantly arriving; many of those who came to see Ernest she'd barely glimpsed before, except from the café door. Some treated her like strangers, eyeing her with curiosity as if they'd heard something detrimental about her which they were keeping to themselves. They came and shut the anteroom door behind them until it was time for departure. Often she heard raised voices and laughter coming from inside while, banished to the sitting room, she struggled to concentrate on the Scrophulariaceae, and grappled with Lousewort both leafy and beaked. In the kitchen she battled with intransigent objects requiring transformation into edibility. Fish stared at her from the paper, defying her to gut them. Lappets of liver, cushions of brains came under her quivering hand. She ran for advice to Mrs Kertesch on how to cope with kidneys, or convert calves' feet into jelly. Ernest's taste for invalid food was insatiable; he wanted *lockshen* soup, and soup with *knaidlach*, and *blintzes* he couldn't eat because they hurt his mouth. He was constantly saying how weak he felt, but she supposed it was part of his plan to stop her leaving. Looking at her the doctor said she too should do her best to spare herself, suggesting she might later try to take a few days away from home. Since the only place to go she could think of, was into the arms of Frank, she wrote that she might, after all, be coming to visit him soon.

His reply shocked her again into the realization that he was still waiting for her to commit herself entirely to him. He told her he felt like asking her not to come but to leave him the hope that if he really needed her urgently she would drop everything for him. If she came in the manner she suggested, she would only have to leave again.

OF COURSE I'D COME AT ONCE. HOW COULD YOU DOUBT IT? was the telegram she sent, followed by letters in which she mentioned Ernest only in passing, and asked if there was any news of the Girl. He replied that the Girl had sent him Amy's reply complete with underlinings, and that like all letters covered with pencil marks, it had its defects. He spoke about Conrad; about Stacey and Jay who'd shown him a plan of her apartment. He sent thanks for the photo and told her she looked like a girl soon to come out of the convent.

He sent her flowers through Mrs Kertesch who shook her head saying they were serious things, but there was no nourishment in them. Quickly she sent him a telegram of thanks and followed it with a letter . . .

Fancy thinking to placate me with flowers! When they arrived I heard those tiny alarm bells begin to ring, saying 'Does he love you?' And when they're my favourites I have to send telegrams saying 'thank you' quickly, before the awareness of the unanswered question rises again. How many problems you always give me, Frank.

At night, sitting alone in the big bed among the night shadows, she wrote of the solitariness of her life. So much for the 'great household' of which he'd written and which consisted simply of a place not to eat in, not to sleep in and not to work in, while she spent her free moments talking to him, thinking of him, reading the books he liked and answering his questions to the best of her ability.

Like him she felt that their treatment of the Girl could have been kinder, for she could see how her whole life had been shattered. But when she considered – as in saner moments she could – the size of the universe compared to the puny scale of their little world, she thought the matter quite slight. Nonetheless she still felt the pain of accusations unjustly made, especially since there were other, closer people who were accusing her.

She refrained from telling Frank yet of the brooch. Paul had called to say that a solicitor had been briefed by Rose's mother. Ernest was starting to fret that his name might be mentioned in connection with theft. He was also hearing from various visitors that they'd received letters from Amy accusing them of spreading lies about her.

And he was getting better. He was becoming more critical. He wanted the house cleaner, saying that even a speck of dust got on his chest. When she came to sit beside him to talk he said she ought to be at her desk. When she tried to apply herself to work, she would find him standing at the door in his dressing gown complaining of being neglected. They would make plans to go to Paris where he'd study and write, and she'd forget all about someone unworthy of her. In the next breath he'd compare himself unfavourably with Frank, saying he'd never disliked him; his only fault, as far as he could see, was trying to take someone's wife away from him.

When things were quieter she went in search of future work, calling first on Laurie. Her reception was cool, but when she'd sworn on Mona's head that she'd written no letter to him, they made their peace and he hugged her. He told her she was looking bad and said he'd never believed the handwriting was hers anyway. But whoever's it was, they certainly wished her ill. He gave her two illustrations to do, with the plea that she should finish them before she actually faded away.

To Fox she delivered what she'd done of the alpine work, promising the rest as soon as possible. He said mountaineering always took a lot of effort. He gave her a vignette to draw for one of Frank's stories, wondering whether she was able to do it in her present condition. Could she put her mind to the problem of depicting a trapeze artist seen from far below? He wanted such an effect of distancing that she might be miles beneath him. She said she knew the condition only too well. The sight of Fox's bright and intelligent face made her want to tell him other things, for which he seemed to be waiting. He looked at her for a long time in silence and she tried to formulate a way to begin. But he stood up suddenly before she had got the words right. His height took him away from her and she finally said nothing.

At night when hash smoke went curling into her thoughts, then she could envisage a possible future with Frank without fearing sexual frustration. He cared for her more in the way a brother would have cared, and like a brother's, his love would last. When her body was quiet she could so easily contemplate that miserable half hour in bed in that miserable hotel as nothing more than men's business – something that happened from time to time when two bodies weren't in tune. He couldn't always be that way, loving her as he did.

If there was any fault in him at all it lay in his dedication to what he saw as truth. He was so uncompromisingly honest, so sensitive. The task of weaning him away from this rarified existence lay with her. But she was afraid. Who was to know how much of his writing stemmed from this source? And how much from his giving in to an illness which – if Leon were to be believed – had reached a really serious stage? Time and again he seemed to escape from her and her life of simple love and simple jealousy back into those regions of which she knew so little.

On nights when she trembled like Frank on the brink of indefinable fears, she appeared at Ernest's door, saying she was the ghost of Happiness Past come to give him his sustenance. Sometimes he refused the proffered box and told her to go back and keep her own nightmares company. At others he invited her to bed, took the box and the blade and chopped at the white powder like a demon. Its effect was always instantaneously good, bringing her straight back into excitement, Ernest into high good humour, and both of them into the old, overwhelming need for each other. The smell, the feel of him. The being drawn into the most ancient, most potent of all magic through the simple spell of happy dust. The hearing him saying again that she was the most desirable woman in the world. The living goddess of creation. Hearing his words as if she'd never known them, or never lost them. Listening to him telling her his need. Telling him her love; the colour of her passion. Inventing a language to match the rhythm of their heart-beats and their twinning. The jumble of their crazy talk lost in each other's mouths. His tongue probing her mouth, his lips moving over her chin, her cheeks. His breath on her eyelids: her closed eyes seeing heaven bands. His arms and legs enfolding her so close they were coupled on an Indian temple wall, fused together in flaking stone. Shapes in sinuous motion, constantly changing, now breast to breast, now mouth to mouth; their bodies fitting exactly into one another's curves and hollows. They would weld and never separate, for she was the female principle spreading out space, time and universe before her partner. In his open mouth she saw straight into the continuing act of creation; yoni and seed with no magnitude: all different phases of the creative process existing at once, beyond the flow of time. She was the power holder, breaking all his bonds save those with herself. And she could never lose him. They were Shiva and Shakti lost beyond Time together. Through *Canchala* and *Sukhapadma* their furious energies combined bringing them to that wild climax that was always the same and never the same.

And not until the cocaine's effect had worn off did they

plunge into sleep, their exhausted bodies so totally immobilized by their exertions that they lay where the last contortions had thrown them. Waking just before dawn she would extricate herself from his slippery limbs to search for the precious powder, and rouse him from sleep to begin the ritual again. Often she failed to wake him, or he begged for reprieve, accusing her of trying to kill him with kindness. Then she carried the paraphernalia back to the big bed in the shadowy room, to sit like a miser huddled over gold, chopping and scraping the shining grains into One and One. Nobody but herself then to experience the rush and freeze, to see her smile at the gift of exhilarating energy, the fantastic ability to think great thoughts and do whatever she wanted.

Her surges of energy burned themselves up in letters to Frank of purest love, in which she tried to share with him the experience of feeling totally at one with someone. To the distant would-be lover she transmitted words never murmured to the sleeping husband, which she knew would be remembered longer than one wild night. She pleaded with him to forget his office duties and lie to them. Her need was greater.

Ernest found Frank's letters a week later while he was clearing the anteroom prior to quitting it. He came into the sitting room carrying them. He was dressed for going out. He held out the bundle with a slight raising of the eyebrows and a 'Might these be yours?' look on his face.

She nodded and took them and went back to drawing arnica.

'I suppose there are more?' Ernest said.

'There will be. He writes every day. And I write to him.'

'Very touching!'

'I'll take them with me when I go.'

'By the look of you, you'll not get very far!' He went to the sideboard and began to search in the drawer. He looked hunched and pale. She noticed his collar seemed too large.

'What's the matter, Ernest?'

'Nothing to concern you.' He put some money in his jacket pocket. 'I'm off to the doctor. Mightn't be a bad idea if you came too.'

She knew he was right. Knew all the signs. She was a downhill racer. 'I'm fine,' she said.

He shrugged but persisted. 'I'll ask him to call,' he said. 'Wouldn't do for us both to go under.'

When he left she sat staring at the letters. Frank had turned away from her as much as she'd turned from him. And he'd done it with three words: 'I can't come'. With another three he'd made certain of their separation: 'I can't lie'. He couldn't lie because he wasn't unfairly treated at work, and because the office was to him a living person who looked at him with innocent eyes.

So what did it matter what she wrote? All the effort, all the trying to be cheerful and seem normal. What did it matter if she sent him books and papers; that she'd bothered to comment on Leon's latest book? Nothing mattered. She'd told him she was ill. Why not, since he spoke so much about his own health, and Leon had confirmed again that his friend needed to go to a sanatorium if he was to be cured at all?

Among the alpine flowers lay her half-written letter to Leon, saying how alarmed she was at his news, and begging him not to think badly of her. Slowly she put the pen to the page again and began to explain how she thought Frank got something good from her. That was the greatest happiness. She said she'd come to see him in the autumn if there was no other way, and they'd send him to the sanatorium together. She said the story of her marriage was too complicated for her to tell then: all she could say to this stranger was that she couldn't leave yet, perhaps not at all. But she was always looking for a way out that was both good and right. What was more important than anything else in the world was that Frank shouldn't suffer.

Her mind wandered. To keep a hold on such distant events was like trying to grasp the beams of light in front of her. They lit her and warmed her, then clouds came and they were gone, leaving her staring at a page of meaningless words and a half-finished golden flower supposed to cure bruising.

She heard the knock on the door but didn't answer it. Later she found a note lying in the hall. It was from Paul. He had arranged a meeting with Rose's mother – just herself and Amy. She would be at the house at three o'clock on Friday. 'Be very calm,' he'd written. She smiled to herself, holding the letter gingerly as if it were alight.

10

It all seemed so far away; sky with scudding clouds, grey roofs of houses thinning out to where the green began. Cloud shadows speeding over playing fields and undulating across broad bands of trees in thick summer foliage. The long avenues and the chestnut trees, their blossom turned brown. The grid system of a not-so-radiant city in which one could lose one's way. Walking had taken a long time and much of her energy. She was on the outer edges of the suburbs going along a road she dimly knew, past high walls and fences surrounding enormous gardens, enclosing houses built like fortresses. So this was Rose land. At the end of the last avenue she saw the park; the dark clumps of trees up where the road wound out of sight, the single roof visible, the tea room where she and Frank had sat. She was in the same road she'd been along on a spring evening several million years ago. Her wrist had healed, leaving a thin white scar.

The walls of Rose's house were as high, the iron gate as massive as the one she'd entered the last time she was here. When she rang the bell it sounded deep and far off, but the gate opened on its own and let her in. The same gravel drive and ornamental urns bordering acres of razored lawn. The house startlingly white stucco, pseudo-Greek columns and pediment around the purple front door. This too opened as if by magic, revealing a grey-haired woman in an overall. Her eyes flickered quickly over Amy's paint-stained blouse and skirt before she stood back to let her in. She led the way across parquet reflecting darkly the violet of the walls, opened another door at the back and nodded sharply for

Amy to enter. The door was closed, leaving her standing in a room like a public library; books from floor to ceiling, the same parquet floor with rugs shining silkily in the light from tall windows hung with velvet swags. A leather-covered desk, brass lamp and pen set which looked as if they'd never been used. Outside a tiled patio, white iron chairs, the edge of a striped umbrella leaning inward to block the view of a lawn and cypresses set like soldiers. She saw the back view of a man in overalls busy hammering at a fence post over on the edge of the grass where magnolias lit the sky.

'At least you're on time.' Rose's mother appeared in the doorway and walked towards her. She looked smaller and more fragile than Amy remembered. The cream dress made the blonde hair look faded, the hair made the face look grey, or what could be seen of it around the dark glasses she was wearing. 'You know who I am,' she said. The red lips parted in a non-smile, revealing the finest of dental work. She neither held out her hand nor offered Amy a seat on one of the precarious looking chairs set in a row against one wall. Her fingers went up to her neck and fiddled with the rows of gold chains which did little to disguise the wattling. 'We'd better get down to business,' she said.

She went over to the desk and sat behind it, the high back of the leather chair dwarfing her. Amy stood saying nothing.

'First of all, I'd like to hear from your own lips what you have done with the brooch you took from my daughter. Then I'd like to know what you are going to do about its return.' She was already plucking at the edges of the leather blotter, the long red nails tapping crescents into the soft paper. 'Because if you can't produce the brooch I'm afraid you're in for a great deal of trouble.'

Amy wondered whether it was an opportune moment to faint, decided against it and, feeling slightly dizzy, went and sat on one of the chairs against the wall. Rose's mother stared and waited for a reply. When none came she began to explain what might happen after the solicitor's letter had been sent, including all the adverse publicity leading up to, and resulting from, a court case. She said she knew Amy wouldn't want to harm her growing reputation. What most amazed and horrified her was that someone with such obvious earning power should take what wasn't hers. She thought that Amy's husband, whose position at the bank surely depended upon complete honesty, might soon find himself in difficulties.

It was clear that she was just getting into her verbal stride. Her voice rose as she continued speaking, sentences rushing out with such speed that some she never completed, while her fingers continued to destroy the desk blotter. She said her daughter was sensitive and truthful, unable to cope with the present situation because of the treachery of her friend. She wasn't used to being let down. They were a close-knit family who stood by one another and never kept things secret. They were concerned over what was theirs and – this repeated several times – given to seeing justice done. She was in the middle of saying how much she deplored Amy's temerity in writing to her, when the front door slammed with a bang.

She started as if she had been hit, scrambled to her feet with a small cry and rushed to the door. Amy saw the flutter of her skirt and the flash of gold shoes as she wrested the door open as if her life depended on it.

'Is that you?' she called in a querulous voice. Footsteps approached. 'You must speak to her, Eric. She won't say anything. Nothing at all! I can't get her to say anything . . .'

The open door swung inward, revealing Rose's mother standing looking up at her invisible husband. His hands were on her shoulders – white cuffs, dark grey sleeves. He pushed her backwards into the room, keeping his hands on her shoulders. Amy saw the white shirt, the handsome, tanned face and prematurely grey hair. His wife let out a burble of sound, pleading with him not to leave her but to stay and sort things out. He put his arm around her, bent his head and said a few quiet words in her ear. Having calmed her sufficiently to release her, he came over to Amy with outstretched hand and introduced himself.

'We've met before,' Amy said. He chose not to acknowledge the statement.

His wife had removed her sunglasses, revealing a face puckered with nervous concern. She looked at her husband with a mixture of fear and vexation, then at Amy, her look changing to one of suspicion.

He turned to her and smiled brilliantly. 'This can be sorted out quite peaceably, I think, without any histrionics.' He shot her a look of warning as her mouth opened to speak, and took a single step towards her. She flinched as if he'd struck her, then she stood her ground.

'Not this time,' she said in a high voice. 'You promised, Eric. You've got to stay. Do you hear? You owe it to me. And Rose.' The corners of her mouth were twitching.

'I have no intention of leaving it to you.' His voice was low and placatory. 'Why do you think I'm here?'

'Because you had no choice.' The reply was defiant, and Amy knew that her presence had momentarily been forgotten. 'And you're to stay while we have it out!'

His face flushed but he kept his voice quiet. 'I'd be very grateful if you'd leave us, Joanna.'

Startled by his peremptory tone she took a step towards the door. He walked over to it and held it wide while she decided what to do. She hesitated. He rattled the door handle slightly and looked at his wife coldly. As she left he helped her through the doorway with a light push at her waist. Her last words as he closed the door on her were, 'Be sure to be firm with her, Eric.'

Amy sat silently waiting.

He stood without speaking for a moment, looking at her. Her face felt expressionless. She was watching something in which she had no part. She could hear the sounds of hammering coming from a long way off.

'Now what?' he said at last.

'I've sold it.' It was curious how few feelings she had about the matter.

He made certain the door was firmly shut, then came towards her smiling warmly and watching her intently. 'So I've heard. Never mind. She'll get another like it in due course.' By the time he'd reached her he had lowered his voice to a near whisper. 'If not like it, at least of equal value.'

'I thought it was beyond price,' Amy said, the man's behaviour of more interest to her than the brooch.

He put a finger to his lips, stood up straight and looked around. 'This is my so-called study. Sinister, isn't it?' His smile was charming. 'So let's find somewhere more appealing.'

He went over to one of the tall windows, struggled with several catches and opened the lower half. 'Shall we?' He indicated that they should step outside.

They went through the window and out onto the patio, his hand under her elbow. He set two chairs side by side, carefully avoiding scraping them on the stone. 'Doors have ears!' he said with another smile.

When they were seated Amy said again, 'I thought it was priceless.'

'So will the next one be. A compensatory gift from you!' His smile was so openly cynical that Amy felt a wave of sympathy for the absent wife probably crouching outside the door in the hall.

'Why isn't Rose here? She wouldn't lie in front of me.'

'Rose is a little like her mother. She is spontaneously generous, but erratic at remembering afterwards. Naturally she can't face you.' He gazed into the distance. 'Now she says you took it off the table . . .'

'That's true. She ran to meet you. Don't you remember that day? But when I shouted after her that she'd left it, she called to me to keep it.'

He raised his hand as if to quieten her. 'Exactly. But I've had enough trouble with that day already.' He drew his chair closer, so close that she was looking straight into his eyes. They were bloodshot. 'I'm sure you understand . . . ?'

She said nothing.

'Now I'm personally quite ready to believe that it was a gift. And, frankly, Rose can't remember exactly what happened. Unfortunately she said something different to her mother. You can understand why. And once my wife gets something into her head, well . . .' He smiled, showing a set of pure white teeth. 'She has a very strong will, my wife. And that includes trying to impose it on the rest of the family . . .'

He was still watching her closely. 'None of us is safe.' He sat back and crossed his legs and put his hands in his lap. Silence settled again as he studied his rings.

Then, looking over the grey garden he said, 'She labours under the burden of certain . . . delusions. One of them is that people are always trying to steal things from her, such as jewellery . . . husbands . . . and the like!' His half-closed eyes were small and intense. He was waiting. She looked at him and presumed he was mistaking her numb silence for deep thought. The only thought that came was that he was on the borders of old age, when the face slips from interesting lines to sagging features and flabby skin. She could think of nothing to say.

'The reason I'm speaking to you like this is because you artists are broadminded.' His voice had become business-like. 'This is strictly between us, you understand, but I knew instinctively I could depend on your silence. That's why I ran the risk of leaving it so long before coming to the rescue!' Amy wondered whom he was rescuing. 'As I said,' he went on, 'I needed a little time to make the necessary financial arrangements to buy an equivalent brooch.' He sat up and put his hand into his pocket, bringing out a small box. 'I have it here . . .' He began to remove the lid.

'I don't want to see it,' she said quickly.

He closed it again. 'Well, be that as it may, this will be given to Joanna when you've gone. It goes without saying

216

that it will be a gift from you. That has been the purpose of your visit.' He stared at her hard, not certain if she was comprehending. 'There will be a few . . . difficulties, but she'll come round in the end. And we can call the matter closed.'

She felt mild anger rising but all she could manage to say was, 'I didn't steal it. And I sold it because it was mine. That's all. How you sort it out is your affair.'

'Good!' He stood up as if the meeting were at an end. They were side by side when he looked down at her with the same brilliant smile. 'You have lovely blue eyes, my dear, which look honest to me.' He bent and whispered into her hair, 'And lips which I am sure don't know how to lie. Or tell tales.' He stepped away from her. 'I can depend on them to keep silent.'

She got up, feeling desperately tired. She said she thought she ought to go. He suggested it might be better if she left the house by the back way, and she thankfully agreed.

They walked across the patio, he holding her arm and saying in a low voice how hard it was to keep the balance between an adoring daughter and a possessive wife. He helped her down terrace steps and along the side of the house, through ornamental arches, across the wide lawn and onto the front drive. He said that when she saw Rose again she must remember how much she loved her father. She saw him last at the front door, fiddling in his pockets for his key.

Outside, looking back, she thought she saw Rose's face peering out from an upstairs window.

On the way home she called at the post office, rather out of habit than the wish to find a letter there. She felt vaguely sick, and in urgent need of bed.

Frank's letter contained money she hadn't asked for, but few words. He asked about pills. What pills? He mentioned headaches. Her head was aching so badly she couldn't remember what she'd told him about them. All the letters flowing into one another in her mind – a positive life history.

Or not so much flowing as zig-zagging up and down like a temperature chart moving towards some fearful climax. But what if the climax, when it came, was nothing more than a return to their first cool and formal way of corresponding? There were times when she herself (supposedly the strong one) couldn't stand the strain of this relationship that slipped so strangely from the intellectual to the passionate and back again.

She went to bed with the curtains drawn, and lay wincing at street sounds and the shouts of the Italians upstairs. Pain killers did little to bring on sleep, only sending her into sad reveries. There were all-too-clear indications that her symptoms were identical with Frank's: the cough, the tendency to spit blood. The dictionary spoke about cold perspiration and night sweats and regular rises in temperature. She had them all. And didn't her temperature fall below normal early every morning? Frank was constantly writing about headaches. One could positively wallow in ill health. But there flickered at the back of her mind that in reality she was a survivor, whatever she may have written to Frank about wanting to die, and the situation nearing its end. Who didn't want to die at three o'clock in the morning when one was reeling dizzily to bed, coughing and groaning and swearing not to touch another grain?

When she woke Ernest was standing over her. She heard him say, 'Possible lesions . . .' and sat bolt upright. He was talking about being ill. She couldn't bear it. When he said something about falls in arterial oxygen she thought he was speaking of Frank. But he was telling her that his lung had been affected by chicken-pox. She noted how cheerful he seemed and thought of the joke about the hypochondriac's gravestone on which were engraved the words, 'Now do you believe me?' He then calmed her worst fears by saying that he'd have to have occasional oxygen therapy, be off work a lot longer, but not be confined to bed. Her headache had disappeared.

Feeling slightly better, she was able to speak about the

brooch. Without going into details she said merely that Rose's father had decided not to prosecute. Ernest seemed uninterested, only remarking that storms in teacups weren't his cup of tea.

In the evening after she'd prepared supper and dutifully washed up, she fainted.

For the next few days she lay in bed giving herself up to the task of breathing in and out, and opening and closing her eyes. She tried to think of nothing deeper than why the sun took so long to creep around the room or why, every time she woke, Mrs Kertesch was bending over her with another spoonful of chicken soup. Ernest appeared in the morning to say hello, then left for what he called 'a short walk', not returning until the evening to do justice to Mrs Kertesch's cooking.

One evening he came into the bedroom to stand at a distance and enquire how things were with the sick. Having compared notes on respiratory problems he leaned against the wardrobe, only his glasses visible in the gloom, and talked about the progress of work with Irwin. They were making plans to establish greater contact with philosophers abroad, he told her, in an effort to find a more collective point of view. It was difficult to follow his train of thought, which moved so rapidly between epistemology, ethics and action, while she was still considering the whiteness of his lenticulars. She could only content herself with thinking how well her present narrow world of simple sensory perceptions fitted his theories.

She would never work again. She knew it. She was like a skeleton in the desert, picked clean by predators and then dried by the wind to a fine, clear emptiness. Ernest's voice blew over her with the abrasiveness of a simoom, echoing in her hollow skull, whistling through its orifices, polishing and reforming the set of bones on the bed which had once been hers. Only the hands had survived; she admired the fan-shaped formation of the ligaments and the complication of knuckles and joints. How could Ernest know that while he was talking so seriously, silica grains were building up between her fingers, wearing away the only skin left; smoothing and rounding the fingernails until they were paper thin and ready to drop like petals onto the coverlet? She watched the gold of her wedding ring getting brighter and brighter as the trituration continued. Next he would notice that she was married. He would ask whether she had a child. And whether that child had a Jewish father.

'Unfortunately not!' she says, watching the look of astonishment on his face. He tells her the Gestapo aren't used to such answers. What can she reply but that she isn't used to such questions? She doesn't think of danger. She has been interrogated before. The articles she writes are always subject to the closest scrutiny. They are translated into German for the benefit of the Sudetan censors, who miss the Czech subtleties and let them pass. When printed they are savoured and saved by comprehending readers of *Přítomnost* who wonder how on earth she's got away with it. Sometimes an article comes into the hands of von Wolmar, a German observer to the Press department. He is not so easily bamboozled. He calls her into his office where, once a week, he can indulge in one of his favourite pastimes – political argument with a worthy opponent.

This time he wants to know if she has ever heard German soldiers singing '*Soldaten auf den Kanonen*'.

'Why not?' she says. She doesn't tell him that she and Fredy searched a long time for something as suitably ironic and counterfeit as Brecht's song. She says she's surely heard it sung somewhere or other; its fine, rousing quality ideal for her article on the virtues of the German soldier. She has written in praise of his military mien which makes the population quake when he passes. She has compared his unquestioning obedience with that of the poor Czech soldier who is always given reasonable explanations for his orders. She has imagined him singing the stirring song in unison with his fellow Germans as he marches.

She has gone too far. Von Wolmar won't be made a fool of by her or a threepenny opera. He warns her that she's reached the limits. He begins to shout.

But the only thing to do is to keep writing. There is no other way to stay in touch with her fellow countrymen and women as the only mediator between events and the people. She will write until she is forbidden to, and then will continue to edit the paper until it too is banned in August 1939.

She'd never work again. She would lie in the dark waiting to be carried off. Waiting for the order to come.

She looked down at it. It lay on her chest when she woke one morning. A fine start to convalescence. When she opened it she thought it crackled more drily than usual. The folded paper was as brittle as his words. So few of them, and so well chosen. 'Dear Daughter' must have stuck in his throat. But he was explicit. She must leave the life she was leading immediately, if she was to take advantage of his natural readiness as a father to help. Naturally he was sorry to hear about her illness, although it seemed that much of it was self-inflicted. But degenerate company bred degenerate ways. Most if not all of her present predicament was due to incomprehensible obstinacy on her part, therefore any suggestions he might now have for her future well-being would contain definite conditions which would have to be adhered to. If she agreed, then an arrangement might be organized to remove her from the influences which, for the past three or more years, had been so reprehensible.

She couldn't believe his incomprehension. His first real letter in three years did nothing but confirm his obduracy. When she'd told him of their daily struggle to make ends meet, tempering it with what she'd supposed was humour, he'd eventually received it with a fatalistic 'you see'. For what else could she expect, having run off with a Jew?

She wrote to Frank at once. She was frightened. She wanted him by her side for reassurance.

She took from under her pillow the several letters she'd written to him during her stay in bed. She'd told him how her illness had brought her closer to him. Sex had been put aside. She'd said she was experiencing a feeling similar to that which existed between herself, Stacey and Jasmine when they were at school. It was a pure kind of love transcending the physical; the kind of love which she knew Frank felt for her. Now she could see more clearly how little he needed his fear of the flesh, for if he looked towards the future like her – in a clear, uncomplicated way – he would recognize that staying calm was the first step towards a more natural existence.

Her mood didn't last, as she knew it wouldn't. Why else should she have mentioned Frank again to Ernest but to put his feelings to the test?

'He wants me to meet him again,' she said. 'Half-way, as it were.'

'Half-way in the literal sense?'

'Yes, of course. Trains etcetera. It means that neither of us would have to travel so far.'

'And are you fit to travel?'

She didn't know. Her body seemed to respond only when she pushed it. But she badly wanted to see Frank again before she either slipped back into inertia, or took up the old battle with Ernest.

'You'll be wasting your time,' he said.

'How can meeting a friend be a waste of time?'

'You know what I mean, Amy. If you think you'll get anywhere with him, then you are deluding yourself.'

In reply she lifted the letters with a slight smile.

He sighed. 'Why do you imagine you'll be any happier with him than with me?'

She thought. 'Because I think he is capable of greater love than you.'

'Must you always talk of "Love"? You're in love with the idea of it. You can't just fuck the fellow. You've got to take the affair onto some higher plane.'

His look was petulant. 'It's quite nice to know where one stands with one's wife. Whether she's staying, or leaving. Whether one can make plans that might include her.'

'Now you know how I've felt sometimes when you've been serious about one of your lady friends!'

He raised his voice. 'That's different. What we're discussing is whether you know what you're letting yourself in for. The fellow's an invalid. Do you know what that means?'

'I should!' she shouted back.

'I suppose you see yourself as some kind of ministering angel? Some saint!' He had gripped the chair back as he spoke. She could see his knuckles whiten.

She paused a moment, trying to stay calm. 'I'm not the saint,' she said. She said she thought Frank was. He was essentially good, in a world where goodness was dismissed as irrelevant.

Ernest was smiling slightly. 'Does his goodness have a form? Or does it just emanate from him like ectoplasm?'

She said that there were some people so wooden-headed they wouldn't recognize goodness even if Saint Francis himself arrived complete with a bevy of perching birds.

Ernest burst out laughing. 'Well then,' he said, 'he's certainly not the chap for you!' He seemed very pleased with himself. 'I wonder if he's ever heard of "Alienation of Affections"? He'd run a mile if he thought he'd be running into trouble.' He looked at her to see how she was taking this.

She decided there and then to stop Frank coming to see her, should he still be considering the idea. If Ernest found out, she wasn't sure what he might do. Another telegram would have to be sent revoking her last request. Their letters were in such a muddle that she wasn't certain any more of their proper sequence. And since none of them was dated and the envelopes thrown away, she had to rely on her own poor guesswork.

The most beautiful of his letters she could remember

perfectly: the way it had arrived at the exact point when she most needed it. It was a love letter in the true sense, saying how he loved her as the sea loved a pebble in its depths. He tried again to explain about his fear, asking how he was supposed to leap the abyss separating the day world from concerns of the night. It was black magic that he needed if he was to catch what every day offered. And that was why he was so grateful to her; by her side most quiet and unquiet, most inhibited and most free, and why he had renounced all other life.

He should know, she replied, that love at its best had no divisions between body and mind. But was it possible to achieve it? Was it necessary?

Lately her mind veered alarmingly, often leaving her frightened by the speed with which she forgot her last thought. Perhaps the cocaine had bitten into her brain with the ferocity it ate away the nasal linings. Its bitterness lingered, reminding her of her need of it, and her promise to herself not to start with it again. On it could be blamed her violent changes of attitude towards the man she considered to be the most worthwhile person she'd ever met, yet to whom she was still unable to commit herself unhesitatingly.

She wrote of meeting Jasmine again, and of her friend's strange behaviour. It was as if Jasmine, while keeping up a flow of chatter about her impending marriage, was grappling with some hidden turmoil. She was no longer the friend who had read the same books, liked the same music, worn the same clothes, adopted the same handwriting. Amy remembered letters people had received purported to have been written by her. The thought of asking Jasmine about them came and instantly left as she watched her friend trying to simulate the old intimacy. But the urge to mention Frank's name had been irresistible when she discovered where Jasmine was going. She spoke about the possibility of her visiting him, only to have it greeted with reluctance.

Everyone was leaving the city but herself. And Frank, who continued to equivocate. Her pen scribbled words as they came into her head. She threatened to fetch him with urgent telegrams again, and couldn't remember what the last ones had said.

The memory was going. She wondered how long before her body, like her mind, would show real signs of the disintegration she felt inside. At that moment she decided to go and have her photograph taken, for Frank to see exactly what state she was in before it was too late.

She arrived tired at the photographer's studio, and sank into the proffered chair under his impersonal gaze. As he began to shine strong lights on her, he spoke about the wonderful weather, and how he longed to be far away from city streets. While he was still setting up the shot, a young boy came into the studio to talk to him. They spoke about stamps which his father had evidently forgotten to bring home for the boy, and which he promised to collect as soon as he could. She could see by his face that the son was used to his father's forgetfulness, yet slightly ashamed to have it shown up in front of a stranger. He left quickly while his father was still apologizing for his bad memory, and the light from an arc was burning steadily into her face. Impulsively she took out Frank's latest letter. She said the stamps were quite valuable and he might have them. The photographer thanked her profusely, accepting them as if they were the rarest objects in the world. She promised more when she came to collect the photograph.

The visit left her sad. She witnessed again how the relationship between father and child might be, where the father's desire to please the child stemmed from real affection. How to explain to one's own father that such a situation might exist if trust replaced contempt? She had put off replying to his letter, hoping meanwhile for some advice from Frank. When it came she knew he was right in what he said: that the best reply to her father would be the truthful one. That all she asked was not to be wilfully

225

cut off from him. Although her life was sad, nevertheless it was as healthy and calm as any spent in a sanatorium – her father's euphemism for an asylum for the insane.

He would never get her back inside one again. When Frank's friend Leon had written to ask her for proof of injustice done to one of the inmates incarcerated with her, she tried to think clearly of ways to aid his release. She would be willing to swear, she'd replied, that the man could live in the world, but she had no proof of it sufficient for official channels. Psychiatry misused was a frightful thing, where everything could be abnormal, and every word a new weapon for the tormentor. What tormented her now was the fear that one day she might definitely conclude that her father had put her away not from a paternal desire to protect her, but from sheer racial hatred. Frank was right when he'd said in one of his letters that to her father there was no difference between him and Ernest; to the European they both had the same Negro face.

She asked Ernest how he would raise a child of his own, and he replied, 'With love'. She said that when she had a child she'd do her best to love her for what she was, rather than what she expected her to be. 'Take Milena's child, for example . . .'

'I didn't know she had one.'

'Haven't you been reading the books? It's August already!'

'I consider it as secondary to write little articles for you Amy, especially now it looks as though you've packed the whole thing in.'

She felt inexplicable panic, as if he were trying to snatch some beloved object away from her. 'I'll finish the second panel in no time.'

'The first is hardly what you might call God's Gift to the World of Biography . . . pretty as it is . . .'

Now he was irritating her. 'Her life wasn't "pretty" Ernest. Anything but. One of her problems – or one of her strengths, whichever way you like to look at it – was that she was extraordinarily sensitive to what was happening around her. She saw the way Europe was heading towards war long before it came. She saw that fascism had to be fought, and she joined the only party which seemed to see it too.' She could hear her own voice rising. 'And she was strong enough to leave the Communist Party after the Zinoviev Trials, and still continue to fight.

'She travelled all over Czechoslovakia to see what was happening at first hand,' she continued. 'She edited *Přítonmost* herself after the usual editor was arrested. And when it was banned altogether after the Nazis entered Prague, she joined the Resistance. She helped hundreds of Jews to escape . . . Oh, and she ran an underground newspaper.'

Ernest raised his eyes heavenwards and formed his hands in mock prayer. But he was listening seriously.

'Don't you ever feel terror when you think what might have happened if people like her hadn't existed?'

He nodded. 'But hard to imagine what being a Jew was like then. Would I have felt like a second-class citizen? Maybe I'd have grown used to it. One day your neighbour starts hating you for no reason at all. And before you know what's happening, you have to go into hiding in the town you were probably born in. If you're lucky someone gets you out and smuggles you across the frontier.'

'Or you're rounded up and transported to a camp some-where,' she said.

'While your neighbours watch and do nothing. They believe in the "law" and they're seeing it in action!' His smile was grim. 'And they never liked you anyway!'

'I wonder how many people would lift a finger if it happened again. How many Milenas are there today?'

Ernest said, 'History moves sideways – it's on you before you know what's happening.' He noticed her frown. 'But she was exceptional, I agree. Although I'm profoundly suspicious of anyone who behaves heroically. One always suspects their motives.'

'Perhaps she already knew so much about fear that it was of no consequence. She went into the streets, you know, wearing the yellow star on her sleeve, in solidarity with the Jews of Poland.'

'Maybe she wanted martyrdom – self-inflicted mortification to atone for feelings of guilt about the past.' Ernest began to cough quietly. She recognized that he'd unwittingly demonstrated too much consideration of psychological states for one who professed to despise them.

'She suffered from feelings of guilt all her life. She wanted to be better than she was, which isn't so bad, I suppose. And she couldn't easily hurt people. Or let them down. That's why she stayed in Prague instead of escaping when she knew she was in danger. I think her life was one long attempt to control her emotions – to channel them into what she considered worthwhile.'

He groaned. 'I smell "Duty" coming up. Save us from that, Amy! Save us from your inherited hang-ups being foisted off onto her!'

'When the war started in '39, Ernest, she was forty-four. And she'd come through more emotional upheavals than most.'

'Not such a great age,' he said somewhat huffily.

'Who thinks about the future when they're faced with such a dangerous present? The tendency is to think more about the past, isn't it? She must have done some thinking: what it would be like if she hadn't run off with Pollak: what it would have been like if she'd had the courage to start a new life with Kafka . . .'

'Didn't he die soon afterwards?'

'In 1924. Thank God!'

'If she knew he was going to die, she surely could have faced it for a couple of years if she was that fond of him.'

'Don't be cynical, Ernest! Nobody thinks that somebody is really going to die. She was torn completely between the two of them. If she'd decided to commit herself, it would have been total.'

228

'Hmmm.'

'And all those letters she wrote . . . One must admit there was an obsessive side to her character.'

'Looks like you're running her a close second,' he said, without rancour. He had lately begun to settle more into his old, neglectful ways, save for the occasional flurry of concern when he caught her writing another letter. He couldn't know how many times recently she'd been on the point of packing her bag and leaving him. How many times she'd changed her mind and pleaded again with Frank to drop everything and come quickly because she needed him.

The problem was that she was making a problem out of something which, if she'd wanted to do it badly enough, she would have done by now. But if she did, she might alienate herself so totally from her father there'd be no hope at all of a reconciliation. She didn't tell Ernest she'd formulated a reply to her father, knowing he would have disapproved of its tone. She followed Frank's advice almost exactly, trying to keep out any querulous note of self-pity, and stating concisely that all she wanted was understanding. It took several attempts before she was satisfied with it. And she was still unsure enough to delay its posting. Finally, she decided to send it on 10 August in celebration of her birthday.

The photo turned out less well than she'd hoped. She looked at it dispassionately and saw self-possession in the face, combined with a peculiar vulnerability which had something to do with the breadth of the cheeks. Some people might look at her and wish to confide all their weaknesses. Others might see in the broad expanses of flesh something which gave them the right to inflict certain wounds on her, to force out tears. The eyes were clear enough, though.

In sending Frank the photograph, she wondered if his reaction to the new image might be the same as Ernest's: seeing it lying beside the still-open envelope he had picked it up with mock horror, held it at a distance and tossed it down without comment.

She'd stayed silent, successfully fighting back the customary refutations. She could see how put out he was by her new attitude.

He began to walk slowly round the room, tapping at objects as he passed. She heard the 'ping' of his fingers on the glass table top. He stood by the bookcase, picked up a pen and tapped on the wood with it. 'Called off the famous meeting, has he? If you send him that he'll run in the other direction!'

She left a long pause, before deciding it was better to reply, than infuriate him by complete silence. 'Nothing's been called off, Ernest. We're waiting until I'm fit enough to travel, that's all.'

There was silence again. Suddenly he started to cough. He coughed again. A pause, then the cough came louder with a racking sound from deep inside his chest. She thumped him on the back until the paroxysm subsided, massaged his shoulders until he returned to normal, fetched water and made him drink. He said he'd been feeling better recently, but there was still a patch on one lung. She begged him to go to the doctor that evening, and he promised he would.

He left the flat soon afterwards, a sorry expression on his face, saying he was going to Irwin's office to collect him for lunch. Minutes later he returned, put his head round the door and said that he might eat with Morris instead.

She was playing the flute rather breathlessly to herself when Ernest returned in the evening. She asked him why he was so early.

Casually, he said 'Had a word with the doctor about you.' She was surprised. 'Told him you weren't coming along as well as I'd like.'

'Really, Ernest . . .'

'No.' He held up a hand. 'It's true. Look at you. Working too hard.' He ignored her amazed look. 'He agreed . . .'

'Did he now!'

'Well, ask me with what?'

'With what, Ernest?' She thought his smile a shade false.

'With my idea about your having a little holiday. Oh, we knew you'd like the idea. And Laurie thought it would be marvellous. Says you love the children, and they love you . . .' He stopped and watched her face, then gave her his best smile. 'Two weeks by the lakes . . . Mountains . . . Your favourite landscape. No worry about money. Laurie says there's plenty of room there. And they're taking the car.'

She felt a pang of guilt that Ernest didn't know about the money Frank had sent her. She felt even worse that he should want to go to such lengths to prevent her seeing Frank. The eager look on his face, the appeal that she should comply with his plan moved her more than any overt plea to stay with him. He was telling her in his own way how much he needed her.

While he talked his way through a detailed list of persuasions, she knew she felt as much love for him as she'd ever done. When he'd finished, she agreed wholeheartedly that she needed a holiday. Only not quite yet.

The dividing line was her birthday. A whole year brought in with the breakfast tray by Ernest. She said she felt one hundred instead of twenty-five. He told her cheerfully she was catching up. He kissed her on the forehead, wished her a happy birthday and said he was going to put in a few experimental hours at the bank, just to show willing.

At the post office she posted the letter to her father. No money was waiting from Frank with which to buy herself a present. All that came was his reply to her remarks that fear was the opposite face of desire. Nor were there any cheering birthday wishes. It might have been nice to have had him at least acknowledge the day was special. Instead she found herself starting to read the dispiriting tale of his first sexual encounter with a shop girl, when he was twenty. She wasn't sure she wanted to read about it while standing in so public a place as the street, but she did so anyway, unable to resist it.

She found herself immediately engrossed in the story. The poor girl, he said, had made some small, repulsive gesture in the hotel; uttered a trifling obscenity, which he knew had drawn him to her in the first place. That was what he couldn't bear – the desire for some small, specific abomination; something with a sulphurous smell. He said it had something in it of the eternal Jew wandering senselessly through a senselessly obscene world. His body, sometimes quiet for years, would occasionally be shaken by this unbearable need for this specific abomination.

But there were also times when his body, although not calm, was under no compulsion. It was a good, quiet life, disturbed only by hope. Previously during those times he'd always been alone. Now he was finding for the first time in his life that he wasn't alone, but had her, whose physical proximity he found so quieting and disquieting. What he was saying, she surmised, was that desire – which he equated with obscenity – was lacking, but not sufficiently to leave him without fear. He called it the 'usual' fear. He lived with it, and would surely bring it with him when their next meeting eventually took place.

He said he wanted to make sure she'd come. He'd be waiting on Sunday morning in front of the station whether it rained or not. For some reason she'd told him she wouldn't be coming if it was raining. Thinking back she could only assume she'd been feeling weaker than of late. Her strength had been sapped a little by the arguments with Leon.

She hadn't wanted to fight with Leon. But since their first correspondence she'd suspected he neither liked the fact that she was a gentile, nor that Frank was mixed up in what looked like a *ménage à trois*. She thought Frank's friend pompous, and put it down to a total lack of humour, strange in one so constantly in the company of Frank's quick wit. On the subject of his health they were united. On literature they were chillingly polite, although she wondered whether Leon suspected her of trying to curry favour by writing to him so fulsomely about his latest book. It was his Zionism she found hardest to take. She said she knew from bitter experience with her father how nationalism could turn the sanest of men mad. She, who had renounced her home and country, felt empowered to speak on behalf of those who wished to break down frontiers, not rebuild them.

Frank had intervened as diplomatically as he could, reminding her that Leon, being a Jew, had to think of seeking a homeland because he had none, while she had the power to choose. She could guess how many complaints Frank had received from his friend about her letters.

He seemed to understand human jealousies as little as he understood sexual drive.

233

What to do on one's birthday? By rights she ought to be home and working, catching up on all the illustrations half-started, put aside, begun again or found fault with before completion. She would have liked instead to visit Fox; sit near the warmth of his arm and say, 'It's my birthday today, Mr Fox,' just to see what he'd reply in that ridiculous accent of his. But she owed him work which was long overdue; his silence about it was more ominous than threats.

There was always Laurie who might be pleased to see her, despite the fact that she owed him a drawing or two and he might explode in a less than gentlemanly way if she couldn't produce them.

She rang him from a 'phone box instead. Their conversation was short, and consisted of shouted questions and yelled replies. The connection was bad, and Laurie's telephone manner similar to that he might have employed in handling a rabid dog. He asked if she was calling to say yes about the holiday. They intended leaving for the lakes in two weeks' time, he said. She began to explain that it wasn't so simple. He cut her short with a few shouted 'What?'s then said the best thing was to talk to Mona. He rang off before she had a chance to tell him the importance of the day.

Mona was working in the front garden, wearing an incongruous felt hat from which her hair flowed out like water from a fountain. She was struggling with a mound of reddish earth which stuck to the spade as she endeavoured to dig. She didn't seem very pleased to see Amy, and after saying a perfunctory hello kept on digging. Her face was flushed with effort. 'Books are too much. Laurie says the garden's a mess. OK, so it is. But *he* never does anything about it. All he ever does is pull a face at it as he passes through on his way to work. Then he brings home a book on gardening that weighs a ton, and goes off smiling again!'

Amy noticed the book on the edge of the lawn, its pages

showing signs of damp. 'Can't you wait until the soil's a bit drier?'

Mona stood up and looked at her. 'Can't wait, can we? Going on holiday, aren't we?' She kicked at a lump of mud. 'Well, are you coming with us?'

'I really don't know, Mona. You see, it's difficult . . .'

Mona stood up straight. 'Personally, I won't mind if you don't come. But Laurie seems to want you to.' She put a hand up to her mouth in horror. 'Oh dear! Foot in it as usual! Sorry, Amy.' She dropped the spade and kicked it. She had a dirty mark on her face. 'Start again . . .' She took a breath. 'It would be lovely if you came with us, Amy. But . . . for myself . . .' she put her hand on her heart, 'I thought it might be nice to be alone with Laurie for a change. Get the kids off to his sister's, and have him to myself. For a change.' Her expression was wistful. She looked hopefully at Amy. There was a pause. 'It was just an idea,' she said.

Instantly Amy said she wouldn't come. Wouldn't dream of it.

'Now I feel terrible!' Mona snatched off her hat and her hair sprang out like a halo. 'After all that Ernest said about your being weak and needing sunshine and longing for a change.'

Amy gently touched her arm. 'No. Ernest is worried about my leaving him. So he wants to get me away with friends – reliable friends who'll look after me and see I don't get into mischief!'

Mona was still standing looking at her seriously. 'Amy, are you sure? Sounds frightfully old-fashioned and not Ernest at all.' On her face was complete disbelief.

'To tell you the truth, Mona, I'm not sure enough. One day I think I can leave him. The next, I don't know.'

'No, no, no!' Mona was shaking her head. 'I mean, are you sure he's worried about you in that way?' She stopped and thought for a second, looking up at the sky, then grabbed Amy's arm and began to pull her towards the house. 'Come on. A fortifier is called for. And a cigarette.'

As she led the way indoors, she remarked with amusement that she'd just given up smoking and had been finding it a bit of a bore.

Over cigarettes, brandy and coffee they talked. She said quite frankly she thought Amy was going up a blind alley if she believed that Ernest still cared for her. As for doing anything to please him, at the end of the day he'd neither think about the sacrifice nor thank her. All he might do was conclude that his wife could be manipulated in any way he desired.

'But why should he want to manipulate me? Or anyone for that matter?'

Mona groaned. 'I'll tell you what I think, so hold onto your hat . . . because you know me.' She put her palms flat on the table and said decisively, 'I think Ernest wants you out of the way.'

'Whatever for? He does just what he pleases while I'm there!'

Mona lit another cigarette from the butt of the last. 'It would be a bit risky — to say the least — if they were seen. And they've got nowhere to go now.' She looked straight at Amy with candid eyes.

Amy paused, drew a deep breath. 'Ernest has never cared who's seen him,' she said. 'He's never been a hypocrite.'

Mona's hazel eyes were glittering with excitement. 'You're not telling me he wouldn't mind losing his job? He's not getting any younger.'

'You may be wrong, Mona,' she said, trying to disguise her ignorance, and wondering about recent discussions of moving to Paris.

Mona sat back looking as holy and remote as a Burne Jones could with a cigarette between her fingers. 'If the manager finds out, he's for the chop. And he's bound to put two and two together soon. Everybody else has.' She paused. 'After all, why should your husband be the only person to catch the chicken-pox? The manager's wife had it first.'

'Who told you this?'

Mona continued. 'And it's not as if she works at the bank . . . Naturally Morris didn't tell me her name. But it's obvious. They'd been using his flat. Then Irwin's. But Irwin became terrified of germs and infected Morris – so to speak! Now the poor couple are outcasts with no place to go!

'So don't let Ernest fool you again into thinking he's changing his spots . . .' She smiled as she saw the joke. 'I say, that's rather good isn't it?'

She went to the stove and rescued the coffee pot which had boiled over. 'How's the affair with the Great Writer?'

'Fine,' Amy said, her mind racing with questions about Ernest's recent behaviour. She felt Mona's arm around her shoulders.

'I'm so sorry if I've hurt you, Amy,' she was saying in a contrite voice. 'But somebody's got to cure you, so it might as well be me.' She put a fist to her forehead. 'Oh dear! Laurie'd be furious if he knew what I've just done.'

Amy spent several minutes reassuring Mona that she hadn't minded being told; forgave her for it and wouldn't bear her a grudge. While they were drinking their fifth cup of coffee, she told her friend that she definitely wouldn't be going on holiday with them. It wasn't, she said, because she wanted to keep an eye on Ernest. From now on she had to be certain that each and every decision she took was her own, and not someone else's taken for her. And one of the first things was to meet Frank again as he'd asked, and make up her mind what to do about him.

'You're too serious, Amy,' Mona said. 'I don't know why you don't go and live with him and see if you like it. It doesn't have to be forever . . .'

'He's talked about marriage, Mona.'

'Ghastly mistake, all this high-minded stuff!'

'It would kill him if he thought I was taking it so lightly.'

'Oh dear,' Mona said. 'You and Laurie are exactly the same. Perhaps that's why I'm always trying to drag you both down to my level!'

Amy could see by Mona's pensive face that her mood was changing to one of self-pity. She thought it time to change the subject.

'Where are the boys today?'

'With Laurie's sister. She's ghastly, but she's got a horse.'

'And have you found a job yet?'

'Not with fashion. Can't you tell?' Mona gripped the front of her grubby jacket. 'But I've been earning a few much-needed pence doing something fairly shady.' She grinned into her cup. 'You ought to try it. Do you the world of good. Knocks one's principles sky high!'

'All right Mona, tell me!'

All she did, she said, was report to a little room above a record shop in one of the seamier streets of the city. There, with a tape recorder and a few sound effects, she created pornographic tapes. She said the plots were simple, involving simply a man and a woman meeting, talking and going to bed.

'I usually start them off in a bar. Clink of glasses and so on. Suggestive conversation!' She lowered her voice to a deep bass. 'Hello darling! Have I got anything you want?'

'Do you have to do the man's voice as well as the woman's?'

Mona nodded. 'Far cheaper. You'd be awfully good at it, Amy. Your voice is deep enough. I tend to get hoarse after a bit. Very authentic!' She said the only difficulty was varying the smutty conversations; there was a limit to their range.

'Anyway,' she said, 'after the chat in the bar, I get them as quickly as possible into bed!' She laughed. 'I like that bit. Lots of heavy breathing, and bed springs going up and down!'

'How on earth do you manage that?'

'There's a bed-spring machine. They're very proud of it. Research is going on all the time, you know!' She pulled a face. 'I thought of something marvellous last time I was there . . .' Her hand went up to her forehead in a mock dramatic gesture. 'That's the trouble – I keep thinking of better ways of making the wretched tapes. You know what it's like if you're in a job . . . you want to improve things.' For a moment her face became serious.

'I have this ghastly fantasy of being so successful in the porn business that I wind up being the boss!' She put her head back and laughed loudly. 'How could I tell Laurie the magazine's solvent again because his wife's a great pornographer?'

'For someone who keeps telling me I need curing of my fixation, you think too much about that man,' Amy said.

Mona's laugh subsided. 'Don't I just? But good men are hard to find. Look at the way he forgave you when he thought you'd written that rotten letter.'

'Have you still got it, Mona?'

She finally found the envelope tucked into a vase on a kitchen shelf. She handed it to Amy saying that Laurie had thrown away the contents in disgust.

At first glance Amy could have believed the letter was hers, so closely did the writing resemble her own: the nearly parallel downstrokes, the ornate flourishes to the letters. But almost as instantaneously she knew who had really written it. She handed it back to Mona saying no more than that she hadn't seen it ever before.

'Well, whoever it was,' Mona said, 'they were awfully jealous of you.' She put her head on one side and stared thoughtfully. 'I can see why . . .'

She suggested that Amy spend the day with her. And if she liked, they'd make her a dress for her meeting with Frank.

It was a good afternoon sitting working and talking, while outside the clouds turned to rain which beat softly on the windows. They smoked, ate and drank a great deal.

The dress was constructed speedily and not too well through laughing conversations that lasted until Laurie came home late for dinner.

He was sorry to hear that Amy wouldn't be coming on holiday with them after all. He tried to get Mona to change Amy's mind, but Mona said she was adamant.

When he took her home it was after midnight. Ernest was waiting and in a temper. He'd had a table booked for two in a very good restaurant. She said he might have let her know. He told her she ought to have realized something was up when he hadn't given her a present that morning. If it hadn't been for Laurie standing watching them, she might truthfully have said that lately she'd taken nothing for granted. It was Laurie who broke the news that she wouldn't be going on holiday with them. She watched Ernest's face for signs of further frustration, but apart from staring hard at them both for a second, he remained tight-lipped but polite. Standing between them she felt she was being fought over in some unspoken way, although Ernest merely nodded as Laurie repeated that she needed a good holiday. Ernest's final reply was that she was a big girl now and must make up her own mind.

Laurie squeezed her hand as he departed, whispering 'Stay cool!' Ernest was already on his way to the bedroom before the front door closed. He spent the time it took to get into bed saying he wished she wouldn't go telling all and sundry about herself, as if she were hard done by. Not only did she find it curious that he should be so mild in his attack, but that he should be in her bed at all. She wondered if he still loved her.

She chose the bathroom the next morning as the most neutral place to begin her questioning.

'Ernest,' she said, 'are you having problems at the bank?'

He continued cleaning his teeth.

'Are they so delicate that you'd rather keep them to yourself?'

Still he said nothing. 'I'm wondering if all your talk about Paris only means you'll be taking off with someone other than me . . .'

He stood up, toothbrush in hand. 'Cleaning one's teeth isn't the best time to hear what someone's saying.' He hadn't heard her.

At breakfast she said, 'What are you going to do today, Ernest?' She wanted to hear him lie. He said he might put in an appearance at the bank. Later in the day he was due for an X-ray. At this mention of his illness she was smitten with guilt. It was too bad of her to torment him.

He was smiling at her over the top of his newspaper. 'Laurie's right,' he said. 'You do need a holiday rather badly. Why didn't you fancy going with them?' She could detect nothing but mildness and concern in his manner.

'Maybe I'll go after all,' she conceded. 'But on my own.'

She said she'd rather not be tied to a noisy family. Peace and quiet were preferable. 'Unless you want to come with me?' she added as casually as she could.

He thought for a moment. 'Mightn't be a bad idea.' He cleaned his glasses on the tablecloth. 'How about you going first though, and me following later?' He hadn't even asked where she was thinking of going.

'When will you go?'

'Soon,' she said with a tiny smile.

He got up, put on his glasses, and folded the newspaper under his arm. He came round the table to kiss her on the forehead. 'Your roots are growing out. See you tonight, eh?'

She heard him whistling cheerfully as he slammed the front door.

The empty canvas of the second panel still stood in a corner of the sitting room. With paper and pen in hand she stood staring at the shadowy shapes created by what light there was coming from the balcony window. The shapes meant nothing. Only she could read into them the shady history of Milena's last weeks of freedom. There was no way she could think of to communicate a state of siege; a state of living in such constant fear that it became the norm. And that fear not for herself, but for the fearless ignorance of Honza whose attitude to danger, as to everything, was to laugh at it and go her own sweet way. There must have been around the child voices by the score, saying from morning until night, 'Don't speak if they talk to you', 'Don't tell them your name or where you live'. So the intelligent girl would do as she was told and not tell the Gestapo anything when they found her at the printers. All she would do was run home and describe to her mother the excitement of a real raid. She had no idea she was being followed.

The child stands in the middle of the floor, looks sulky and simple and shakes her head at the questions. Her mother sees how furious she really is with the men in uniform for being cleverer than she. She tries to divert the attack on the child to herself by accusing them of illegally breaking into her flat where she is trying to work in peace. She prays that Honza will keep standing over the spot where the documents are hidden. She keeps up a barrage of questions in answer to theirs, for she has had dealings with the Gestapo before and isn't frightened for herself.

The search of the flat begins. The questioning continues: first the child; then the mother; then the child again. When an officer suddenly strikes Honza the mother grits her teeth, clenches her fists and keeps silent.

But there is sufficient evidence to incriminate her. All documents relating to Jews she has protected are taken away. Before she too is taken away she tells her daughter to go to Fredy's, who's been prepared for months for just such an occurrence. She sees the child smiling bravely at her as the door closes. It is October 1939.

The day was a grey one. It invaded her first efforts to shake off Milena. It settled over the pen as she wrote 'Dearest Frank'. For an instant she had removed herself into the confines of a prison van, and was rattling through the autumn streets on her way to Pankrac prison. She got up, walked once around the room and back, sat down and began to tell him about her visit to Mona. It was time, she said, that he studied carefully the letters he'd received from her. Some of them might be fakes. And still she hesitated over mentioning Jasmine by name, wondering whether Frank was strong enough to hear her condemning another person without condemning her for doing so. But the evidence being so definite she said, she had no option but to speak. In detail again she explained how both she and Stacey – not to mention the rest of the class – had accepted Jasmine's slavish adulation as normal. Now she could see how the abnormality had been carried over into adult life, leaving her high and emotionally dry. It was her opinion, she added, that an attachment like Jasmine's was totally unhealthy. It was to be avoided at all costs, for it led to the danger of personal collapse should the under-pinning be removed. If Frank read into this her own weakness in clinging to Ernest, then she must take the chance. Not until they met again could they sort out which of his letters had been replies to fakes, and how they had influenced her own responses.

At the post office she found two letters waiting for her at the counter. One of them had evidently been written on her birthday. He told her he couldn't recite lengthy congratulations without coughing, but he just gave thanks that she existed in the world where he wouldn't have suspected she could be found.

He asked if she knew she'd been given to him as a present on his Confirmation: he was thirteen when she was born. He was always making her smile. The truth of what she'd read somewhere came to mind – that women would do anything for a man who made them laugh.

His other letter amused her too, with its lengthy and detailed timetables. He'd worked out that it would be possible to have between fifteen and twenty-one hours together. There, he told her, they'd talk about the father. Which one he didn't say.

It was Rose she collided with when she left the post office. Rose was flung against the outer door, and onlookers rushed to brush her down, but her main aim was to escape from Amy's restraining hand. Amy firmly held her arm until they had walked several paces along the street. Rose looked frightened. They stopped in the doorway of a shop, where inconsequential questions about what she'd lately been doing served to calm her down. Her expression of alarm gradually gave way to one of dubious hope that Amy might not attack her.

'I was going to post a letter,' she said at last.

'So you shall, Rose. So you shall.' For the second time that day she behaved with insincerity. The sensation wasn't pleasant.

'You look wonderful,' Rose said.

'I look terrible!' The laugh caused Rose to smile in surprise, uncertainty still showing in her eyes. 'Never mind. I'm going on holiday soon.'

Rose gazed up at the lowering sky, still unable to meet Amy's eyes. 'How is Charles?' she said.

'Oh, fine I suppose. I thought you'd given him up.'

Rose blushed and looked at her shoes. 'Yes. Yes . . . there's somebody else . . .' her voice trailed off. 'Mother says . . .' It trailed off again as she foresaw the approaching quagmire.

'How is your mother, Rose?'

She was looked at sharply. 'Very well, thank you.'

'And your father?'

This time the look was more defensive. 'He's very well too, thank you. But working too hard, as always.' Rose was looking at passing traffic. Amy wondered when she would mention the return of the substitute brooch, and how thanks would be proffered. 'He never stops, you know, from morning till night. I think he's ruining his health. There should be a law that says a man can only work so many hours each –'

She had to stop her. Her hand on Rose's shoulder caused

her friend to start as if she'd been shot. 'We might as well get it over and done with, mightn't we?'

Still gazing hard at the traffic, Rose spoke defiantly. 'I really don't know what you mean.'

'I mean that you know I didn't steal the thing!'

There was a pause, then Rose said, 'You took it all the same. You should have kept it and handed it back to me some other time. When I wasn't so preoccupied.'

'But you got it back anyway. Sort of!'

'No thanks to you!' Rose was confronting Amy like a ruffled chicken. 'Do you know something?' She put her face close. 'He is one in a million! Do you know anyone else who would have done what he did? Do you know anyone else who would have scrimped and saved, and searched and searched to find one like it?' Her eyes were shining.

'He told you that?'

'No. He didn't tell me of his own free will. I had to get it out of him. Do you know what he wanted?' Amy waited to find out. 'He wanted me to believe that *you* had bought another brooch to give to mother. You! Without a bean! Of course I wasn't fooled. And do you know what he made me promise . . . ?'

Amy interrupted her: 'He wanted you to promise not to tell me, your mother, or anyone else what he'd done. What a generous person your father is!'

Rose continued to praise her father, her laudation increasing with every sentence.

'Wasn't your mother a trifle surprised that I could afford to return such a valuable piece of jewellery?'

'She was,' Rose said, 'until he told her you'd had to sell a painting. When she asked me privately whether you'd got any pictures of any worth, I remembered the one with the leaping dog.'

It had been on the tip of her tongue to describe Rose's father's secret activities, but another look at her insecure face was sufficient to quell the deed. What occurred to her at the same moment was the thought that the painting was definitely a saleable commodity on which she might raise much-needed cash for her pending holiday, should Frank not send any more. What he was sending was weighing heavily on her conscience each time she read how ill he was. When he eventually went to a sanatorium he'd need every penny for himself.

'Well, one good thing has come out of it,' Rose said. 'I know more than ever now what a wonderful person he is . . . Whatever mother may say about him.' She gave her hair a shake, with a gesture Amy thought theatrical. Poor Rose.

'You can go if you like,' Amy said suddenly. She'd had enough.

Rose nodded at her, thankful for the release. She disappeared through the post office door, leaving Amy staring blankly after her, then at the shop window in front of which she was standing. It was a jeweller's.

She hurried to the station, feeling that the sooner she got her ticket, the sooner she'd accelerate the day she'd be on her way to someone whose honesty was without question. She stood in the ticket queue pondering what to do after meeting Frank. Where to go.

From the travel agent she collected brochures of places with sanatoria to send to Frank. She would tell him to take them to Leon for discussion. Of one thing she was certain: that Leon would do his utmost to see that Frank got well. So many places to see, yet he would be stuck on his back, filled full of injections and looking at the wide-framed sky. She supposed he'd have to go for the cure soon after their meeting, thus leaving her with the choice either to come home again to heaven-knew-what, or take herself off on her own private holiday. She grabbed at handfuls of coloured holiday offers, making up her mind to be dynamic.

Reading the letter she'd written to Frank she discovered it looked a little scrappy. A petulant note had crept in of its own accord, and she had mentioned money again. Why had she done it? All the time she had to put Frank to the test. She said there still wasn't sufficient for the holiday she was planning; wondering what his answer would be, and hoping he wouldn't give one. Always when things looked like settling she had to come along and flick them into motion. Neither he nor she liked dormant dust. They liked to see it sparkle and dance. But recently she'd detected in his letters a more tired note, as if he were pleading for a little rest from it all. He was fatigued.

In the letter with the brochures she enclosed several stamps for the philatelist friend in Frank's office.

The money came. Ernest was told a few days later that not only had she decided to go on holiday, but she'd be leaving on the following Friday night. As she showed him the picture of the lake with the background of trees, she came to the definite conclusion that nothing would be gained by telling him of the complications of her route. First she had to travel to meet Frank, stay with him for a day and a night, and on the following day continue on to her real holiday.

'Why there?' Ernest asked.

'Why not? It's all shades of blue. I love blue. See . . . even the fields.'

He laughed indulgently. 'As good a reason as any, I suppose.' He lifted the picture close to his glasses. 'Nice hotel. Can't say I'm keen on spotted sunshades.'

And still he didn't ask her where the money had come from. Nor did he say anything about joining her there. She was glad. Frank had been told, and been given the task of booking a room for them for one night in a suitable hotel. She'd begged him to be very careful in the selection. No more bed bugs. He had also been warned that should she be late, he wasn't to blame her. The present state of the country was such that at any moment there might be a rail strike. Already the postal services were being delayed by unofficial stoppages. She could see a clear case for the workers. When they met, she said, she'd like to talk about political attitudes, for the subject had never occupied them – that is, if he wouldn't think her unromantic.

Politics had lately been more on her mind; a feeling that one couldn't escape them, and that ultimately they were what guided one's life. All she had to do was turn her chair, and she'd be faced with the invisible yet tangible evidence of politics. Behind her on the easel was the blank canvas of another woman's history. One victim selected from the mass to represent what could go wrong when despotism flourished. She still didn't know how to give it form. To festoon the whole work with barbed wire would do no more than cause the viewer to retire to a safe distance. At least that is what William said.

He and Charles paid a surprise visit while she was putting the finishing touches to the silky hairs of a Spiked Wormwood.

Charles asked why she was in such a good mood. 'And you're putting on weight!' he said. 'You must be loved.' She told him she was going on holiday, but didn't elaborate on her plans.

William said the blank canvas was intriguing. Were the faint scratches on it part of the finished design? She said she wasn't sure. She thought he'd drop the subject, but he persisted until she was persuaded to show him the first panel. Charles looked on and said nothing.

'Are we your first audience?' William said. 'Apart from Ernest, that is.'

Only Mrs Kertesch had seen it properly. The old lady, always full of surprises, had stared at it for a long time with her hand in front of her mouth. Then she'd announced that it had some of the qualities of Rauschenberg at his best.

'Mrs Kertesch understands,' she said.

William smiled. 'So the details of Milena's life aren't so important.'

'No. As long as her strength is evident.' She looked hard at him to see if he was serious. 'She must shine, you see.'

248

He nodded. 'And in the second panel you're afraid the horror will eclipse her. That's why you can't begin it?'

He understood. She searched for lost photos and clippings to show, apologizing for their ruined state. She said she'd been unable to find a picture of the Petschek Palace where they'd interrogated her. It had been in her mind to draw a long corridor in fast-diminishing perspective; at the end, the back view of a tiny Honza walking away beside an official of the Gestapo. Milena's last sight of her child. But who wants clichés? It had to be composed in blocks, overlapping and intercutting in a non-figurative manner. Strips of newsprint of the period might suffice as divisions between the various oblongs and squares.

'Or rags,' she said to an attentive William. 'You see, it's prison and prison camps from then on. Nothing else. A camp at Benešov for Jewish sympathizers. A prison in Dresden.' She picked up from the table a felt-tipped pen, and rapidly drew a harsh rectangle in black.

'Easy. One cell made to measure for a middle-aged woman with a bit of a limp. Not much walking to do in a cell that size.' For some reason she felt the need to show off. She knew Charles was watching her keenly. Beside the rectangle she drew an overlapping square of a larger area.

'Pankrac prison again,' she said. 'She thought she was being brought home for release. But 9,999 others were in the same situation: sent to prison or concentration camps.'

'And where was she sent?'

'To Ravensbrück.'

In the following silence she distinctly heard the sound of single raindrops falling on the plants outside.

'Let's talk about something more cheerful!' Charles had put his arm around her shoulder and was looking into her eyes. 'Let's discuss that heap of a friend of yours.'

'Oh dear. Don't tell me we're going to drag up Rose.'

'Heaven forfend! No. Dearest Jasmine was who I had in mind.' But he said he didn't mind admitting that Rose had given him the information.

They sat in the kitchen listening to Charles's version of events. He said that he too had received one of her letters. Without going into details he said it had contained the information that the writer (supposedly Amy) had wilfully destroyed the garden because she hated him and his family. It was as weak as it sounded. Not at all Amy's style. He'd thrown it away without giving it much more thought, thankful his mother hadn't found it.

'Why didn't you tell me about it?' Amy asked.

He was cross with her at the time, he supposed. There wasn't much communication going on between them, except of the mud-slinging variety. 'And you were awfully busy with You-Know-Who.' Charles eyed her with a slightly malicious look, while William's glance went from one to the other.

'It's all right, William,' she said. 'He wants you to know about my affair with Frank.'

'If you can call it an affair!' Charles was looking faintly victorious. 'He knows anyway,' he said. He patted William's hand. 'They're having what might be called a "passionate correspondence".'

William said he thought he might be in the presence of something called jealousy.

She took the subject back to Jasmine, who'd gone home to visit her aunt. Charles said he'd heard reports that things weren't quite right with her. Somebody had sighted her – possibly Conrad, but he wasn't certain – and said she was showing signs of paranoia. As she continued listening to Charles's description of Jasmine's present sad state, she decided that something would have to be done for her. She would ask Frank to speak to her. It wasn't right to allow her to suffer when it could be alleviated. Charles thought Jasmine deserved it. William said he'd always hated to hurt anyone, especially a woman.

Amy said, 'How condescending of you! I must remember to do something bad just to test you.'

'Try me!' was William's smiling reply.

Charles sat watching them, looking from one to the other with an amused expression. 'Am I by any chance witnessing the start of a beautiful friendship?'

Nothing was the same. It was never going to be again. He had gone home, leaving her with the memory of his puckered, smiling face just visible behind the glass of the carriage window. And rain streaking down so furiously that it kept washing him away. She had waved and waved at nothing, and wondered whether it had been the kind of dream he was fond of describing; she seeming to beckon him to come nearer; he trying to tell her important things about how he felt; her indifference finally defeating them. It wasn't true. Such a heartfelt desire as hers to do right by him could never be called indifference. In a way she was trying to protect him from those aspects of their relationship he couldn't yet see might be detrimental.

He was ill, she could see that. Thinner and slightly bent. His colour paler, the perspiration evident on his forehead even on the short walk back with her to the hotel. Her first sight of his tall form, overcoated and scarfed against the inclement weather and standing alone in the road, had excited and moved her. He'd nearly swung in her arms with the force of her greeting. He felt the same. He smelled the same. His kiss was the same, promising so much. He'd seemed tired to exhaustion even after waking from the sleep she'd made him take; she sitting beside him until his eyelids had flickered and closed. Later when she'd asked if anything was the matter, he'd said he always felt a deadly tiredness and emptiness when anything delighted him. His voice was huskier and lower. At lunch she found herself having to strain her ears to hear the worst he was saying. It was as if by speaking quietly about their misunderstandings he could diminish them. He told her she was looking thin and beautiful. He made her eat what she didn't want, and ate little himself.

He didn't want to stay in the hotel all day, he'd said. He wanted to walk and talk as they'd done before. She wondered how his strength would hold out, but once on the country roads he'd regained some of the old energy. It had taken her a little time to detect beneath his habitual modesty a cheerful possessiveness. She was afraid of it all that day as they'd tramped the unfamiliar lanes in the mist, talking as usual as if their lives depended on it. It had showed itself in the way he'd received the news that she wanted him to find Jasmine and talk to her when he got back home. He'd said he thought he could do it, if it meant an end to the letter affair.

All he needed was advice on the best tone to adopt. She'd told him to use his best judgement in the matter. What he must bear in mind was that Jasmine should suffer no further because of what she'd done. He'd suggested that Jasmine should be asked directly if there were any unposted letters in her possession. If so, they should be burned.

'If possible,' she said, 'and without making heavy weather of it, try to tell her that I still love her.' He said he'd do his best.

About the commission she'd wanted him to fulfil, he hadn't been quite so certain. He'd had the sympathy to smile at the irony of his getting money for Ernest to go to a conference, typically missing the point that with her husband away in Paris she might be more available to him. He couldn't understand why Amy should want him to act as intermediary. He'd said he was willing, but still didn't understand why someone who was, after all, a distant relative, should not know that the loan was intended for Ernest. She could remember the exact spot at which they'd stood when the discussion took place. She had stared at the distant mountains lit by a weak and dying sun and committed the peculiar bleakness of the scene to memory while she'd tried to imagine the transaction in Frank's dubious care. As for collateral – if collateral were needed – back along the same route would go 'Flight into the Grove'. He'd held her very close and whispered that he'd do whatever she wanted.

They'd gone to sit in the field under an oak where they could watch the last of the light. Side by side, stretching out their legs, they had talked up to the tree's foliage, sometimes overlapping and drowning the other's words. He'd spoken about a friend in his office, but her thoughts had been back in Art school days with the man who'd lain under the tree with her then. Once Frank had begun to cough, a dry convulsive cough which was quickly suppressed. He'd told her not to be alarmed, but accept it as he did. She'd said he was asking an impossibility. The evening had come early, forcing them to leave the field to creeping mist and the promise of rain.

She had wondered how they would spend the rest of the evening, but he'd taken her up to their room unhesitatingly, and she'd been pleased to see how clean and agreeable it was. They had sat side by side on the sofa, letting the dark take over the room, their eyes growing used to the gloom. He had held her hand, and from time to time kissed her gently on the face and neck. She'd noticed how excessively hot he was, and remarked on the change in his temperature.

What had first reassured, then alarmed her, was a complete lack of passion on his part. Along with it had disappeared the unnerving bouts of shaking when she touched him. His kisses had been of the calmest kind. His words were evidence of his love. But where was the sexual spark? Trying to excuse his lack of physical interest in her, she'd begun to wonder if he'd been trying to go to bed with someone else. To her question, 'Have you been faithful to me?' he'd replied with a simple yes, letting the word hang alone in the silence of the grey and unfamiliar room.

About the Girl he'd been more forthcoming, telling her how badly she'd taken the breakup. The old claim had been reiterated that she wasn't mentally strong enough to bear what had been done to her. She'd felt a special tension coming through his arms as he'd spoken, which had transmitted itself to her. All the muscles in her neck had tightened so firmly she'd hardly been able to turn her head in his direction. Not that she could have seen him except as a smoky shape beside her, speaking slowly and softly and sadly about his failures, while the heat coming off him had made her wonder if he was actually glowing in the dark. It was then she'd tried to break the spell by standing up decisively, putting on all the lights, and begging him to come to bed. 'Don't ask too much of me,' he'd said.

What had happened in bed had been beautiful, he'd told her next morning. She'd had to agree. He had slept all night. He'd told her how sweetly. How was he to know that she'd lain beside him staring at strange shadows and room shapes, and the ripple of the patterned curtain as it began to undulate like the sea? Trying not to disturb him she'd lain for what had seemed like hours, straining her ears for familiar sounds to soothe her. She'd heard the wind start in the hills and take over the trees. A far-off train had rumbled away into the rolling thunder of a gathering storm that had broken over them in the hour before dawn. In the white lightning glare that had hit the room at the height of the storm she'd seen him beside her lying on his back, eyes closed and mouth open, arms by his sides, so corpse-like it had frightened her. She'd felt his hands and they were ice-cold. At the next illumination he'd sighed and moved, and she'd left him sleeping. For a while she'd sat in an armchair, wrapped in a blanket and staring from window to bed while the light flashed photographically, printing the scene on her memory. Fears and bad thoughts had come and gone, 'what if?' following 'what then?' until she'd gone back to lie beside him and hold him and fall asleep to the sound of rain lashing the windows.

It had been impossible to leave the hotel next morning. They'd been trapped by a downpour which had shown no signs of let-up. Instead of the walk they'd planned, they'd been forced to sit in the curtained confines of a sun parlour, inappropriately named for it faced the wrong direction. Both had been aware of the speeding clock on the wall which had ticked its way through their conversations. It had punctuated the silences between his questions about future plans, and her hesitating replies, all concerned with Ernest. His own plans, he'd said, were fairly simple considering the complexities surrounding them. First a sanatorium, then – should the doctors have made the mistake of letting him live – the possibility of life together with her. She had never heard him speak so positively. He'd insisted he wasn't trying to persuade her. How could he? If persuasions were necessary, then all was lost between them. She'd had the feeling that beneath the positive tone lay desperation. If she tried to remember his exact mood now, all that came was the sense of herself as mother having to soothe a feverish child with vain promises. Yet she'd promised nothing, only not to desert him and not to think ill of him for speaking as he'd done. She'd asked if he could live sharing her with Ernest, knowing before asking what the answer might be. But she'd asked it just the same. She'd asked why they couldn't be lovers first, and let things go gently as they would. He'd smiled sadly, parted her hair with his hands, kissed her forehead and said her roots were growing out. He had shaken his head several times after that, saying no more but standing close to the glass and looking out at the pouring rain.

Over lunch his paroxysm of coughing had interrupted her in a long tirade against her father. Coughing and holding a serviette to his face, he'd hastily retreated, and after half an hour she'd gone to look for him and found him upstairs lying fully clothed on the bed, his fists in front of his face. As she'd entered he'd struggled to his feet with apologies for his behaviour. What was left of their afternoon was spent on the bed, his head in her lap, while she listened to the steady gush of rain rushing along the gutters and down pipes, interrupting the flow of his voice. He'd spoken about her father and his; about mutual friends like Conrad and William and Charles; about learning Hebrew, and about Israel. He'd touched lightly on the novel which had been occupying him for several years – saying little more than that the problems of a certain land surveyor were proving altogether too much for him. Once he had reached for her wrists and held them tight, as if he'd been reminded that the time was quickly coming when they would have to part.

At four o'clock when they were out of the hotel and huddling together in the lee of a station pillar, he'd pulled a bulky packet from his pocket and thrust it into her hands. His instructions were for her to read it and not think too badly of him afterwards. It was the letter to his father. He'd said she would understand. It had crossed her mind that his sense of drama was still intact. At four-thirty his train had arrived and eight minutes later it had gone, leaving her alone to stare down the track, wondering if the tiny disappearing black spot was really the end of the carriage, or floating vitreous matter, or a mere trick of water and light.

After that there had been the most urgent necessity to escape the place. To pack her bags with the speed of the hunted, brave the rain and the terrible Sunday travel services, just to put some distance between the event and what she hoped might be the rest of a reasonable holiday.

She shouldn't have opened the letter on the train. What he'd already told her about the relationship was fresh in her mind. But the dreadful letter from Frank to his father showed more permutations on the horrors of it than she'd been prepared for.

Twice she'd read it in its entirety, having to give up at certain points to draw breath, while staring at the drowning countryside that was passing, before she could find the courage to read on.

There was nothing about his childhood, his family, his feelings he hadn't touched upon. Incidents tiny in themselves had been cherished and churned into solid accusations against this one man – the despot who ruled in Frank's house. Everyone there had suffered, and was suffering still, from the impossibility of living at peace with him. Yet did Frank, seeing the hopelessness of it all, really still feed on the sad relationship, and consider his writing nothing more than a long-drawn-out leave-taking? It was preposterous. She knew of his father's contempt for whatever Frank did, including his aversion to his son's literary career, but what shocked her was Frank's admission of secret pleasure in his father's attitude; his finding in it confirmation of the indictment, as if he really didn't want any other outcome but the one he so clearly saw. Was it true he desired nothing more than minimal comprehension from him? He knew how brutal and boorish and perverse his father was, and yet he still longed for some contact. No wonder he understood her predicament. But where was the optimism? She kept turning to the end of the letter to read his last cheerless words which, with dry intensity, hoped for so little from this gigantic outpouring; only a little reassurance, now that the truth had been spoken, to make their living and their dying easier.

She felt weak in the face of such desperation, much as his mother must have felt when she'd read the letter. But although he'd written of his mother's unfailing goodness and kindness, he must have caused her bitter pangs of remorse with his accusations. He said that with the passing years she had, more and more, blindly and emotionally adopted her husband's attitudes. Had his mother liked being compared to a beater during a hunt, secretly shielding her son, and so driving him back into the guilty worthlessness he felt before his powerful father? She wondered if the woman had ever before been faced with the exposure of such raw feelings. It must have shocked and amazed her that her husband's casual advice to his son all those years ago, on how to avoid sexual danger, should not only have been long remembered, but held to be symtomatic of the contempt the man felt for the boy. And if she was a simple woman she would not have clearly understood her son's contorted reasoning when he stated that his marriage was both an escape from his father and, by its very nature, the act most clearly connected with him.

These were the lines Amy thought over the longest, trying to read into them other than what she saw. She saw that he would never marry; his father had closed that door by saying his son belonged in the dirt, at the same time demonstrating – in Frank's eyes – how far above him he was himself. Frank saw in marriage a way of proving to his father he was as pure; that he was his equal. And yet he didn't want to be his equal, for everything his father was, he held in contempt. And his father was married. It was all too terrible. No wonder the mother had handed the letter back to her son without having let her husband see it. Yet his son still considered it the most important thing he'd ever written. Frank had kept the letter for two years now; treasuring it, setting such store by it as representing his true feelings that he'd given it to her, the woman he was saying he wanted to share the rest of his life with.

She thanked heaven she was on neutral ground now, safe from both Frank and Ernest, in a hotel so impersonal she might have been a battery hen for all the individual attention she elicited. And rain bathed everything, coating the hotel windows so opaquely there was little chance to admire the view of the lake which other visitors told her was unique. She was content. She wanted what she'd got – a cube of dry space in which to rest and pause and confront herself. The only possessions she'd brought with her were a few clothes, pencils and brushes and water-colours, and the obligatory writing paper and pen. Old habits died hard. There was no resisting the urge to write to Frank instantly on arrival. It was an action as reflex as the daily cleaning of her teeth.

She kept it brief, telling of the journey through what she feared might become major flooding, and which had worsened the closer she'd come to arrival. The whole countryside was saturated with rivers overflowing their banks, and the lakes taking over. Comments on his letter to his father she must save, she said, until the mixture of thought and feeling and fear had been separated into recognizable shapes. The letter turned out to be as neat and circumspect as her room, a model of correct, descriptive language and affectionate regards. When it was finished she looked at it hard, wondering how it had come from her pen.

To Ernest she sent a postcard of the hotel standing among bright flower beds and impossibly viridian lawns. On the back she wrote that as yet she hadn't been able to confirm the exterior, but since the hotel was on the higher slopes of a hill, they might not be washed away by morning. In the next sentence she told him she'd met Frank half-way as planned. She signed it 'Amy'. He could pick the bones out of that!

The astonishing thing was that Ernest replied, rapidly by express letter. To her amazement it was a serious, un-ironic, loving attempt to communicate his feelings for her. It wasn't often, he said, that he had a chance to write to her. And since she was the one who loved receiving letters, he was making it his business to see that he was the first. Not being face to face he wanted to try to tell her what perhaps she'd become unsure of, and that was his love for her. She stared at the magic words wondering whether the contents of the silver box had played a part. He went on to say that when she'd married him she'd been aware of his positive views on open marriage. He'd mistakenly thought she'd shared them. Most of their problems had stemmed from this. But he had wanted to marry her, not anybody else; to *marry* her, because he wanted their lives truly linked. This was still the case. She shouldn't doubt it. What she should bear in mind was the indissoluble nature of their bond. He ended by signing himself 'E'. She felt she had been addressed by a superior; liked the thought at first; disliked it for several days afterwards, then came round to the notion that truth was expressed more vigorously through action than words. Theoretically Ernest's next move should be to come to her.

She waited for him and was bored. The rain continued dropping unabated from a grey sky as low as the tops of the trees on the obscured mountains. Each day all there was to do if she wasn't to stay trapped indoors, was to brave the slide down the slushy hillside whose paths were running with rivulets of peat. Once at the bottom of the hill there was only the lake to stand by, to watch the roll of mustard-coloured waves slopping between the sodden slats of the jetty. She gave up trying to arouse sufficient enthusiasm to bring out an already soggy sketch block to paint soggy scenes. Better to stay indoors waiting.

Between bouts of doing absolutely nothing, desultory conversations with guests, unmemorable meals, or short walks to a newly discovered nearby café, she wrote her letters. The rain continued. And because Ernest hadn't yet come, her mind kept going to him even while she was writing to Frank. What would happen to Ernest if the winter were bad? There were already signs of a swift autumn. The damp weather was chilling to the bones; add to it the cold winds, and trouble might arise. What would it do to a man with a patch on his lungs and a few on his boots, who was forced to go to work each day in arctic conditions? Twice Ernest had been ill, she said, and twice she'd been responsible. Now she was giving him more worry. What was all this talk of a new beginning for herself and Frank? He knew it would never be. There was something horribly hopeless about it. She had to be honest with him . . .

For whatever you or I may talk about or plan, we always come back to the same thing – my worries over Ernest, and this fear of yours. You said once it was fear of self-abuse. Such a strangely antique and over-simplified way of explaining fear of a more complex kind. You make so much fuss about purity that in it lies the clue to your suffering. If one is afraid of sex, then self-abuse (as you call it) is surely preferable? It seems to me that desire and fear are powerful enough feelings to disturb anyone's tranquillity.

She went on to quote Ernest's letter to him, well aware of the harsh tone she was using. It wasn't cruelty that prompted her, only the wish to show him how complicated living in the real world could be. Added to which, she badly wanted his opinion on Ernest's letter. He had a way of going to the epicentre. She asked if she could send it to him.

On some evenings, instead of watching television, she drew pictures. She produced meticulous drawings in black and white which she presumed were reflecting the new clarity of her mind. The good little girl sitting at the high table, her arms barely reaching the drawing board: mother beside her guiding the pencil. From memory she drew the city's cupolas and spires and triangular roofs, putting in the thin towers and decorated domes of her own imaginative geometry. She drew St George ramming the dragon; the wrought-iron well head with the lion; the curious three-dimensional clock, just as her mother told her. The old fountain surrounded by four angels with drawn swords. The church on the corner of the street that ran only as far as the river. The bridge with many arches and the statues sacking-wrapped in winter. The river on misty evenings, shifting the rowing boats on their moorings. And everything in motion – rippling water, flying curls of clouds, flocks of birds migrating, flows of leaves from trees being stripped bare by the wind. She had to have something to hang onto.

It was the only direction in which to break out of the terrible oppression of the camp. The only part of the prisoner existence that couldn't be torn from one. Except for self-respect. She kept hers somehow. The friend she found in Ravensbrück said it was the most astonishing thing about her. Some by their attitude or behaviour brought terror down on themselves. She was never servile. She was one among thousands who lived with no rights and no privacy, packed like animals into huts, subjected to starvation, cold, and cruelty, who achieved the miracle of remaining human.

She drew Milena small as a doll standing in a labour gang, waving her headscarf to her friend, in full sight of the SS guard. She tried to show the two friends in the darkness, crouching in the corner of a hut within sound of three hundred occupants and guards, risking death for the luxury of conversation. Milena at a desk in the sick bay, forging medical cards to save the lives of women with venereal disease automatically condemned to death. She drew the bent head of a gaunt woman arguing: Milena threatening the Jehovah's Witnesses with the wrath of God if they didn't take bread to her friend in the punishment cells which she couldn't get to herself. Milena welcoming new arrivals with the only smile they'd seen since the start of their ordeals. Milena trying to make political contact with other prisoners as they arrived in their hundreds day by day. She hadn't it in her to depict anything but the surface of it all: who could show beatings and torture; the monotony of constant terror which built to a slow and deadly climax as the war years rolled on? How could she bring herself to describe death on such a scale: death *en masse* of the old, the unstable, the sick, gipsies, new-born babies, and political undesirables? No artist would ever do it, unless memorable images were the only intention of the commemoration. There was more to her than that. There was the woman who had come through the ultimate test unscathed. It had been simple to present her early life in the form of a beautiful collage. But the next section was still beyond her.

Her present reality was a quincunx of sketches in a neat and tolerably competent style. She sent them to the Tribune editor who knew her work, more to get them out of sight than with any hope of publication. What she herself had achieved so far in Milena's name could stay in the flat with Ernest while she moved into the uncertainty of a new awareness in a strange and novel place.

Still Ernest didn't come. She supposed rain was delaying him. Or a bad case of amnesia caught from a woman whose bed he was sharing. Her body had begun to feel shaky and sensitive; exposed, but prepared for whatever was likely to happen. Nothing happened. No letters from him. None from Frank.

She began to look around at people in the hotel: couples alone, couples with children, couples with dogs. Couples curious. To drink with them at the bar in the evenings was mutually tolerable as long as the conventions of formal intercourse were adhered to. Women were wary of her. It was eventually preferable to go to the café along the road and sit damply drinking coffee and feeding the juke box. One evening a young and muscular man came along to feed it for her, and sit opposite her and be interested in why she was there. He said he was learning to build houses. 'There's no half-way house,' she told him. 'It either stays up, or it doesn't.' He thought she was very witty. She let him kiss her outside in the pouring rain. 'Are you married?' she asked.

'No. Why?'

'Do you want to share my bed?'

He said he didn't mind if he did. She took him back to her room where they struggled together in the dark until he gained the upper hand. All she got from him was a nasty cold, and the guilt of the deserted who deserved it.

And still no letter from Frank. She continued to write, becoming more frantic with each communication . . .

Am I such a trouble to you that you ignore me? Ignore even the innocent postcards I send with trembling hands? By the time they've dropped from my fingers into the box at the end of the slippery path, it's already too late for me to snatch them back. I should get a can-opener to the letter box but I can't. I can see the look of bewilderment on your face as you stand with those pieces of paper in your hand. No, you didn't deserve the bombardment. All right. You're hurt. You've done nothing to deserve it. Nothing my friend, my love. What you have done is by default. You've done nothing, and that is bad enough.

And now I'm unable to get beyond the point where I see you standing in the dark in your parents' hallway looking perplexed at the thing in your hand. It's only a piece of card with a totally inexplicable picture of some parakeets on it. Why should this thing have come to you just as you've mustered all your energy to get yourself moving down the stairs and onto the damp, morning streets? You did nothing to deserve it. You hold the card stiffly and peer at it closer. Good Heavens! There are words on it! What is the mad woman saying now? You can't face another attack. But now, dear Frank, the mistake is made: you read my words as if they are said in your ear; shouted at you down your hall corridor.

But don't you see how late it is? Too late. You would have been too late had you stood beside me in the lane and helped me push it into the box. Even then my frantic need for you had been in the process of transforming into a piece of card, and into the non-existent hearts of those colourful parakeets. Now even you can see this situation isn't good enough. It can't go on. If you don't deign to respond by the smallest blink of an eyelid to those pieces of card, then all is lost. Isn't it?

A question, Frank: is it lost? For first there must be some gain. And did we in those four days together, and in that one other separate day not altogether together – did we gain anything? My gain involved loss – the loss of peace of mind and outward calm. Before you came I had troubles so familiar that I existed inside them in a kind of calm. That's gone. You've taken it. You stand in the hall in your coat and you've unwittingly put on with it my lost calm. It becomes you. I'll let you use it as a gift. It's all you'll ever take, I know, and I suspect you can't make use of it.

And maybe now I can arrive at what is behind all this. In my tortuous way I'm saying how jealous I am that such a man can exist without me. He doesn't even need me. He looks askance at the cards I write, and the letters, and mildly wonders why he's receiving things from a mad woman.

What was inexcusable about the bitter words she sent hurtling one after the other was that none had been written under the influence of anything but panic. She couldn't believe he would desert her so simply and so cruelly. It mattered deeply much more than Ernest's not totally unexpected neglect. Much of her time was spent in wondering exactly which letter, which specific card had done the final damage. Was it the card with the jovial tram conductor on one side and on the other the awful complaint about his not caring? Or the late-night accusation that with her he was only conforming to a planned pattern of courtship, engagement and let-down, in which all his pleas not to be deserted actually disguised a wish to the contrary? Or he may have been unable to face the novelty of unusually controlled letters giving calm reports of her daily activities; the awfulness of everything cloaked in good humour. When was Frank ever fooled?

Her cold became worse, yet self-pity disappeared. She sneezed her way through several more days of contemplation, arriving at the conclusion that equilibrium was being achieved. She was becoming objective. There was no need to stay any longer. The first sight of a slip of blue sky below the nimbostratus made her pack her bags before the holiday was officially over. With a sense of relief and achievement she took herself to the station.

It was risky coming home unannounced. She slunk into the flat half expecting the roof to be rising with the sounds of wild rumpus. The least she'd been prepared for was a pair of strange knickers on the bedroom floor, the remains of a dinner for two in the sink, a few blonde hairs in the bathroom. There was nothing but the stale smell of unopened windows, and dust. She went to question Mrs Kertesch. Ernest had said he was lonely, was the report. Mrs Kertesch wouldn't lie.

Ernest in person was a different matter: his greeting perfunctory, his manner slightly formal. The Paris plans were happening he said, due to an inflow of funds for which he assumed she was responsible. While not objecting to the loan in principle, he did object to the accompanying implications that relatives weren't such an easy touch as they might seem. And what was all this about a painting changing hands? He'd received an urgent note from her father's solicitors instructing him not to part with the work to any other member of the family. She told him as best she could how the plan had gone wrong, without mentioning

Frank's part in it. Nobody, least of all her father, should have been aware that she'd been asking the family for money. The picture, if it had to go – and it hadn't been asked for yet – was none of her father's business. Anger at Frank's ineptitude was rising. Now she knew why he hadn't dared write. But he'd certainly be hearing from her.

'Aren't you back a bit soon?' Ernest asked.

'I was in danger of drowning. There were lifebelts in the bedrooms!'

He tut-tutted. 'So what does the Peasant-at-Heart do when she finally gets to her beloved countryside? She rushes straight back to the smoke. I bet you didn't once put your head out of doors.' He stared at her. 'And you still look awful.' He took out his handkerchief and held it to his face. 'I mustn't catch a cold.' The tone was accusatory.

Looking at the bloom on him she wondered first why she was feeling few pangs at seeing him so, and second, whether she had the right to spoil his pleasure.

'I'm going to the post office to see if there are any letters from Frank,' she said, trying not to linger to watch his surprise at her honesty.

A pile of letters was waiting. And a parcel of books. She hadn't thought to put the new address on her letters. A week must have passed before she'd used an hotel envelope with the address printed on the front. She stood at the counter feeling numb. The clerk said the books were a little late for her holiday, then asked if she'd actually been. She could see by his face he didn't believe her.

She shut herself in the anteroom to go through Frank's letters in peace. The early ones were full of meetings with Jasmine; what she'd said about burning the fake letters; how she'd talked about the past; how she was now hiding away from everyone. Enclosed was a letter from Jasmine pathetically pleading for forgiveness, which she found distasteful. It was obvious that he'd upset her friend more than was necessary by the fervent way he'd carried out instructions. He said his visit had pleased Jasmine; his departure had pleased her more. Instead of quietly suppressing the affair, here he was, blowing it up into the biggest, most complicated of exculpations she'd ever seen.

Irritated, confused, amused and touched by turns, she continued the long reading. But through long letters and short, through notes, through facts and feelings there came as clear as bells several reiterated passages; she was tormenting him beyond the bounds of his strength; he still loved her deeply and was afraid of losing her; he understood her unhappiness. She had read them all before, but added to these was a newer, more disturbing message and one she couldn't ignore: the receiving of her letters was becoming a burden.

Poor Frank. He told her it was better not to write daily. He said he could reconcile himself to not hearing from her as long as he himself could still write to her. Some consolation.

This time fear wasn't allayed by rushing off to the post office to send the old placatory telegram. Instinct still said it was the only thing to do, but as she handed it through the grille she knew she was at the start of a holding operation. From now on the stony but level road before her had begun to slope dangerously away. He wrote that he'd resumed an old rhythm of work: he slept in the afternoons, went for a walk, then stayed up as long as possible writing. The real prize, he said, lay hidden in the depths of the night. But so far there'd been no results. He'd need half a year in order first of all to loosen the tongue, then to realize that it was over. He remarked that the cough intervened. Always these days the pessimistic conclusion. From it all she could see how he was slipping away; telling her that what strength he had left must be reserved for writing.

The worst part of it was that another packet of letters was yet to come. She waited with trepidation for the hotel to send them on.

Now there was Fox to worry over, telling her she was

unreliable and threatening not to give her more work. The trapeze artist came to light looking the worse for wear. She reluctantly completed it, begrudging any time not spent poring over Frank's letters trying to extract the maximum from each one. The letters from the hotel arrived, and in these his mood was obviously changing. He said autumn was playing him up. She wrote to him in encouraging tones, trying to take his mind from his ills. She wrote about old friends, but he replied that getting other people mixed up in their letters had caused all the trouble between them. She tried cheerful discussion of the books he'd sent, and ran into his comfortless claim that, should he lose her, he would have less than Robinson Crusoe: he would have nothing he said, not even his name.

In other letters written at night when the oppressive sight of a sweetly sleeping Ernest made her want to escape to Frank, she reverted to attack. She abused him for mishandling the loan negotiations. He replied simply that she was right; he was an unclean pest, an obstacle, a hindrance. To prove his point he told her how everything he'd touched – the Jasmine affair, the loan, Amy's argument with Leon, their last meeting – were all demonstrations of how he didn't belong in the place where she was. Again on the attack, and in an attempt to stop such self-destruction, she told him she'd never properly understood his fear of love and living. To call her the knife which he turned in himself was to place her so inevitably out of reach that she could only shout across the void that there were people who hadn't the strength to love.

Ernest said she was showing signs of dementia. She said it was only a mild dose of the 'flu. 'Look at you,' he said. 'The Human Heap!' He was right. Compared with his ordered appearance and restrained manner, hers were extraordinary to say the least. But she had always been excessive. And how was he to know that great changes were taking place in her?

'Writing, writing, always writing!' he said.

She didn't tell him that all her energies were going into fighting a battle to save someone. He said there was an obvious link between the disorder of her dress and her mind. Taking umbrage at such hints of moral degeneracy, she accused him of talking like a bigoted Christian. His anger lasted several days but he still returned at a reasonable hour each evening, and still shared her bed. She asked why he bothered.

'I should have thought my letter made that evident,' he said, looking slightly disdainful.

'You think it explained everything, then? You don't see any discrepancies at all?'

He sighed heavily. 'Constant inquests, Amy, can drive a man mad.'

It didn't seem worthwhile to explain that what he thought or felt wasn't a matter of life and death to her any more.

She had already written to Leon trying to explain how she saw Frank's dilemma. She knew what was wrong, she said. The world was a mystery to Frank. He was incapable of living in it in an ordinary way. Others were capable of living, she said, because they could take refuge in lies, blindness, enthusiasm and optimism. But Frank had no sheltering refuge. He was like a naked man among the dressed. He was compelled to asceticism by his terrible clarity of vision, purity and incapacity for compromise. She said she thought that Frank would never get well.

She began to search for a way to mitigate the pain, and found it in a new desire to work. In the following days while she worried about the impossibility of committing herself totally to him, she found herself able to create some shape out of the chaos. She began to see that her talents as an artist offered her the best, if not the only chance of facing the uncertainties, and finding strength.

Frank was weakening. He wrote that he had, after much trouble, booked a room in a sanatorium. He was coughing for an hour at a time without stopping. A few days later he said he was delaying his departure. It was if he couldn't make up his mind to be made well. Back and forth the letters still went, hers trying to buoy him up with continuing promises of a shared life; his fending her off. He asked why she still wrote about a common future which would never be. He knew they would never live together. He saw this with the certainty he saw himself unable to get up the next morning. But with typical Frank-ness he added that she shouldn't take him literally. She still clung to the idea of another meeting: suppose he came to see her on his way to the sanatorium? Her suggestions came and went like leaves floating past on an icy wind. He was too ill. She urged him to keep up the regime of work he'd imposed on himself. Work was good. He said how impossible it was. Wasn't he the most typical of Western Jews, with not one calm second granted him? Everything had to be earned – present, past and future. But he hadn't the least particle of strength for such obligations. How could he carry the whole world on his shoulders when he could barely stand the weight of his winter overcoat?

This edging towards death was the frightening thing. He replied that he was only terribly afraid of pain. To want death but not pain was to him a bad sign. He wanted to continue the discussion of physical suffering started when he'd written the long story she found the most compelling and disturbing of all. It was increasingly obvious that he'd been describing his writing and his life when he'd depicted the execution machine which etched a labyrinth of lines on the victim's body. She wanted more than anything to pull him away from this many-faceted vision of horror. She told him as forcibly as she could that she didn't understand his submission. It was an illness of the spirit – and she had read his letter to his father – an illness manifesting itself in the physical ills by which he hoped to cut himself off from her, and therefore any chance of survival. He believed, he told her, that the therapeutic part of psycho-analysis was a hopeless error. Illnesses were a matter of faith (in the religious sense), the efforts of souls in distress to find moorings. These moorings pre-existed in man's nature, and continued to form his nature. There was no cure.

Contrarily, her health improved as his worsened. She took on September and fought it, finding in the exceptionally cold weather a necessary opponent. She went again in search of work, and applied herself to it with skill and a new awareness of her worth. No longer did she feel a mere adjunct to her husband. Ernest had settled into a period of adjusting to the old bank routine, tempered by the knowledge that at last his philosophical studies were connecting with a wider scale of intellectual sympathizers. He was making preparations for the long-awaited trip to Paris by which he set so much store. His other activities troubled her less and less as her work became more demanding. Fox was now employing her regularly. Laurie was using her talents in an earnest bid to stay solvent. Tiredness now came from long hours at the drawing board, or days spent in discussion in offices where she was more than welcome. Her letters to Frank were becoming less tolerant of his wish to sink into oblivion.

'Isn't it time you got that thing out of here?' Ernest had noticed the greying canvas in the corner of the living room. To her it had become so much part of the room's character that she'd rendered it almost invisible. If one looked at it in one way, its presence was an improvement on the room. Only when she sometimes caught her heel in the easel did she remind herself that one day something would have to be done about it.

'She's not doing you any harm.'

'She's not there,' he said, running his finger down the empty space in a black track.

'I know where she is,' she said.

She is still in Ravensbrück. Conditions in the camp are getting worse, and she is getting weaker. More prisoners crowd in every day. Sixteen huts have become thirty-two;

272

eight hundred women to a hut. The systematic killings have become as much a matter of routine as the hunger, brutality and endless labour. She drags herself to work in the sick bay every day, afraid that if her deteriorating health is detected, she too will be given a fatal injection. She is partly reassured by the arrival of a sympathetic doctor who has admired her father.

Her friends do their best to protect and sustain her. On 10 August 1943 they contrive to give her a birthday party. She fingers the gifts lovingly fabricated from what scant materials could be found, stares at the smuggled flowers in disbelief, and wonders whether this will be her last birthday. But good news is coming from the East where the Russians are gaining ground. And only a week has passed since half of Hamburg went up in flames during relentless Allied bombing raids.

'She's still fighting,' she said. She knew he wasn't listening. He was at the window, holding the curtains bunched in one hand, and looking down into the street. All she could see from where she sat was his smooth head outlined against the grey of an October afternoon. There was something different in his stance.

'I am going to leave you.' He turned around briskly, still keeping his grip on the curtains. She presumed he was looking at her with a special expression, but it was too dim to make out more than the movement of his mouth and eyebrows. She continued working by the light of her lamp. 'Did you hear what I said, Amy? I'm thinking of leaving you.'

She didn't look up again. 'When, Ernest?'

'I don't know.' His voice was surprised. He came over and sat down beside her. She waited. He tapped out a beat with his nails. 'I thought you'd take it differently.' He sounded almost disappointed. His tone, devoid of irony, made him seem vulnerable. 'Don't you care?'

She chose not to answer him. Instead, she got up and left the room while he stayed as he was, sitting and staring through the glass table top at his distorted feet.

She made no mention of the incident in her letters to Frank. And since Ernest continued living with her and sleeping with her, and behaving generally as though it hadn't happened, she chose to concentrate on more important matters. Frank was again suggesting he might come to her. This time she knew he wouldn't. She told him so forcefully, still attempting the impossible task of keeping him in the real world.

Having once accused him of insincerity, she now accused him of lying to her. And being Frank, she said, his lies were not the simple kind, but made up of frightening tales of being too sick, too heavy, too overcome by cosmic fear to function. She said he'd told her he felt like someone who, before he could take a walk, had to sew his clothes, make his shoes, whittle his walking stick and so on. Didn't everyone at one time or other feel the same, she asked. But he claimed he was lost, finished, hopeless. What he was saying to her – if he was speaking the truth – was that he had been broken. And since she could see no other causes for it she could only assume, with the deepest desperation, it was against her that he'd broken. He told her she was only tormenting herself when she wrote such things. It was true. He had always been able to see more honestly than anyone she'd ever known.

'I hope you're telling him the truth,' Ernest said to her one morning. He found her in the kitchen writing to Frank while eating a hasty breakfast.

'What is the truth?'

'That I intend leaving you,' he said in the polite tones he'd lately begun to use.

If it hadn't been for the fact that he cheerfully took off his coat as he spoke, she would have believed him. He rescued his cup, sat down and poured himself some coffee.

He told her the situation had become untenable. He spoke at length about incompatability. She agreed. She asked if what he was saying precluded retaining the good feelings between them. He said his feeling was for someone

274

else with whom he could see a new future. He sounded very positive. But he said she mustn't suppose the new relationship had anything to do with the breakdown of the old. She stirred her coffee nervously, hoping he wouldn't say too much.

'Why do you act as though you're completely helpless?' he asked.

She didn't mean to. 'How must I act otherwise? What must I do?'

He said he wanted her to show some normal emotion. But knowing her track record, he wasn't quite sure what normal was with her. She didn't tell him she agreed, knowing it wasn't exactly normal to feel so dissociated from what was going on. Any nervousness she was experiencing seemed to spring simply from a desire not to see Ernest exposed as too much of a charlatan and liar.

Instead of going to work, he stayed behind in the kitchen to talk, doing his best to extract the old, familiar reactions. She would have liked to oblige out of kindness, but having spent herself so completely in Frank's cause, all that was left was the sensation of being present at someone else's confrontation. He accused her of having driven him into the arms of countless women. Her extravagant ways were also responsible for their failure to live happily.

All morning he elaborated on his themes, standing over her as she started to work on urgent illustrations, insisting that he wanted freedom.

'Then have it!' she said at last.

He looked at her suspiciously, and asked how he was supposed to put it into operation.

'Just go, Ernest. Go! Stop hanging around pleading your cause.'

'This is my home too, Amy.' He told her she must face up to things. She said she did. He clearly didn't believe her. He said it would be wonderful if she could be honest for a change instead of hiding behind a façade of jokes.

'Isn't it strange,' she said, 'that here you are, saying what

I might have said once? All this soul-searching. Why don't you go, Ernest? Just go and get it over with.'

His face took on a stubborn expression. He put his hand over hers to stop the brush. 'You'll not keep me here with those tactics,' he said.

He stayed with her all day. He brought her coffee and sandwiches and sat beside her and talked. She knew he was trying to goad her into the old, violent reactions. Once he told her he was in love, and the smile she couldn't suppress made him explode with anger. He said her behaviour was despicable in the circumstances and that he wouldn't tolerate it. 'Then you must go,' she said, as sincerely as she knew how. She looked him full in the face.

He bent and whispered in her ear, 'You'll not *drive* me away.'

Escaping from his new attentions, she chose to write to Frank in the park. The air was cold and crisp, and her fingers couldn't properly grasp the pen. She asked him why he was driving her away. The malformed words seemed ideally suited to the question . . .

Why do you drive me away? You've done it, that's for sure, and there's no going back. Shall I tell you what I think? You did it purposely and maliciously because I have fulfilled your purpose. In me you saw an escape from that other situation with the Girl. I rescued you superbly. And wasn't I the ideal replacement for her, being no real threat to your habitual way of life? And wasn't I the catalyst for what you're writing? Presumably it is so well advanced that by now I've outgrown my usefulness. So our affair, you've decided, is at an end.

She stared at the words. Who was she attacking, Frank or Ernest? That she was performing an exorcism was certain. She stared at the sentences as if she hadn't written them, wondering whether the Maria Theresia yellow of the paper had been a conscious choice, or merely a scrap snatched from the table as she'd fled from Ernest's insistent voice. She folded the letter with meticulous creases, and slipped it into the envelope as if it were a razor blade.

When she'd posted it and was still standing by the letter box staring at collection times she knew by heart, she decided Frank mustn't read it. The telegram she sent after it demanded the letter back unopened.

It took two days for the reply to come back from Frank, during which time he'd received the telegram but not the yellow letter. Of course he'd return it unopened, he said. She read on, unprepared for the violence of her emotions as she read what he had to say next.

He'd be terribly mistaken, he said, if the idea that they now ceased writing to one another didn't turn out to be a good one. She smiled grimly at the negatives. And he wasn't mistaken. What she was to him couldn't be found in daily scraps of paper. They couldn't do anything but produce misunderstandings, humiliation, almost perpetual humiliation. What was decisive, in his opinion, was his powerlessness to reach beyond them – one thousand letters on her part and one thousand desires on his couldn't disprove this. And what was more decisive to him was the irresistibly strong voice, her voice as it were, which begged him to be silent.

It was crazy. He couldn't mean it; there was no way of breaking such a bond as theirs. All she could do was send a pleading letter, then a card, begging for a stay of execution. In the throes of real panic, she'd forgotten that she was pleading with someone so ill that it was as much as he could do to get up each day.

She knew his replies before they came. To be silent, he wrote, was the only way to live. She herself had said, half-unconsciously, the same thing. What did it matter if the living was in sadness? It rendered sleep more childlike and deeper. But torture, he told her, meant driving a plough through sleep – and through the day. And that was un-bearable.

So there was silence. All she could do was respect his request and not write to him any more.

Days later, in the strange calm that settled without him,

277

she went back to his letters for comfort. It was then she noticed the last postmark, and realized he'd left home without telling her, and had written from the sanatorium. What they did to him in such places was torture, he'd told her. When he'd written about it he was already there. Her letters had been part of it. What had she done to him?

For her own peace of mind she made one last attempt to understand. She wrote to Leon, with the faintest of hopes that he might be able to offer enlightenment. She wanted to know if she was the kind of person who had made Frank suffer the way he'd suffered from every other woman he'd ever known. Was it through her his sickness had grown worse, so that he'd had to flee from her in fear? She had to know whether the whole thing was a consequence of his own nature. Leon was the only person who might answer her, and she begged him with all her heart to try and do so.

His reply attempted to give her comfort and brought her none. It was couched in the reserved tones of someone suffering for his friend, who had little sympathy to spare for the hysterics of a distant woman. At best, he said, a miracle could save Frank, and therefore all conjecture about the past was now futile. She should stay calm and do her best to comply with Frank's wishes by remaining silent.

But each day, sometimes consciously out of hope, sometimes out of habit, she continued going to the post office for news from him. Each day the clerk shook his head. Each day Ernest asked her where she'd been. She told him no more than that Frank had stopped writing. The news seemed to please him.

'Concentrate more on work,' he said. 'Keep occupied all the time.'

'I seem to finish everything too quickly.'

'Then go back to Milena.'

'I can't,' she said. 'She died, you see. After an operation

278

in January 1944. She died of kidney failure.' Tears came to her eyes.

'Come now!' Ernest said. 'I thought this was supposed to be a celebration.' He tapped the dusty canvas, then rubbed it hard with his elbow. A large and dirty mark showed on his sleeve. He didn't seem to mind. 'Finish it,' he said. 'At least then we'll have the choice of how we see her.' He bent forward and looked hard at what he'd revealed. 'Apart from all those lines, isn't there something already there?'

Heads together they stared closely at the dirty smear.

'Perhaps a face,' he murmured. 'Could that be hers?'

'If it's like the organ grinder's monkey, then probably it is.' The little monkey with the sad eyes and the floppy hat that performed outside her father's house. 'That's what she said she looked like at the end.'

Ernest stood up. 'Dear, dear!' he said loudly. 'Can't we do better than that?' He began to rub the surface vigorously with his finger. 'This is no way to celebrate her. Give her nobility. Put some energy into it. And finish it.' He kept his eyes averted as he spoke. 'Who knows, maybe we'll eventually see her in some gallery.' She wondered if he was serious.

'If it's any good when it's done I may take it on myself to write a foreword for the catalogue. Give it a bit of depth.' She almost replied that he'd have to do some research, and that all the books could be put at his disposal.

She picked up the panel on its easel and placed it in a good light. There must be a way to make a new start. But nothing came. Between her and the canvas came only Frank's words. Try as she might to suppress them, they kept intruding: sometimes, he said, he had a vision. Her face was covered by her hair. He succeeded in dividing it and pushing it to right and left. Her face appeared. He moved over her forehead and temples, then held her face between his hands.

279

It was a strong face and a real one; the face of a woman who was courageous enough to stand up on her own. What beauty there was in it came from its sensitivity and its lively look. One could tell from looking at her that the world had gained something from her existence.

'I shall definitely begin with the face,' she said.